Joy Gill lives in Altrincham, Cheshire with her husband and pet greyhound. She has two grown up children.

The Alphabet Tour is her first novel.

The Alphabet Tour

The Early Years

Joy Gill

G&H Publications

ISBN-978-1-734445-1-9 (paperback)
ISBN-978-1-7384445-0-2 9 (ebook)

G&H Publications
Timperley
Cheshire

To my husband who never stopped encouraging me and believing in me. This is for him and my children for all their love and support always.

And of course for *The Alphabetties* without whom this book wouldn't exist. You know who you are and I love you all.

Preface

Although a great deal of this book is fictitious or based loosely on real events, *The Alphabet Tour* is an actual annual occurrence usually taking place in September or October

Acknowledgements

Huge thanks must go to the following people, without their help I would never have got this far:

My dear friend Katherine Steer for been so patient and sharing her thoughts and insight. She had faith in me when I didn't.

Philip C Quaintrell for sharing his wisdom and experience and answering my many questions.

Sharon Davies for making sure the words I eventually wrote were comprehensible.

Table of Contents

Prologue

Before they all met these women never thought they had anything significant missing from their lives. They never thought they would become part of a voyage to new destinations taking many years to complete. They never thought they would be entwined with the lives of others for so long. They certainly never thought it would start at antenatal classes on a typically wet morning in the leafy suburbs.

What they became a part of is *The Alphabet Tour*, an association in the making being built over twenty six years. The women it has brought together have a common goal, to provide love, support, humour and the enjoyment of fun without judgement. Although not usually perilous, they have been on many exciting journeys and a bond has been forged between them which grows stronger each year. *The Alphabet Tour* helps them to cope with whatever life throws their way.

It is a fellowship based on friendship and its strength comes from its members each of whom have their own unique character and story to tell. There is nothing secret about *The Alphabet Tour* – in fact keeping its members quiet about their exploits would be difficult – but it is exclusive. It consists of five members:

Zoe, who tells this story, is the oldest of the group but just by days. She's not tall or fat but is far from skinny and is afraid of artificial intelligence. She is a northern girl through and through and reckons she has a good sense of humour. She considers herself to be fairly creative and artistic. She has sufficient computing and mathematical skills to get by but spreadsheets do nothing for her. She likes to think she is empathetic and a person people can turn to and rely on. She finds Ewan McGregor very attractive and at her funeral she definitely wants at least these two tunes played; "Boogie Wonderland" (Earth, Wind and Fire) because it always makes her dance and "Always a Woman to Me" (Billy Joel) because it always makes her cry.

Zoe is married to a Geordie called Frank and between them they have produced two children, Holly and Eric whom they adore. Her best friend is also an *Alphabettie* but she is blessed with many friends from all walks of her life. She considers friendship to be a very precious commodity.

Faye is the second youngest of the group. Although not a stereotype she has blonde hair and blue eyes. Her generosity is legendary and she is kind and greatly enjoys communing with her fellow man. She doesn't sleep well but never appears to let this get to her. She too isn't tall but has a penchant for high wedges and is rarely spotted in completely flat shoes of any kind. She is inherently stylish and carries it off with ease. She is a big admirer of Jack Savoretti and *Strictly Come Dancing*. Although a slow reader she has a quick wit. She will always laugh at herself and is never afraid to make a fool of herself.

Faye has been with Clive since she went to university and they are married with three children, Chloe, Noah and Amelia. She originates from somewhere in the Midlands but is definitely more at home in the vibrant, exciting city that is Manchester. She is fun and excitable and embraces all opportunities in life. She is a person people confide in, a quality which has served her well in all aspects of her life.

Maggie is tall with a beautiful smile and a huge heart. She is non-judgemental but doesn't tolerate cruelty or stupidity. Like Faye, she is a poor sleeper but is happy with her own company. She is well travelled but loves her home, husband, and girls passionately. She is married to the love of her life Shane, and has three daughters, Scarlett, Jennifer and Samantha.

Her taste in many things is offbeat and surprising, often seeing something others have missed. She loves to laugh and bizarrely finds Noel Edmunds attractive. She has taken charge of her own destiny and forged her own path changing the things in her life she didn't like. Like all *The Alphabetties* she is fiercely loyal.

Sally is the tallest *Alphabettie* and wears it well. With dark hair and dark eyes she has a presence which can't be ignored. Although passionate about her Scottish heritage she has lived her adult life south of the border. Her work is important to her but she never lets it get in the way of the chance to have a good time. She is sporty and enjoys the outdoor life but her body isn't quite a temple. She certainly enjoys food and drink particularly wine about which she has a great deal of knowledge.

Sally has two daughters, Abigail and Charlotte, who are a credit to her and with whom she spends as much time as she can. Her outlook on life is very positive and she has a strength of character way beyond average. She is very intelligent and a pioneer in her mostly male dominated field.

She loves a romantic sitcom and a good book. She has a good relationship with both her siblings and religiously keeps in touch with all her friends.

Kate is a force of nature. She always tries to see the positive in any situation or a way to solve a problem. She has a wicked laugh which thankfully is heard often and which adds to her attraction. She has an ample bosom, sparkly eyes and fabulously glamorous nails.

She is very clever although would deny it and excels at logistics – she enjoys nothing more than a complicated spreadsheet. She loves a glass of wine and *Les Miserables*.

She reads a book in one sitting and generally takes life at full pelt.

Kate is married to Max and has three children, Francesca, Vincent and Katherine. Although born in London all her immediate family now live in south Manchester or thereabouts. She is the beating heart of her family and the glue that binds them together. She hates to forego any occasion and will go through hoops to try and ensure she doesn't miss out on anything. Her life is definitely for living and she is going to pack as much into it as she can.

This story goes back to the origins of *The Alphabet Tour*, its early years and its place in each of the lives of these founder members.

Chapter 1

Initial Thoughts

"As soon as I saw you I knew, a grand adventure
was about to happen."
Winnie the Pooh

Zoe was musing on thoughts of the embryonic days of her babies and her *Alphabet* friendship group. She should have been trying to summon up the energy for the final supreme effort of actually dragging her body from the bathroom to the bedroom and into bed. Bed was where she wanted to be. It had only been the strains of a Sky documentary theme tune that had stirred her. She couldn't face the thought of an hour following the police on the streets as they hunted down drug lords so had headed upstairs. She had to be asleep, or at least in bed pretending to be before Frank wound his way upstairs. She loved him deeply but really couldn't be bothered to have sex tonight, sleep was a much more attractive prospect.

However, despite the threat of mid-week sex she still couldn't get into her pyjamas and actually go to bed. Her mind was racing and took her to thoughts of this year's *Alphabet Tour* and how dear her fellow conspirators had become to her. She could hardly believe it was over thirteen years since they had all met. God, so many things good, bad, infuriating, disappointing, happy, and sad had happened over that time.

It felt like yesterday. Zoe could recall walking into the local health centre for her first ever antenatal class. The room was barren, unlike the women in it and filled with a collection of moulded plastic chairs which were hideously uncomfortable whether you were pregnant or not. Although decorated in the early NHS style, this austere room was to be the setting for not only the mechanics of multiple deliveries but would give birth to a friendship group that would thrive and grow with highs and lows alongside the children these women would produce.

Zoe laughed to herself as she remembered seeing Faye, perfectly turned out, looking immaculate even at seven months pregnant. Her blonde hair was in a neat updo, and she managed to pull off the then popular M&S cheesecloth maternity dress with style – unlike Zoe who when she wore one looked like a small walking marquee! On seeing, Faye, Zoe thought she looked a little stand-offish and potentially a closet snob – they didn't exchange words at the initial meeting. The large house in a leafy suburb, progressing career, successful medical husband, beautiful clothes, and a penchant for Moet & Chandon should have fuelled this initial impression. However, over the years, Zoe's fears about Faye have been well and truly dispelled.

Strangely Faye had felt apprehensive about going along to the antenatal class. She had recently moved to the area due to Clive's work – Clive being her husband and a vascular surgeon. Clive is a good few years older than Faye and much as she loves him, he could have a knack of sometimes making her worries seem insignificant or foolish. So, she hadn't discussed her anxiety over the ante natal class with him; she knew he would be thinking for Christ sake's Faye how can meeting a few other pregnant women be anything to worry about, try doing my job for a day!

Faye hadn't had the time to establish any friendships yet and her family, what was left of it, were in another part of the country, so she couldn't just pop to see them for support. However, she wasn't usually worried about making friends as this had never been a problem for her. Not wanting to blow her own trumpet, Faye possessed alluring social skills and she could put anyone at ease. Genuinely likeable and attractive, she had a knack for engaging with people and bringing them in to the conversation. On this occasion she put her nervousness down to pregnancy hormones and the possibility that she could end up in a group of younger or more stylishly pregnant women – she had nothing to fear on either score.

On the adjacent wall of the Health Centre room sat Maggie seeming slightly wary with a look of Princess Diana circa 1990. Maggie had a beautiful smile and gave off a vibe that she was someone you could trust. Although taller than Zoe (most people are) she wasn't in any way threatening but you could tell she could produce a sense of authority if necessary. She and Zoe just clicked, got on like a house on fire and other similar clichés. This was mainly due to their shared sense of humour, and ability to see the funny, offbeat side of life. Zoe loved this trait in people as it brought back to her positive, happy memories of her mother.

Maggie proved to be extremely generous and kind. It turned out she did own an export company, but you'd never know it apart from her proclivity for going on cruises. Zoe wondered if this affinity with large ships had originated when Maggie and her siblings were dragged across the world by their parents on the *Ten Pound Passage* to Australia. A large part of Maggie's extended family ventured down under along with over a million other Brits. Maggie and her family became *£10 Poms* and were in the prestigious company of the likes of Hugh Jackman, The Bee Gees, Olivia Newton John and Kylie Minogue!

However, some years later, despite been relatively successful, Maggie's family had returned to the delights of Manchester. Selfishly, Zoe was glad their new life hadn't worked out, as it made her sad to think of a life without Maggie in it. Mind you, at that first clinic, although positioning herself alongside Maggie, Zoe did leave a strategic chair between them – she didn't know Maggie was kind, trustworthy and generous then, she could have been a complete loon. Plus, they were both over thirty weeks pregnant by this point so sitting on the chair immediately next to Maggie, or indeed anyone, would have been a bit snug. They just smiled at each other and continued to read the information posters above Faye on the opposite wall.

Maggie had married, not quite her childhood sweetheart but near enough when she was in her early twenties. So, she had been married longer than most when having her first child. It wasn't that she or her husband had fertility problems they just wanted to enjoy some married life together without Rugrats running around. Zoe and Frank didn't have the luxury of child-free married years together as they were older when they tied the knot and, as your grannie would say, the biological clock was ticking. Nonetheless they had hoped to have a year or so to enjoy married life pre children, but Zoe had 'fallen' pregnant alarmingly quickly. Zoe hated that expression, she always thought it sounded like the bizarre outcome of tripping over your shoelaces and landing on some random naked guy lying around with a permanent erection! Becoming pregnant so swiftly after getting married and relinquishing birth control made Zoe realise how reckless she had been with contraception in the past and how lucky she had been not to have had a completely unplanned pregnancy! However, despite the speediness of conception, from the moment they found out she was pregnant, they were both thrilled and Frank went around boasting about his super sperm – and still does if an opportunity ever comes up in conversation!

It still made Zoe titter out loud as she recalled how she had managed to drag Frank along to this first antenatal group meeting. She lectured him with:

"You have to experience the whole pregnancy, so you'll be able to bond with the baby and it'll be easy for you to accompany the mother of your child as you work from home".

Of course, this was complete twaddle but made him feel so guilt laden, that he reluctantly agreed to come along. But it did occur to Frank that there may be the possibility of a breastfeeding video which might have some points of interest to him! He only lasted one meeting but Zoe was still proud of him. As much as he enjoys spending time with the opposite sex, there was far too much discussion about feelings and areas of the female anatomy he really didn't want to know about. After that first class Frank was quite emphatic that he wouldn't be accompanying Zoe to the remainder of the course telling her

"I really don't feel I need to know any more about amniotic fluid, antepartum haemorrhaging or the contents of the birth canal. I'll be here for you every step of the way Zoe, but I don't need an encyclopaedic knowledge of women's bits to do that!"

He did have a point.

Zoe had met Frank at a fancy dress party in South Manchester. She'd been invited by a friend of a friend as she had just moved back 'up north' having worked 'down south' after university. Despite this being a sympathy invite and regardless of the fact that Zoe was proving quite capable of making her own new friends, she went along. After all, in the late 1980s Manchester was the place to be (and still is but even more so then). She was bound to bump into *New Order* or *The Stone Roses*, that was a given. So off to *Madchester* she went and what a fateful decision it turned out to be.

Not only was that night fancy dress but it was also themed as a wear a uniform party. Frank had rocked up as a *Thunderbird* - Gordon for the nerds. And really a drunk, leery Gordon. Zoe wasn't sure at first whether he was actually drunk, or whether his loose-limbed movement was to add that Gerry Anderson puppet authenticity to his persona. But no, after watching Frank further for a very short time, Zoe knew he was well on his way to being very pissed and not method acting!

At the start of their first encounter, Frank was in the process of chatting up a younger lady who would have fitted in seamlessly on any ridiculous couples reality television show. As Zoe was nursing a hangover from the previous excellent night out with some of her own new friends, she was refraining from the delights of alcohol so she could drive home to her bed and recover from a weekend of overindulgence. Her delicate state had also made her very unimaginative when putting together a costume. She had staggered to the local costume hire shop, grabbed a gold braided jacket, thrown on some black trousers and Doc Martens and hoped to look vaguely like someone from the *Charge of the Light Brigade*. Not sexy but she really wasn't in the market for any sort of liaison that night.

Trying to escape from inane small talk and inebriated dancing, she'd ended up in the kitchen, as one often does at parties. There she had hoped to wait until it was reasonable to leave without appearing rude or a bore. The kitchen proved more entertaining than she anticipated as that was where was Frank trying out his best chat-up lines on the young lady in a very tight, body-hugging costume. Zoe could certainly understand why a healthy full bloodied male would be drawn to the young lady rather than her good self who resembled a cavalry officer in the 17th Lancers!

Zoe's eavesdropping had never been subtle, and she was now standing close enough to hear every word of the conversation between Frank and the curvaceous recipient of his seduction. Zoe's close proximity didn't seem to put Frank off and in fact he had quite a lot of witty banter along the lines of: "I might be dressed as a Thunderbird but there's no strings on me pet!"

However, most of his efforts were sailing a long way over the head of the pretty but thick girl who, by now wasn't even attempting to understand anything he said. Zoe on the other hand was finding it hard to suppress her amusement and was laughing out loud at some of his particularly pithy quips.

Clocking that his efforts weren't falling completely on deaf ears, Frank eventually abandoned the lovely but vacuous young lady, deciding to enjoy a two-way conversation with a woman a bit older but with something between her ears.

They bonded from that moment on and proved the old adage that women are attracted to men who make them laugh. Mind you Zoe finds Rowan Atkinson and Bill Bailey funny, but she wouldn't hop into bed with either of them! Frank had shown Zoe to her car when she was leaving. Zoe liked how tall he was when she followed behind him through the packed party to the door. As they stood awkwardly by her car, he had then ventured "Can I see you again?"

Zoe recalled been surprisingly pleased he had asked and as usual been totally uncool when it came to flirting with men, she had blurted out "What socially?"

Despite her ridiculous response, Frank wasn't put off and in fact resurrected her clanger in his wedding speech! They now have two children, Holly their eldest and Eric.

Several years after that fateful night, in readiness for Holly's arrival, Zoe had applied the antenatal class ethos to the letter. She had her birthing plan all prepared in a wipe clean pretty A4 folder. The plan clearly stated no needles as Zoe hated them and had to be held down in a half nelson to get through her schoolgirl vaccinations. Frank had lovingly put together a birthing CD of peaceful and calming tunes to play during what would, of course be a short and relatively pain free labour. Bless him, Frank had also bought some linen baggy trousers to wear so he wouldn't get too hot in the delivery room. Zoe had purchased a huge t-shirt to deliver in which had to be green for no explicable reason other than pregnancy hormones. Also, she had a new crisp cotton nightie to show off her maternal glow, whilst holding her perfect baby when visitors arrived after the birth. She'd even carefully chosen a coming home outfit for her and the baby.

It was all just going to be so beautiful and magical. Then she went into labour!

After twenty-three hours and her mother taking every labour pain relieving drug on offer, by needle or otherwise, baby Holly eventually made her appearance. To be fair it had all started as envisaged at antenatal classes with Zoe slowly walking around the delivery room and Frank occasionally rubbing her back when she squatted on the floor. But after several hours of this, during which Frank had eaten all his carefully prepared sandwiches, her body decided that she was far too comfortable and cranked up the pain levels. Zoe vocalised this shift with "Jesus Christ what the fuck!"

She turned in to a drug-crazed mad woman, gnashing her teeth and refusing to relinquish the gas and air which the pretty nurse gave her, the young one she wouldn't kill later. Then, bodily fluids never mentioned at antenatal classes began appearing from all her orifices in disgusting quantities. The room was awash with vomit, pooh, snot and tears and echoed to shouting, Neanderthal grunts, graphic swearing, and several high-pitched screams from Frank when Zoe squeezed his hand with demonic strength. She had even begged for an epidural and duly had one administered. Zoe, who previously felt queasy at the thought of a needle in her back, would happily have been harpooned in the spine if it would have stopped the pain.

Predictable though it sounds, Zoe fell instantly in love with Holly when she finally made an appearance and wept uncontrollably when Frank held his precious little girl for the first time. The torture of the birth, and the following stitches that meant she would never pee in the same direction again, were all worth it. Not even the fact that the stitches to what was left of her labia were administered by a very young and handsome doctor who quipped, "now what goes where?", could detract from the unconditional euphoria she felt.

13

Speaking of her husband, Zoe had just heard movement from downstairs. Frank was shuffling around doing his nightly chores before coming upstairs. These chores comprised of switching the dishwasher on and turning off a few lights but in Frank's eyes constituted a major part to the day to day running of the house and family. But bless him, he did earn a nice wad of cash to keep them off the breadline. Frank's late night domestic efforts were certainly a trigger for Zoe to finish her ablutions and get to bed. Thankfully, Frank was knackered and in his incredibly annoying way managed to be asleep and snoring like a dragon before Zoe had managed to apply her various lotions, pills and potions and start reading the same page of her book she'd read last night and indeed the night before. This was always a sign that the book she was attempting was too intellectual for bedtime and she needed to go back to a novel somewhere just above Jilly Cooper but well below Dickens or Austen. She tended to 'read' the classics in the car on audio books on her way to work. Having *Great Expectations* read to you by a man with a lush voice, who is apparently revered in the world of audio books, is easier than trying to wade through Dickensian descriptions of a misty landscape or an aging gentleman with a limp, yourself. Although Zoe did always feel as though she was cheating somehow.

Anyway, her inability to get into her book allowed her thoughts to again return to that first visit to the Health Centre. Sally had arrived late. The group had moved on to another equally uncomfortable but bigger room with rubbery mats on the floor to try out positions for labour. Zoe always felt that these mats were particularly unpleasant and were installed not for comfort but in order that any leakages from heavily pregnant women could be wiped up easily. Consequently, she found this class rather disconcerting and spent most of it focussing on her bladder and controlling her wind whilst Frank tried to make her considerable bulk comfortable.

Announcing herself with a loud "Hello, sorry I'm late!", Sally had made quite an entrance and she had brought her three-year-old daughter, Charlotte with her. As Charlotte strived to completely disrupt the class by noisily moving all the NHS furniture around, there was much tutting and frowning from the other, then childless, women. My, how their views would change! They would all soon discover that no parent's life is complete until their child has thrown an epic screaming fit during the speeches at a wedding or flung themselves to the ground in Sainsburys with a deafening cry, beating the ground with both hands and feet!

Sally was in fact a highly respected career woman and with her Scottish accent and statuesque frame she made an impression on the other women. Being in her second pregnancy, Sally was also to be remembered as the one who everyone thought was being alarmist and over dramatic as she tried to tell the antenatal class what the reality of childbirth was like. She dropped tactful hints like "I wouldn't rule out pain relief" and "I found gas and air really helpful!"

Most of the first timers were by now contorted on the floor thinking "I won't need these drugs, ridiculous positions and breathing exercises. My baby will just pop out painlessly like a champagne cork."

Although this was her second pregnancy, Sally had come along to the class as she liked to be sure she was doing all the right things at the right time. She liked nothing better than crossing items off an agenda and trying to keep her life in order. She was attending antenatal classes again to ensure she had all the relevant knowledge available to her so she could make intelligent decisions about the birth and try to be in control - this despite already having all the life experience of bringing wee Charlotte into this world.

Kate, also on her second pregnancy, failed to make the first class at all but insisted Zoe pointed out that she would be coming in future – although Zoe got the impression that the midwife taking the register thought she was making up an imaginary friend. Kate is Zoe's dearest friend. They have known each other from pre-marital days, long before antenatal days when they were steadfast drinking and dancing pals. Kate is a doer, an instigator of action and over the years Zoe had happily become her loyal sidekick. Although being pregnant at the same time was merely a coincidence. Zoe didn't do everything that Kate did when Kate did it!

Kate always wants to get as much out of life as possible and as a result has the worst FOMO (Fear of Missing Out) Zoe has ever come across. Kate, although already having one child and a job was trying to get to these antenatal classes in case something came up that she would have regretted missing. Not because she wanted to be sure she was still au fait with the most current methods for baby massage or breast milk extraction but to ensure she didn't miss out on any social opportunity. But as it was to turn out Kate's FOMO radar was spot on.

When they first met, Kate had a big perm to match her personality and a curvaceous figure, which Zoe could relate to. They both had ample bosoms and decent sized booty which overall they both considered assets being as they were at that time in their late twenties/ early thirties and the bits around the boobs and bums were still firm. Kate was one of three children all of whom and their parents, lived locally. Although they had their moments and various traumas and revelations, they were on the whole a very caring and supportive family. Zoe would always be deeply thankful to Kate and her relatives, for welcoming her Frank, Holly, and Eric into their fold. Zoe's parents had died when she was in her twenties, when they were only in their sixties. Her siblings were great but not physically available on a day-to-day basis and Zoe was immensely happy to have Kate and be a part of what came along with Kate.

As she was beginning to feel sleep taking her over, Zoe tried to recollect the other women in the antenatal group besides her now dear friends. It was proving tricky, but three others did pop into her tired mind. There had been Sheila, a little lady who proved to have absolutely no idea how to look after a new born. A fact which Zoe and indeed a lot of the new mothers found disconcerting as she was a paediatrician! Then there was Susan Werner-Nielson who always said her surname very quickly as if she was ashamed of if been hyphenated. Not only was Susan Werner-Nielson attending NHS antenatal classes, but she was also a devotee of alternative, homeopathic methods of childbirth. Although Zoe was open to anything which helped women through pregnancy and to get the baby out of their body as painlessly as possible, she did think these ideas were bonkers. Anyone who thinks sucking on ice cubes is a viable form of pain relief during childbirth and spends hours making organic vegetable puree for their offspring needs to get out more. This, in turn, reminded her of Deidre Tilly who was also a bit of a hippy when it came to labour pains and rearing small children. Zoe remembered vividly when it had been Deidre's turn to host the post birth coffee morning. The proud mothers with their new-borns all duly arrived and were treated to Deidre explaining how to make a homemade mobile for baby's cot from biodegradable environmentally sourced household items. Zoe laughed out loud thinking of the lunacy of this causing Frank to grunt and roll over. Excellent! She wouldn't have to feel the horrid rush of warm air on the back of her neck every time 'Frank the Dragon' breathed out!

Chapter 2

From Stirrups to Truth Chair

"We meet the people we're supposed to
when the time is just right."
Alyson Noel

When Zoe woke to the sickening sound of the alarm her mind immediately went back to her train of thought from the night before and those early pre–*Alphabet Tour* days. She continued to puzzle over how the antenatal group had been whittled down to the hard core which had become such firm, unshakeable friends.

After much naval gazing as she had breakfast, dropped the kids at school and then drove to work, she recollected a step up in the game from coffee mornings to a night out. As the babies were by then older and husbands were trusted to look after them, a meal at a local French restaurant was proposed. This meant the consumption of alcohol as breastfeeding was a thing of the painful past.

Zoe winced at the mere thought of lactation. She had been an advocate of breast feeding, but due more to its convenience than for the nurturing mother's nipple baby bonding malarkey. However, Zoe's boobs, which had grown exponentially during pregnancy much to Frank's delight, hadn't wanted to play the game. It wasn't that she couldn't produce milk, in fact quite the opposite. She churned the stuff out at a ridiculous rate, too fast for poor Holly to drink it. She always took several spare t-shirts with her when she eventually ventured out of the house, for when the inevitable, embarrassing seepages occurred. You can't fully pull off the proud mummy, beautiful baby combo when you're sporting large wet patches where your ridiculously huge nipples have decided to let loose from both barrels.

What's more, the overproduction in the Zoe Sloane milk making factory caused the stuff to back up, block her tubes and trigger hideous discomfort in the form of mastitis. God, Zoe hated her knockers. Not only was feeding her beautiful new baby far from a pleasant experience but the treatment had involved shoving Savoy cabbage leaves down her bra all day. Despite his protestations, Zoe would send Frank out at all hours to buy the weird combination of giant sanitary towels and a large cabbage! She often sat on the sofa with her sleeping baby in her arms whilst she sobbed and cursed her malfunctioning mammaries - all accompanied by the smell of school dinners. Zoe, and therefore Holly, succumbed to the bottle after visiting the doctor with a second bout of mastitis. As she sat in his surgery, once again crying, he told her firmly, "You are going to stop this now aren't you Mrs Sloane?". To which Zoe replied, "Yeeeesssss" through a lot of tears, snot and the staggered breathing that crying makes you do.

Nevertheless, her badly behaved breasts had meant that Zoe was up for a drink and was a definite for the night out. Coffee mornings were lovely, but as she explained to Frank as she walked out the door, "Nothing beats the amazing healing powers of a cold refreshing gin and tonic with ice and a slice"!

However, her mind set had not been shared by most of the antenatal mums. Six of them turned up that fateful night. Yes, you've guessed it Zoe, Kate, Sally, Faye, Maggie and Sheila – the seemingly inept paediatrician and a wild card none of them had expected to see. Sheila turned out to be a strange one and developed a more than passing obsession with Sally whom she saw as some sort of role model. Sally would get calls from her with annoying regularity asking things like:

"Where do you get your hair cut Sally, I like the style and think I'll try it."

And

"Can I give Sunshine Orange to the baby for breakfast. I know she's only four months old but that'll be fine, won't it?"

It was all a bit disconcerting for Sally and rather than another new mum asking her advice, it had a stalker *Single White Female* vibe about it! Zoe could completely understand why you would choose Sally as a role model. She certainly had presence, topped with confidence and wasn't afraid to voice her opinion. She had just had her second child, whilst still staying on a successful career path. With her attractive, angular features, thick brown hair, and ridiculously long legs she certainly portrayed the unshakable, successful businesswoman. However, Sally was to have issues. At this early stage of their friendship nobody had any reason to perceive things weren't as great as they seemed between her and Gabriel – even Faye with whom she was to become very close. When Sally had met her future spouse, she had been attracted to his free spirit and sense of 'what will be will be' – qualities which her parents had never encouraged. Although having British parents, he had been brought up in California and had that relaxed vibe and attitude to life.

Despite the Church of Scotland suffering a decline when Sally was growing up, her parents were devout churchgoers. Long Sunday church services, Sunday school and bible study often dominated the weekend. What's more her parents also ran a newsagent which meant long hours in the shop and very little free time to relax, never mind have fun. As a result, although feeling loved and secure, Sally's upbringing, and definitely her teenage years, were spent with limited freedom.

So, when she met Gabriel, it made her excited to be with a man who did what he wanted without thinking about the consequences but just seizing the day. Not only was this the antithesis of her childhood, but it was also far from the corporate world that Sally inhabited at work. Her world of commerce required she spend her days ensuring the right person was doing the right job at the right time and in the right way to ensure the job was done correctly at the right moment. Not much room for spontaneity and a 'devil may care' attitude in her line of work. Back then Gabriel, Gabe, was like a breath of fresh air.

As that first social evening progressed and the drinks flowed, despite idolising Sally, it soon became apparent to Sheila, and everyone else, that she was out of her depth, and she chickened out after the food and at about ten o'clock she left saying,

"I must go, my husband needs to get up early."

The remaining five were now getting into their stride and if they were honest, not giving their husbands a second thought. After finishing off the delightful French food which had been laden with the previously forbidden pleasures of runny, smelly cheeses and cream, and lots more wine, Sally made sure the frivolities continued by declaring, "Let's go back to my house, we've got loads of wine!"

The girls didn't need to be persuaded and Sally's house very handily was in walking distance, so they weaved their way back through the quiet residential streets - only on arrival did Sally realise she hadn't got a key.

Zoe instantly had real estate envy. Sally's home comprised a beautiful three storey period brick-built semi. Zoe loved her 1930s home, but when she was at university, she'd always imagined herself living in a house like Sally's abode. Mind you back then she had also imagined she'd have a home by the coast, a bottomless bank account and be with a man who would do anything just to please her. Her boobs would always be pert, and her bottom and tummy firm all accompanied by an amazing sex life free from UTIs and orgasms anywhere and everywhere. As she stood outside Sally's house not yet wearing her pre-pregnancy clothes and still trying to get rid of the pesky hemorrhoid Holly had brought with her, it took her a little while to realise that she was indeed blessed and 'it's not what you have' etc.

The home Zoe now lived in and cherished, was originally Frank's house which he had bought mainly as it had lots of storage. When purchased the interior was completely painted grey, with vertical blinds and nasty badly fitted cheap wardrobes in all the bedrooms. Frank had bought the house from a family who were leaving the country to run a bar on a Greek island, which initially made Zoe very jealous. However, from information passed on via the neighbourhood grapevine things did not go well in paradise and the couple had divorced. Nothing that surprising there but, in fact, the husband then went to Thailand to take a walk on the wild side, and he became she. Many years later when Zoe was working from home, she spotted an unusually tall and let's be nice and say distinctive looking woman walking past who went to call on one of her near neighbours. Zoe later heard that this was in fact the former owner of her home making house calls to spread the word about their new identity. The myth along the street was that one neighbour when surprised by the former resident had declared prior to slamming the door in their face, "No of course I don't recognise you! Last time I saw you, you had a full beard and a pair of testicles!"

This curtailed the enthusiasm of the lady to reintroduce herself to the rest of her former neighbours and she didn't come knocking on Zoe and Frank's door. Overall, that was a relief as Zoe felt sure she would have said or done something politically incorrect or that the former owner would have criticised what they had done to the house which would have really galled her.

She now had her name next to Frank's on the mortgage and they had changed the house beyond recognition. As the family had extended, so had the house and Zoe had put her mark on the décor and Frank had done likewise in the garden. Worryingly, it turned out that Frank had a secret liking for statues in a taste not dissimilar to Del Boy Trotter. Zoe had to keep this desire in check, or the back garden would be overrun with weeping angels and topless maidens carrying urns of water that light up at night just to reiterate their ghastly presence. Zoe reckoned Frank had developed this trait during his previous job when the only shop he could get to at lunchtime was The Range! He still often sends her images of gruesome statues from garden centres asking her things like, "What do you think of this? It would look great by the buddleia."

 Zoe has never felt these messages warrant a reply.

The predicament Sally found herself in having invited the girls back for drinks was somewhat embarrassing, but she remained undaunted. Clearly, she couldn't ring the bell as that would wake up the children which, of course would be breaking the first cardinal rule of parenting - if the baby is sleeping do not wake it. So, she got creative - nay Shakespearean - and began throwing small pebbles from her driveway at the front bedroom window, where Gabe was tucked up in bed. This was accompanied by that whisper shouting you only do when you're drunk which you think is so quiet.

Thankfully, Gabe had become attuned to waking when hearing the slightest noise at night and shortly appeared at the window looking somewhat bewildered. Zoe remembered thinking how different this was to Frank who had selective hearing. He could sleep through the baby crying during the night and wouldn't have appeared at the window if a brick had been thrown at it! But bizarrely he could always hear Zoe putting the kettle on when he was in the shed at the bottom of the garden, or the rustle of chocolate being opened over a similar distance.

Despite having been so rudely awakened, Gabe kindly traipsed downstairs and opened the door for his wife and her drunken friends. In fact, Gabe found the whole thing very entertaining and cheerfully asked, "Anything else I can do to help girls?"

He would have been more than happy to join the group if Sally hadn't swiftly ushered him back upstairs saying, "Thanks Hun, that's great but now go back to bed we have serious female bonding to do!"

This statement made Gabe's face light up and made him even more keen to stay downstairs with his unexpected guests. But after a few minutes of inane banter Gabe made his exit.

This was the first time most of them had met Gabe and Zoe had expected him to be taller – she reckoned he was probably about the same height as Sally. His general persona and accent were what you would imagine but although attractive he wasn't the living embodiment of the stereotype guy from the Pacific coast of the USA. Zoe had conjured up a different image in her mind for a man named Gabe Miller. She had him pigeonholed as being at least six foot six with shoulder length blonde locks, being an excellent surfer with a six pack, permanently tanned and sporting a leather shark tooth necklace. Gabe was more Silicon Valley than Venice Beach.

After Gabe's departure they had settled themselves in the lounge, opened a bottle of wine from Sally's collection and resumed chatting. The alcohol was certainly making the conversation less inhibited, and this was the night the *Truth Chair* was introduced. This wasn't a difficult concept. A chair was chosen and when a person was sitting in it, they had to answer truthfully any questions put to them. As this was the first night out, nobody wanted to lose face or had the courage to say no, so they all took their turn in the aforementioned chair. But back then the women didn't know each other well enough to ask any probing or enlightening questions about each other. Instead, they stuck with teenage schoolgirl humour and established that they all preferred receiving and not giving oral sex, none of them had a Brazilian, two of them owned a vibrator and one of them lost their virginity to a bass player in a dodgy early 80's new romantic band.

Then, completely unprovoked, Kate announced, "I had sex on a train once", to which Faye added she'd done non-specific 'stuff' on a beach on the Costa del Sol. Despite a lot of alcohol, Faye's inhibitions were still not relaxed enough to give details of her early sexual shenanigans. Maggie said, "I can go one better than the train Kate, I'm in the mile high club!" which it was then assumed meant Shane was too, although this has never been confirmed.

Then Sally shared that she had once been creative in an art gallery but again the details of the other participant were never revealed. As everyone was so freely sharing, Zoe was desperately trying to come up with an exciting location where she and Frank had got down and dirty. Although Zoe and Frank's sex life was great, and she thought quite exciting, it did tend to stay within the confines of their own home! However, in a flashback to a pre-marriage holiday on a hot sunny foreign beach she did recall a particularly pleasant interlude in the sea where the water helped compensate for the considerable height difference between the two of them. "That'll do" she thought and gleefully proffered it whilst in the *Truth Chair*.

The *Truth Chair* was one of several games the girls came up with over the years which was far more entertaining when alcohol was added to the mix. There was *Snog, Marry, Push Off a Cliff* and *If I was a (insert item here e.g., Sweet) what type of (item) am I?* One of the enduring favourites is *Red Man, Green Man*. Again, not a very intellectually challenging game but one which can be played almost anywhere. This game - albeit shallow and often tactless - does reveal a lot about your taste in the opposite sex. Maggie had been found to have the most offbeat taste in men. Amongst the opposite sex she confessed to finding sexually attractive were Robert Plant and Eammon Holmes. This was an eclectic mix the girls hoped were based on good hair and a great accent. Maggie's husband has neither of these attributes.

Shane is a man obviously in love with Maggie and has been for a very long time. He had worked for Maggie's father in exports since leaving school and was being groomed to take over the firm. Shane had embraced the role and taken to international business like a duck to water.

When playing the *Red Man, Green Man* Faye has more of a penchant for the younger rather than older guy and isn't ashamed to flirt outrageously. Annoyingly she did this with some success. She kept herself very toned and fit and Zoe had often driven passed Faye pounding the pavements in her Lycra. In her past Zoe had had a couple of very good-looking boyfriends. However, she had never been truly at ease in these relationships, as she could never quite believe someone so good looking would be interested in her. A sad reflection on her self-esteem which had meant that many years had been wasted trying to please men when she could have had an absolute ball just being herself. This revelation came to her when she headed back to the North after a foray working in the South and she'd set about catching up on lost opportunities. One such opportunity turned out to be Frank, whom she found very attractive, one reason being he wanted Zoe just as she came, warts and all.

The night at Sally's house was to be the first of many get togethers over the next three years during which time several more children were produced. Maggie had beautiful twin girls to join their beautiful sister, Faye had a bouncing baby boy to keep their little girl company, Kate had another gorgeous girl bringing her total to three, two girls and a boy and Zoe also produced an adorable baby boy to complete her set. In her mind, Zoe was now done. A healthy girl and boy. She knew she had always wanted children and remembered the exact moment when she felt that even if she got pregnant accidentally and didn't want to partner up with the father, this wouldn't be the earth-shattering problem it would have been earlier in her life. She had a reasonable job; had bought her first little house and she was in a state of mind where she could cope with whatever life threw at her. Well life threw Frank at her, so all was well, as he was happy to get married and do things in the conventional order.

Despite the birth of her second child being considerably quicker than the first – her labour being reduced to five hours rather than twenty three – Eric's arrival had caused some complications. About three to four months after having Eric, she had received a letter from her doctor's surgery saying she was due her routine smear test. So, notwithstanding the very unappealing thought of yet another NHS employee messing about with her down there, she dutifully went along to her appointment. The process was somewhat more uncomfortable than usual, but Zoe just put that down to the fact that not long ago she had pushed an eight pound baby out of that particularly small orifice.

A surprisingly short time after this event she received another letter from the NHS. This letter informed her that her smear test had shown the presence of some abnormal cells at the neck of her cervix, and she should report to the local Gynaecology department for a colposcopy appointment. Luckily, this appointment was only days away as Zoe had immediately gone into a worst case scenario spiral – she had cancer, how would Frank cope with a toddler and a baby when she died!

Frank, bless him, stayed remarkably calm, on the surface anyway and accompanied Zoe to the hospital. Her appointment was with a gynaecological consultant called Mr. Farrell who until this point had been an almost mythical figure. During both her pregnancies, Zoe knew Mr. Farrell was her appointed consultant but she had never seen let alone met him. Now he was standing in front of her, very tall with his hand outstretched in a double-breasted pinstripe suit. Zoe shook his hand and Mr. Farrell greeted her with, "Now Mrs. Sloane, just because we have found abnormal cells in your cervix does not necessarily mean you have cancer. My expert team and I are going to look more closely today and see what's going on."

Zoe had to stop herself leaping up and kissing him. The ego of this man was huge but his obvious absolute confidence in his ability and that of his colleagues was just what she had needed. If he had been a small, wimpy man who spoke very quietly and couldn't make eye contact she would have probably just disintegrated. At this point Frank also let out a deep breath which he had obviously been holding for some time. Mr. Farrell took Zoe into the examination room whilst Frank took up his post in the waiting room. Mr. Farrell then left her in the capable hands of one of his team – a lovely woman with a reassuring manner.

Once again Zoe stripped from the waist down and put on a gown. However, this time she sat with legs up in stirrups as the speculum was inserted and then the colposcope brought in for Mr. Farrell's colleague to have a microscopic look at her cervix. After only a few minutes the reassuring lady pushed back the equipment, removed the speculum and told Zoe she could take her legs out of the stirrups before she left the room. She returned moments later with Mr. Farrell who told her that there was definitely an area of abnormal cells which they could see needed to be removed and if she was happy to go ahead, they could do that there and then.

Although she already knew she wanted this to happen Zoe had asked if Frank could come in to hear what the consultant had said and what was going to happen. With Frank holding her hand Mr. Farrell told them that although the cells were not at this stage cancerous, he considered that if they were left for any length of time they would be. He then explained to them a procedure called LLETZ (large loop excision of the transformation zone). Under a local anaesthetic this involved a heated loop of wire being used to remove the abnormal tissue – usually an area about the size of a fingernail. He went on to explain that this was a very common, simple procedure and he was confident it would remove all the abnormal cells present at this time. Her treatment that day would be followed up with regular screening and smear tests.

Zoe definitely didn't want to wait any longer than was absolutely necessary to remove something abnormal which could turn into cancer from her body! Frank looked pretty white but agreed with her completely. So, they consented to go ahead and then Zoe was led away to another treatment room by the reassuring lady and Frank once again took up his seat in the waiting room. This time Zoe got to lie down. Mr. Farrell came in accompanied by his registrar and asked Zoe if the young woman could carry out the procedure under his supervision. Although she wasn't thrilled by this she agreed and lay back with her knees bent once again and a pad was attached to her thigh to ensure a safe path for the equipment and to avoid any injury. She was then given a fast acting anaesthetic which to say smarted a bit was putting it mildly!

Despite the presence of three members of the expert team, nobody had actually told Zoe what was going to happen. So even though the reassuring lady was holding her hand and trying to distract her with inane chat, Zoe was very perturbed, and her heartbeat was racing when she could smell burning and saw smoke rising from her vagina! Mr. Farrell and the registrar were engrossed in the procedure which seemed to be making a small bonfire of her pubic area. However, Zoe's shock and increasing distress were noted by the nurse – who's hand Zoe was now squeezing very tightly. She tentatively suggested to the consultant that he could maybe just explain a little to Mrs. Sloane what was going on down there, although Zoe certainly didn't want his attention diverted from the registrar who was practicing this highly inflammable procedure on her bits! Luckily Mr. Farrell managed to keep an eye on his trainee whilst he told Zoe that the cells were being burned away and the smoke was quite normal, and it wouldn't take much longer - Zoe did want to retaliate with, "Having smoke coming out of your fanny is definitely NEVER normal!" But she just lay there and tried to go to her happy place!

Once everything was finished and she had very tentatively got dressed, she was told that obviously she would be quite sore in that area for a few days and should refrain from amongst other things, having penetrative sex for about six weeks. Zoe immediately doubled that time in her head. There was no way after everything her lady parts had been through in the last few months – giving birth and a forest fire - that Frank was going to get anywhere near them for quite some time. Other than that, they were confident that unless she had any unusual bleeding, discharge or pain, she would only need to be called for another smear test in a year – but to contact her GP if she was at all concerned. Although not the greatest afternoon of her life Zoe, and Frank walked away, very slowly, from the hospital feeling very happy indeed!

It was a few weeks after this that one of the most memorable and messy nights of her life and that of her friends, took place. It had become a tradition that after each new baby appeared a night out would be organized to celebrate, and the latest mother would be treated to something which they would particularly enjoy. For instance, Kate is a bit of an amateur thespian with a marvellous singing voice, so they all went along to see the Rodgers and Hammerstein classic *South Pacific* which was on at one of the city centre theatres. Zoe was not one for musicals, people breaking into song every few minutes just to tell you they were going outside is not her bag. Zoe thought that *South Pacific* must hold the record for repeating the same song within a musical format. How many times did the audience need to hear "Some Enchanted Evening" for Christ's sake! However, this was Kate's treat and she seemed to thoroughly enjoy it.

Anyway, at that time Zoe was a vegetarian and, as it happened there was a highly rated vegetarian restaurant owned by a notable TV chef, not far from where they all lived. A table had been booked at the place where "*your taste buds not your lifestyle are important*" and the group met up in a local wine bar for aperitifs. Much to Zoe's delight and amazement a limousine had also been organized to transport them from drinking place to eating place. However, it seemed churlish to make such a short journey in such a magnificent vehicle with such an obliging driver. Zoe recollects this guy been called Timmy but that could probably just be the name the girls adopted for him. So, to lengthen the journey they took the limo back to show Frank and take photos of themselves sprawled daintily across the bonnet and then went to the local supermarket – where else!

Pulling into the supermarket pick-up zone it was just as well that several drinks had been consumed in the wine bar as they drew a lot of attention. Faye and Zoe were dispatched into the store to buy champagne to complete the whole limousine jet set lifestyle image the evening had aimed for. Consequently, by the time the limo pulled up at the restaurant the passengers who alighted were pretty much three sheets to the wind. Nonetheless they swaggered into the rather elitist restaurant and - much to the horror of the staff - it was confirmed that they did have a booking. Not many of the vegetarian customers arrived quite so paralytic as this group who clearly had been drinking more than a small glass of vegan organic wine.

Now to say that Zoe was the only member of the party keen on a vegetarian meal was an understatement. They were shown to their table which unfortunately for the staff was bang in the centre of the restaurant. But it goes without saying that the group wouldn't have been missed wherever they had been seated. They all examined the menu. All except Zoe were decidedly under impressed with it. The alcohol consumption seemed to have fueled their carnivorous tendencies and the vegetables really weren't hacking it. Faye said in a very indiscreet or just loud voice, "What the fuck is Jerk Jack Fruit?" and Kate added incredulously, "How can you have Halloumi Buffalo wings?"

After many more not so subtle derogatory comments they finally ordered and quaffed a few more drinks whilst they waited for the food. Whilst the organic veggies were cooked the wine had a more ominous effect. Several of the group began to feel less bolshy and more bilious. Sally stood up and said, "I just have to pop outside" rapidly followed by Zoe.

There was a conveniently dark alleyway running down the side of the restaurant which they felt suited their current needs. There they were both quite loudly and violently sick but thought nobody would notice, given the darkness of the location. Turning to rejoin the party inside they both thought 'oh shit' as, to their horror they realized that there were in fact several tables outside the restaurant. To the right of the door customers were taking advantage of the warm summer evening and the romance of eating under the moonlight. Several couples were now gawping at Zoe and Sally whom they had just heard hurling in stereo. The girls desperately tried to regain their decorum praying there was no vomit on their shoes and casually re-entered the restaurant to find their friends.

Inside the situation wasn't much better. Maggie, Faye, and Kate, in a moment of lucidity, had decided that given their smashed state it was pointless serving food to them especially given their distinct lack of enthusiasm for vegetarian food. However, they had hit a problem with this suggestion as the food was already being cooked and the chef was understandably a bit pissed off. The waitress was insisting that the drunken women have the food they had ordered, although they had offered to pay for the food just not eat it. By the time Zoe and Sally joined the fray a full-scale row was well under way with Maggie actually saying the immortal line,

"DO YOU KNOW WHO I AM?"

Even in her seriously inebriated state Zoe's butt clenched as the words left the lips of her co-conspirator. Given the look on the Maître D's face and the potential for police involvement being thrown around, at this point a taxi was summoned and a dramatic - if not wobbly - exit was made from the restaurant. There was an audible sigh of relief from the staff and customers who weren't quite sure what they had witnessed. Even if it had been explained to them that the women involved had all recently had children, still had hormones rushing round their bodies and were seriously out of practise at drinking alcohol, Zoe didn't think they would have generated an ounce of understanding from the cream of the local vegetarian elite.

Zoe had fallen asleep in Kate's ample bosom on the return journey and was deposited back home first. Frank immediately sent out a message to the other husbands to warn them to be prepared for the imminent arrival of their similarly disgraceful spouses - "it's messy!" Legend has it that later that night one of the parties, who shall not be named, rolled over in bed and was sick on her sleeping partner's face. Gruesome!!

Chapter 3

And so it begins, AMSTERDAM.

"Fill your life with experiences. Not things.
Have stories to tell, not stuff to show."
Anon

Some of life between tours.

Kitty took her first steps after a worrying period of bum shuffling!

A few weeks after giving birth to Eric, Zoe attended the christening of a university friend's baby. Whilst there she was asked when her baby was due and promptly burst loudly into tears. The baby blues are a bitch!

Charlie fell off her bike in spectacular fashion and broke her collar bone. Both Mum and Dad vehemently blamed the other for this lapse in parental concentration.

Clive turned forty and is patiently waiting for his new life to begin!

Samantha and Jennifer picked up impetigo from nursery. Maggie's home was turned into an isolation ward.

Faye started to develop insomnia and began trying different ways to help her sleep. To date a solution has not been found.

Zoe decided that as Eric is now five months old this would be a great time to take the family to visit her sister in South Africa. What in God's name possessed her!

The flashback to Zoe's ante and early postnatal days had now turned into a marathon rather than a quick jaunt down memory lane. Despite the distractions of her job, the house being full of children and a husband intent on some kind of 'suicide by wife' mission, she still found herself preoccupied with events from years gone by. Zoe wondered, "How did that first weekend away materialise?"

She could recall that back then when she was getting to know her now staunch friends, it was baby brain that bothered her. Zoe's first meeting, shortly after returning to work following Holly's birth, was still firmly imprinted in her mind. Her boss at that time was a tall guy with dark curly hair who swaggered about the office in a navy pinstripe suit and cowboy boots. To say he fancied himself was an understatement. He used phrases like "let's touch base" and "let me just run this up the flagpole". Most people in the office just thought he was a bit of a prick who had come up from London.

Zoe had managed to get suited and booted for her first meeting which was to be chaired by *Swagger Boots*. Miraculously she had got into her work suit thanks to Rosemary Conley Diet and Fitness Classes and a bout of mild postnatal depression, and she felt like she was back in the game. She took a place at the large meeting table with the obligatory cup of coffee and rustled papers with the best of them. Some of the faces around the table were new but those that recognised her said encouraging things like "Hi Zoe, glad you're back" and "It hasn't been the same without you! How's the baby coming on?".

As the meeting progressed, she began to feel that, despite having taken months of maternity leave she could actually do this, she could return to the workplace and be a full-time professional woman and an amazing hands-on mother. Piece of cake. So swept up in these self-confident thoughts was she, that, at item three on the agenda, Zoe raised her hand to catch the eye of *Swagger Boots* so as to contribute to the grown-up discussion.

As soon as she opened her mouth, she instantly regretted her boldness. Like a hideous out of body experience she could hear herself saying to the gathered colleagues, who were mostly men or childless, single, self-assured young women, "As I recall the officer that dealt with the application was, oh what's his name, you know thingamabob who works for oh shit, what's his name?"

She had wanted to die. She had been horrified as everyone looked bemused and then, after an interminable pause, just carried on with their discussion as if she wasn't there. To top off her day and put the final nail in the coffin of her confidence, when she took off her jacket to drive to the nursery to collect the child that had caused the untimely genocide of her brain cells, there was a large patch of dried baby sick running from the left shoulder and down the back of her suit. Fucking perfect!

Nowadays though, Zoe worries more about the early onset of dementia and growing old. She can't for the life of her remember when, where or how the first venture overseas for the antenatal friends had come about. Clearly, the window for having all your mental faculties is a small one and one which opens and closes throughout your life. When you're a child your mind is like a sponge from an unpolluted coral reef absorbing everything it can and processing it successfully. Then, well in Zoe's case, the discovery of alcohol, boys and the occasional puff of wacky baccy comes into play and you lose it a bit and don't fulfil your O and A level potential. You still manage to get to university where your brain takes another serious hit during Fresher's Week and the window to your cerebral faculties closes again for a while. Then you start to show some interest in what you've chosen to study, and the brain cells are revitalised with a curiosity to learn and gain knowledge. But then it's second year and your brain goes into more of a ticking over phase doing enough to get by and just about managing to fend off the regular barrage of house parties and cheap club nights. Then it's final year and the window to your mental capability is thrown as wide open as possible and you cram as much information as you can into the space between your ears.

This technique paid off for Zoe who got a degree and, as it was the 80's, a job shortly after and her brain was once again keen to learn and absorb the world around it. Then after a few years in Local Government her brain was switched to automatic pilot for several hours a day and began to focus on finding a life mate. This time though, she called on the knowledge her brain stored regarding the opposite sex and found herself a life partner rather than a shagging partner. The window to her intellect having been opened wide then got well and truly closed when she got pregnant and to be honest hasn't fully reopened ever since. It took another hit with the birth of Eric but revived somewhat when she started her own business. But having started this trail of thought she was now wondering where she was going with it which highlights the point she had been trying to make in the first place! Suffice to say that Zoe could take comfort from the certainty that the other girls would definitely not have a clue about when and where the trip abroad was organised. So as life is short, she decided to gloss over this chronological detail and to just go ahead and reminisce affectionately about Amsterdam. For that is where the group first went.

The numerous children of those going on the trip were still very young. By now there was Holly, Eric, Francesca, Vincent, Katherine (Kitty), Scarlet, Jennifer, Samantha, Chloe, Noah, Abigail (Abi) and Charlotte (Charlie). Handing over the responsibility for the safety of the various offspring was quite a daunting feat. Zoe had made Frank so many lists that she had thought even he, a man who likes nothing better than ticking things off a to-do list, might freak out. There had been a list for getting the children up and dressed and what they should wear. There had been a list for breakfast and other meals and what to do if he decided to leave the safety of the home and go out for a meal. There had been a list of what to take with him if indeed he did leave the house. There had been a list of places the children liked to go and a list of places they didn't. There was a list of contact numbers in the event of a) an emergency, b) he would like to meet up with other grown-up people to ease the load, c) a list of people not to contact in either scenario (obviously she didn't think it was explicit enough to just leave them off the other lists) and d) all their flight, hotel details and the mobile numbers of the whole group. Also there had been a list of what was in the fridge, freezer and cupboards which had all been stocked for a year long siege!

The other girls were similarly preparing for their first child free trip abroad together. Maggie had gotten almost uncontrollable with excitement. Since those fateful, antenatal group meetings she had given birth to twin girls Jennifer and Samantha, bringing her total to three under three! She was by then desperate to have a weekend to herself without holding a baby in each arm whilst trying to entertain her toddler. She had been exhausted since before she could remember and just wanted to think about nobody else but herself for a few precious hours.

At their eleven week dating ultrasound scan which confirmed they were having identical twins, both Maggie and Shane had gone into shock – though it wasn't a complete curve ball as Maggie had older twin siblings. Shane had hung his head as he contemplated the rest of his life potentially surrounded by four women and said, "God help me!" Maggie had spluttered "What are we going to do?"

She had spent the next couple of years in a blur. On one notable occasion, when she actually made it out of the house with the three baby girls, to a birthday party for the perfect child of one of her peers from nursery, her twins were much admired. They were gorgeous and still are, having huge blue eyes and mops of luxurious, bouncy curls. One particularly fawning guest had asked the girls names. Maggie had looked at her for a cringing length of time before she replied, "Do you know I can't remember!"

She then walked away to get a large drink! It turned out that the guest who asked the deeply probing questions was the host's prized celebrity friend who regularly appeared in a long running TV soap opera. But given Maggie's mental state, it could have been the Queen and she wouldn't have recognised her. What's more she wouldn't have given a flying fuck who they were!

After everything they had been through together since the birth of the twins, Maggie had been confident she could rely on Shane to keep their family safe – well at least for a weekend! If nothing else he had a sense of humour albeit fairly warped and her mother loved him and would have helped if absolutely necessary. This was another thing Maggie and Zoe had in common; both their mothers lacked a strong maternal instinct. Zoe's mum was dead so she couldn't have offered to help out with her grandchildren, but Zoe knew from her siblings' experience that it wouldn't have been forthcoming. Maggie's mum was to an extent similarly begrudging and generally only helped with the children if Shane asked her.

To be honest come hell or high water Maggie was going on the trip. She wanted to be recognised as an independent person again. As did all the girls and they had all voiced their thoughts on this at a pre-trip planning meeting. Maggie implored the most, having twins and Scarlet to cope with, she had felt stripped of her identity. What's more, whilst she had taken a career break to have the children, Shane was rising through the ranks and working closely with her father. Business trips abroad had already started for Shane, which would feature heavily throughout their married life. Meanwhile Maggie was increasingly tied to home.

Although Maggie had envied Shane's relative freedom, as he left the house every day to go to the office or fly off to meet clients, she wasn't missing her old job. She had worked for a chemical company in sales. She'd been given a certain amount of responsibility managing customer's accounts, but it wasn't really in her nature to be a driven sales professional – which was partly why she'd never shown a great deal of interest in the family export firm. Maggie was perfectly capable of doing her old job and had accrued a competent level of technical capability, but in her heart, it wasn't where she wanted to be. So, in the rare moments she had when all the girls were asleep, she had spent time contemplating where she wanted her life to go.

Also, like the others, she had made sure she'd had the time to plan the weekend like a military operation and prior to leaving had handed explicit instructions to Shane. He'd looked at the sheet of paper with some incredulity but said nothing. The woman he'd seen in front of him then was not the Maggie of old. She looked possessed and told him. "I don't give a shit about the pressure you are under at work or that most of the things on that list are a mystery to you. You owe me this and you will spend this weekend bonding with your daughters whilst I spend time thinking about me, OK?"

Shane had sensed he shouldn't answer that question.

Having checked Frank's lists and her own list, Zoe too had felt ready to leave the nest for her venture abroad with her friends. She remembered how they had all felt like excited schoolgirls again. As she sat thinking about how wonderful it was to feel that way, she also realised that she had subliminally started doing Kegel exercises to prepare her pelvic floor for the laughter which was inevitably going to follow. Laughter was always a major component when they gathered and given the richness of the material on offer at their chosen destination, that first weekend was to be no exception. As she tried to remember their exploits her mind flitted from one incident to another and who did what, when and why. It had started to feel like one of those films that use a fast-cutting technique when hundreds of images are flashed up on the screen in rapid succession until a character screams in a deranged fashion. Fun though this random thinking was, she had considered that maybe if she put her musings in a more coherent order and wrote them down, it would be fun for all the girls to relive the edited highlights of their group outings.

So, Zoe then started to think logistically about how to do this and the more she did this the more she thought, "When the hell will I find time to do this amongst everything else?"

Then she had argued with herself that these were treasured memories and a great reason for a get together to revisit them if nothing else. What's more it is a damn fine excuse not to do something infinitely more crap. So, she thought "sod it, carpe diem" and whilst Frank handled the kids for a little while, she had gone upstairs to what they generously called the study, switched on the computer and began typing.

All that Zoe could remember about their arrival at the airport was the giggling and euphoria that this had actually happened. Only a few short months ago she had felt she was never going to leave the house. Eric had had a terrible reflux thing going on and would throw up with alarming regularity and seemingly for no reason on God's earth. One morning he vomited three times before even getting out the front door and Zoe had sat crying on the floor of the hall whilst Eric also cried and continued to throw up. She had thought she would never leave the house again, it was just too hard; but she was lucky. Kate's middle child, Vincent had been able to projectile vomit like something from *The Exorcist*. There was one particularly memorable incident when out doing the family shopping, Kate was preoccupied trying to focus on what fruit and veg she needed to keep her growing family free from vitamin deficiency. Then Vincent, who had been sitting placidly in his car seat across the top of the shopping trolley, projectile vomited over the aisle onto the display of handpicked fruit and vegetables; a distance of at least six or seven feet. Other shoppers had just gawped unashamedly at this devil child and then scuttled away before he could have made eye contact with them, and they were turned to stone! Kate horrified but resigned had just told the staff, "Terribly sorry but my child just vomited all over your Maris Pipers". She then left her trolley of shopping, got in the car, banged her head on the steering wheel a couple of times, went home and told everyone, "Takeaway for tea guys!"

ⵁⵁⵗⵔⵁⵁⵁⵁⵏⵁ…⸱⸱⸱∶⸱⸱̈⸱̈⸱ⵁ⸱∴ⵁⵁⵁⵁⵁⵁⵁⵁⵁ

When the girls first went away together it was in a different century when getting through airport security was a very minor inconvenience and there was plenty of time for pre-flight drinks and purchasing duty free goods. All passengers had their luggage checked in, none of this hand luggage only business, and after getting your passport checked and a quick frisk if you were unlucky, you were through and officially on holiday. Subsequently, by 11.15am the group was settled in the airport lounge with their first drink of their child free weekend.

Whilst they passed through the terminal Sally had needed to purchase currency. She had asked Gabe several times to pick up some guilder but like many things she asked Gabe to do, it didn't happen. That morning when she had asked him, "Where are the guilder you got for me, I need them?" Gabe had replied, "You never asked me so there aren't any."

Sally had sighed and inwardly once again thanked God that she had employed Margaret, a wonderful nanny/home help/housekeeper/personal shopper who kept her sane. She had briefed Margaret to keep an eye on things whilst she was away from home, which she often was for work. There was no denying Gabe was a great dad with imagination and excitement in spadefuls, but the everyday reality of bringing up a family wasn't his forte. In fact, this point was to manifest itself the next morning.

The girls were enjoying a childfree lie in at their lovely hotel when the phone rang in the room occupied by Zoe, Kate and Maggie. Zoe begrudgingly answered it only to hear Gabe's voice on the end of the phone asking to speak to Sally. Through gritted teeth Zoe pointed out to him that Sally was in a different room. He then stated without any apology for waking them, that he couldn't find the girls ballet shoes, and could she go and ask Sally where they were. It took all Zoe's strength to remain polite and not to tell him what she thought about the ballet shoes. Instead she politely but firmly said, "No Gabe I'm not going to do that for you, I'll put you back through to reception - OK?"

Despite being in a different country Gabe knew he didn't have a choice.

Before reaching the hotel, the group had enjoyed the pleasures of flying in the nineties. Back then it was the era of free drinks on all flights - even a swift up and down to Holland in economy class ; and after a couple of G&Ts, before they knew it, they had touched down in Amsterdam. Curiously as they had gone through the terminal at Schiphol Airport the girls were greeted by a short, dark young woman who grinned emphatically at them and asked where the rest of the party was.

Kate, who being a control freak had taken on the role of tour leader at an early stage, told the little Dutch girl, "There isn't any more of our party, this is it and be assured it's quite enough! I don't think you are meant to collect us."

Despite Kate being fairly assertive the woman told her that she had instructions to take a party of English ladies to their hotel by coach and it seemed she wasn't going to take her finger out of this particular dyke!

As the conversation got nowhere Maggie had calmly suggested, "Maybe, in order to smooth relations with our European friend we should just take the free ride into the city centre. The little Dutch girl will be happy, and we save on taxi fare".

Maggie was often the one to see clearly through situations the girls had got themselves into and to suggest a solution, this suggestion certainly had legs. So, it had been explained that they were staying at The American Hotel and that after some discussion amongst their party they'd be happy to be driven to the hotel on her coach and the little Dutch girl was asked to show them the way.

Old habits die hard, and the girls headed straight for the back seat of the coach. This is, of course, where the cool girls are to be found on any school trip drinking vodka from a Panda Lemonade bottle and gobbling up their packed lunch before leaving the confines of the school grounds! Zoe felt quite reminiscent as she sat at the back of the bus, although she never quite made the back seat at school, she was usually back seat adjacent. She thought wistfully of one theatre trip for O level English Literature to see *Julius Caesar* at The Leeds Playhouse. The coach ended up on fire and the pupils had to be evacuated onto the hard shoulder of the M62. They were then given a lift the rest of the way by a bus load of rugby supporters who had seemed more than happy to help out a load of excited schoolgirls!

The Dutch lady's coach had far fewer passengers than any school trip, but the noise levels were still quite high. Five, at that time, youngish women let loose without their small children and husbands, fuelled by alcohol and excitement made a hell of a noise. This brought many fraught glances and nervous smiles from the little Dutch girl and, as the journey progressed towards the centre of Amsterdam, she realised - and indeed prayed - that these weren't her passengers. Despite what had clearly been a major cock-up on her part, the little Dutch Girl decently dropped the girls off at their hotel. She had last been seen berating the confused driver as the coach headed off at speed back towards the airport!

□□ꔟ⚡□□□□∩□……⋯∶.⋅˙˙⋅.□∵□□□∪□□□□□

Cities, towns and buildings had been at the heart of Zoe's career, and it was she who had recommended The American Hotel. It was one of the few things she could remember distinctly from her first visit to Amsterdam. Almost unbelievably, when Zoe had been at university for her third-year foreign field trip, the professor permitted twenty or so reprobate students to be taken on an educational visit to Amsterdam – a city with a cannabis culture and liberally scattered with great night clubs and sex shops! What was he thinking? Apart from enjoying all the obvious attractions and attending very few of the academic events organised, The American Hotel really stuck in Zoe's memory. One of the long-suffering tutors who had recklessly gone on this trip, comically called Dick, was a very sweet guy and had recommended to the students that they should visit the hotel, go into what was then called the Reading Room and just take it all in.

This intrigued Zoe and her motley university crew, and they had done as Dick suggested. What they found was an incredibly stylish Art Deco room with a unique ambience. It was the place where Zoe could genuinely recollect being in awe of interior design for the first time. To her this room beat hands down the stuffy tapestries, gigantic portraits and ugly gilt furniture of the Tudors or Stuarts. She had fallen in love with its eclectic shapes and colours, and the way everyday objects were made wacky and memorable. She hoped the room would stay like that forever.

⬜⬜�Ⱶ⬜⬜⬜⎾⬜…···⋮.·¨·.⬜∵·⬜⬜⬜∪⬜⬜⬜⬜⬜

When Kate, Faye, Sally and Maggie walked into the lounge with Zoe all those years later she announced, "Don't you just love it, it's incredible don't you think?"

The impact on them may not have been as profound, but they had certainly been impressed and saw why she had insisted they stay there. Zoe was really pleased that Faye appreciated the interior design as she greatly admired her taste, and she thought Faye's house was particularly beautiful. What's more, Zoe was relieved that the Art Deco masterpiece hadn't been destroyed by corporate branding and was still as magnificent.

The lounge had made a great setting to begin their first night in this unique city and the girls had sipped a few Genever gins there. This was after they had prepared for their night out in a luxurious, self-indulgent, childfree state, drinking wine and being women again rather than mums.

They had got dressed and applied makeup without having to bathe kids at the same time. They didn't have to stop their husband perving over the young babysitter or apologise to them about the unusual smell in the kitchen. They hadn't to explain the intricacies of the TV controls or pray to God the babysitter didn't invite her boyfriend round as soon as they'd stepped out the door.

But Maggie could tell the tale of one such night when her go-to babysitter had indeed invited her boyfriend around whilst she and Shane had gone out. The young lady in question had looked after their girls many times and Maggie and Shane had no worries about leaving their daughters in her capable hands. However, it turned out that the babysitter's boyfriend had quite capable hands too. They returned home to catch them in a state of undress and indulging in what was referred to at Maggie's comprehensive school as heavy petting. But it got far worse when the babysitter later informed Maggie in confidence that she hadn't had a period since that fateful night. Maggie had never experienced being worried about someone else's menstrual cycle before and she also mused that in nine months' time she would still be paying off her interest free instalments for the damn sofa! Luckily for the babysitter it wasn't long after her confession that the curse fell upon her, and Maggie could breathe a sigh of relief that their three-piece suite had only been the site of foreplay.

De Wallen, also known as the *Rosse Buurt* to Amsterdammers and the Red Light District to visitors is actually the oldest part of Amsterdam, an interesting fact about the area to which the girls had been drawn like moths to a flame after a meal and several drinks. Despite the area being dedicated to adult entertainment, the girls had felt and acted like children, peering in windows, pointing, giggling and gasping. Although not adverse to wearing high heels and the odd bit of gentle role play, Zoe had never come across most of the products offered in the local retail outlets. Sally, who was quite worldly on this subject, was also quite perplexed by many of the items on offer. Never before had they seen so many rubbery, often ugly, big, vibrating supposedly erotic things. And why do so many vibrators light up at the end? Sally willingly informed the group that the vibrators Gabe had acquired for their joint pleasure were far prettier and a lot less rubbery!

However, outside the sex shops, the area had been much more scenic than the girls had imagined. Although sordid with prostitutes sitting in windows and live sex on offer every few yards, the shimmering reflection of the red lights in the water of the tree-lined canals had made it all quite picturesque. The area had been vibrant and alive, and people weren't skulking around looking ashamed. They played music in the streets and young couples held hands whilst they wandered passed establishments selling erotica and unlimited ways to climax. Mind you, things got a little too vibrant for the girls when they narrowly missed being flattened by a large television which someone had decided to throw out of the top floor window just as they walked by! A television in 1998 was a substantial piece of equipment, and after a collective exclamation of, "WHAT THE FUCK!" the girls then decided to take refuge inside.

Zoe had thought maybe a nearby bar would suit this purpose, but no, Kate had other ideas. She had spotted an establishment called The Moulin Rouge with a gentleman outside proclaiming, "Live Sex, Very Safe, Family Show No

Animals!" She had then grabbed Faye by the hand and announced, "Come on girls if we don't do this it would be like going to Blackpool and not seeing the lights" and made the rest follow along behind her into the club like frightened sheep! Zoe felt Kate's analogy wasn't going to be quite true but thought trying to protest at the time would have been a pointless exercise.

When they entered the murky underworld of live sex, the first performance was underway. A nubile young woman dressed as a cowgirl in bottomless chaps had taken a no doubt willing male participant from the audience up onto the stage. From their allocated seats stage left, obviously for those visiting for the novelty rather than to get fired up, it had appeared that she had straddled him and was just writhing around on his bare stomach.

The group thought this seemed quite tame with Maggie saying, "I don't see what the hell all the fuss is about?" until that was, the cowgirl and the fella stood up. She had managed to write "YEEHAR!" in capital letters across his midriff with a magic marker that she hadn't held in her hand! The first thing that had come into Zoe's mind was the impressive penmanship and how tight the performer's pelvic floor muscles must be - there was no way on God's earth, after giving birth, that she could have done that! She also thought that Frank would probably just wonder what the hell was going on if she decided to write things on his belly wherever she put the pen!

After the arrival of the free drinks they had been promised as they had paid to come in (which were very watered down), the show had continued with a lesbian display carried out by two girls dressed as New York cops and then a very large Caribbean lady firing fruit from her lady parts. Then the girls braced themselves for the grand finale and "live fucking"!

Pitiful, puny, particularly unattractive with a very long, very skinny penis is a brief description of Mr Salami, the male half of the supposed highlight of the show that night. Zoe had never been keen on salami and now her dislike was very much assured. The look the couple went for was Roman emperor and slave girl. Though the girls were confused at the choice of music that accompanied this tableau as it had all been acted out to the familiar strains of Ravel's *Bolero*. At a total duration of 15 minutes 50 seconds, Zoe hadn't known whether to be impressed or horrified that the couple might keep at it for the whole of the musical piece. Certainly, they bore absolutely no resemblance to Torvil and Dean as the performers had got down to it in a graphic fashion. Far from being charged with sexual tension, Zoe just kept thinking of the practicalities of the whole scenario. How had they rehearsed? How do had they interpreted the music? What if he couldn't get it up on the night, how did they improvise?

Several minutes into the performance, which clearly hadn't been of enough merit or athleticism to have held her attention, Zoe had found herself looking around her alien environment. She thought how sordid and astronomically different those surroundings were to that first day in the antenatal clinic. She scanned the women around her that she already knew were now going to be friends for life and as she had got to Faye, she let out a hoot of laughter at what was probably a very inappropriate moment for Mr Salami and the Slave Girl. Faye had held her free gin and tonic as though her life depended on it and drank it through a straw, her eyes the size of saucers with a look of sheer incredulity. She had resembled a scared rabbit caught in headlights, petrified but transfixed!

Faye did have a naivety which didn't show itself very often. Generally, she appeared full of confidence and the life and soul of any occasion. But little things she mentioned

53

would surprise the girls. For example, when they all found their seats on the Amsterdam flight she announced,

"This is only the third time I've been on a plane", something you certainly never would have thought from her. The live sex show had obviously been way out of Faye's comfort zone and from a world she never thought really existed. Zoe certainly got the impression that, very much like herself, Faye wasn't overly adventurous when it came to sex, and she possibly spent time trying to keep Clive's desires at bay. Mercifully, certainly for Faye, Mr Salami and the Slave Girl had indeed cut Ravel short with a much abridged version of his masterpiece and reached a climax both literally and artistically in well under fifteen minutes. Credit to them though, it was a hell of a way to earn a living! The girls, somewhat dumbstruck, ticked off one of life's experiences and scuttled out of the seedy establishment pronto.

The next day, continuing last night's theme, the girls had decided again that 'when in Rome…'. So, like millions of visitors before them, they'd gone in search of the other illicit thing which Amsterdam so readily has to offer: on the whole, an unfamiliar field to them all, it did bring to mind an ex-boyfriend of Zoe's.

⬜⬜Ⱡ⁂⬜⬜⬜⬜∩⬜……⋯⁚.⋅˙˙⋅.⬜∵⋅⬜⬜⬜∪⬜⬜⬜⬜

He was a few years older than her and a former pupil of the school where her brother had been a teacher. The old flame was a moderately sized fish in the small pond of her hometown, rode a motorbike and generally wanted to be regarded as a bad boy. She had no idea how this relationship came about and recalls it being short-lived having ended after her brother got wind of it! But her enduring memory of this dalliance was that he grew cannabis inside the chimney in his bedroom. He had it all kitted out with fluorescent lamps, lined with aluminium foil and two or three plants happily growing skyward up the chimney! All of which had been hidden from his parents behind a board. Quite ingenious really - shame he hadn't applied the same intelligence at school.

Ironically, Zoe's brother had taught her to roll joints for him and his mates when she was a little girl during the many hours he spent looking after her. She could remember they had a little machine into which you first placed the cigarette paper and then the 'special' tobacco. She became quite adept at it but had not really made much use of her early learning since.

□□Ⅱ⅄□□□□∩□....···⋮.·˙˙·.□∵□□□∪□□□□□

Sally and possibly Maggie may also have had the odd puff of wacky baccy, but the group were pretty uncool about buying cannabis! As none of the girls officially smoked, they'd agreed their best bet was to visit one of the many Amsterdam Coffeeshops. Not to be mistaken for a coffee house or café where they wouldn't have found what they were after. Looking back, their process of selection for a Coffeeshop should have been more thorough, but they'd been girls with limited time and many things to see and do. So, they chose the Coffeeshop they had spotted across the *Leidsplein* from the hotel. Since they were all mothers, they also thought this was a sensible location, in case things went tits up with their exploration of marijuana!

Although really, the girls had given very little thought to this activity and didn't follow any of the advice they would now give to their grown-up children. If either of Zoe's kids had asked her for advice on sampling the usually forbidden delight legally on offer in Amsterdam, which obviously was very doubtful, she would have proffered; "don't underestimate the effects, check out the price, strength, and quality, ease yourself in slowly". The girls didn't heed any such advice and just marched in, sat down, and ordered five space cakes with coffee. The coffeeshops aren't allowed to sell alcohol as well as cannabis which disappointed the naïve group. When the goodies arrived, they hadn't looked the most appetising, being rather bland and slightly green, given the content. Kate, the chef of the group, was very disappointed at the taste and texture of the cake, and they all agreed the space cakes weren't a patch on anything she could have produced for the school fair! Nonetheless, the cakes were polished off and every last crumb eaten. Having eaten their weed, the girls waited for something to happen. Clearly, they were women of the world and knew that instant gratification was a myth but after five minutes they had hoped that at least one of them would feel like they were 'floating man'. Nothing. So, they'd gone back to the hotel, wondered what all the fuss was about and regrouped a short time later for cocktails in the beautiful hotel bar.

It was only many years later that Zoe read on a website that even if you have tried cannabis products in the past you should still be warned that selections in Amsterdam coffeeshops are quite strong. She also gleaned that after eating an 'edible' containing marijuana, it is absorbed into the bloodstream through the stomach and then the liver. Since this absorption process is much slower than in the lungs the effects felt through an edible will be less potent but could last much longer – sometimes between four to six hours. Also, the liver can potentially strengthen the strain, usually resulting in a greater sedative effect. This explained a lot and maybe they should have done this research prior to indulging.

As they'd sat sipping cocktails in their sophisticated art deco surroundings, randomly and completely off topic of the conversation Kate had announced quite loudly, "My arms are really long!" She'd looked very bewildered as she held out her arms and was turning them over and over examining them as if she had acquired two completely new body parts. They'd all started to laugh at Kate's bewildering predicament but some more than others. Zoe found that once she'd started laughing, she couldn't stop. For the next hour and a half at least, she laughed pretty much continuously. This sounds like a great night out and a rather sweet reaction to the cannabis which was then clearly passing through their livers and sending a stronger strain to their brains. But although it was enjoyable for about twenty maybe thirty minutes, laughing then starts to become painful and somewhat embarrassing. Sally and Maggie were just more mellow than usual, and Faye had become hyperactive.

The stereotyping had continued as the girls became ravenous with the onset of the munchies. Fortunately, earlier in the day, a dinner reservation had been made at a Lebanese restaurant recommended by one of Sally's well-travelled friends. Those members of the party that weren't laughing or dragging their imaginary knuckles along the ground had managed to navigate them all to the restaurant. Once ensconced at their table in the rather upmarket and busy eatery, the group had ordered copious amounts of food. Faye normally ate like a bird and had been known to hoover a pizza just scraping off the topping and leaving the evil dough base, but she too placed a request for at least two courses. When the food arrived, they hadn't held back and set on it as though they hadn't eaten in weeks. It was reminiscent of a scene from *The Night of the Living Dead* when a herd of zombies comes across a freshly wounded victim. The biting, chomping and tearing of flesh and the accompanying lip smacks and swallowing noises drew the attention of the other diners and indeed the staff. Maggie had been particularly protective of her king prawns and almost growled at the waiter who came over to check everything was OK. They'd assured him that despite appearances everything was fine. With food in their bellies their blood sugar levels calmed down and normal service resumed. Although Sally and Faye did invoke another outburst of hilarity when they engineered it so that Zoe, of limited height, was dancing next to an extremely tall man in the nightclub that followed on from the restaurant. This was the same venue where despite the music being at usual nightclub volume, Kate and Maggie managed to fall asleep in a corner booth!

□□⊔⅄□□□□∩…⋯∶.⋅¨⋅.□∵□□□⊔□□□□□

Zoe was often thought of as the short member of the group. At a mere 5 foot 2 she will admit she isn't tall. However, Faye isn't much taller if at all but wears killer heels all the time, favouring a pair of wedges. With this Zoe cannot compete as ninety percent of the time she opts for comfort over fashion. As a result, she is stuck with the perception that she is the shortest member of the group. Mind you she should be used to it now as, until her eighteenth birthday she was no taller than four foot eleven and spent much of her later years at school responding to *Short Arse*!

□□⊔⅄□□□□∩…⋯∶.⋅¨⋅.□∵□□□⊔□□□□□

Sitting in the study recapturing the girls' inaugural trip abroad, Zoe mused over the trivial details of the adventure but then she remembered another incident - a classic she felt was worthy of recording. Having experienced the underbelly of Amsterdam they had spent some time doing something more highbrow. The Van Gogh Museum houses the largest collection of his art in the world including two paintings worth £100 million which were stolen and then supposedly retrieved from the Italian Mafia. So, the group had thought this venue would not only raise the intellectual level of their activities but would also be a quiet, gentle environment in which to nurse their post cannabis headaches and aching tummies.

Once inside the iconic museum, they'd mulled around and admired the world-famous paintings of sunflowers, bridges, portraits of Van Gogh himself with one or both ears and a plethora of other less famous canvasses. Many people visiting used audio guides to talk them through the priceless collection. Zoe had sat nursing her abdominals whilst contemplating a particularly pleasant painting when Faye had plonked herself down on the leather bench next to her.

After they passed various inane comments to each other and chose their favourite masterpiece, Faye had come up with something priceless herself. In all seriousness she turned to Zoe and asked, "Why are so many people using their mobile phones?"

Now bear in mind this was 1998 and the phone of choice was a brick like Nokia with push buttons, a fixed aerial, no camera and no internet. But it had still taken Zoe a few moments to grasp what Faye was talking about. When the penny dropped, she'd thought how much this comment reflected their first world background! The mobiles to which Faye had referred were the museum audio guides and Zoe hadn't held back the condescension when she explained this to her ditsy friend. However far from being embarrassed by her ineptitude the explanation merely made Faye and Zoe laugh loud and long to the annoyance of the more serious art lovers that were present. Faye, bless her, could always take a joke at her own expense and to be fair was equally good at taking the mickey out of her companions – she possessed wicked observational skills and wasn't afraid to use them!

The final lasting impression Zoe recalled about Amsterdam involved silver lurex. Never a forgiving fabric, Zoe had left behind in the late 80s anything made from lurex or its equally body-hugging counterparts. Since giving birth, clothing that clung to her body was still a no-no and would be for some time to come. However, it was and still is the go-to material along with Lycra for costumes of entertainers, acrobats and sportspeople. When Zoe had first met Frank, he was partial to Lycra clothing as he was then a keen cyclist - not an acrobat clearly. In fact, his firm, sharply defined thighs were a definite plus when they were courting: but when he went cycling Zoe always had difficulty with the concept of shorts that had chamois leather padding in the crotch. It just conjured up images of far too much sweat in areas of Frank best avoided.

No, this ditty related to the street entertainment which the girls had been treated to whilst they enjoyed their last cup of coffee al fresco in the *Leidsplein*. The surroundings were not as idyllic and relaxing as you may have just summoned up. The group tried to chill after a frantic morning buying souvenirs for all those at home and to curb the guilt of having enjoyed themselves so much without them. Unfortunately their efforts had been thwarted by a man in very close proximity to them who had juggled with whirring chainsaws. At the time the only medical qualifications the girls could have mustered between them would have been Faye's BSc (Hons) in Optometry, so they would have been no help really if a mishap had occurred! The atmosphere was tense, and the girls had wanted his routine over with.

What's more, there had been a man high up above them in the nearby trees doing acrobatic and precarious things with a rope. This sounds tame compared to the chainsaw guy, but the treetop acrobat had only been wearing the smallest, silver lurex thong. Although his glutimus maximus had to be admired, having his lunchbox dangled in front of them wasn't the lasting image they had wanted to take home from their trip to the Dutch capital!

Chapter 4

Barcelona - The Alphabet Tour is born!

"Friends that travel together stay together."
Anon

Some of life between tours.

Eric's turn to take his first steps and after a slow start there was no stopping him. He went at top speed everywhere!

Abi had a 4th birthday party at the local Wacky Warehouse. To Sally's horror one of the kids invited had a poo under the party food table. Not a great thing to have to tell the parent when collecting the child. Not surprisingly said parent is suitably mortified!

Sadly Faye's Godmother died. She took it badly as they were very close.

Charlie and Abi were spoilt rotten during a visit from Stuart's parents from California. They mentioned they're toying with the idea of moving home to the UK. Sally isn't sure how she feels about this, although it would be lovely for the kids who adore them.

Maggie and Shane went on the first of many family cruises.

Frank grew a goatee beard which comes through ginger and made him look like a serial killer. It didn't last long!

The success of Amsterdam had pretty much cemented Zoe and her four antenatal cohorts as life-long friends. It provided masses of material for reminiscing, which the five of them had done several times over many, many glasses of wine. Of course, they were also eager to plan their next trip. With lives full of nappies, work, school runs, studying and general domestic chaos, it was great to have something to focus on and look forward to. As Zoe began to gather her memories about the girls' second overseas adventure, she realised that even back then, these trips were an important lifeline. Something for themselves and an opportunity for each of the five women to retain their personality and individuality.

Although Zoe didn't appreciate it then, Frank was, and still is, a great husband and dad. Even so she had still struggled to varying degrees with motherhood - especially after Holly's birth. She went back to a full-time job that demanded a long commute, having convinced herself she could do it all. The night when she broke down in tears at 9pm with a trolley half full of shopping, by the chiller cabinet in the supermarket, she realised that perhaps she couldn't. She felt so ashamed that she couldn't be a good mother, wife, sex goddess, friend, cleaner, children's entertainer, confidante, loyal daughter-in-law, sister, aunt, cook, decorator, nurse and work full time. She was a woman - she thought being a mother would just come naturally. So why did she feel so shit and cry so much? Why couldn't she do it?

Holly was a beautiful baby but sometimes it was just so hard. Often when Holly wouldn't stop crying Zoe had to put her in her cot, close the door and walk away, just to stay sane. In Zoe's mind, middle class people living in leafy suburbs shouldn't feel like this. She thought all her friends could cope, why couldn't she? Thankfully, although she didn't know where it came from, Zoe had the strength to recognise this wasn't just the infamous 'baby blues' and that she needed help. She took herself off to the doctor and blurted it all out; her feelings of inadequacy for not breastfeeding; how was it that she could feel anger, even rage with such a gorgeous baby?; her lack of euphoria at having had a healthy child; why did she crave time away from her baby and how does a baby produce so much pooh and vomit, and cry so loud, for so long?

After her torrent of woe, punctuated with many tears, the short rapid breathing and, of course, a lot of snot, the doctor gave her a tissue and his diagnosis. He told her that in his professional opinion, like countless new mothers, she had a mild case of postnatal depression. Zoe had to confess to herself that she probably felt that depression was something you could snap out of and that it was a sign of weakness or self-pity – now she knew how wrong she was. Growing up the media had helped to fuel her misconceptions by often portraying people with mental health issues as violent criminals, deranged strangers mumbling about where the body was buried or bitter, evil women snatching babies from their idyllic homes. These characters were always taken away to some institution never to be seen again.

The doctor very calmly explained that she wasn't a freak, or a failure, that depression is an illness not a weakness and that she had a chemical imbalance in her brain. Much to her relief he confirmed she could get help. He then got out his prescription pad and began talking about the drugs she could take to help.

Although again probably misguidedly, Zoe heard alarm bells – she didn't want to add drug addiction to her list of things to deal with then. So, she politely declined medication and asked:

"What other options are on offer?"

The doctor then arranged a meeting with the counsellor attached to the surgery whom he said should be able to help without chemical intervention. Zoe remembered leaving the practice hopeful that her shitty, dark state of mind and feelings of despair and inadequacy would soon be a thing of the past. However, the meeting with the counsellor proved to be the opposite of what she had hoped for. With some trepidation Zoe had arrived for her session on time – arriving anywhere on time was quite a feat at this stage of her life - and had been shown to a room at the back of the building. She already felt as though people were treating her as if she was mad and this special, tucked away room only made it worse. Zoe sat alone for at least ten minutes in this uninviting room before an officious woman came in. She had to assume this was the counsellor, as she made no attempt to introduce herself. Her opening gambit to Zoe, her new patient with a mental issue was: "I only have forty minutes; I have to pick up my son from lacrosse practice."

Although Zoe could relate to the woman's tight family schedule, this approach didn't put her at ease. She certainly didn't want to tell this anonymous, clockwatching stranger her innermost feelings and fears. She made her excuses and left, feeling devastated and even more of a liability than before. On her return home, infuriated and out of despair and anger, she rang the surgery and complained to her doctor. The person he had sent her to, had made her feel stigmatised, not understood and may as well have just told Zoe to pull herself together. A few days later, having listened to Zoe's complaint the doctor got in touch and asked if she would be prepared to speak to their practice nurse who had counselling training. Somewhat reluctantly after her last experience she agreed.

The practice nurse turned out to be a marvellous woman who could empathise with Zoe, helping her realise she wasn't alone. She was older than Zoe and looked very much like Nerys Hughes in *The District Nurse* - both of which were qualities Zoe instantly found comforting. She told her reassuring facts like one in ten women experience postnatal depression within a year of giving birth. She talked about ways she could help herself without using antidepressants and how talking with other mums and your family really helps. But it was the anecdotal advice and her empathy which Zoe took the most from. Although they were grown up, the nurse had children of her own so was understanding and compassionate. She made Zoe relaxed and comfortable, not rushed and an inconvenience. The nurse told Zoe that once she had asked her now adult boys whether they would have changed anything when they were growing up, they had replied:

"We wish you hadn't spent so much time cleaning and had spent more time playing with us."

This was something which Zoe would remember all her life and since then whenever there was an opportunity for fun with her family, she'd taken it – often whether the family wanted to have fun or not!

The nurse also imparted that most women out there, new mums or otherwise, struggle to varying degrees and a lot are hanging on by a thread. Comforting though it was for Zoe to know she wasn't completely useless as a mother, it was worrying to think there are so many women wandering around the world who at any minute could completely lose the plot.

For the record, it turned out that the doctors' surgery had been waiting for someone to complain and the counsellor was subsequently "politely asked to find an alternative place to practise."

During the year since Amsterdam things had moved on for all the girls. Unlike Zoe, when Kate had gone back to work, she'd managed to retain all her faculties. She'd started working for her uncle, well uncle by marriage, Geoffrey. He was married to Auntie Fern, on her dad's side who many members of her family said Kate really looked like – although Zoe had never really seen it beyond a passing family resemblance. Kate had made every possible effort to shed her baby weight and her hair had grown longer after cutting it short following the birth of Francesca – a knee jerk reaction to try and help make her life with a newborn more manageable. Geoffrey was a really thoughtful gentleman and when a part time vacancy had come up at his firm, he thought Kate would be ideal and that she may like to get back to work. He certainly had that right.

Despite having a houseful of small children to keep her busy, Kate hated having nothing to keep her ever active brain occupied. However, since she had started looking for work again after having Kitty, she had realised that the computing world she had left before taking maternity leave had changed. It was then the late 1990s, a radical new era in the world of technology and communication. With the ever-increasing power of the internet and the world-wide web, everything was rapidly evolving. Cell phones, computers at home, Amazon, Apple, SMS messaging were all starting to become commonplace. And along with all this the skills of those working in the industry had had to adapt – Kate's hadn't. In her short period of maternity leave, to her horror a lot of her CV had become obsolete.

But Kate still had aspirations and ambition and wanted to accomplish things. She was not a person to be told she couldn't do things. She had two daughters now and she wanted to be able to inspire them as they grew older. Her mum, Louise, had been an amazing role model to her, having been a teacher, businesswoman and mother – she wanted to carry on that legacy.

So, the offer from Uncle Geoffrey had come at the perfect time. He knew from first-hand experience that Kate had amazing logistical skills which coupled with her economic background would make her an asset to his office. He also knew she wouldn't have any trouble picking up the new skills required for the advanced computer age. So, after her initial panic that she was professionally antiquated, she grabbed the opportunity to get back into the working world. She had reasoned that the children weren't young forever and, with the help of her family support network she would make being a successful working mum possible. If anyone could do it, she could and she'd thrived on juggling roles, commuting three days a week and loved organising her life and Max and the kids.

Wanting more from life than looking after the children had been infectious that year as, completely independently from Kate's venture, Maggie had also started in a completely new direction. Having had three babies in rapid succession, she had decided she wanted to know more about the miracle of life. She completely switched her career path from sales and had applied to university to study midwifery! Since having the twins Maggie had come to realise that at that time there wasn't a great deal of support for those who'd had multiple births and the unique issues it presented. People would often make comments to her about how lucky she was to have two babies but just one pregnancy and how beautiful it must be to have an instant family. Maggie's usual thoughts were more along the lines of, if she managed to get to the end of the day and they were all still alive she'd done a good job. Although, through the power of a great community midwife she had found a group of mothers with twins that met once a week in a draughty church hall to share their unique predicament and offload their problems to someone who could truly relate.

Inspired by her midwife and the women she met at this group, Maggie's interest was spiked in the difficulties other women experienced after and during pregnancy and not just those having multiple births. Pregnancy wasn't always the wondrous thing it was painted, and many couples went through traumatic experiences both before and after the birth. She had decided long before then that she wasn't going back to her career in sales and had known in her heart that she wanted to care for people rather than pitch them new products.

With her calm demeanour, kind heart and ability to be non-judgemental, the girls knew she had what it would take to become a midwife. Zoe for one could not have coped with the physical logistics of this job. As far as she was concerned the only saving grace about giving birth was that you didn't have to see what was going on at the business end of proceedings! Maggie was waiting for offers from local universities. Of course, she couldn't apply too far away as she still had to get home easily for her babies and Shane. This was going to be multi-tasking at the highest level.

□□Ɫɫ入□□□□∩□...···∶.··.□∵·□□□∪□□□□□

For their second weekend away, after many discussions fuelled by G&T, wine and fizz, the girls had decided on a trip to Barcelona. They reckoned it had something for them all. There was architecture and the beach for Zoe, Cava and shops for Faye and good food for Sally who does like a nice lunch and Kate and Maggie were happy with all the above. However, the timings of this trip were such that the group had to fly from Liverpool airport. Every time Zoe goes to Liverpool airport and sees the John Lennon classic lyric – 'Above us only Sky '- emblazoned across the terminal, she has the same thoughts. Somehow in this context the words seem crass. Then she starts to think of other lyrics that could go up on an airport wall –" Come Fly with me, let's fly, let's fly away" Old Blue Eyes or possibly "Fly Away" Lenny Kravitz or at a push "Flying without Wings" by Westlife. But ironically not "Leaving on a Jet Plane" by John Denver, given the nature of his untimely death. As the girls had headed across the concourse, Zoe had felt pretty sure she was the only one thinking like this and kept her musings to herself – something she found she was doing increasingly more often as she grew older!

⬚⬚Ⅱλ⬚⬚⬚⬚∩⬚…⋯⋮.·˙˙.⬚·∵⬚⬚⬚∪⬚⬚⬚⬚

As Zoe sat once again in front of the computer, she found that she was really enjoying recording her memories from her travels with her crew. Although she did feel a bit selfish spending time tucked away in the study. Frank was now working in Leeds everyday which was a hell of a commute. So, when he was home, she felt she should be looking after him more, not leaving him with the kids whilst she wrote down the details of her adventures with her female friends. Obviously, Frank also had friends, but he wasn't one for organising get togethers. He'd go along to things if invited no problem but was unlikely to be the instigator of social events. Zoe and he differed in this way as she loved nothing more than inviting people round and being with people. Although to be fair to him, Frank often came up with the best ideas for parties and always put in a great effort with costumes and decorations. Although he was dressed as Gordon the Thunderbird when they had met, over the years Zoe had got a little concerned about his particular delight at dressing up as a pirate! Overall, Zoe felt Frank was happy with his own company and that of his family and close friends, so her guilt wasn't too deep rooted.

As she wrote, it also became clear that, as a diarist Zoe was more Adrian Mole than Samuel Pepys, with greater poetic licence than historical accuracy. And when Zoe referred to the girls as her crew, she wouldn't have dreamt of trying to be the leader of this group of headstrong women. Kate is a self-confessed control freak with an amazing grasp of logistics. Maggie often goes with the flow but has amazing clarity when the group reaches an impasse. Faye usually gets her way through charm and flattery. Sally doesn't take any crap from anyone and is the first to step up in a fight and usually gets what she wants in a polite but assertive way. So quite happily, Zoe usually took on the role of backup, reiterating what the others had said or done. And she tittered as she thought of the numerous occasions when she had witnessed poor souls being subjected to the girls using all the above skills at the same time.

Although she found as she got older, she had become increasingly intolerant of bad behaviour and poor service – often much to Holly and Eric's embarrassment.

⬚⬚⊔⅄⬚⬚⬚⬚∩⬚…⋯⋮·⋯⋅.⬚∵⬚⬚⬚⊔⬚⬚⬚⬚

Indeed, when the group had arrived at their hotel in Barcelona, just off *The Ramblas* there had been the potential for the collective might of this group to materialise. They had got off to a good start when, on arrival, the door of the hotel airport transfer minibus was opened by a porter who'd greeted them and showed them to reception. However once at reception they had been told that they could no longer stay at the hotel. They'd been instantly riled and, as one, had taken a step forward. Given the level of menace that had suddenly materialised, the receptionist had quickly explained that there had been a flood in the night and the ladies had been relocated to an equally good hotel nearby.

As they had been handed vouchers for free drinks at their new accommodation the girls had graciously accepted the new arrangements and traipsed across the street with the sweet porter coming along behind them with all their luggage on one of those tall, brass trolleys that are always shown in American hotels on TV.

Once installed in their respective rooms, the girls had headed out. *The Ramblas* had been throbbing – not a word Zoe uses very often. Throbbing is up there with moist, both words make her grimace slightly. But on this occasion, it seemed appropriate as the place had indeed been vibrant and pulsating with life. Well, that is apart from the human statues of which there had been many. It had to be said these had varied in ability. Some had been absolutely brilliant and even the odd pigeon had been fooled into landing on them. Others had been quite frankly, crap and if Zoe had covered herself in silver paint she probably could have stood still for longer.

The girls had been more focused on finding a sunny picturesque spot for lunch. After consulting their travel guide a couple of times, they'd located *Placa Reial* - a beautiful, enclosed square lined with palm trees, a charming fountain, restaurants, and bars and dotted with people enjoying the Spanish sun. Perfect. The girls had chosen a table strategically half in the sun but with an umbrella to provide shade. The group are divided on the sun/shade issue. Kate and Faye love nothing better than to gently roast themselves in the hot sun. The others Zoe and Maggie in particular, just get a bit agitated and sweaty and much prefer their sunshine filtered.

□□Ⅱℵ□□□□∩□…∵∵⋮∙∙⁚∙∙⁚∙.□∵∙□□□∪□□□□□

When Zoe was younger, she could lie on the beach for hours covered in what was essentially cooking oil. In those days skin cancer wasn't a general concern and if you went anywhere sunny on holiday it was vital to come back to England with a tan – preferably all over. Zoe had even been known to sunbathe topless in the good old days when her boobs didn't disappear towards her armpits when she lay down. She also wore a bikini or a costume that was so high cut she looked like a trapeze artist. She sighed as she thought of the days of being slim with perky boobs and a healthy glow. Now that she's of the age when, if she wears a swimming costume it doesn't attract the attention of young men but covers her up because of the threat of melanoma and holds everything in. But going on holiday is actually a lot simpler. Her costume is more comfortable, there isn't anywhere near as much preparation required, removing hair from here and trimming it there or worrying about tan lines. She just makes sure her pubes aren't too scarily bushy, and her armpits are hair free. Mind you she does still get her toenails painted. A habit she developed not to be glamorous but when she'd had an outbreak of nail fungus after which her toes had never looked the same!

As she wrote down her thoughts from Barcelona, Zoe realised that it was where and when she'd had an epiphany. Sitting there in *Placa Reial* under the parasol sipping sangria with her friends, she'd known she'd finally reached the age when she was content and, passe though it sounded, she was happy in her own skin. There are very few people in this world with whom you can be your unreserved self. Frank, of course, was top of this list for Zoe, followed by Zahra, her very precious friend whom she'd known since junior school and, of course, Kate. But the rest of *The Alphabetties* were rapidly gaining a place close behind them. Back then in Spain, from the look on everyone's faces and their body language it seemed to Zoe that the other girls had developed similar feelings. The ambience and alcohol inevitably meant they'd begun to discuss once again how marvellous their weekends away were. They laughed out loud as they'd recalled their exploits in Amsterdam, often causing those nearby to stop and turn to see what was causing the commotion. Then, from nowhere, and it's never been established from whom, they've probably all taken credit for it when telling this tale to other friends, one of them said:

"A for Amsterdam B for Barcelona - we should work our way through the alphabet!".

It had instantly been agreed that this was **an absolutely fantastic idea** and, much to the waiter's delight, a jug of Cava Royale had been ordered in celebration. Everyone thought that this was brilliant, and they must do it. So, there in *Placa Reial*, off *The Ramblas* in Barcelona, Catalonia, Spain, 41.39 latitude and 2.16 longitude at elevation 47 metres above sea level, Europe, Earth, Milky Way Galaxy, *The Alphabet Tour* had been officially born. And thus, without hesitation, the girls had sealed their friendship for at least the next twenty-four years!

Having mapped out one weekend of their lives for the next couple of decades, Zoe, Kate, Maggie, Faye and Sally – from now on aka *The Alphabetties* – had thought perhaps they should get on with making some memories ready to recount next year. This in mind they'd ambled back up *The Ramblas* to their hotel for a quick nap (because they could) and change for the evening's exploits. However, once back in the hotel room, and having perused the room service menu, Zoe, Kate and Maggie – who often shared a room - decided a sneaky bottle of wine would be marvellous.

They'd ordered a bottle of chilled Vino Blanco Catalán – the girls always liked to support the local industry – and very soon there had been a knock at the door. Maggie had leapt up to answer it and, to Zoe and Kate's surprise, had shown the waiter in. Maggie has a devilish streak and had let the waiter enter, knowing full well that her roomies were relaxing on the bed in just their bra and knickers. To be honest, despite Maggie finding it amusing, the other two hadn't even flinched. Zoe had reckoned an experienced hotel waiter would have seen a lot worse in his time. Though on this occasion it had been a young man who'd blushed profusely and tried to avert his gaze from Kate and Zoes' sizeable bosoms – bless him. Zoe recollected thinking, "Thank God I'm wearing my half decent underwear!"

☐☐Ⅱ⅄☐☐☐☐∩☐…⋯⋮.⋯⋅.☐∴☐☐☐∪☐☐☐☐

In years to come, Zoe would look back on that moment in front of the young waiter and think how illogical people could be, in particular she would think of when she eventually went for her first mammogram. As a woman, one of the small delights of growing older is the reduced frequency of having cervical smear tests. But then once you hit fifty, regular mammograms kick in. When the appointment had arrived for her initial breast screening Zoe hadn't immediately thought of how great the NHS was or "Oh my God they must think I've got breast cancer!" No, her mind went straight to, "Shit I'll have to find time to go and buy a new bra and pants."

Frank had never shown any great interest in Zoe wearing sexy lingerie. She had tried on the odd occasion to spice things up a bit, but Frank was happy just to get everything off and get matters underway! So, the smalls Zoe possessed, whilst being quite pretty, were reasonably priced and comfortable rather than expensive and lacy. Also, Zoe had to admit to herself that a lot of her bra and pants were that horrid grey colour that all underwear seems to go eventually. So new items were purchased and off she went to the fabulous new breast screening clinic at her local hospital.

Once there, she realised that the new underwear had been a complete waste of time. She'd been ushered into a very small room to take off all her upper clothing and then gone through a door at the other end of the room, boobs proudly on display, straight into the screening room. Not a soul had seen her new balcony bra with lace trim and easy fastening and her new knickers had never featured in the process at all. The lady waiting to carry out the screening had been lovely, and despite being quite short, had managed to explain things without looking at Zoe's chest once. She'd asked:

"Have you had a mammogram before?"
and explained that it wouldn't take long:

"But there may be some discomfort."

Well, that had been an understatement! In the past, when her breasts had been examined, it had been a very gentle laying on of hands, at the most a little circular pressure. Not that time. Zoe's breasts were flopped one at a time onto the scanner and squashed as flat as they would possibly go as the lid of the machine just kept coming down. It really hadn't been pleasant at all. She'd never seen her knockers resemble thick scotch pancakes before - horrifying. As the scanner kept squeezing her breast, it reminded her of a scene from a Bond movie when he's strapped to a table with a laser coming between his legs getting closer and closer to his private parts! Mercifully it had been a very short procedure and things bounced back to their normal shape straight away. Zoe had put her beautiful new bra back on but what she'd really wanted to do was wander into reception displaying it to all the clinic staff to show she'd made an effort on their behalf!

As Zoe had left the clinic, she'd told herself that what she had just experienced was so worth it and was much better than the alternative. Fairly recently Maggie had confided in the girls that her elder sister had died of breast cancer a couple of years before she had met them. Maggie's family were shattered and although they weren't torn apart by her death, the relationships within the family had never been the same, like a shadow had been cast over it. Her sister's death was devastating, especially as she left two small children behind.

Having two brothers, Maggie and her sister were naturally close; they had a unique history. They had grown up together and she had known Maggie in a special way, different to those who had only known her as an adult. She was Maggie's oldest friend, protector and confidante.

Her sister was also a twin with Maggie's eldest brother and her sister's death had meant a redefinition of the family. Maggie was now the only daughter and her relationship with her parents had changed. Over the years she would be expected to look after them, become the main caregiver and they would turn to her when they needed support.

Adult siblings are sometimes called the 'forgotten mourners' – their grief somehow not seeming as great as that of the spouse, parents or children. People had asked Maggie and her brothers how her parents and her sister's family were coping, expecting them to be stronger somehow to deal with this momentous unfair change. But when the time finally came, grief had hit Maggie like a train and had just kept rolling over her since her sister's death. To Maggie's surprise she had also felt fear – fear of what would happen if she too developed cancer or any other reason that led to her dying unexpectedly. She hadn't been afraid of death before, when she thought it would happen when she was an old lady going doolally in her twilight years. But now she had the frightening reality that it could happen anytime. What would happen to Shane and her beautiful girls?

For a while she had found this fear overwhelming – she had been wounded and it had taken her time to heal. She'd also felt that the loss of her sister had fuelled her desire to help people and had definitely contributed to her career change. She knew she wanted to have a rewarding, value driven life.

☐☐⊔⅄☐☐☐☐∏☐…∵∴∴∴∴∴☐∵☐☐☐⊔☐☐☐☐☐

After they'd changed into evening attire, *The Alphabetties* had regrouped in the hotel bar to spend the free drink vouchers they'd received on arrival. Glasses of cava and a couple of G&Ts were ordered from a fresh-faced waiter. The waiter had taken their order in perfect English and made Zoe think once again how lucky we are as a nation, that the international language is our home tongue. She also thought how lazy our history had made us when it came to learning another language. She had failed French O Level which her mother blamed on her poor brother. Apparently in her mother's eyes as he was a French teacher it should have been his responsibility to ensure his little sister could string a sentence together in French!

Indeed, there were moments on tour when communication went astray. Clearly during this tour, a knowledge of Spanish would have been useful. For instance, when the group wanted another round of drinks, Maggie had caught the waiter's eye and asked for: "The same again please."

Zoe smiled as she pictured the puzzled faces when a tray of five cooled glasses of Saint Miguel lager turned up.

Apparently, at the time of *The Alphabetties* second adventure, according to some of the world travel press *"the city that never sleeps"* was a nickname that had been given to eight global twenty-four-hour cities; New York, Buenos Aires, Sao Paulo, Tel Aviv, Belgrade, Mumbai, Madrid, and Barcelona. Having discovered this gem in their background research, the girls had been confident that they'd have a good night whilst in Spain's second city. Their guidebook had shown plenty of bars and restaurants in the Marina/Seafront area which were also relatively close to the Olympic village – that had seemed like a good place to head for. Undeniably, they'd found plenty of places to eat in this area, not surprisingly many of which specialised in fish and seafood. Although fish was not Zoe's first choice, they'd all found something to order on the menu. She didn't like eating seafood or shellfish or anything slimy and uncooked. And, despite their reputation, oysters just seemed to her like a complete waste of time as a food source. However, she did recall that the other girls had been more adventurous, ordering octopus and Faye had had a side dish of *Arros Negre* or Black Rice. This is a Catalan delicacy made with white rice, garlic, paprika and squid ink – the ink enhances the seafood flavour and gives the dish its distinct colour. Zoe, and in fact all the rest of the girls, had steered clear. Faye had polished off the lot, which had been impressive for a girl with the appetite of a mouse. It was only the next day that she'd regretted her actions. She'd arrived at breakfast the next morning walking a little strangely after visiting the loo and announced that she thought she had bowel cancer!

⬜⬜Ⅱℷ⬜⬜⬜⬜∩⬜…⋯∴.⋅ ̈⋅.⬜∵⬜⬜⬜∪⬜⬜⬜⬜⬜

Obviously, Faye was in very good health and her figure had gone back to being as great as it was pre babies. She was also back at work, where she certainly felt her visual image was part of her brand. Faye is the perfect advocate for presenting an attractive, up-to-date, professional image that represents how you want the world to see you – after all first impressions are supposed to be made within the first tenth of a second of meeting someone. That said she definitely didn't support cosmetic surgery or fad diets but looking after herself and presentation were important to her, and she did both very well although she would never admit that herself.

Having gone back to work, she'd decided it would give her more flexibility to do locum work rather than be tied to one practice full-time. This meant on her return, despite still limiting herself to locations close to home, that there were a lot of new faces, many of whom were younger than her and still full of ambition. In one very trendy opticians' in fact her furthest venue from home, most of the staff looked like they had just stepped out of the pages of *GQ* and *Cosmopolitan*. Nonetheless they'd all been very welcoming, and Faye had soon been invited to social events which pleased her and boosted her ego. Outwardly Faye oozed confidence and certainty. But like many women, inside she was often nervous and needed reassurance. Little things like being invited for drinks by her younger peers told Faye she was doing OK.

⬚⬚Ⅱ⁁⬚⬚⬚⬚∩⬚…··⋮.·¨·.⬚∵⬚⬚⬚∪⬚⬚⬚⬚

One good thing about Zoe's chosen career path was that it had allowed her to indulge her love of buildings, such as the American Hotel when they had visited Amsterdam. She wasn't interested in the technicalities of construction, just what they looked like and how their aesthetics impacted our lives. So, for her, going to Barcelona had another dimension, Antoni Gaudi. His work in Barcelona has been globally recognised and designated a world heritage site. Zoe completely agreed with this recognition. To her, his work was wonderful, free flowing, colourful, natural and above all, wacky. She wished all architects could be allowed to express their imagination more. When she was working full time, Local Government had been confined by ever decreasing budgets and infiltrated by bigoted, uninspired councillors. This in turn meant that many planning authorities had played safe and more blandness had permeated the built environment. Frustrated, she often wondered where the vision had gone? Why can't the built environment respect its surroundings and create wonderful buildings like Gaudi with curves, individuality, and eccentricity? Thankfully things seemed to be changing with amazing buildings like The Sage in Gateshead, The Gherkin and The Shard in London, The Imperial War Museum in Salford and Urbis in Manchester, cities are once again featuring modern but iconic buildings. Coincidentally one of Gaudi's first design projects were the lampposts for the *Plaça Reial*. Zoe liked that and felt he'd given the *Alphabet Tour* his seal of approval!

So, when it had been decided that the group would book an open top bus tour of the city, Zoe had been delighted as it took in several of Gaudi's works. This included the *Sagrada Familia* where they had alighted for a closer look. Funnily enough, on arrival, the first exclamation from the girls hadn't been: "Wow what an incredible monument to postmodern geometric stylistic experimentation." Rather it had been: "It's not finished!"

Zoe had told the girls to give the Catalonians a break. They'd only been at it for a hundred and sixteen years by then and they weren't scheduled to finish until 2026. After further examination of the cathedral, they'd all agreed the place was amazing inside and out – even unfinished!

Of course, Faye, being uber fit had wanted to climb up to the highest viewing point within the structure and, as ever, she had managed to persuade the rest of them that this was a good idea. At about two thirds of the way down one of the many *Sagrada* towers, some of the girls had begun to wish that Gaudi had thrown in the occasional straight wall and staircase. The curvaceous nature of the spiral staircase and its slight but definite camber had meant a couple of the group had felt distinctly nauseous.

Much to Zoe's delight, the open-topped bus had also taken them to *Park Guell*, passed *Casa Mila* and *Casa Batllo* before returning them to *Placa de Catalunya*. Zoe had spent the trip, probably annoyingly pointing out rooftops, façade details and architectural gems to the girls. The results of this had been the adoption by the group of a Zoe inspired mantra when visiting foreign parts: "Look up girls, always look up!"

By the end of the bus tour the group had been ravenous and had agreed that it had reached the time to try another local speciality, tapas. They'd all had the British version of tapas before, but they'd felt sure it would be a step up in its country of origin.

The search for food on tour had meant that, as a unit, the girls did an exorbitant amount of aimless wandering in pursuit of the perfect location for any given meal. Kate and Zoe eat pretty much anywhere if they're hungry and the food looks decent. Faye, Sally and Maggie are definitely choosier about where to eat and drink. Hunger is a signal that the brain needs more fuel. It's triggered when the level of nutrients in our bloodstream begins to drop. When the brain runs dry of fuel, it stimulates a stress response. In Zoe it meant she became snappy and irritable and would generally get pissed off after the third or fourth eating place had been rejected. Being Zoe's BFF, Kate had come to recognise the signs that Zoe was getting hangry – hungry and angry- such as muttering, "oh for fuck's sake" under her breath and huffing a lot. Kate had learned to skilfully spot a decent restaurant that would hopefully satisfy everyone's sensitivities and at least serve a palatable bottle of wine that would ease any mounting tension.

On this occasion, group hanger meant that they were rather foolhardy and had ended up in a tapas restaurant on *The Ramblas*. However, it had a table available in the window to watch the world go by and an efficient waiter had brought them sangria almost before their bums had touched the seats. A collective sigh of relief had gone out as the hangry group were to be fed imminently. The menu had a good selection of recognised and new tapas which the girls had been hoping for and the order was placed. The dishes that were brought out included the usual *patatas bravas* and *albondigas* which had been fine. However, some of the other dishes were not. Although Zoe and Kate aren't in any shape or form, highbrow about food they have their limits. The *pincho morino*, was supposed to have been a Moorish flavoured chicken kebab. Maggie had been convinced the chef had nipped outside and killed a pigeon perched on one of the many human statues and had stuck it on a skewer. The *patatas a lo pobre*, potatoes in a creamy sauce with pimento, had tasted uncannily like a can of Heinz vegetable salad that was served up by your mum in the 1970s (usually followed by tinned fruit cocktail and Dream Topping for dessert).

Normally if Zoe thought about food or watched a cookery programme on TV, she would get hungry. For example she and Eric now have a guilty pleasure of watching *The Great British Bake Off* together. The last episode they'd seen was caramel week and the pair of them had been nearly salivating. However, not surprisingly recollecting this tapas experience hadn't triggered the same reaction at all. Zoe recalled that increasing hunger had driven the girls to eat some of the disappointing dishes soon followed by fury when they were presented with the bill.

Everyone knows that eating in a prime tourist location is going to be more expensive, but this, given the standard of the cuisine, had been insulting. The waiter had made the mistake of presenting the astronomical bill to Sally and oh, she hadn't been happy! Whilst the others muttered about being ripped off, she'd marched off, and almost squared up to the concierge, whom she dominated over as she had reached her full height. As Zoe watched the exchange from a safe distance, she could see why Sally was so successful at her job. She was a force to be reckoned with.

The bill for their meal of small, shared dishes had come to the exorbitant price of, in current money, forty euros each. Even with sangria – which was also mediocre – this had been outrageous and Sally had let loose. She'd approached the head waiter and politely said:

"Excuse me I think our bill is incorrect."

Despite speaking English perfectly well when the girls had arrived, he now started to behave like Manuel from *Fawlty Towers* and just replied "que?". Sally had repeated her statement several times getting closer to him and shoving the bill under his nose, getting more and more frustrated. Eventually the waiter managed to string together "No, no this is what you must pay".

Whatever Sally said to him he just kept repeating it back at Sally. Despite her frustration – she'd felt like giving the guy a slap – she had returned to her more cowardly companions with steam coming out of her ears. She had explained the situation and bar fighting their way out, the girls had realised their only option was to pay this ridiculous bill – minus the optional service charge. They'd left the restaurant with a worse feeling in their stomachs than when they'd gone in!

Although the stand-off in the tapas bar had highlighted that Sally seemed to be the one that didn't take any shit, she too had a vulnerable side and sometimes she tired of being the one who had to hold it together. Occasionally she just wanted someone to put their arms around her and take all her cares away.

Despite a lovely singsong accent her mother had never been a particularly demonstrative woman and with her more pessimistic outlook she wasn't a warm, cuddly mum. Sally was determined to give her girls all the maternal bonding both physical and emotional she could. This was undeniably one of the reasons she had been attracted to Gabe whose public displays of affections were numerous and always available. When they had first met, Sally and Gabe couldn't keep their hands off each other and would happily snuggle no matter where they were. Sally loved showing the world how comfortable they were with each other – she was proud to show everyone their loving bond. But as the years had passed, she was beginning to feel they were less important, certainly to her and questioned for whose benefit they were?

□□⫙⫙⫯□□□□∩□…··∴.·˙˙.□∴□□□∪□□□□□

Later, in order to banish the tapas debacle, the girls had headed out into the Barcelona night on a mission to have a good time. More by sheer dumb luck than judgement, they'd found the perfect place to do just that. Again, having a senior moment Zoe has no real idea where in Barcelona they'd gone, but the girls had found what they came to call *The Disco Bars*. Located together in a row, there had been several nondescript looking, glass fronted bars. Despite their bland appearance, which made them stand out in this city of fabulous architecture, these little drinking holes had been very popular, and people spilt out of them onto the street. Zoe wondered whimsically if these *Disco Bars* were still there today, or whether they just popped up that summer and were always moving to wherever there were some empty units - like a much cooler, Catalonian version of calendar shops at Christmas!

The girls had wandered passed a couple of them and then decided they had to find out what all the fuss was about. These places weren't big, and the interior design was basic, but they'd persevered. Once they had purchased drinks, they'd found a bit of space to stand, as seating didn't seem to feature. Then without warning the music was turned up and the clientele had all just started dancing.

The music had been great, no euro-pap thank God and in no time, they too had been boogieing away. Although alcohol was flung everywhere as the dancing throng had become more animated, it hadn't mattered – there'd been no posh furniture to worry about and nobody had seemed to care. The atmosphere had been great, and everyone had been really friendly and had just had a good time. The girls had all let loose and thrown away their home-based inhibitions and danced until their feet hurt.

According to researchers at the University of California Greater Good Science Centre, dancing is fantastic for both your body and your mind because it causes the release of the very chemicals that are good for your brain. Zoe felt *The Alphabetties* dancing session had done more than that, it had found and released their collective soul. They had all just gone with the music and the atmosphere and had the most free, wonderful time with no malice whatsoever just mutual love and friendship.

Chapter 5

C for Champagne

"There comes a time in every woman's life when the only thing that helps is a glass of champagne."
Bette Davis

Some of life between tours.

Francesca's front teeth fell out – great school photo!

Max turned forty – in denial!

Chloe managed to get chewing gum in her hair and had to have her gorgeous strawberry blonde locks cut to get it out. Many tears fell!

Abi had an outbreak of sibling rivalry. Sally found her quietly and systematic burying all of her little sisters clothes in their sand pit.

Gabe was thrilled as his efforts to improve his golf game have paid off and he was registered with a commensurable handicap of just two. Impressive!

Kate was called in for first time to see the headmistress about Vincent! Bless him he isn't a naughty child but as the years go by it becomes apparent that he is often in the wrong place at the wrong time and has the strength of character to take one for the team.

As the years were going on, Zoe was having to immortalise the antics of the *Alphabet Tour* when she could grab time. This was usually after Holly and Eric were in bed and before she had to succumb to sleep as well or whilst the kids were at one of their many activities or when Frank, bless him offered to give her some peace and took them off somewhere to try and exhaust them or pay to sit through the latest Disney or Pixar offering. Whilst carrying out her labour of love during these snatched moments, Zoe had come to realise that when you have children, the passage of time changes. Sleepless nights with babies crying each last a lifetime. Days when they are at school, and you're not working and can have some peace pass in an instant. Primary school years doing school runs last an eternity. High school years go by in a heartbeat. Before you know it, your babies have grown and flown the nest. Then you're desperate to have them back again to cuddle and hug and love.

This in turn made her ponder over, not only how *The Alphabetties* had all gelled together, but also how the relationships within that group had developed. Life decisions, location, logistics and background had all influenced the group and made it inevitable that some girls had grown closer to each other. Faye and Sally both lived in a very desirable postcode within which their children attended the same nursery and primary school. They also discovered early on that they had mutual friends and so socially had begun to move in the same circle.

Sally and Gabe had always enjoyed entertaining. Gabe always wanted life to be pleasurable and not a chore. Initially this was a quality Sally had adored in him. Although her job was secure and well paid, it took her away a great deal and she needed to know Gabe was there for her at home. She knew he loved his girls without question, and it was just the other mundane stuff that she felt Gabe found less enamouring. Sally had by now started to confide in Faye about her relationship worries although only on a fairly superficial level as she wanted the friendship of the two couples to grow. She hadn't wanted to frighten her away by painting a not quite so rosy a picture of her relationship with Gabe. But Sally could sense that Faye would be a receptive ear and would be a confidante she could trust.

Although Faye's work didn't take her abroad, her return to work had introduced her to a new social circle and she loved going out with a younger crowd and relished the attention she received. Clive, like many men, wasn't one for paying many compliments and she'd forgotten how nice it felt to be flattered. Although she couldn't always go along to social gatherings due to Clive's work schedule or doing 'mum duties', she was always asked by her colleagues, "Fancy a drink/something to eat after work Faye?" Actually, it was usually a colleague called Bridget from the opticians where Faye was probably one of the oldest, who organised things of this sort and asked Faye to come along. Faye made a mental note to do her best to go on these occasions as she got the impression Bridget was disappointed when she didn't make it. It was nice to feel wanted for herself and not as a mother or wife. Strangely Faye had also felt like she had known Bridget a long time. It was a welcome expansion of her world where others genuinely seemed to value her company and opinion.

Maggie and Zoe had shared the experience of being in hospital together when they gave birth. Maggie had the first of her three daughters two days after Holly was born. Maggie had always said how much she hated Zoe for being up and walking around when she first saw her after delivering. She still felt like shit and Zoe was about to go home. Zoe had also been happy, as that morning she had managed to do her first post birth poo, which is a milestone only those having given birth will understand! Luckily Maggie's loathing had been very short lived, and the nearness of the girls' appearance in this world meant Zoe had a special bond with Maggie as did their eldest Holly and Scarlet.

The way it had panned out over the years had meant that often Maggie, Kate and Zoe had shared a room when on tour. Kate and Zoe being friends from long ago usually share a double bed and Maggie, bless her, had spent many a weekend away on the put-me-up. Ironically, as with her family she has over the years travelled the world in a luxurious fashion, this has led to the group referring to her as Dobby of Harry Potter fame - knowing her place and being less comfortable. Dobby is also described as selfless and quirky, two more attributes that Maggie shared with the mythical creature. Although of course Maggie bears no physical resemblance to a house elf whatsoever! Maggie is attractive, tallish with blonde hair – the length of which has varied over the years. She has great teeth and super skin. So, no wonder her three daughters are particularly gorgeous. She doesn't like being the centre of attention and is happy for her girls, or anyone else for that matter, to take the limelight.

Chronologically one of the reasons to remember the third *Alphabet Tour* was that it was the first in the new century. Zoe distinctly remembered New Year's Eve 1999 when half the population thought the world would grind to a halt as technology couldn't cope with Y2K and the other half was optimistic and excited about the new millennium and how things would change for the better. In her mind's eye Zoe could see Holly in her purple sequinned party dress staying up till midnight for the first time, all excited and fizzing on sugary drinks and snacks. And going to wake up Eric, her then one-and-a-half-year-old brother, who was sleeping peacefully, so that he too could see in the new century.

Clearly waking a sleeping baby was not something which Zoe would advocate or had done lightly, but this was definitely a once in a lifetime event – well for her and Frank anyway.

Kate had certainly kicked off the new century with a bang. Although she loved her kids dearly Kate always felt that she could have had more children. However, after three she knew it was sensible to stop procreating. She isn't an 'earth mother' into breastfeeding till they can walk or anything. In fact, of all the girls she is the only one to have had a caesarean although not from choice. The other *Alphabetties* were now all back at work in some shape or form, and it was as if Kate had a confidence crisis and needed to prove her worth somehow: she certainly didn't have to do this to Zoe, who brazenly looked to Kate as a life mentor. It was more to herself – if she wasn't going to have more children, she had to do something more than the job she was doing for Uncle Geoffrey – something exciting to kick off the year 2000!

So, when most people might decide to set themselves a personal challenge, perhaps a sponsored walk up Snowdon or learn Tai Chi, Kate in her 'spare' time decided to study for a law degree. Kate doesn't do anything by halves and her bar is set so high most people could only hope to reach it with the help of a stepladder. So, she too, like Maggie began to study again, she hit the books and became a master at spinning plates. Although she did recognise how lucky she was to have a support network close by. Her mum, and dad were a godsend and were always there to help her out. After Kate had been away to university the first time, it was to a greater extent the draw of her family that had brought her back to glorious South Manchester. One of her two elder brothers had done the same – the other never left. So, her family were a tight knit group and a very important part of her life and how she went about it.

Funnily enough the world survived that momentous New Year's Eve 1999 and managed to carry on with the new century. This year the *Alphabet Tour* had reached C and Faye requested they visit the Champagne region of France – for obvious reasons. At this stage Zoe stupidly didn't like champagne but this was not to last for long. Faye and Sally made it their mission to help Zoe see the error of her ways. When Faye found out about Zoe's lack of love for fizz, the conversation kind of went along the lines of:

Zoe: "I'm not keen on champagne really, I'm more of a G & T girl."

Faye: "Well although I too enjoy a gin, that's just ridiculous, any friend of mine must enjoy champagne and should take advantage of me when I buy it, which I do regularly!"

Champagne being Faye's area of expertise, she had been entrusted to organise the trip. Although they'd all agreed they would stay in Reims, the capital of the world-famous wine region. Faye had stepped up eagerly to take on her duties as leader for the third trip. She assured them all she would get everything sorted and given her good taste and liking for the finer things in life, the girls had no reason to doubt her. Clive was usually the one who dealt with the organisation of holidays for the family so Faye had really looked forward to organising something the way she wanted it to be. And despite Clive's misgivings and trying on numerous occasions to muscle his way in on the act, Faye had stuck to her guns.

Everything started off brilliantly as the girls had been greeted on arrival at Charles de Gaulle Airport by a very pleasing on the eye young Frenchman to drive them to

Reims. Seeing the young man holding up a card with "*Alphabet Tour*" written on it Faye had announced:

"See girls I really did make sure I got things the way I like them!"

She'd then begun flirting outrageously with the handsome chap. But everyone had to admit this had been a much better start than the strange Dutch lady in Amsterdam.

Once on the road someone in the group asked, "Where exactly are we staying in Reims?" as Faye hadn't actually divulged details. Faye rummaged around in her oversized handbag and had found the address. Everyone nodded enthusiastically having, no clue where it was that Faye had just read out – all except Zoe who'd noted the crucial final detail. As they drove through the French countryside, Zoe seemed to be the only one in the group who'd appreciated that this location was strange and said:

"Girls don't you think that's odd as we're meant to be staying in Reims?".

She'd then pointed out to Faye, and the rest of her fellow passengers that Èpernay is in fact a different town to Reims located some 16 miles (or 25.5km as they were on the continent) south from their expected destination! Faye had gone a bit pale, muttered "*oh shit*" and then frantically began rummaging in her oversized handbag again to check she hadn't cocked up anything else.

As it was, they'd all quickly resigned themselves to going to Èpernay, it cemented the idea that so long as they were together it didn't matter where they were. Although Zoe suspected that this statement had been made with them all knowing that there wasn't a hope in hell of the group going to Butlins in Skegness or an all-inclusive weekend in Benidorm! So, most of them had nodded off until they'd arrived on the outskirts of Èpernay. And as it turned out Faye had played a blinder! The hotel she had unwittingly booked was within a stone's throw of both the **Moët** & Chandon and Pol Roger Wineries! Faye had instinctively been drawn to her spiritual home!

☐☐⊔⅋☐☐☐☐∩☐…⋯⋮.⋅˙˙⋅.☐⋰☐☐☐⊔☐☐☐☐

Faye's penchant for champagne does epitomise her liking for the good things in life. But she has had her fair share of life's vagaries. Like Zoe, Faye's parents had died when she was relatively young. And despite being a well-respected optician Faye can come across a bit ditsy. Things like world geography (clearly) and foreign languages are a mystery to her. Faye's children are her priority and - like all her fellow *Alphabetties* with all their children, of which there were now many - she profoundly cares for and protects them.

Although Zoe had loved her dearly, her relationship with her mother probably wasn't quite the same as Faye's was with her mum or indeed any of the group with theirs. Zoe is considerably younger than her siblings and clearly an unplanned pregnancy, her mother been forty when she had her. Zoe once asked her Mum if indeed she was a mistake. Her mother casually replied: "don't worry darling, you all were!"

Funnily enough this response didn't make Zoe feel any better about herself!

Zoe's mother had been a practising alcoholic for many years until Zoe was seven. As a baby and a small child, to a large extent it was up to her brother and sister to take care of their unexpected sibling. Obviously, Zoe was blissfully unaware until she was older of their sacrifice and the strain it put on the family. When Zoe was nearly three her sister, Helen, being the eldest, left the family home understandably heading off to Liverpool University and the escapism of studying English Literature. She had been fifteen when Zoe appeared on the scene and people leapt to the conclusion that she was a teenage mum. Zoe always assumed this situation couldn't have been easy for her and must have justifiably fuelled tension and resentment. Many years later when clearing out her parents' house Zoe found one of Helen's diaries which of course she read. As you can imagine a great many of the references to Zoe weren't particularly favourable as it appeared poor Helen had to take Zoe along with her on many dates with her now husband! To be clear Helen and Zoe now get on very well and Zoe misses her big sis as she lives on the other side of the world.

Her brother, Rich, whom she worshipped from a very early age and still does, had to stay a couple of years longer. Apparently, our ability to understand childhood recollections comes from our episodic memory – what we personally have experienced. Some evidence suggests that young children do have episodic memories of their infancy but lose them later. Zoe has never lost the clear memory of her brother sitting patiently by her cot trying to do his homework, keeping her safe as she stood and cried whilst their mother was out socialising in The White House Hotel when her father was home on leave.

For so long Zoe couldn't understand why her mother drank. But since having children of her own and looking back at what her mother had to cope with, she could sympathise with her actions and has in the past, to a degree, had thoughts of *"there but for the grace of God go I"*! Zoe's mother was a very intelligent woman and when she was young, she had dreamt of going to London to study at a world renown college which produced exceptional personal assistants for CEOs, diplomats, Captains of Industry and the like - which of course in those days were all men! Her mother's elder sister, Winnie, had previously broken the mould and the prejudice of the era and gone to university in

Reading. So for Zoe's mum leaving home shouldn't have been a problem: but then things changed. Zoe's grandmother died, leaving behind not only Zoe's Mum and sister but of course her grandfather and a son with mental illness, Timmy. And the Second World War started. Zoe suspected her mother didn't choose to but was made to stay home and look after her father and brother, and her plans for the future were well and truly thwarted. She had taken a job working in the local tax office in a building with black out windows in their hometown in the back end of Lancashire – far, far away from the excitement of living and studying in London. As it came about, the college her mother dreamed of attending was bombed and many students were killed. Part of Zoe thinks that even knowing this, if given the opportunity, her Mum would still have taken her chances.

Zoe's parents' relationship wasn't exactly conventional. When war broke out, her father was training to join the Merchant Navy. Zoe had always regretted never asking her mum how they had met but during the course of the war they fell in love, were married and in 1947 Helen came along, followed in 1950 by Rich. Zoe's paternal grandfather died at some point and so her widowed grandmother was added to the list of those her mother cared for. By now Zoe's Uncle Timmy had been moved to what was then called a mental asylum and her grandad had moved into the family home.

All this, Zoe's mum dealt with whilst her father rose through the seafaring ranks working for British Petroleum (BP) and was soon Chief Engineer on an oil tanker. He was a good-looking man, not very tall but with a charming personality and gregarious nature. For want of a better description he was 'a man's man' fixing engines whilst sailing the world and exploring foreign lands and meeting exciting, often important people. As well as being practical he was artistic and made sketches of Zoe's Mum, making him seem very romantic. He also learnt new skills from the other crew members – like the Chinese carpenter who taught him how to make furniture. He rode a motorbike and smoked cigars. His name was George, but everyone called him Hank – another thing Zoe never found out about.

When he was home, her mother's life would instantly change from the mundane to the glamorous, socialising with her father and their friends, drinking, smoking, dancing and making up for lost time in all ways. Then he would leave again for months on end travelling to places her mother could only imagine. Her father was still in the Navy when Zoe was a small child. She can remember being so excited when he would come home, or they received giant packages from exotic lands. She idolised him – how could a child not put such a character on a pedestal. It was only years later that it became clear to Zoe that he wasn't completely the wonderful man she imagined. Cliched though it is, it turns out he had girls in, not every port but certainly had his share of dalliances - a Swedish ballerina being particularly memorable.

Hard though this was to come to terms with, it did open Zoe's eyes to everything that her mother had had to face and she could completely see how one or two G&T's to get you through the day could escalate in to a bottle or two without the tonic. Things came to a head when her mother was found in a heap at the bottom of the stairs. Her poor brother had to tell their father to come home and take care of his wife and family – a very heroic act but not seen as such by their father and one which did nothing to heal the widening rift growing between them. But thankfully things did change.

As *The Alphabet Tour* approached their hotel it had looked marvellous, just like the mansion from *The Addams Family*, with magnificent wrought iron gates and railings, mysterious attic windows and wide stone steps up to the oversized front door. As the Peugeot people carrier passed through the entrance on to the driveway, you'd have almost expected the gates to close on their own with an eerie groan and shut with a menacing clang. But they didn't and they'd all jumped out without fear or foreboding. Although every single time Maggie and Zoe passed through the gates, they'd sung the theme tune to the 1960's series and clicked their fingers accordingly – predictably the pair of them had also laughed every single time.

Once inside, *The Alphabetties* were met not by Morticia but by the owner, a formidable lady called Madame Woda, who'd swept across the foyer to greet them in an impressive cascading, colourful ensemble – very Isadora Duncan. As she'd approached she had announced:

"Bonjour et bienvenue dans notre hôtel. J'espère que vous avez passé un bon voyage et apprécié votre séjour".

To continue their imaginary creepy theme, Maggie and Zoe had been convinced, she'd said:

"Ah fresh meat, I'm starving! Come, you can check into our hotel, but you will never leave!"

It hadn't surprised them that Madame Woda only spoke French – she probably thought English was too plebeian. But the girls had been surprised when Sally had begun chatting away to their host in what seemed to them to be flawless French. Sally's elder sister is married to a Frenchman and lived in France, and she had visited them on many occasions. Sally's talent had obviously been forgotten but the girls had been extremely glad of it as it had made the trip go far more smoothly. Madame Woda had seemed delighted that Sally could speak her native tongue and took her to one side and gave the rest of the group a very disparaging look. The lesser mortals did have a very basic smattering of French which consisted mainly of useful phrases such as *"Ou est la bibliothèque?"* (Where is the library?), *C'est un aspirateur"* (that is a vacuum cleaner) and *"Va te faire foutre!"* (loosely translated as go fuck yourself). So, on the whole Sally had done most of the talking to the locals but funnily enough everyone had still figured out how to order drinks whenever necessary.

After a fairly lengthy discussion with the flamboyant hotelier involving the reallocating of rooms due to a particularly fussy gay couple, Sally had turned to the girls clutching keys and assured them that Madame Woda was very pleasant and not a vampire – Maggie and Zoe had not been convinced! Once again, Zoe shared with Kate and Maggie and Sally had been in with Faye. The rooms didn't disappoint continuing the wacky, eccentric, Art Noveau theme. The three-person room had a very cosy (small) double bed, a single bed and a large skylight with wooden panels painted in a vaguely Clarice Cliff style. There was plenty of space to accommodate all five of them for prinking and an ensuite bathroom albeit without a door. During their stay, Kate, Maggie and Zoe tuned their whistling skills whilst performing ablutions and even broke into song if it was necessary!

Whilst in Èpernay many, many glasses of champagne had been sampled. The region is home to some four thousand growers who make their own wine and *The Alphabet Tour* had been on a mission to taste them all! They'd already established that the official capital of the Champagne region is of course Reims – the expected destination. So, having booked tours at a couple of champagne cellars in Èpernay for the next day, they'd headed to Reims to see what they were missing. For over a thousand years the kings of France had been crowned in the magnificent *Cathedral of Notre Dame of Reims* and the city boasted UNESCO world heritage site status. Cathedrals the world over are undeniably awe-inspiring and when entering them Zoe always felt very insignificant. Although, even as a lover of architecture and man-made places, she couldn't stop herself thinking what could have been achieved with the money if the cathedrals hadn't been as lavish and not quite so grand.

Following their ecclesiastical experience, it had been agreed that a stop for a cuppa would be a fine idea - yes, tea not champagne. Over the years of the *Alphabet Tour*, a number of running jokes have become established and this innocent café in Reims became the home to one of them. Surprisingly, for a French café this one sold a very comprehensive selection of teas. To Zoe's bewilderment, Faye and Kate had wanted flowery teas which she hated - Earl Grey is about as exciting as she gets. Sally and Maggie opted for something more traditional. They'd all managed to order a tea of their choice and sat sipping their various brews at a table opposite a wall covered in a decorative display of tea caddies, each with the word *'thé'* on them. Zoe observed that when read out loud in French, the tea caddies formed the lyrics to the Mel and Kim disco classic "Respectable"! Obviously, a rendition of the 1987 top ten hit was rapidly forthcoming with – *"Tay, tay, tay, tay, t-t-t-tay-tay, tay, tay Take or leave us only please believe us we are never gonna be respectable".* However, their musicality wasn't appreciated by either the staff or other customers, so they'd exited fairly hastily.

In-jokes often arise in groups such as these antenatal friends and are often bewildering or even annoying to those outside the group. Reims proved to be a rich seam of such in-jokes, many standing the test of time. Zoe, and indeed all of *The Alphabetties* like to think they have a better than average sense of humour and like to go along with a good joke. Whilst growing up Zoe had been affectionately nicknamed *Titch* and to this day her offspring take the mickey out of her unmercifully just for being small and generally going about her daily life. In Reims her misfortune had once again proved to be hilarious and had gone down in *Alphabet Tour* legend. Late that evening, after having run up a truly enormous bar bill in the hotel they thought was going to be their home for the weekend, prior to Faye booking Madame Woda – they were all ravenous and had decided to seek out a restaurant. They'd all been very vocal, loud and finding everything uproarious, as they'd staggered through central Reims. None of them had really paid attention to where they were going and unfortunately, it had been Zoe who'd walked straight into a cast iron bollard. It'd struck her right in the pubic bone causing her to bend double and a tear to appear in her eye. In response to this incident Maggie had come out with, the never to be forgotten and often to be repeated expression:

"She's hurt her Doris!"

◻◻Ⱡ⅄◻◻◻◻∩◻…··⁙·˙¨·.◻·∴◻◻◻∪◻◻◻◻◻

Zoe really hates many of the slang/swear words associated with this area of the female anatomy, but *Doris,* she and the others really liked and still use whenever a reference to that part of the body is needed. To Zoe the slang words for the male reproductive parts sound comical and light-hearted – *knob, cock, willy* and *dick* are all quite fun. Whereas the equivalent words for the female reproductive area are almost aggressive and angry – *pussy, twat* and the worst of all *cunt*. If you say someone, usually a bloke, is a bit of a *knob* or a *dick*, although insulting you generally just mean you think they're an idiot. But if you said someone is a *cunt* or a *twat* you really dislike them. According to one website Zoe had looked at, *cunt* was described as definitively the worst swear word around. Furthermore the male anatomical terms are even somehow easier to hear – penis, testicles and scrotum don't have the same yuk quality as the feminine labia, vagina, and clitoris. In fact, Zoe wanted Holly to call her two pet goldfish Tess and Tickle for their comedic value!

Maggie had picked up the term *"Doris"* on her midwifery course which she had now started at a local university. Although the first year of the course was a lot of science dealing mainly with the anatomy and physiology of the body, Maggie was loving it and she couldn't wait to start her placements on the wards. The eager new students were taught by fully trained midwives, who readily imparted their extensive knowledge - this knowledge was often dotted with work weary jargon such as the aforementioned *"Doris"* or *"Wookie"* (a tall lady with unkempt pubic hair).

Being a mother put Maggie in the minority on her course, as did her age – although her tutor told her the oldest student she had taught began the course at forty nine! Obviously, most of her fellow students were in their early twenties and didn't look to have had enough life experience of their own to take on the challenges of bringing new life into the world. But nonetheless, regardless of age, Maggie had found all the girls were welcoming.

Maggie had attended as many of the non-curricular activities as she could given her unique situation amongst her fellow students. She could easily have felt like everyone's mother – well favourite aunt maybe, at these events. But Maggie embraced this and through listening to the girls she found she became a confidante and a go to person for many of them as they struggled with some of the trickier aspects of the course and university life in general. Likewise, the other students also came to realise Maggie was far from a prude and could certainly hold her own on a night out, although she usually drew the line when they hit the nightclubs – she had three very small children, a husband, her parents, and her in-laws to sort out the next day.

⬜⬜Ⅱ🕭⬜⬜⬜⬜⋂⬜…··⋮.·˙˙·.⬜∵⬜⬜⬜⋃⬜⬜⬜⬜

The Alphabetties' visits to the champagne cellars had certainly provided plenty of opportunity to have met some of the aforementioned *knobs*, although more for being pompous than idiotic. The young man who had greeted the champagne loving tourists, as they'd arrived at Moët & Chandon wore a blazer and what Zoe's dad would have called slacks. He had a very large Roman nose, down which he had looked at all of the assembled sightseers. However, the formal young man had known his stuff and the tour had been very informative. They learnt that Moët & Chandon was established in 1743 by Claude Moët, and today owns 1,190 hectares (2,900 acres) of vineyards, and annually produces approximately 28,000,000 bottles of champagne; the pressure in a champagne bottle is 90 pounds per square inch; and Faye's personal favourite fact champagne can help prevent memory loss - according to new research (origin undisclosed), one to three glasses of champagne each week could counteract memory loss associated with ageing!

The champagne for the tourists to sample at the end of their visit was served on trays and had been strictly rationed to one glass per visitor. This aspect of the tour the girls had found somewhat disappointing and a bit tight. Moet is part of the LVMH French luxury conglomerate (Louis Vitton, Moët Hennessy) which regularly has profits in the billions. Therefore, the girls felt they could've risen to more than one free glass of fizz for those who had made the pilgrimage to the hallowed winery. But they'd had a stroke of luck with their particular tour group. Alcohol intolerance is an inherited metabolic disorder – clearly one which the girls in this group didn't have! With alcohol intolerance, drinking just small or moderate amounts of alcohol causes unpleasant sensations. Alcohol flushing syndrome is a typical reaction. The skin on your face, neck and chest may become red and warm immediately or soon after you drink alcohol. People of Japanese, Chinese or Korean ethnic groups are most likely to experience this reaction. For that reason, the syndrome is known as Asian glow or Asian flush.

Their tour had comprised to a great extent of Asian tourists whose exact origin was never established – in her head Zoe did wonder why so many Asians had taken the tour, given the potential for them to have an adverse reaction and break out in blotches. The important thing was the Asian tourists had all declined their free class of Moët & Chandon. Like a ninja, Kate had swept in with impressive stealth and secured the rejected glasses for her thirsty chums. This is probably when Zoe first began to acquire a taste for the world-renowned beverage - perhaps it was tastier being illicit! However, as they'd stood drinking their ill-gotten gains, the aforementioned tour guide with the large nose, blazer and slacks had come over to their huddle. He'd asked all the expected questions: had they enjoyed the tour? Where were they from? Although a little uncomfortable they'd engaged in his small talk and praised him and the winery appropriately. But then he'd said:

"You wouldn't believe, even here, how many of our visitors have the cheek to pinch more than one glass of champagne at the end of the tour, unbelievable!"

Now you'd have thought at that point at least one of the girls would have spat out their stolen bubbly. But none of them had missed a beat and all had looked suitably horrified and disgusted at such behaviour. To this day Zoe can't make up her mind as to whether he saw Kate pinching the spare glasses but even if he did, she hoped they went up in his estimations for retaining their appalled persona!

□□ЦЖ□□□□∩□……··∶.·¨·.□∵□□□U□□□□□

This reminiscence in turn got Zoe wondering which champagne her fizz loving friends prefer now that it is many years on since they'd visited the prestigious vineyards. Predictably Faye's champagne of choice is Bollinger – *Bolly* darling! This iconic drink is synonymous with elegance, excellence, and James Bond. Maybe these aren't adjectives that would immediately spring to mind describing Faye. But "having an independent spirit "and "being particularly suited to ageing in a cellar," possibly! What's more, reportedly Queen Elizabeth II had drunk a glass of champagne before going to bed each night and Bollinger had been one of her favourites. This is a habit Zoe can imagine Faye taking up – if she hasn't already!

Maggie too is a *Bolly* fan – the woman who with three small children became a midwife and was always by Shane's side to take on board all the trials and tribulations of keeping the business her father built up successful. She certainly deserved the best life had to offer.

Sally and Kate were both advocates of Veuve Cliquot with its distinctive yellow label. Both these girls were to become very successful in their chosen career paths and deserved all they achieved. So, it is fitting that they prefer a champagne which sponsors a prestigious businesswoman award won by many inspiring women, Anita Roddick among them. This particular entrepreneur was picked out as Zoe owed Ms Roddick and her creation Body Shop a great debt. Anita's henna powder led to her hair being the best it has ever been, a great colour with shine and a fab shoulder length bob. A look which amongst other things caught Frank's eye and he referred to her as *henna head* for many years.

After her late start, if she had to choose, Zoe would say Lanson. Another of the Queen's favourites, it is described as "fruity and truly unique" – an epitaph Zoe would be happy to have on her gravestone!

On the last day of the visit to the Champagne region the girls had wanted to finish off with something typically French to eat and drink and if possible, locally produced. During the weekend they'd spotted what looked like the perfect venue for this feast. A little bistro full of local people wearing berets and reminiscing about their time in the Resistance. Well not quite!

They had the foresight to book (or rather French speaking Sally did) and on arrival had been shown to a cosy part of the rather intimate restaurant. It wasn't the venue for sweeping hand gestures otherwise plates would have gone flying – very restrictive for a nation famed for its gesticulation. The menu duly arrived and was literally just what they had all hoped to order and when the champagne list (not wine list) arrived Faye had nearly wet herself. It had been an enormous tome far out sizing the food menu. Pages and pages of champagne from all the local vineyards. During the course of this tour, they'd gone from feeling decadent at ordering a bottle of champagne between them to ordering a couple of bottles if they were under £20.00 each (approximately £34.00 each in today's money!) as that had clearly been a bargain. Credit cards were dangerous things even before the days of contactless transactions!

There was one other notable incident from the trip to Èpernay that year which always made Zoe laugh and has become a long-standing in-joke but just between her and Kate. It occurred on the second night once they had all finally decided to get some sleep and Kate and Zoe were snuggly tucked up in their 'double' bed. The three of them, Maggie had been in this room too of course, had all been slumbering peacefully when Zoe had been awoken. She had felt a gentle but definite kiss on her shoulder. This was new! She'd lay there trying to clarify where she was and what was going on when Kate had muttered in her ear:

"Do you love me because I bought you champagne?"

Now Kate is her dearest friend whom she does love deeply and would do anything for; but Zoe had never felt any feelings of this nature for her. Zoe had rolled over to try to break this news to Kate and tell her she did love her but not that way – Zoe was rather taken aback as she did think Kate would have been the last person to have deep rooted lesbian tendencies. She'd turned over expecting to see Kate facing her, lips puckered ready to continue with their foray into the world of LGBTQ. But thankfully Kate was by then facing the other way, had begun to snore quite loudly and had obviously kissed Zoe in a dream state – a state in which we'll say she was dreaming about her husband Max.

◻◻Ⱡⱡⱥ◻◻◻◻⌒◻……⋯∶.˙ˉ˙.◻∵.◻◻◻⋃◻◻◻◻

Other than Zoe mistakenly thinking Kate could no longer resist her, she'd only ever had one other approach from the same sex – but on that occasion she was ignorant of what was going on and had to be told later. It was quite early on in her relationship with Frank, and she had accompanied him to the wedding of a friend of his she'd never met. These situations are always awkward as you don't know anyone and have no history with the other guests to dip into for topics of conversation. So, when Frank left her alone to go to the bar she was pleased when another female guest began chatting to her. She was really friendly and seemed to be genuinely interested in what Zoe had to say – they were getting on like a house on fire! Frank had been side tracked by old work colleagues, so Zoe was glad of the company. At least she wasn't standing there on her own like a lemon.

Eventually Frank returned with drinks and Zoe introduced her new acquaintance to her boyfriend. The new friend smiled, shook hands and then announced that she should do some more mingling and left them alone. Just as Zoe was about to tell Frank how nice the other guest was, he said: "I see you were getting chatted up by the token lesbian then."

Apart from being taken aback that Frank was being very politically incorrect, Zoe was also shocked and contested his announcement. But seemingly Zoe's new acquaintance was an old friend of the bride, now training to be a police detective who had come out in lower sixth! This news brought on a mixture of emotions from Zoe; flattered that the other guest had found her attractive, slightly worried she looked like a lesbian (whatever that might be clearly Zoe didn't know) and oddly annoyed at Frank that he hadn't been jealous and rushed to her aid earlier.

Finally, on the subject of champagne, Brigitte Bardot has said that it is the one thing that gives her zest when she is tired. *The Alphabetties* can certainly see where she is coming from with that and when thumbing through other quotes regarding fizz, Zoe found the following two ditties which she felt appropriate to this chapter of her reminiscences:

"Champagne because no great story starts with someone eating a salad!" – Unknown

and

The Alphabet Tour – The Early Years
"If you have to ask if it's too early to drink champagne,
you're an amateur and we can't be friends." —Unknown

Chapter 6

D for Dublin

"I hope that people will finally come to
realize that there is only one 'race' - the human
race - and that we are all members of it."
Margaret Atwood

Some of life between tours.

Eric at the age of three decided "Sex Bomb" by Tom Jones is his favourite song and performs it at any given opportunity. He has quite a talent and enunciates the words very clearly and even mimics the singer's gyrating hip movement perfectly. His parents get questionable looks.

Noah's first hair cut turned out to be a complete disaster and mainly due to the barber's ineptitude and not Noah's wriggling!

Kate's parents, now retired, went trekking in the Himalayas.

Maggie temporarily lost Scarlet at the local aquarium during her 6th birthday party. Luckily she is returned by the aquarium mascot aka Shaky the Shark before her parents went into complete meltdown.

Francesca managed to turn upside down whilst swinging vigorously at the park and scraped her forehead on the floor. Kate and Max have some concern that the incident may result in a slight Harry Potter type scar!

Max took on an extra job as a security marshal at entertainment venues in the City. His imposing stature earning some cash and discounted tickets!

Over the course of Zoe recording the *Alphabet Tour*, history good and bad had inevitably been made.

We all realise when an event occurs which will be a flashbulb memory – an event so powerful, with such an impact that people know exactly where they were and what they were doing when they heard about them – like a flashbulb has gone off in your head. Zoe can remember as clear as crystal when the hijacked American Airlines Flight 11 and United Airlines Flight 175 were intentionally crashed into the North and South Towers of the World Trade Centre.

After she had Eric she worked from home on various enterprises, one of which was as a private consultant for her old employer. It was great, she could take the kids to nursery and school, work from 9.00am – 2.00pm, have some lunch, then pick the kids up from school and if necessary, she could finish work in the evening having put the kids to bed. That fateful day, as she sat down to have her lunch, she switched on the television expecting to watch some mindless but addictive daytime TV. Instead, the BBC news was reporting a story far more outrageous than any fiction imaginable. At 13.45 British time the first plane had crashed into the North Tower of the World Trade Centre in New York. Zoe instantly picked up the phone to ring Frank to tell him what was happening – at this point it was still thought to be some sort of awful accident. As she was trying to explain to him the magnitude of what was unfolding, unbelievably, the second plane hit the South Tower. She was speechless as Frank was demanding to know what was going on, shouting at her down the phone. She couldn't believe her eyes, she just stood there in her safe, cosy lounge in suburbia unable to say a word to Frank just staring at the television. As we all know this wasn't the only horror, which was unfolding that day, none of which will ever be forgotten.

114

On the Thursday of that week Zoe had had her own little, personal disaster – having gone to the file where the family passports were kept as she prepared for this year's tour, she couldn't find them and had realised she had thrown them all away! Again, she found herself standing, speechless in a cold sweat having realised exactly what she had done. Earlier in the year Zoe and Frank had taken his Mum, Edna, to Jersey for her first and only flight on an aeroplane – Zoe suspected that after Edna had watched the recent world news, she'd never have flown again even if her health had permitted it! Holly and Eric and Jean and Henry – Frank's sister and husband – all came along. It was quite a party. Zoe had overseen bookings and logistics which as those days weren't paperless meant a sizeable wodge of documentation had been accumulated. When they had all returned safely after what she could proudly say was a smooth, incident free, very enjoyable holiday, Zoe thought she didn't need her 'Jersey' file anymore and threw it in the recycling.

Recycling then wasn't a home-based activity. You had to take your saved-up paper, glass etc to the recycling stations usually located in a library car park or at the local supermarket. That critical day Zoe had taken their recycling to the garden centre before taking the kids in to run around and annoy all the pensioners wandering among the plants and the aisles of The Edinburgh Woollen Mill outlet. She felt sick as she pictured herself stuffing the holiday wodge through the mouth of the paper only skip. Zoe became distraught, her tummy churning and feeling sick as she began thinking she was going to miss an *Alphabet Tour*!

She'd immediately rung Kate who always knew what to do – or certainly appeared to. Kate hardly recognised Zoe as she had hysterically sobbed down the phone:

"Kate I'm such a stupid cow I've thrown my passport away. I can't come to Dublin. I'm such an idiot, I can't believe I'm so stupid!"

Zoe was by then suffering with what she later came to learn is called stuttering inhalation. Medically this means the diaphragm shoots down, interrupting the airflow to the vocal cords and the sentence produced is far from fluent – in layman's terms t, blubbering. Once Kate had fathomed out what Zoe was saying through the high pitched whimpering, she'd instantly gone into action looking up alternative ways to get her chum to Dublin. She looked up ferry times and train timetables to get Zoe over there at approximately the time of the plane and before Zoe had known it, she was nearly booked on the Holyhead overnight ferry! In Kate's world leaving a man behind wasn't an option – although why the ferry alternative wouldn't need a passport was not discussed!

After the initial panic induced flurry of activity, they'd begun to think more calmly. Kate in a moment of clarity had said:

"If you're a European National travelling within the European Union, do you actually need a passport?"

In those heady days before the madness of Brexit, they'd decided to contact British Airways for a definitive answer. Why they contacted BA Zoe later questioned as the only time she had flown with BA they were sadly pretty crap. Anyway, on that rather fraught occasion she'd spoken to a very nice lady who, after having consulted her colleagues, said she thought it should be OK to travel to Dublin with an alternative form of photo ID. Zoe had then rung Kate back and after consulting the rest of the group it was decided she should risk it and try to fly to Dublin with the other *Alphabetties*.

For the next hour or so Zoe had gathered every piece of identification she could find, with or without a photo. She'd even put in her recently acquired Toys R Us loyalty card – she'd felt sure the al-Qaeda wouldn't be regular shoppers at this retail outlet and anything would help. She hadn't slept well that night. The next morning, they all gathered at the airport.

□□𝕃𝕃⚓□□□□∩□……⸱⸱⸱⦂⸱⸱ ⸱⸱ ⸱.□⸫□□□Ս□□□□□

Zoe was full of trepidation and had expected to be waving the others off as they went through security without her. However, at this stage at least, her worries had been unfounded. There hadn't been a whiff of a request for a passport from any of them. But they had been informed that all flights from Manchester Airport, and pretty much every other airport in the country and indeed Europe, would be subject to delay. Friday 14th September 2001 had been declared a National Day of Mourning across Europe for the victims of 9/11. At 11.00am there was to be a three minute silence. *The Alphabetties'* flight had been due to depart at midday, so they hadn't had much hope of leaving on time and resigned themselves to the forthcoming delay.

As they'd approached customs and security, Zoe again broke out in a sweat. However, it had transpired that a pregnant woman heading for Dublin was far more interesting to the staff on duty that day, than a panicky woman clutching a Toys R Us loyalty card. Despite the minute amount of radiation involved, in her obviously pregnant condition Faye had got it into her head that she did not want to go through the full body scanner at the airport. Although this maternal instinct may have been somewhat misguided, she'd still asked politely if she could be excused from passing through the scanner. The security staff had said in that case she would have to be thoroughly frisked – apparently women around the world have been known to fake pregnancy to try and smuggle all kinds of things including drugs, jewels, explosives, puppies, kittens and even a rhesus monkey!

Nonetheless the security officer asking Faye if she'd come with them to a private room, was a rash move. Most people are aware that pregnancy can trigger a whole gamut of emotions and cause mood swings which are often nobody's friend. In Faye's case, moodiness was a euphemistic term for anger! Whilst pregnant she could see red at the drop of a hat. So, a couple of butch, unempathetic security officers wanting to take her away from her friends to a private room to touch her and interfere with her beautiful baby bump was not a good move. She had, not so politely, declined this offer using the pent-up rage of a woman who hasn't been able to get comfortable in any position for the last four months to vocalise her displeasure. Although the female security officer had gallantly tried to calm Faye saying: "the key focus of our assessment is the health and well-being of the mother and the baby."

Most airlines require a certificate after twenty eight weeks, confirming that any pregnancy is progressing normally, that there are no complications and the expected date of delivery. To be fair to the poor souls at the airport that day, they hadn't asked for this and did eventually show some discretion. Although somewhat degrading they'd searched Faye very swiftly, gently but thoroughly in front of her four trusty companions and it was soon established that Faye was indeed genuinely pregnant. There had been an audible sigh of relief as *The Alphabetties* moved away towards Duty Free.

Once through Duty Free, they'd entered the food and drink area which was rammed and at least four people deep at each bar. Despite Faye only moments earlier having been cleared as a drugs mule, it was decided that her condition was now definitely worth exploiting for their personal gain. Faye had been pushed in front of them and they'd let her, her baby bump and her winning smile clear a path to the bar. It takes a brave person to stand in the way of a pregnant lady trying to get refreshment. Apart from a number of disapproving looks when she'd ordered four gin and tonics with her sparkling water, Faye had managed very smoothly to get them all a drink – the next thing was to acquire seats for the wait of, as yet undetermined length of time until the flight was called.

Faye again put on her best hopeless pregnant face and waddled over to a member of staff. The sympathetic woman informed them that an extra lounge had been opened upstairs, seats were available up there and pointed towards a lift. The room the lady had described as a lounge was really a windowless holding pen full of people feeling they shouldn't be cross because of what was happening that morning but inside they couldn't help themselves and were fuming!

As the girls had sat with the other resigned fellow travellers it had occurred to Zoe that there was no way of knowing from this featureless room when the official day of mourning three-minute silence was going to begin. Zoe has a somewhat irrational insistence on respecting occasions when the general public should be quiet. She's one of those people who will "Shhhh" people at the cinema and glare at people if they are talking during a wedding speech. So, the thought of all these people, admittedly through no fault of their own, talking all the way through a silence that was to be respected by hundreds of thousands of people across Europe was too much for her. As the eleven o clock deadline approached she got up and went to investigate if there was to be an announcement piped through every room of the airport or if indeed those in the herding pen would be forgotten.

Zoe had found a member of staff who'd told her nobody was supervising the herding pen and they'd just have to do it themselves. She could remember looking around for someone who appeared authoritative and charismatic who, just by slightly raising their voice, would be able to silence the room full of international passengers – someone like Winston Churchill, Bill Clinton, The Queen or Superman. She'd drawn a blank, not surprisingly this kind of person is few and far between. So, calling on her inner Erin Brockovich, she told herself "It's up to you Zoe!".

The other *Alphabetties* were understanding but had been surprised at how much she had got her knickers in a twist. She'd loitered in the corridor outside the characterless room, straining her ears ready to hear the announcement in the airport concourse below. When it came, she'd pulled herself up to her full height (an impressive 5ft 2inches whatever her sister may say) and walked purposefully into the room and had loudly announced that the three minute silence for those killed in New York was underway and had declared:

"PLEASE BE QUIET!"

It had worked to some degree, but she did have to follow that up by going around the room doing a lot more "shhhing" and pointing at her watch. Although several people didn't have a clue what was going on and had completely ignored her, many didn't ignore her and fell silent in respect. As Zoe had again loitered by the door waiting for the announcement that the silence was over, she'd felt quite proud of herself. When she returned to *The Alphabetties* they'd all patted her on the back and said well done – she had been glad she was with them or she may not have had the courage to have even tried. This feeling happens a lot on *The Alphabet Tour*.

Of course, her euphoria was short lived as they touched down in Ireland and had to get through passport control – irrationally they'd all felt getting into a country would be trickier than getting out. Scenes from *The Fugitive* had been running through Zoe's mind and she looked around for alternative escape routes. However, despite the events of only two days previous Irish passport control had been more cavalier than they'd anticipated. That coupled with a stroke of good luck meant all went well. Just as she had been about to reach the Border Control Officer and begin explaining the situation, a very tall gentleman to her left had been called to the desk. Kate had swooped in from behind, grabbed Zoe's arm and muttered *"just keep walking"* which she'd done whilst waving a Toys R Us card vaguely at the official. Phew they were in!

󠀀󠀀󠀀󠀀󠀀󠀀󠀀󠀀󠀀󠀀󠀀󠀀󠀀…󠀀…󠀀:.·˙˙·.󠀀·:·󠀀󠀀󠀀U󠀀󠀀󠀀󠀀󠀀

Kate had always been there to support Zoe's arm and her life in general. They had become close friends through a car share commute to work which was at best a good forty-minute drive down the motorway. There were three of them who made this journey day after day – Kate, Zoe and a male colleague of Kate's whose name has long been forgotten. They would both admit they were very rude to this poor soul. When it was his turn to drive, they would both sit in the back and gossip away like he was their own private chauffeur. In fact, it was in the back of the forgettable guy's car that the two of them had planned Zoe's wedding.

Frank and Zoe were short of parents. Hers had both died by the time Zoe was thirty and Frank's dad had died shortly after Zoe's mum. Edna, Frank's mum, was still with them but not in a position to pay for a wedding. So, on the whole Frank and Zoe had to pay for the event themselves and looked for ways to make things fabulous but cheap! Kate and her mum proved invaluable in this department. Kate, amongst all the other things, helped her mum run a bridesmaid dressmaking business. Louise is an excellent seamstress and had very kindly agreed, with Kate's help to make Zoe's wedding dress. Zoe was ecstatic. She had been looking through wedding magazines for some time and had fallen in love with the most magical dress which, in 1994, if bought from a retailer came in at £1000 – roughly £1400 today. It would never have happened without Kate and Louise.

Luckily there was a stockist in a town not too far away. So, off the three of them had gone to see the garment in the flesh. The shop was very select and a lady in a Chanel style suit and pearls had greeted them at the door. Zoe described the dress she had fallen in love with and Chanel and pearls lady immediately nodded and smiled with pound signs in her eyes, then disappeared to the back of the shop. She returned saying her assistant was taking the dress to a room upstairs where Zoe could try the dress on at leisure. They had then been shown up the heavily carpeted stairs to a well-lit room decorated in the style of the court of Marie Antoinette. Zoe tried the dress on, and it looked beautiful - everything she had hoped it would be. However, prior to arrival at the bridal gown shop the three of them had conspired and hatched a plan. Whatever the dress looked like, Zoe was to appear somewhat disappointed with the style once she had it on. So, after much twirling and umming and ahhing she then asked: "I'm not convinced, do you have anything else in this price range that you think might suit me better?"

Once the plan was instigated the assistant smiled and said "of course" and trotted off downstairs to bring more dresses. At this point Louise was like a dressmaking ninja. She whipped out her tape measure and was on the floor taking measurements and examining fabrics and stitches like a woman possessed. She had just stopped crawling around looking up the skirt of the dress and returned to her seat when the assistant entered laden with other dresses for Zoe to try – many of which wouldn't have been out of place in the live action version of *Cinderella.*

Zoe was able to make her excuses at this point saying the dresses she had brought were very flouncy and not to her taste. She expressed her disappointment at the other dress not working out, even going a little teary eyed for authenticity. The assistant looked gutted at having lost a potential sale – but that was never going to happen. After many fittings in the much more comfortable surroundings of Kate's family home, standing precariously on a kitchen stool, Louise produced the most wonderful dress - more wonderful than the one in the shop as Zoe knew how much care and love had gone into it.

⬜⬜Ⱡⱡ⚡⬜⬜⬜⬜∩⬜…···∴·˙˙·.⬜∵·⬜⬜⬜Ս⬜⬜⬜⬜⬜

Despite the hotel in Dublin not being the best *The Alphabetties* had stayed in by far, they'd been very glad to finally arrive. However, as they'd wearily stepped into the hotel lobby, they were greeted by what seemed like hundreds of women of varying ages but mostly of more advancing years. The girls had arrived just as a sea of Daniel O' Donnell fans had been washed up in reception. In Ireland, women of a certain age worship the Irish singer and TV presenter and he was appearing in Dublin that weekend. His doting fans are believed to have provided 'Wee Daniel' as he is also known with a net worth of thirty one million euros. The fans range from a twenty six year old Colleen from Cork, who was jailed for running a cocaine lab, to superfans, The Gallaghers, who owned the Daniel O' Donnell Museum and Visitor Centre in County Donegal. Sadly, the museum closed down in 2012 – clearly a blow to the Irish Tourist Board. Zoe knew very little of Daniel O' Donnell and if asked to categorise him, would have lumped him in with Val Doonican and Cliff Richard. These were not men that set her heart a flutter and if a man describes his greatest achievement as, being Donegal Person of the Year 1989, she will continue to happily give Daniel O' Donnell and those of a similar ilk a wide berth.

⬚⬚�⬚⬚⬚⬚⋂…⋯⋮⋅⋆⋆⋅⬚⋰⬚⬚⬚∪⬚⬚⬚⬚

The only one of the group who may have seen the attraction of Daniel O Donnell was Maggie. As has previously been mentioned she has a questionable taste in men – Shane actually being an exception. Although now been well into her midwifery course, not surprisingly her taste in men was not something she had shared with her fellow students – even though none of them would have a clue who Daniel O' Donnell was. Likely under the influence of alcohol, over the years Maggie had vocalised her attraction to the likes of Alan Titchmarsh and Robson Green in whose company the other *Alphabetties* agreed Daniel O' Donell wouldn't have looked out of place. However, at this point in her life Maggie had very little if any time to fantasize about male celebrities: or even Shane for that matter. She had to make every waking minute count, often working late into the night. After a day at university, she would come home to feed her family, put the kids to bed and then get down to finishing an essay. By now the course was tackling maternity related complications, emergency medical disorders in pregnancy and childbirth and neonatal nutrition and sexual health. All of these being complex and often harrowing subjects at the best of times.

Shane was often travelling to the other side of the world with work and Maggie was wrestling to keep up with her coursework and trying not to blame her young family for not letting her reach her full potential. She knew she had Shane's support despite it being a tough decision to go to university, she and Shane knew it was the right thing for her to do. But often she couldn't help but feel guilty if she went out socialising, even more so when Shane was home. He would return home from Africa or China and not surprisingly want to spend quality time with his family who were growing up whilst he was in meeting rooms with clients and interpreters. But Maggie knew that the need to go on *The Alphabet Tour* was unquestionable – a lifeline to keep her sane to forget for just a few days all the hard work she was doing at home. Just to have some fun without judgement.

Kate too was well into her studies and taking on the academic world – in fact she wished she had risen to the challenge of law when she had initially gone to university instead of her accountancy degree. Choosing a degree when you leave school is very different to choosing to go back to university to do something you really want to. Kate and many others, including Zoe for sure, had done degrees based on their best – in Zoe's case far from brilliant - A level results and what the careers officer had advised them to do to make sure they got a job at the end of it. But now, despite the challenges of a family and a job, Kate was loving learning about something she had a passion for. It was far from easy, but she was driven.

Having both these qualifications would make her even more of a force to be reckoned with. Mind you she had only one day a week at university and the rest of her course being independent study was taking its toll, even on someone as capable as Kate. Gone were the days of studying through the night with Pro plus as your closest friend. She had to be

125

incredibly disciplined and run her life and that of her family, like a military operation. Thank God she was a logistical wizard who could think many steps ahead and could work out solutions to pretty much any problem. A redeeming feature which many of those close to her, Zoe included, often exploited – Max maybe too often!

Before he met Kate, Max had been married before albeit briefly. Very soon after leaving university Max had married the housemate of one of his university football friends. She was always there at sports socials, house parties, and hungover nights sleeping on his friend's floor. She had flirted outrageously with Max making it pretty clear how she felt for him. He'd succumbed and a relationship had started which continued after university life had finished. Most of his crowd had managed to get jobs locally and had stayed fairly near to their old university haunts. Max had thought he could spend the rest of his life with his former wife who knew all his former friends and fitted in. But when he met Kate he realised that he had proposed when he was too young and hadn't known what true love really was. Once Kate came into his life a few years later, he realised that he'd made a mistake and was being unfair to his then wife as their marriage was based on the wrong reasons.

Max and Kate had met through work and had an instant attraction which both had found impossible to resist – a feeling Max had never had before. They began to have what Kate described as a passionate and exciting affair. Kate had been through a nasty breakup not long before she met Max and she wasn't looking for another long-term relationship. But although she knew he was married and it was wrong, she couldn't help herself as far as Max was concerned. Inevitably Max's wife found out and after several heart wrenching discussions Kate found a new job and moved away to try to let Max and his wife rebuild their marriage. But it was too late for Max, he had fallen head over heels in love with Kate, left his wife, tracked Kate down and as the saying goes the rest is history. Seeing them now, it's hard to picture Max with anyone else, his love for Kate is obvious to anyone who meets them.

☐☐Ⅱ𝔁☐☐☐☐∩☐……⋮.·¨·.☐∵·☐☐☐∪☐☐☐☐

Having eventually made their way through the 'Wee Daniel' fans and checked in to their rooms, *The Alphabetties* had really needed some food and headed out into Temple Bar. Normally the busy riverside neighbourhood would have been full of crowded pubs and buzzing restaurants. But that particular day Temple Bar had been closed. Dublin had been no exception, and it too had respected the 9/11 day of mourning. Again although the girls had felt bad about the circumstances, they were getting fractious and hangry by this point. It was mid-afternoon and their distant breakfast and snack on the plane just weren't staving off the hunger pangs. Faye in particular was getting very peckish as she was eating for two. Her distress had been so apparent that a passer-by took pity on her and had thrown her a packet of crisps, for which she was most grateful.

From a reconnoitre of the restaurants in the vicinity, the girls had gathered that most establishments would be re-opening at 5.00pm – it was 3.45pm. Not normally being ones to queue they'd concluded that this time they had no choice and decided to lurk outside an Italian/ Mexican restaurant until opening time – other than the hotel with its Daniel O Donnell contingent there really wasn't anywhere else to go. The eatery, outside of which they'd lingered did have a view of The Liffey so was reckoned the best in the vicinity. To begin with, as a group standing rather forlornly outside a closed restaurant, they thought *The Alphabetties* must have looked a bit sad. However, as the minutes went by more groups of hungry people began to appear outside other restaurants all making sure they were going to be the first to get food as soon as they could. Once eventually inside the restaurant, the menu was extensive and the food, when it came was perfectly acceptable – although that may have been something to do with them being ravenous. This type of restaurant is now trendily labelled fusion, cuisine that combines elements of different culinary traditions that originate from different countries. The girls didn't care what it was called or where the food was from so long as it was tasty and arrived quickly.

◻◻Ⅱλ◻◻◻◻∩◻…··∴·˙˙·.◻∵◻◻◻∪◻◻◻◻◻

After eating it had been time for those of the group who could drink to sample the local Temple Bar hospitality. Not being able to drink when you're pregnant is one of the many things which Zoe felt was a kick in the teeth for women. Not only are you growing another human being inside you, but you can't have a glass of wine to chill out whilst you're doing it. The sperm donor, in her case Frank, obviously didn't experience such restrictions and indeed often took great pleasure in exploiting Zoe's condition by, if nothing else saving on taxi fares.

There is a time during pregnancy when women are said to be 'blooming', their skin is unnaturally smooth and spot free, their hair shines like no product before or since has been able to achieve, their eyes are bright and they are generally happy and thrilled to be fulfilling the role nature intended, producing a beautiful, perfect baby. However, Zoe found that during her pregnancy this blissful episode was short. She spent a lot of the nine month gestation period either ensuring she knew where the nearest toilet was or using said toilet; at night after about week twelve sleep was erratic but during the day she would fall asleep at her desk; she couldn't stop eating with a particular craving for Galaxy chocolate and chicken coronation sandwiches so that by the time she gave birth she looked like Mr Blobby; she developed piles; it was physically impossible for her to paint her toenails which had to be done for the labour ward or the world was going to end; she cried a lot and bizarrely worried frequently about dying and how Frank would be able to cope with the new baby; she farted incessantly and extremely pungently; her boobs grew to the size of small Zeppelins (another benefit for Frank) and there was a continuous metallic taste in her mouth. And she was lucky. All these side effects of pregnancy were completely normal, and she was fortunate enough to have two trouble free pregnancies and give birth to two healthy children.

So, credit to Faye as she traipsed along with them to the bar which that night was giving all proceeds to the New York Fire Brigade – at that time you couldn't have found a more worthy cause to which to raise a glass. By this stage of her pregnancy Faye was still working but carrying out limited duties as it's not easy being a heavily pregnant optician trying to stare deep into people's eyes and avoid crushing them with your baby bump – or indeed subjecting them to the other effects of pregnancy discussed earlier. Faye also feared that her pregnancy would deter her newly found workmates from staying in touch once she went on maternity leave. This happened to varying degrees, but it didn't put off Bridget who seemed remarkably interested in how she was feeling and what she was up to. In fact, Bridget had ventured over to Faye's a couple of times when she had finally gone on maternity leave. This was despite Faye subjecting her to inquisition like questioning about what everyone was up to in her absence. Bridget had even met Clive when he unexpectedly returned home early from work whilst they were still having coffee – well it was probably hot chocolate for Faye as this was her drink of choice whilst pregnant. Faye wasn't great at sitting around waiting for her baby to appear, which was made worse when she went over her due date. So, visits from Bridget were more than welcome and talking about something other than pain relief and stretch mark cream was a blessing.

Sally on the other hand seemed to be increasingly busy and much to her disgust was having to take work calls whilst on tour. She was definitely beginning to make her mark in the IT Sales and Marketing world and was instigating her campaign to make women a force to be reckoned with in this predominantly male dominated field. She loved the adrenalin rush of overcoming the discrepancies prevalent in the workplace and despite being held to higher standards she was still outperforming many of her male colleagues.

Conversely home life was for her, travelling down a rockier road. Gabe was still great with the kids, enjoyed his job and generally seemed happy with their married life. But Sally's feelings towards him were changing and she couldn't explain why. Despair was an emotion Sally hadn't really felt in her life before, but for this seemingly inexplicable reason she was feeling it now.

□□ㄐㄐ⅄□□□□∩□...···∶·˙˙·.□·∴□□□∪□□□□□

Dublin is indeed a fair city, and the gang did cover many of its streets broad and narrow during their stay. However, one thing that they found disappointing had been of particular relevance on this tour. Frequent urination is a common early pregnancy symptom, but it can also reappear later on during pregnancy as your uterus and baby grow, and your baby's head puts pressure on your bladder. Faye had definitely been at this latter stage and had needed to pee with alarming regularity. What's more the group of women she was with would also need to go to the loo as soon as anyone mentioned it - once the seal was broken it all got ridiculous. Sadly, pretty much all the public toilets they had tried in Dublin were rank – very smelly and often dirty. So, you can appreciate that Zoe was pleased to come across an article published many years later in 2018 in the *Irish Sun* pronouncing "Dublin to get first public toilets in more than 20 years as council to spend €200,000 on new loos by River Liffey". *The Alphabetties* considered this move by the City Council had come twenty years too late.

Nonetheless, the girls had all agreed that Dublin was a city with a host of charming features many of which they enjoyed from the vantage point of the City Tour Bus. The Tour Bus had been opted for on this occasion partly due to Faye's pregnant state and partly due to the inclement weather. *The Guinness Factory*, the *Molly Malone statue*, the haunts of James Joyce and many more were all taken in from the top deck of a bus. Faye was still annoyingly svelte and energetic enough to get up to the top deck of a bus. At that stage of pregnancy, Zoe wouldn't have had a hope. In fact, she did actually get stuck in Frank's car when she was pregnant with Holly.

□□ℿℷ□□□□∩□......⋮.·‥·.□∴·□□□∪□□□□□

When she met Frank, he was the proud owner of a silver Nissan 200SX, a very sporty number which was his pride and joy. It had to be said Zoe was impressed on their first date when he drove over to take her out. To say it had any influence on her decision to go on a second date would be shallow, but probably true. As the car was lower down and more comfortable than the Land Rover Frank had decided was needed as a family car, she often drove the Nissan to work when she was with child.

However, one day she realised that although hauling her, by then considerable bulk up into the Land Rover was a pest she was going to have to take that option. Zoe had taken Frank's car to work, parked up as usual and then turned to open the door. To her horror she couldn't get out, she couldn't get her baby bump around the leather steering wheel and out of the bucket seat. She was trapped. Irrationally she began to panic, mainly because the need for the loo was ever present, her baby pressing very unkindly on her very full bladder.

After various unsuccessful attempts to squeeze her body between the steering wheel and the seat, it came to her that surely a flash vehicle like this would have some mechanism to adjust the steering wheel to achieve the optimum driving position. She was right and after having pushed and pulled several buttons and levers she found one that allowed the steering wheel to be raised sufficiently to allow her to slide her extra large girth out of the driver's seat. However much to her embarrassment Zoe ended up on the ground on all-fours next to the car sweating, red faced and swearing. The car park had filled up considerably since she'd arrived, and a couple of people came over to her aid – they thought this poor woman had gone into labour and was going to give birth there and then. Just to complete the indignity of this episode Zoe had to explain to these kind people that no, she was fine she wasn't in labour yet, she was just too enormous to get out of her car!

Chapter 7

E for Edinburgh

"Be happy while you're living, for you're a
long time deid."
Old Scottish proverb

Some of life between tours.

Zoe turned forty. Frank whisked her off to Venice for a romantic weekend - bless him. Kate was a marvel and her and Max looked after Holly and Eric!

Sally started Kick Boxing classes – it helps with her pent up aggression apparently!

Gabe also turned forty. He still looks pretty much like he did when Sally met him – bastard!

Frank volunteered as a marshal at the Manchester Commonwealth Games. God love him but he looked incredibly camp in his official shell suit and beret!

Faye and Clive had welcomed baby Amelia Some months earlier. To their surprise she was sleeping through the night. They think this is amazing, then begin to question whether something is wrong; this hadn't happened with the other two! They speak to a paediatrician friend who examines her and tells them she's fine and to count their blessings - . lucky buggers!!

Kate joined the school Parent Teachers Association Committee – along with her trusty sidekick Zoe of course. She pretty much reinvented it and set about raising more funds for the school than ever before. The maternal force is strong in this one!

Once again Zoe began to carry out her annual labour of love and commit the *Alphabet Tour* activities to paper. From what she could remember mistaken identity or mistaken identification was the issue which had hounded Sally when the group went on tour to Edinburgh. Sally had by now racked up many air miles through work but here "Where Scotland meets the World" in Edinburgh Airport, for the first time, she had become the victim of lost luggage or more accurately mistaken luggage.

After all the other passengers had collected their cases, the five girls had found themselves standing watching a familiar looking suitcase go around and around the carousel. Eventually they succumbed to the obvious realisation that this case was similar to but not Sally's case and that some other random person had picked that up and walked off with it. Before they went to the Airline desk, the *Alphabetties* felt they could justify having a look in the unlocked imposter case. Tentatively, Kate had proffered that: "Maybe we should have a look inside to see if there is an address and have a nosey at what's in there – we could be dragging drugs or body parts to the airline desk for all we know!"

Clearly such items would have been discovered by staff at departures but nonetheless the girls felt they should get a feel for the kind of person they could possibly end up dealing with and potentially establish the whereabouts of Sally's case – which to be fair was almost identical to the suitcase they were about to rummage through. After they had opened the case Sally had had mixed feelings. Firstly, it was immediately apparent that it had been a woman who had mistakenly taken her suitcase and indeed a woman with very good taste. The clothing and particularly the lingerie had been very high class, more Agent Provocateur than M&S – having her belongings accidently taken by someone with good taste somehow made the situation feel better. But the fact that this woman was a dress size or two smaller and judging by the underwear selection, potentially having a far more active sex life than Sally, indeed any of them, didn't make her feel so great. They had decided the owner of the case must be a high class prostitute and had then handed it over to ground crew.

Sally had remained characteristically philosophical about the suitcase debacle and after leaving her contact details with staff, she took on her role as Tour Guide and they headed for a great little bar in the heart of the city. As she is Scottish and has a relative or two living in the city, Sally had spent a lot of time in Edinburgh. She took the group to what would now be described on TripAdvisor as a 'cool and quirky' basement bar for champagne where she recommended the mulligatawny soup. Zoe has a penchant for retaining useless pieces of information and recounted to the group that it is a little known, and bizarre fact that according to Alfred in the Batman franchise, mulligatawny soup is Batman's favourite food. And after tasting it for the first time on this, the fifth *Alphabet Tour* it also became one of Faye's favourites too. Faye had never before sampled the delights of this Indian soup and was so blown away that she ordered a second bowl. For Faye to eat seconds of anything was a rare, if not previously unheard of event.

Faye always keeps herself in great shape and is universally acknowledged as the fittest of *The Alphabetties*. Although, as we all know by now, she does enjoy a glass of champagne, she counteracts this by taking in lots of water and being mindful about what she eats. She has been known to hoover a pizza, eating the toppings and leaving behind the evil, calorific dough base. Even after the birth of her third child, her fitness regime meant that her figure had returned enviously quickly. Faye was now back at work after the birth of Amelia or usually Amy – who, being the third child was put into nursery at the soonest respectable opportunity. Faye went back to optometry part-time, limiting herself at this stage to working out of one fairly local practice. So, this meant she didn't get to see the young trendy crowd she'd enjoyed socialising with prior to maternity leave. However, Bridget had kept in touch and Faye really appreciated this and delighted in hearing about her friends that were completely separate from her life with Clive. She'd met Clive at university and so he knew pretty much everyone in her social circle then and ever since. Not that Faye didn't enjoy socialising with Clive. Outside the confines of work, Clive was often great fun and as gregarious as Faye. He too had a penchant for good food and wine and, some would say uncharacteristically, Clive also enjoyed wearing fancy dress and would often do so to parties whether or not required. Nonetheless Faye still found that sometimes just getting away on her own was great.

□□⊔⅄□□□□⌒□……⋯⋮.·˙˙.□⋱□□□⊔□□□□□

Luckily, by the time the group of friends had arrived at their hotel, the high class prostitute had realised her error and Sally's case was waiting for her at reception and she was able to get changed like the rest of them, in readiness for the evening ahead. They met for drinks in the hotel bar, and it was then that Sally's second incidence of mistaken identity had occurred. As they all merrily sipped their early evening fizz, looking out on to an open, to be honest uninspired piazza style space in front of the hotel, Sally leapt to her feet, shouting: "Oh my God, I'll be back in a minute girls!" Although somewhat surprised, the rest of them didn't move mainly for fear of spilling champagne but also, they were now of an age that they really didn't have to jump up to see what the drama was – they'd find out eventually. Plus, they could easily see their friend running across the characterless space shouting something at a tall, dark haired chap who at this point had his back to Sally. Annoyingly being so tall with long, slim legs Sally looked rather graceful and her long strides meant she caught up with the chap quite quickly. As their glasses were refreshed, they could see Sally tap him enthusiastically on the shoulder clearly excited at having spotted someone she knew. Then, as he turned around, her expression changed from euphoric to mortified. Evidently this person wasn't a long lost friend but a complete stranger, who from behind had looked like a long lost friend. Sally backed away, apologising and made her way swiftly back to the bar rather red faced. As it turns out she should indeed have been embarrassed, as it wasn't just a friend she thought she'd spotted but actually her brother. Although she did have a twinkle in her eye as she admitted the unknown stranger had turned out to be far more handsome than her brother!

❑❑ⅠⅠⅹ❑❑❑❑∩❑……⋯∶.˙˙˙.❑∵❑❑❑⋃❑❑❑❑❑

Recounting this sequence of events prompted another reminiscence from Zoe that happened way back in her days at university. She was walking back to the campus having met a friend who attended what was then called the polytechnic for lunch. Nowadays such establishments are all universities with ridiculous names like De Montfort or Bishop Grosseteste and describing themselves as places where "instinct ignites action" and "where hearts beat as one". And have videos on YouTube to attract foreign students and their cash.

Zoe had been minding her own business when, it being 1st March, St David's Day and their national day, a couple of drunk Welsh men pointed at her from further down the street and shouted, "Is that her?" To Zoe's horror the girl with them screamed:

"Yes that's the bitch!"

Zoe was rooted to the spot as these two substantial Welsh men hurtled towards her. The bigger of the two then unceremoniously picked her up, threw her over his shoulder and carried her back down the road to the agitated girl with the foul mouth, where he pretty much dropped her like a sacrificial offering at the girl's feet. Zoe tentatively got up and when she got a close look at her, the foul mouthed girl decided Zoe wasn't the bitch she was looking for. They then carried on down the road without so much as a word of explanation or apology! But given the size of her assailants Zoe didn't kick up a fuss about this, despite the fact that the contents of her backpack were now strewn across the pavement. As she was reeling from the whole episode, she was mighty glad she wasn't the girl they were looking for as she didn't think they intended to show her much love. The episode still sends a nervous shiver down Zoe's spine if she ever sees a bloke wearing a daffodil.

⬚⬚Ⅱ⅄⬚⬚⬚⬚∩⬚…⋯⋮.⋅˙˙⋅.⬚⋅∴⬚⬚⬚∪⬚⬚⬚⬚⬚

The next morning after a leisurely get-up and even a dip in the hotel pool, a request had been made to have breakfast at the coffee shop where J K Rowling was inspired to write Harry Potter and create the world of Hogwarts – the girls thought that maybe they too would be filled with inspiration and go on to find fame and a massive fortune! Kate in particular, never mind her kids, is a massive Harry Potter fan. She was there with all the other *Potterheads* queueing outside the bookshop at midnight each time a new volume was released! Kate read books the way she pretty much tackled everything in life, at full pelt with complete focus. If she found a novel she liked she would often finish it in a single sitting. Although the opportunity for such a period of self-indulgence generally only presented itself on holiday or if the kids went to visit Max's parents.

So, Sally resumed her duty as City Guide and took the group on a scenic route to The Elephant House Café where after a short wait, they were seated amongst all the other Harry Potter enthusiasts from across the globe. The breakfast was marvellous and enormous. It included the usual fayre plus a square of traditional Lorne sausage made from mince with non-specific rusk and spices, plus the option of haggis and black pudding – the girls declined the latter option. Once again stuffed with hearty morsels the group headed out to explore more of Edinburgh, described by Tobias Smollett as "a hotbed of genius". Zoe thought to herself: "Sadly, I don't think *The Alphabetties* will be adding any gravitas to Toby's description!" Although to be fair to them Maggie and Kate were back at university reawakening the brain cells that had gone dormant during the baby years.

◻◻Ⱡ⁊◻◻◻◻∩◻…⋯⋮.·¨·.◻∵◻◻◻∪◻◻◻◻

Maggie, by this time had reached the stage of her midwifery course when the students were let loose on the wards to help them "develop as accountable practitioners". Around six hundred thousand women give birth on an NHS ward every year and Maggie was now out there helping the future population arrive safely. If you say midwife, most people think of a nurse who gets to cuddle new born babies all day, hold ladies' hands and wipe their slightly sweaty brow. Maggie had learnt fast that being a midwife was not a bed of roses and was very far from the picture painted by the media. Long physical hours helping any pregnant woman who came through the maternity ward door from all walks of life was widening Maggie's horizons, increasing her vocabulary of profanities, running her full gambit of emotions and taking its toll on her physically. She was pretty much knackered and was suffering with a bad back – she suspected this would be a recurring occupational hazard. When he was home Shane was a godsend and was supporting her in any way possible, but he was still travelling. In fact, Maggie's father was increasingly relying on Shane to run the business as he was by now semi-retired. So, after shifts at the hospital where the course of events in any one day couldn't be predicted, she went home to try to maintain a routine for her little girls. *The Alphabetties* were amazed she was managing to stay awake let alone keep up with the usual round of continuous, often overlapping conversation, drinking and eating that was now the tour norm.

☐☐⅃⅃ⅈ☐☐☐☐∩☐……⋮.∵˙˙.☐∵∵☐☐☐∪☐☐☐☐☐

After the success of the Dublin Bus Top Tour and given Maggie's midwifery injury, it was unanimously agreed that this should be the next activity and that bus tours should become a regular feature of the *Alphabet Tour* – fortunately, Edinburgh was able to oblige. Impressively, Edinburgh had several bus routes to choose from, one of which went out to Leith, where the sunshine would be – according to The Proclaimers anyway: a band which Zoe secretly very much disliked, she couldn't bear their voices or their identical looks – but she kept this snippet to herself given they were local lads!

As a group the girls happily embrace a bit of eccentricity and indeed often seemed to be magnets for life's oddballs –

collectively and as individuals. So, when they got on the bus and saw the unconventional attire and appearance of the rather mature tour guide it was water off a duck's back. He was clad in a bespoke tweed suit, no doubt from Harris, complimented by tartan accessories. They assumed he would be witty, endearing and quirky in a Frank Muir type of charming way. Wrong. His accent even for Sally was unintelligible and when they did tune in to his dialect, he turned out to be a pompous ass – completely up himself and actually quite offensive towards his passengers. They alighted the Tour Bus and opted for drinks and some of the best chips ever had on tour, in a quayside pub in Leith somewhere not far from the Royal Yacht Britannia.

As was prone to happen, afternoon drinks turned into evening drinks, on this occasion in a previously reconnoitred rooftop bar overlooking the city skyline. It was very trendy with lots of chrome, chic people and uber minimalist décor. But the view was beautiful as the sun set and a rather begrudging guest was asked if they would take a group photo. The begrudging guest managed to take a reasonable photograph of *The Alphabetties* – except for one thing. The angle of the shot combined with the copious amounts of chrome in the bar meant that Kate, who was sitting nearest the camera, looked like she was in a wheelchair and had been purposefully wheeled in, front and centre.

⬜⬜⎁ℷ⬜⬜⬜⬜⌒⬜…⸱⸳⋮⸱⸳ ̈⸳ ⬜⸫⬜⬜⬜⎷⬜⬜⬜⬜

There was a certain irony to this as Kate usually liked to be front and centre stage enjoying nothing better than being under the spotlight and treading the boards. Kate couldn't really say when she gave it up, sometime fairly soon after the birth of baby number three and starting a part-time law degree whilst working, but prior to all that she, and indeed

Max were amateur thespians. When they met, Kate was well and truly established as the go to leading lady in the theatre group local to her parents' home. The theatre group operated out of a lovely little theatre nestling at the bottom of the hill and had a respected and well-loved reputation. Kate and Max, then still in their twenties were the young stars of the ensemble. Max although never having been on stage before, at well over six foot with dark hair, was a ready-made leading man. Kate has a wonderful voice and a personality that landed her many, many roles – her dream character was the cockney flower girl Eliza Doolittle and it was generally recognized in South Manchester amateur theatre that she gave Audrey Hepburn a run for her money! So amateur dramatics became a major part of courtship and early married life for Max and Kate.

The other *Alphabetties* can recall Kate inviting them along to what must have been one of her final performances. The company were putting on *Oklahoma* and not surprisingly Kate and Max were playing Laurey and Curly the main characters and love interest – they were approximately the right age and yes, were in love. However, the rest of the company were somewhat older and there had to be some creative casting. As *The Alphabetties* watched Kate giving a great performance, they also had to refrain from laughing out loud at some of the seventy year old farmhands who were also attending the box social dance. Nonetheless, and despite Zoe's aversion to musicals, they all had a great evening and Kate and Max did sterling work clearly both enjoying the smell of the greasepaint and the roar of the crowd!

Secretly Zoe was happy it wasn't her that was the brunt of the Edinburgh photographic joke. Throughout her life Zoe had appeared in more than her fair share of crap photographs. At least in this day and age you can instantly get rid of the images you dislike. Zoe's misfortunes tended to be in the old days when you got your prints from Max Spielman a week after you got back from your trip, only to find your finger was over the lens in fifty percent of them and the others were slightly out of focus. Or in her case you looked either disgusting, were doing something stupid or resembled someone completely different. Her friends have in their possession images of her looking like Gary Glitter, *Whistler's Mother* and the side of a house – the latter of which there are sadly many. Over time Zoe has come to accept that she is not photogenic. Now with the ever increasing frequency of selfies, she just grins from ear to ear and then deletes or crops the offending photo when it gets sent to her. Luckily for her, Holly, Eric and Frank are all very photogenic, as is their beautiful pet greyhound, so she isn't short of photographic memories.

Zoe pondered whether this new acceptance of things she can't change had come about as she'd turned forty that year – another reason not to get in photographs! She had never worried particularly about growing older and liked to think she would do so with grace. Certainly, she found the thought of plastic surgery, liposuction, Botox or similar quite repugnant and scary. She took far more comfort from the words of Costa Caldes in *Shirley Valentine* after they had made love and he had kissed her stretch marks and she's mortified. He gently says to her:

"Don't, don't be too stupid to try to hide these lines. They, they are lovely, because they are part of you, and you are lovely, so don't, don't hide, be proud."

Zoe was of the opinion that this attitude applied equally well to wrinkles, crow's feet and laughter lines, wherever on your person they might be. Although she did have to admit that her parents had blessed her and her siblings with youthful looks – a gift which she, at forty had much appreciated. However, her children on to whom she had passed this trait, would not have such good things to say about it when trying to get in to clubs in Manchester or purchasing alcohol.

□□Ⱡⱥ□□□□∩□……∴.·¨·.□∵·□□□∪□□□□□

When they were in Edinburgh, *The Alphabetties* were mightily glad they got to see some men in kilts. As a rule, Zoe isn't mad on most things Scottish – which is sacrilege as her ancestral roots are deep in the north of Scotland. But the whole tartan, bagpipes, haggis, Robbie Burns thing leaves her cold. However, she does rather like a man in a kilt, a feeling shared by her fellow travellers. So, it put a smile on their collective faces when on returning to the hotel they found the bar overflowing with sporrans and dirks. A large traditional family wedding was well underway in a function room adjacent to the main hotel bar. A table was free, strategically placed between the two rooms which allowed maximum surveillance of the comings and goings of the wedding guests. They grabbed it and settled down to shamelessly people watch and hope that some drama would unfurl.

Funnily enough five women sat in a row clearly commenting on everyone that went by didn't go unnoticed. Three somewhat inebriated men in kilts wandered over and struck up a conversation with the highly original: "So where might you ladies be from?" Well, that's what they thought they said as their accents were thick and laced with several glasses of whisky. The jovial jocks turned out to be the father of the bride, her uncle and a cousin in his early twenties. They did look impressive in their full regalia and of course Faye had to ask if it was true what a Scotsman wears under his kilt. An audible groan went up from her associates as she tendered the predictable question, followed by a sharp intake of breath as the gentleman lifted their kilts to show them! The two older chaps strictly adhered to the old traditional ways and would be considered true Scotsmen, but the younger lad was in underwear – albeit tartan boxer shorts. The girls' shock at seeing two of those things that there is really no need to see unless absolutely unavoidable, rapidly changed to concern for the young man's safety. His older male relatives were not happy that he was not letting everything hang free and were berating him severely for it – despite current attitudes that it's unhygienic not to wear undergarments. To the girls' horror they were having a go at him so loudly and expletively that the commotion had caught the attention of the bride and she was marching over to see what was going on. The tale of how they had learned that wee Jimmy was wearing *skids* was recounted to her by her now very agitated father and uncle. As her expression became angrier, and she clearly wasn't impressed with five uninvited, female s*assenachs* having caused a disturbance at her wedding reception, the girls made a hasty exit.

The next morning, with all thoughts of men in kilts behind them, Sally had mentioned that her godfather lived in a beautiful apartment up by the castle and as they followed the tourist trail and listened to the one o'clock gun, the group were all hoping they might be able to visit the godfather and sneak a peek at his amazing residence. Sally recoiled in horror at this suggestion – apparently, he is as mad as a box of frogs and can just about tolerate or indeed recognise those he is related to. So, they thought better of it as it didn't sound as though they would get a warm Scottish welcome – and they certainly didn't want to upset another Scotsman. Zoe was curious to know whether he had been diagnosed with Alzheimer's or was just a miserable old Jock – from

Sally's clear horror at the thought of introducing them to him, Zoe suspected the latter.

⬜⬜ↄ⬜⬜⬜⬜⌒⬜…⋯⋮.⋅¨˙⋅.⬜∵⬜⬜⬜∪⬜⬜⬜⬜

Zoe was glad to hear she wasn't the only *Alphabettie* with weird relatives. Although she was positive many other people have them too, Zoe did feel she had been dealt more than her fair share of strange family members. Of the male variety she had (for they are both now deceased) a couple of uncles who stand out in particular. One was Uncle Norman, a six foot five giant of a man married to her dad's sister, Monica, a very petite four foot eleven slip of a woman. He had slicked back hair and a pencil moustache and looked like a World War Two *spiv*. He was from Wigan and had a glass eye, she can't remember which one. The combination of all these characteristics and a generous but loud personality meant he was affectionately known in her family as *Uncle Abnormal*.

He had fallen head over heels in love with Zoe's Auntie Monica whilst working at the shipyard on an engineering contract – and also whilst he was still married. Monica was beautiful and took great pride in her appearance, always dressing with immaculate style. Their forbidden love flourished and by the time Zoe was born they had moved away and lived together seemingly as man and wife. Uncle Norman's legal wife was a devote catholic and wouldn't give him a divorce. So, they lived in sin in suburban Manchester - all their friends there being none the wiser. In fact, many, many years later when Zoe was at university and her aunt and uncle were in their seventies, Norman's wife finally relented and agreed to a divorce. As no one else knew the truth, Zoe's mother had to travel to Manchester to be a witness at their secret wedding on the other side of the city from where they lived. Zoe always thought it was so romantic that they still wanted to get married and declare their love for one another even after all those years. Not long after the happy event they had waited so long for, Zoe's aunt had sadly died – it was like she had waited for their love to be approved of in the eyes of the law before she left Norman's side.

Her other notorious uncle was also on her father's side – his eldest brother, Leonard. He had married a woman called Enid who looked like a cross between Cher and the Mona Lisa. She had long dark hair parted in the middle, pale flawless skin and Zoe recollects her always wearing a full length fur coat. Len had a penchant for wearing leather trousers and jackets which blended into his skin which was also leathery, tanned and pitted with acne scars. His look was topped off with a flock of collar length white hair. He wouldn't have looked out of place in an episode of *Bonanza*. Not long after they had married Enid announced she didn't want to have any children. Uncle Len did and this drove them apart - although they did live together separately in the same house for many years. Why this issue hadn't been discussed prior to their marriage was beyond Zoe.

They would often turn up at her parents' house individually but accompanied by their latest fling. This made for many awkward visits especially when Zoe was a young child and Uncle Len turned up. Young Zoe was fascinated by his leather trousers (which were pretty uncommon back in those days) and she would insist on stroking Uncle Len's leg! God it must have been excruciating for her parents – although Uncle Len never seemed to mention it! Uncle Len was also crap at Christmas presents. He sent Rich the complete works of Shakespeare when he was about eight and she got a twenty piece wooden jigsaw when she was fifteen – perhaps it was just as well Uncle Len never did have children.

Hardly surprising that Len and Enid eventually divorced. Uncle Len later married an exotic dancer named Trudie, whom he first met as she writhed around in a net above his head in a nightclub in Hamburg. Sadly, Zoe wasn't home when Len brought her to visit her parents – Zoe always wanted to know if Trudie matched up to the mental image she had painted of her!

⬜⬜Ⱊⱦ⬜⬜⬜∩⬜…··∴·˙˙·.⬜∵⬜⬜⬜Ս⬜⬜⬜⬜

Despite the lack of a visit to her crazy godfather, Sally did manage to take the tour group to an amazing building by the castle – The Witchery Hotel. From experience Sally had the foresight to book a table for them well in advance in The Secret Garden Restaurant in this amazing, opulent hotel. Located in a sixteenth century building it gets its name from the hundreds of men and women burned as witches on the nearby Castle Hill. The group thought it was indeed wicked and Zoe was pretty sure it would be the only time she would be likely to step foot in this gothic masterpiece – she doubted Frank would be booking them in to share one of the hotel's double rolled top baths any time soon.

Although in the past Zoe and her husband had shared many a bath. When she met Frank, his house, now their home had a ridiculously huge corner bath complete with numerous jets and sprays – it was environmentally unfriendly, enormous and a lot of fun. For their first Valentine's Day together Frank lit the bathroom with candles and floated a bowl of strawberries across the bath and served champagne amongst the bubbles! Sadly, once the children arrived such things went out the window, but they did have family fun in the gigantic tub. When Holly and Eric were very little, they could all get in their together which was cute. But once they were old enough to trust them not to drown Frank and Zoe would refrain from sharing. They did still have to keep an eye on them obviously and not just to ensure they didn't disappear under the water! There was one memorable occasion when Holly and Eric were in the bath together; Eric was quite little but able to sit up and splash around quite happily. Bath time was usually a noisy affair with the pair of them playing with rubber ducks, and squirty toys. But that evening as she was busy putting their clothes in the washing basket and getting towels ready, it went spookily quiet. Zoe turned in a panic. The scene that presented itself filled her with mixed emotions. Eric was sitting happily with a big smile on his face as Holly was playing with his willy like it was a new bath toy! Zoe blurted out:

"Holly don't do that darling!"

To which she innocently replied:

"But he likes it!"

Heartily glad though she was that they hadn't drowned, she then had to come up with a way to explain to a five year old why she shouldn't play with her brother's, or any other boy's willy in the bath, or indeed elsewhere – certainly not for, at the very least, the next thirteen years (or if Frank had his way - ever). After this and the curious incident of the poo in the bath, Zoe and Frank gave up on family bath time and stuck to washing them separately!

Chapter 8

F for Faro

"Close female friends are a particular source of happiness," says psychologist Michael Argyle in The Psychology of Happiness. Female friendships in particular seem to be a great happiness booster: "They're more rewarding to both males and females, and the best predictor of not being lonely, for both sexes, is frequency of interaction with women. Time spent with men makes no difference," says Argyle.

Some of life between tours.

Samantha and Jennifer learnt to ride bikes. Maggie and Shane were crippled with backache!

Maggie and Shane turned forty and felt their age!

Max had an operation on his vertebra to help the pain in his neck and spine. Thankfully it was a success – his golfing career can go on!

Chloe knocked a pupil off the stage whilst been an overly enthusiastic Angel Gabriel in the school Nativity play! There was a slight doubt that it may not have been accidental!

Kate was randomly contacted by a television company to ask if she would appear in the British version of *Wife Swap* – a TV programme where two very different families swap mothers/wives (obviously with no sexual content). Despite the lure of being on the TV and some financial reward Kate politely turned down the opportunity. It took all her energy looking after the family she'd spent years training and wasn't going to be subjected to the habits of complete strangers for anything!

Shane splashed out on a hot tub for the family and friends to enjoy. The kids love it!

As Zoe began work on the sixth *Alphabet Tour* diary, she realised her duty as scribe would take longer this year as the group had progressed to a three night stay - Halleluiah! The children were then aged between eight and one and three quarters, the youngest of these being Faye's third child, Amy. Faye was by now a more confident parent and had no qualms about leaving the children with Clive and didn't worry quite so much about her husband killing their offspring – although coincidentally her mother-in-law usually visited when Faye went away. To be fair to Clive though, this wasn't entirely to do with his childcare skills, but often his work meant he was on call.

Although Faye did tell an after dinner story of their extremely early parenting days which, if their skills hadn't improved, the presence of Clive's mum was certainly warranted. Faye and Clive were leaving the maternity ward, proud parents of newly arrived Chloe, their first born. Clive had pushed Faye to the door in a wheelchair as required then by the NHS, having previously brought the car round close to collect his family. At the hospital door he took Chloe from Faye and carefully placed her in the car seat in the back, locked and closed the door. In those days of course you didn't open and lock the car with the press of a button from outside the vehicle and using a fingerprint or facial recognition were things of science fiction. It was quite possible, indeed quite easy to lock yourself out of the car with the keys inside it. Or in this case, lock you and your wife out of the car and your newly born baby girl and keys inside it! All of which happened in the ambulance bay just outside the entrance to the maternity department. Suffice to say, no harm came to Chloe but Zoe can't actually recount how the situation was rectified as she had been laughing too much by this point of the story to catch the end. She did appreciate that she probably shouldn't have been laughing quite so heartily and should have been horrified. But stories like this are good for the soul of those who have basically bumbled their way through bringing up children and it brings cheer to know that there are many equally as bemused parents in the world.

⬚⬚Ⱡⱥ⬚⬚⬚⬚⌒⬚…⋯⋮·⋰⋅⬚⋰⬚⬚⬚∪⬚⬚⬚⬚

The three night stay had been to Vilamoura on The Algarve. Clearly this does not begin with F, but the girls had flown into Faro airport and that was close enough for the *Alphabet Tour* - 25 km or 15.5. miles to be exact. The main reason for the choice of destination had been that Kate's brother-in-law had said the group could use his company's apartment in Vilamoura - *Alphabetties* do not look a gift horse in the mouth. The apartment was located on a complex among several other complexes, each had a swimming pool, and each was surrounded by its own golf course. Apparently, there are five, eighteen-hole golf courses in Vilamoura – that's a hole for every thirty full-time residents. In Greater Manchester the stats are approximately one golf hole for every fourteen thousand residents! Sadly, all this sporting provision was wasted on Zoe who agreed with Mark Twain that "golf is a good walk spoiled."

⬚⬚Ⱡⱥ⬚⬚⬚⬚⌒⬚…⋯⋮·⋰⋅⬚⋰⬚⬚⬚∪⬚⬚⬚⬚

The abundance of all things golf had prompted Zoe to think of her husband's sporting prowess. Frank dabbles with golf, but he has a regular habit of losing his balls when playing, not metaphorically but literally – it's now almost disappointing if he doesn't. He plays once or twice a year with a group of old boys called the *Forty Niners* which includes their brother-in-law Henry and many of Henry's friends. Frank used to do surprisingly well on these jaunts often coming home with several very tasteless trophies. One in particular had stuck in Zoe's mind – a combination of trophy/wall clock in a tacky mock wood frame that you were meant to display proudly on your wall. It was a bizarre pairing of practical timekeeping and pride at one's achievement hitting a small ball a long way into a hole – it never saw the light of day whilst in Zoe's home!

Max on the other hand, is a big golfer and goes away regularly on golfing trips with a group of like-minded friends. Apparently, according to Kate, it all gets quite competitive, and Max comes home very crestfallen if he hasn't performed to his full capability. In fact, one year he was very sad as there was a fatality – of sorts. Zoe knew not where this unfortunate event took place, but it made her laugh, albeit tinged with guilt, every time she thought of it. Max is a man of considerable stature standing at six foot three and was giving his all and going for a super long drive. This indeed he did but his shot landed in an ornamental pond further up the course killing a resident duck! Max had been mortified. Zoe wondered how they recorded it on his score card and felt it must have been in keeping with all the ornithological jargon that golf entails.

Sally's other half is probably the best of the lot and played off a very small handicap. Over the years Gabe had in fact passed on some of his golfing skill to Sally. She remembered fondly the time he had spent patiently teaching her the intricacies of a good swing and how he'd been pretty impressed with her delicate putting skills. In fact, recently they had managed a weekend away at a Spa/Golf hotel which although they hadn't talked about their life together as much as Sally had hoped, she had let it go. It had been an opportunity to just be together and forget about the stress of life for a while and have fun as a couple again. She also kept to herself the fact that although not bad at golf she much preferred to just go for a run or even a game of netball.

Even after the mounting years of friendship, new things were still discovered on *Tour.* That year it had transpired that one of *The Alphabetties* had an intense, acute fear of birds, Ornithophobia. Maggie is petrified of them. Their first evening in Vilamoura the group had thought it would be lovely to sit on the balcony sip *Vino Verde* and watch the sun go down. The balcony happened to be outside Maggie's room. And indeed, it had been very pleasant, and they'd all begun to mellow. That was until a certain hour when the more nocturnal insects had started to come out which then prompted the appearance of swallows from a nest located in the top corner of the balcony. As they'd swooped in and out of the nest on their evening feeding frenzy Maggie had become hysterical, she'd screamed and leapt around precariously. At first, the girls had laughed as Maggie had been comical to watch. But then they'd seen the look of genuine terror in her eyes. Eventually she moved her chair and took part in the conversation from the relative safety of just inside the room.

Her phobia had all stemmed from when she lived in Australia as a child with her parents and three siblings. Her parents had kept budgerigars in a large, home-made aviary to the rear of the house. Maggie was the youngest of the family and during one school holiday whilst her parents were out at work, her brothers had decided to lock her in the aviary. From what the rest of the group had gathered she had been in there for quite some time with the budgerigars flying around her like a scene from a Hitchcock movie. The horrid brothers had found this all very amusing but poor Maggie had been scarred for life.

□□Ⅱ𝓍□□□□∩□......∵∴.˙˙˙.□∵□□□∪□□□□□

It is fascinating how things that people do can unwittingly affect others. As a child, on visits to the beach Holly had loved to swim in the sea. Through her primary school years, Zoe and Frank spent many a happy day at the seaside watching the kids playing and Holly splashing around for hours in the water. Then she went to senior school and eventually decided to take A Level Film Studies. As part of this course, she had to study some of the great film directors including Steven Spielberg. Of all the films that the teacher could have chosen by this amazing film maker, they opted for *Jaws*. It was years before Holly went back in the sea and only now ventures forth under considerable peer pressure. Why didn't the teacher show *E.T* or *The Goonies* or even *Schindler's List*!

□□Ⅱ𝓍□□□□∩□......∵∴.˙˙˙.□∵□□□∪□□□□□

As well as Kate's brother-in-law having a company apartment, Faye had spent a lot of time on The Algarve at their family timeshare. She had wanted to take them to a lovely restaurant she and Clive had discovered, right on the beach just further down the coast. A taxi had been ordered and on arrival the driver turned out to be a very jolly chap whose cousin owned a bar very near the restaurant. In the spirit of good family relations, he had proposed that if they went to his cousin's bar after their meal, he would be more than happy to come back and collect them from there later. This had all sounded very amicable.

The food that evening was as good as Faye had promised but was somewhat overshadowed by them all been flummoxed when it came to pay. Back in 2003 paying by credit card in the UK involved a duplicated strip of carbon paper been placed in a machine along with your credit card from which an imprint was then taken by a roller that ran over the top of it. You then signed the slip; the retailer kept the bottom copy, and you got the top sheet as your receipt. Simple! In the past the Global Competitiveness Report ranked Portugal forty third out of a hundred and thirty four world economies. The UK had been ranked twelfth. Yet, that night, back in 2003 in a beach bar in a sleepy village on The Algarve it had become very apparent to *The Alphabet Girls* that the British public were falling behind in the world of money transactions.

When they'd come to pay the bill for their delicious meal the restauranteur came to Kate first and had asked her: "Please can I have your chip and pin."

This was an expression never before heard by any of the girls but one which now seems very dated in this contactless age. After much explaining in pidgin English and rudimentary Portuguese, the bill had eventually been paid and everyone in the restaurant was happy but had still been baffled that these English women didn't know about this payment method.

Now chilled, despite the bill debacle, they had listened to the water rushing on to the shore and wandered out on to the moonlit beach towards their taxi driver's cousin's bar. But their peace had been short-lived as before they knew it, Faye had decided this was a beautiful night for a dip under the stars. She'd taken off her obligatory white holiday trousers and ridiculously high wedges and headed for the waves, shouting:

"Come on in, the water was lovely last time Clive and I did this!"

En masse the girls had firstly been surprised by Faye's spontaneity, but more so by the fact that Clive's trousers had come down on a previous visit to this public beach. They knew he liked to dress up when the occasion arose but had never put him down as a man who was carefree about public nudity! This had led to follow up questions of; were the kids there, if not what else went on and did they stop at taking trousers off or go for the full monty – many mental pictures had been conjured up!

Much to the envy of the group Faye had looked fabulous as she'd frolicked around half dressed in the surf but, after what was probably a longer length of time than they should have left a clearly drunk woman splashing around in the Mediterranean, Maggie had said:

"Do you not think we should get her out of there, she doesn't have an ounce of fat on her and she's starting to wrinkle."

So, despite her protestations, Sally and Maggie had dragged Faye back onto the beach and tried desperately to get her garments back on. As has been mentioned before Faye is a very stylish lady and, on this occasion had been wearing a beautiful, crocheted top – not ideal for open water swimming. Sadly, the coveted top had stretched somewhat under the weight of the seawater. On the other hand, her trousers seemed to have shrunk as the whole group had tried to get them back on her wet legs. After a concerted effort they'd made Faye respectable enough to go to the bar for a drink. On arrival, Faye had immediately mentioned they had come in a taxi driven by the owner's cousin and then *The Alphabetties* had become quite the centre of attention. Alcohol had been ordered and consumed at a ferocious pace by the locals and their new friends and things had started to get messy. Luckily, Maggie in a moment of clarity had called the taxi as soon as they arrived at the bar.

Clarity and reacting in the moment were skills which Maggie was now having to perfect as she had finished her midwifery training, was registered with the Nursing and Midwifery Council and was working at a hospital in a local town. The catchment area of the hospital covered all social backgrounds. She had already carried out home visits to footballers' wives in huge mansions, where the only concern was their waters breaking on the cream wool carpets, to seeing women coming in for check-ups who clearly used pregnancy as a method of birth control, the baby being a complete irrelevance. But she was loving it, she had been welcomed by the other midwives and they were happy to pass on their knowledge and take the time to settle in their rookie. The one downside was the commuting which added unwanted time away from her own family, which was hard for them all.

The girls were all incredibly proud of Maggie's achievement and were thrilled when she'd asked if they'd like to join her and Shane for lunch after her graduation. This was an event not to be missed and leave had been booked, and the girls had travelled to her university town and its impressive cathedral to celebrate Maggie's success. Photos had duly been taken to record the proud moment, then Shane in his naturally generous way had sorted a surprise lunch for them all at a very plush hotel. It was a lovely day and one which Zoe felt honoured to have been a part of.

⬚⬚ΙΙ⅄⬚⬚⬚⬚∩…⋯⋮.⋅⋯.⬚⋰⬚⬚⬚∪⬚⬚⬚⬚⬚

Having watched Faye strip off for an illicit swim, Zoe had been reminded of her first time skinny dipping. Long before she met Frank, she was great friends with a couple of guys called Matthew and Douglas. They had met through a work colleague who had been to university with both the boys. Zoe had recently had a bad break-up from a bad boyfriend and really just wanted to have some fun. These guys certainly provided that. They got on famously with no romantic pressure. That summer Zoe had a holiday booked to Corfu and asked if the lads wanted to come along. Matthew couldn't make it, but Douglas came. The two of them had a wonderful time and had gone skinny dipping on a remote beach in a sheltered cove they'd found when out on those ridiculous scooters that you tell your kids not to go anywhere near because they are death traps. In those days Zoe could also get away with topless sunbathing and wearing high cut swimwear – both of which were de rigueur in the mid-1980s.

So really, she shouldn't have been shocked when, one evening as she was getting changed in their twin room to go out for dinner, Douglas suddenly asked if they could have a quick one and started chasing her around the bedroom waving a condom in his hand, pleading: "Oh, go on Zoe, just once!". Bless him the amount of flesh on show in very close proximity but not on offer had been just too much for him. It was Matthew who had supplied the condoms with a note saying: "Just in case, you never know."

It turned out Douglas had been quite smitten with Zoe who loved him dearly and despite a subsequent but very brief try at romance, just hadn't felt that way about him. Life can often be cruel that way. Zoe still often thought of him and the trip to Corfu and always smiled.

The next day the girls had thought they would venture into Vilamoura and surprisingly for *The Alphabetties*, had opted to get there by public transport from the nearest bus stop. After the obligatory confusion over which way the traffic would come and pondering over which side of the road to stand on, they'd finally found themselves at a bus stop with two obviously British ladies in dubious sundresses – they'd reminded Zoe of figures from a Beryl Cook painting. Despite their lack of fashion sense, the ladies had proved to be very helpful informing them which bus to get, how much it would cost and where to get off. The girls had dutifully followed their instructions and thanks to the ladies they had soon been wandering around the rather beautiful Vilamoura harbour.

⬜⬜⊔⋏⬜⬜⬜⬜⋂⬜…··⋅∴·˙˙·.⬜∵⬜⬜⬜⊔⬜⬜⬜⬜

Whilst recording the exploits of "F", Zoe realised that she had the potential to morph into one of the bus stop ladies - definitely not the revolting sundress but certainly having all the logistical details prepared well in advance. She likes to think she's still spontaneous but really, she's not. Since the dawn of the internet and the arrival of Google, everything is at your fingertips. Whenever Zoe travels now, with whoever, she will have bus timetables, local train stations, taxi numbers, recommended restaurants, must see things, quirky-off-the-tourist-trail things to see, all sussed out before she even leaves suburban South Manchester. Her FOMO (second only to Kate's) and a family quite happy to let someone else make the decisions has caused this to come about. She also loves a map. GPS is a marvellous thing, but Zoe likes the tactile stimulation of holding and manipulating a map. She finds it very satisfying to navigate to where she needs to reach a new destination – although like Joey in *Friends* she does have to 'get in the map'! She remembers places this way, plotting a route by landmarks and road names rather than blindly following the instructions of a faceless voice on her phone. And navigating is one of the few times when Kate is happy to hand over the reins and follow

Zoe or anyone else with a better sense of direction. Kate often swears blind that she has never been to places that she has visited before with Zoe - she has even been known to get lost having come out of a department store through a different door to the one she went in!

☐☐⊔⋏☐☐☐☐∩☐…⋯⋮.⋅˙˙⋅.☐⋰⋅☐☐☐⊔☐☐☐☐

The Alphabetties are five strong, opinionated women, so making decisions can often be a trickier exercise than it might be with their own family. But over the years their roles have, to some degree, become defined. Obviously, Zoe is the map woman, having a reasonable sense of direction to get them from A to B and working out where everything is. Sally is the linguist (well she speaks French) and frontwoman in a confrontation. Faye is the charming, sweet talking, restaurant guide. Maggie is the voice of reason, often seeing the obvious solution to a predicament they've got themselves into when the rest of them can't. Kate is the logistics expert, checking out flights and accommodation and getting the best price.

In fact, Kate's logistical talents were becoming legendary at her new job. She was by now working for an insurance firm owned by one of her old 'am-dram' chums. Luckily, when taking on Kate, it had been agreed she continue her studies subject to her staying around for a while once she qualified. Law degrees don't come cheap and she still had well over a year to go till qualifying so this was a great help - taking some of the pressure off funding family life. Zoe reckoned Kate's new boss had still got a good deal, as, despite university day release and pretty much being knackered most of the time, Kate was knocking the firm into shape, increasing efficiency and hence profits and generally helping create a lean, mean insurance machine! Obviously, Kate would never say any of this, but she was making herself indispensable.

□□⛿⅄□□□□∩□…··⋮.·˙˙.□∵□□□∪□□□□□

In Vilamoura the girls had enjoyed a 'nice lunch' and several jugs of Sangria by the side of the harbour before they'd headed to the beach. A 'nice lunch' (a phrase coined by Sally) was something they all agreed on and was rapidly becoming a feature of *The Alphabet Tour*. Over the years it would often turn out to be the discussions over a 'nice lunch' which would encapsulate their friendship and provide 'moments' never to be forgotten by any of them.

The beach had been pretty much as expected for the Mediterranean, blue sea, golden sand and thatched beach umbrellas: but something weird had happen. Once they'd all changed under one of the plentiful thatched umbrellas which hadn't been quite tall enough, even for Zoe, they'd all ventured into the waves together. Faye and Sally had swum out quite a way whilst the others had splashed around in the shallows. But bizarrely, as Maggie had been trying to look graceful and stay on her feet, a couple of 20 Euro notes had slowly floated passed her. Although being somewhat taken aback by seeing the cash in this unexpected location, she had the foresight to grab it and holding it aloft had shouted: "Who's got kitty?"

'Kitty' referred to the collective *Alphabet Tour* purse, a system which had been adopted on the girls' first trip away together. Instead of squabbling over bills and who had the extra slice of garlic bread, they all put into a kitty at the start of each day and meals, tickets etc were purchased from their pooled funds. Frequently kitty took a hammering and credit cards were called for but on the whole the system worked well and to date, there had never been any arguments about money. Finding cash in the ocean had certainly been a welcome bonus for kitty and once dried out in the Portuguese sunshine a round of free drinks had been consumed in a beachside bar.

As that afternoon closed, the girls had begun to think about getting back to their accommodation. Another form of transport which *The Alphabetties* like to frequent whenever possible is the *choo choo* train – those cute little pretend steam trains that wander through many a tourist destination taking in the sights at a leisurely pace and tooting annoyingly as they go. Vilamoura's own version hadn't so much done a tour of the sights as scooped people up and taken them back to their apartment complex/golf course. *The Alphabetties* had jumped at this idea and boarded the train along with several other more elderly passengers. The journey had been nice enough to begin with but then they realised that the *choo choo* train was possibly the slowest form of transport in Portugal and it would have been quicker to walk – well for them, perhaps not the other passengers! They'd also realised that they didn't actually know where their particular complex was or indeed what it was called. So, they sat, and they sat, and they sat as they inched along stopping to let the old folk off at the various apartments, tooting all the way! Much to the relief of everyone, after many stops and complexes Kate had exclaimed: "I think this is us!"

She leapt out of the *choo choo* closely followed by the rest of them. Praise the Lord she'd been right, and they all soon had a much needed glass of wine in their hands – although that evening they'd sat on the patio well away from swooping swallows. Once settled Maggie proposed a toast to her fellow traveller in recognition of her uncharacteristic navigational skill: "To Kate for expertly getting us back here before we became the age of the other *choo choo* passengers!"

The first ever second full day of an *Alphabet Tour* had been exciting as the group had booked a boat trip along the coast. The mode of transport that day had been a large, very sleek catamaran with drinks served on board and plenty of space for passengers to lounge around and soak up the rays. The coastline had been beautiful and with the wind in their hair and sun on their faces, the trip had been very pleasant. The catamaran passengers had given the girls much to talk about. They'd spoken jealously about the younger women aboard, every one of them looking amazing in designer bikinis and not a stretch mark or sagging breast between them. But to counteract this there had also been a number of older ladies on board, clearly several golfers' who, judging by their tans, had come on a lot of these trips. It hadn't been quite the seven stages of woman, but the girls did think that their past, and possibly future selves had all been on that boat in front of them.

After they'd headed out for over an hour, the boat had dropped anchor close to a particularly scenic stretch of coastline and everyone had been invited to go for a dip in the azure waters. Two options had been on offer; one was to jump off the bow of the boat or the other to go down the steps at the aft and gently plop in off the platform at the back. Well, this certainly split the group. Sally and Zoe had been more than up for jumping off the bow. Zoe loves the sea, and this had been right up her street. Sally was just up for the challenge and had been in the frame of mind to do anything vaguely outrageous and not her usual routine. But Kate, Maggie and Faye had been horrified at the thought of launching themselves into the unknown. Faye had vocalised their general feeling: "Are you out of your tiny mind? No way, never, not a chance!"

She'd been pretty definitive and she, Kate and Maggie had chosen to slide into the sea off the back of the boat.

Before that they'd stayed at the bow to watch Sally and Zoe fling themselves into the abyss. However, they weren't very supportive and just muttered that the other two were insane and never in a month of Sundays would they do such a stupid thing etc. etc. By now it had become a matter of pride for Sally and Zoe and there had been no turning back. Although as she teetered on the edge, Zoe had blurted out: "Shit it's high!"

As they had perched on the brink about to jump, they'd both wondered what had possessed them. But then to the very audible shout of "Fuck it!" Sally had gone, and Zoe had to follow.

Zoe had entered the water ok, but she'd seemed to go down for ages. Her life hadn't flashed before her eyes, but she remembered panicking slightly and clambering for the surface - and doing so with a massive very uncomfortable wedgy! Once her head had broken the surface, she still hadn't been cool, spluttering and gasping but she'd managed to swim through the catamaran hulls to the back of the boat to join the rest of them. On the way she'd released her swimsuit from between her butt cheeks – which now seemed to go a lot further up her body than previously, then had caught up to Sally, before she'd reached the others and announced: "That was great!"

☐☐Ц☥☐☐☐☐∩☐…···∴·˙˙·.☐∵☐☐☐Ц☐☐☐☐

Zoe did wonder if her rash decision to throw herself off the front of a very large boat had something to do with her reaching forty that year. She'd never been worried about getting older, but reaching the birthday when life is about to begin had made her reflect a little. Her mother had been forty when she'd had Zoe, who couldn't imagine having another child now. It certainly made her more understanding of why her mother had turned to alcohol to help make her home life bearable. Zoe had far less to cope with than her mother and in far less difficult circumstances, but she could see how a crutch for someone can turn into an addiction. She wasn't saying her life was a complete bed of roses, but she was lucky and appreciated it.

☐☐⊔⋏☐☐☐☐∩☐…⋯∶.˙˙˙.☐∵☐☐☐⊔☐☐☐☐

That evening another unique *Alphabet Tour* event had taken place, a video screening – well several to be precise. The apartment had been equipped with, what would now be classed as an antique, a VHS video player. Kate had organised it so that they had all brought along their wedding videos to watch and mercilessly critique.

☐☐⊔⋏☐☐☐☐∩☐…⋯∶.˙˙˙.☐∵☐☐☐⊔☐☐☐☐

Weddings are certainly big business these days costing tens of thousands of pounds. Zoe felt she was living in a bubble as she found these figures mind blowing. Some of the wedding stories her friends had told her about their relatives or even their offspring had left her dumbfounded and indeed panicking about Holly and Eric entering marital bliss.

People, regardless of their demographic, seem to need to get married in a French chateau or beside Lake Garda in a designer dress with butterflies being released as they put on the rings that were minutes earlier delivered by a passing barn owl! Your wedding isn't so much a statement of your mutual love, but the size of your families combined bank accounts. Her wedding paled in comparison to what you can have when you tie the knot nowadays. You can be married pretty much anywhere from a brewery to a donkey sanctuary, have your bridesmaids escorted by lambs, have personalised Lego figures as your table favours along with a tiny bottle of gin or a temporary tattoo kit of the loving couple in case you forget what the bride and groom look like. Your guests can be entertained by magicians, balloon artists or have their portrait painted. In case this isn't enough, sack races, a bouncy castle, a human pyramid or a craft table are among the suggestions to keep the wedding party amused - none of which Zoe imagined most guests would want to do in an outfit that cost them a small fortune. Zoe and Frank thought they were out there getting married at the zoo and arriving in a vintage Cadillac - apparently this was now pretty tame!

□□Ⱡↅ□□□□∩□......∶.˙ ˙∙.□∵□□□∪□□□□□

Obviously, all the videos had brought back memories for all the girls. Apart from Kate, who had attended Zoe's ceremony, none of the girls had known each other before they got married, so seeing the videos had been really exciting and an insight into the girls' former lives. To varying degrees, they had each had the hallmarks of a 1990s wedding – brides in large dresses with equally large bouquets, bridesmaids in Laura Ashley dresses, grooms and ushers in top hat and tails, tiered wedding cakes on pillars and guests looking like they'd just stepped off the set of *Four Weddings and a Funeral*.

First up were Maggie and Shane who had been married the longest of the group. They were SO young when they had tied the knot and looked like they should have been in school uniform to get married.

Of course, with her mum's sewing skills, her family and exuberance and drive, Kate's wedding was the full works – big dress, big reception, big bouquet and big perm!

Faye looked very innocent, slim and stylish as ever – more silk crepe than taffeta, more Meghan Markle than Princess Di.

Sally looked so young and tall but also with fairly large hair. Of course, with a number of men in kilts in attendance.

They'd all looked so happy, carefree and in love. They were all now at a different stage of life, some of them happier than others, nowhere near as carefree but on the whole still in love - but possibly in a different way and for different reasons. Zoe felt it was a shame they hadn't known each other in time to attend each of their weddings. The hats would have been a sight to see! But then *The Alphabet Tour* had grown from a different phase of their lives at a particular time and place. A time of extreme happiness coupled with hardship and the emotional turmoil of bringing a new life into the world. Zoe certainly had guests at her wedding that she thought would be friends for life but that she hadn't in fact seen since. The shared experience of childbirth, something so uniquely female and enduring, had formed a strong foundation and cemented *The Alphabetties* together, Zoe hoped, for life.

Reminiscing about their weddings made Zoe pensive and thoughtful - where did the time go? The thrill of meeting someone new and the excitement of a first kiss was still a feeling she could recall distinctly. The passion in her first kiss with Frank will always be fresh in her mind. And one of Zoe's greatest fears was that Holly and Eric would fall in love with someone she didn't like and wouldn't have any sort of relationship with.

The screening of the wedding epics had of course been accompanied by glasses of wine and not just champagne. On this trip the group had rekindled not only their love of sangria, which they had first developed in Barcelona - but had also discovered a new tipple, well at least to them,

Mateus Rosé. The girls got through a fair few bottles as they'd watched each other take their vows and reminisced how it only seemed a heartbeat since they had all been young, free and single!

☐☐⫝̸⫝̸⋋☐☐☐☐∩☐…⋯⋮.·¨·.☐∴·☐☐☐⋃☐☐☐☐

Bizarrely, Mateus Rosé was among the alcoholic beverages which were stockpiled in the cellars of Saddam Hussein's palaces and it was apparently a preferred wine of the then Queen – who, from her research Zoe thought had drunk quite a lot! Zoe first came across the distinctive narrow-necked, flask-shaped bottle, as a child. Her parents had a lamp by the side of the bed in their spare room made from a Mateus Rosé bottle and a pink fringed lampshade, which was very trendy in the late 1960s. The questionable lamp was probably a by-product of her mother's drinking habits. If they'd done this with every bottle she drank, Zoe's family house would have been lit up like Blackpool Illuminations! However, when she met Frank, his parents had something which topped even the lamp for bad taste. In their bathroom on top of the toilet cistern sat a doll wearing a large, snot green crocheted crinoline style skirt under which was secreted the toilet roll – just why?

The Alphabetties had discovered Mateus Rosé whilst sitting by the harbour under the Portuguese sunshine. It's funny how you develop a taste for local delicacies whilst you're on holiday. You drink or eat them with great enthusiasm and buy some to take home to share with your friends whom you've told how marvellous it is. Only to discover in the cold light of a dreary day in South Manchester that the delicacy you so loved is actually pretty foul and why in God's name did you buy a litre bottle of it? This happened to Zoe with Ouzo which she now can't even look at but quaffed merrily on her trip to Corfu with Douglas. She also thought Ouzo was blue as she drank it in a bar with neon lights which gave it a cobalt hue! However, Mateus Rosé has fared somewhat better than Ouzo and *The Alphabetties*, well Zoe and Kate at least, still like a glass with lots of ice, in the garden in the summer – although neither of them has made a lamp or any other household item from the empty bottles!

⬚⬚Ⅱℵ⬚⬚⬚⬚∩…⋯⋮⸱⋅˙˙⋅.⬚∴⬚⬚⬚∪⬚⬚⬚⬚

Indeed, it was a bottle of Mateus Rose that the girls ordered to accompany their last 'nice lunch' in Vilamoura before heading for the airport. As this was the final opportunity for them to all genuinely talk for the foreseeable future, Sally took the opportunity to tell the girls that things were going from bad to worse with Gabe. Her career was going so well, and she was away an increasing amount, but she wasn't sure whether any more time together as a family would help. It just seemed to her like they were drifting apart and living almost separate lives now. When she returned from business trips, Gabe would often spend the majority of their free time with his work or golf friends. Sally was beginning to feel like they were just going through the motions of a marriage, despite Gabe still appearing happy with their lot. Although they had managed the weekend away together it hadn't changed how she was feeling. For many women, Gabe would have done nothing wrong, but Sally knew she wanted more, she felt like she was outgrowing Gabe. She saw his free and easy spirit more as lackadaisical and nonchalant. Sally needed someone with more ambition, who would be dynamic and take on what life had to offer head on. But she felt so guilty – Gabe is a good man. She'd had a little weep with her dear friends and then ordered another bottle of the very drinkable pink wine.

Chapter 9

G for Glasgow

"I count myself in nothing else so happy,
as in a soul remembering my good friends."
William Shakespeare

Some of life between tours.

Zoe took over Eric's Beaver Pack. He loved it and it was under threat of closure. Not surprisingly she became the butt of many not very subtle jokes and innuendos. Hope Eric appreciates her sacrifice one day!

Frank is no longer working in Leeds! Gone are the days of the M62 commute. Hopefully he won't be quite so frazzled from now on.

Charlie dramatically announces she has a strong emotional attachment to her boyfriend. They have promised each other they'll get married when they leave school and nothing will stop them! Charlie is nine so we'll wait and see – Sally isn't too worried!

Zoe and Frank's tenth wedding anniversary which they mark with a romantic weekend in Paris. Guess who looked after Holly and Eric – what would Zoe do without her?

Amelia hid in a kitchen cupboard happily eating Coco Pops whilst Faye ran around the house in a complete panic.

Maggie and Shane were asked if Jennifer and Samantha would become part of a control group studying cognitive development in twins. Although Maggie felt guilty about it they declined – she had enough in her life to cope with and the twins thought they were special enough as it was!

This year Zoe began to chuckle before the computer had even found the *Alphabet Tour* file. Once again Faye had been in charge of organisation and Zoe remembered the group had gathered with a certain amount of trepidation! After her Reims or should we say Epernay mix up, the girls were concerned that they might actually end up in Paisley or some other satellite town and not in Glasgow itself. But their doubts had proved to be unfounded as once on Scottish soil Faye had come up trumps. As *The Alphabetties* hadn't had the pleasure of one for nearly six years now, Faye had thought the time had come for the girls to familiarise themselves once again with an activity they all enjoyed. Bless her, outside the terminal they had been greeted by a somewhat ostentatious, but splendid white stretch limousine!

This was excellent and they'd all piled into the outrageous vehicle in a way that made it obvious that this wasn't their normal form of transportation. But Faye hadn't finished yet and had produced a bottle of champagne that she had hidden about her person – not in a smuggling cocaine type of way clearly. No, Faye had casually produced it from her oversized but ever present, stylish handbag. Faye's generosity was, as ever, legendary.

□□Ⱡ⚡□□□□⋒□……⋯⋮.⋅˙˙⋅.□∵□□□Ս□□□□□

Faye's champagne conjuring trick filled Zoe's mind with flashbacks to a TV programme that Frank is particularly fond of about border control at various international airports called something original like *Border Patrol* or *Nothing to Declare.* Although this was mindless TV that Frank watched while Zoe prepared the dinner, she had managed to pick up a few bizarre snippets which made Faye's exploits pale into insignificance. Such as the twenty four year old Columbian woman who was arrested in Germany after being caught with a kilogram of cocaine hidden inside her false breasts. Or the Brazilian man who made an outlandish bid to smuggle drugs into Portugal and was arrested at Lisbon's international airport, accused of carrying 1kg of cocaine inside a pair of fake buttocks.

Faye's generous gestures were among the many reasons Zoe could completely understand why her friend was so popular both at home and at work. She was gregarious and always seemed happy to meet people and entertain. Faye was, by now, back at work but still managing to get a couple of days off each week. Although not back at the trendy opticians from pre-Amelia days, she had crossed paths again with her former colleague Bridget. They had met at a professional development seminar in an upmarket hotel somewhere in the Cheshire countryside. It was great to see a friendly face, so she didn't have to make inane small talk with the other candidates. But as Faye chatted to Bridget there was something different about her yet oddly familiar. Faye shook off the feeling at the time and just enjoyed catching up on all the news. But later that night she nearly frightened the life out of Clive when she sat bolt upright. She had realised what it was about Bridget that mithered her and announced: "Bridget was wearing an exact outfit that I've got in my wardrobe! I have the very same blouse and suit – Oh my God!"

She began to contemplate how weird that was and how annoying as Faye was given the impression when she purchased the items that they were exclusive to that particular shop. But she then had to stop thinking about Bridget and focus on trying to calm Clive down as he was getting excited at the possibility of middle of the night sex.

Zoe suspected all the girls admired Faye's flair and style. Faye in a very unassuming way always managed to look great but never flash, just classy. Faye clearly had an eye for fashion and panache. But she was always the first to compliment someone and also received compliments with modesty. Having said that and although imitation is said to be the sincerest form of flattery, the fact that Bridget had cloned her outfit had pissed her off!

⬜⬜Ⅱℷ⬜⬜⬜⬜∩⬜…⋯∴·˙˙·.⬜∴·⬜⬜⬜∪⬜⬜⬜⬜⬜

Sadly, but not surprisingly, the girls' foray into the world of the super-rich had ended as they alighted from the stretch limo. Unfortunately, their accommodation hadn't matched up to their method of arrival. The hotel Faye had booked for that year was not salubrious despite, in her defence, being located close to the Glasgow School of Art which is arguably the most well-known of Glasgow's buildings. The name of the hotel escaped Zoe but it had been located just north of Sauchiehall Street. The hotel website informed browsers that the establishment was a listed building which is always a good start in Zoe's opinion. The building was in fact a nineteenth century villa located in the designated Garnethill Character Area of the City Central Conservation Area. All of which had sounded promising.

However once inside they'd discovered that the place probably hadn't been refurbished since the 1800s and the staff appeared to date back to a similar period. When they'd tried to check in, progress had been hampered by huge bags of dirty washing as the reception had appeared to be doubling as the laundry. The group managed to acquire keys to two rooms and climbed up to the first floor carrying their luggage - there was no sign of a lift let alone a porter or a trolley. Once on the first floor the rooms hadn't been numbered and as a result, finding their rooms had been challenging and Faye and Sally's room had a peculiar odour.

The décor of both rooms had been early DH*SS* and Zoe could remember praying that her bed wasn't going to still be warm from the previous occupant!

Sally grew up in Glasgow and assured them the choice of hotel was unfortunate and not typical of what the city had to offer. She had assured them that Glasgow was a vibrant, dynamic and friendly city. The girls hadn't yet seen this side of its character, but in hoping to do so they had headed out into the centre and at Sally's request gone straight to one of her favourite eating places anywhere, The Café Gandalfi. Here they did experience some of the renowned Scottish hospitality and amongst the eclectic wooden furniture, wood panelling and soaring ceilings they enjoyed a very pleasant late lunch.

◻◻⨆⨆ℵ◻◻◻◻∩◻…··∶.·˙˙.◻∴◻◻◻⨆◻◻◻◻◻

Zoe loves it when this happens, when you're visiting somewhere new, and you find an eating place which is so unique or charming that the memory of being there stays with you forever. Not wanting to sound ostentatious but her family have been fortunate enough to have experienced this on more than one occasion. Eric recalls a cute little place on the Greek island of Lesbos which was really a takeaway but had one table on a precarious little balcony at the back. When they arrived the table was free, they took it and enjoyed the most delightful Greek yoghurt and fruit whilst taking in an uninterrupted view out to sea. Frank remembered the ramshackled bar they found at the end of a long boardwalk along the Amalfi Coast from Sorrento where all the locals go to get away from people like them. They had gorgeous BLTs and red wine looking across the Bay of Naples to Vesuvius.

◻◻⨆⨆ℵ◻◻◻◻∩◻…··∶.·˙˙.◻∴◻◻◻⨆◻◻◻◻◻

In Glasgow that evening they had decided to take the advice of Zoe's brother, Rich, who had recently visited the fair city with his girlfriend. Apparently, Billy Connolly was staying at the hotel Rich chose. Obviously, this wasn't the same hotel where they were staying and maybe they should have taken his advice on that too! Zoe loves her brother dearly but for a lot of his life Rich's relationship status had been complicated to say the least. At that time he was actually still married to Diana with whom he has two sons. They separated many years ago but never divorced for various reasons and have just never got around to it since. However, their affiliation remains remarkably amicable. They still spend time together along with their respective partners which isn't the norm. But Diana and Rich have now had the same partners for a long while and both seem happy and that was all that mattered to Zoe.

⬚⬚⫫⚡⬚⬚⬚⬚∩⬚…··∶.·˙˙·.⬚∵⬚⬚⬚⫦⬚⬚⬚⬚

The restaurant he recommended was, an Indian restaurant in the West End which had turned out to be a great call. *The Alphabetties* found, over the years of going on tour, that if they were struggling to find a decent place to eat, first try for an Italian and if no luck their staple back up is an Indian restaurant. As she wrote down this snippet of *Alphabettie* trivia, Zoe realised how very English and unadventurous it came across. But she and the others all knew from experience that it is a sure way to avoid long periods of endless wandering and arguments.

After the Ruby Murray the girls thought they'd spend the remainder of their evening in another Glaswegian, architectural gem spotted earlier in the day. The Corinthian Club was housed within one of Glasgow's most impressive buildings, a former bank and high court, then home to a variety of restaurants and bars. As this place had been recommended in the pre-*Google* Guidebook, they'd hopped in a taxi and headed straight there, no messing about. The Corinthian Club had turned out to be absolutely splendid with a bar on the top floor with plenty of squidgy sofas, an open fire and barely noticeable background music. Clearly this was the perfect place for cocktails, and they'd enjoyed many a margarita – each of these varying from its predecessor in quality, why is that? Zoe often found this fluctuation in flavour and taste when she made a cookies on the rare occasion when she baked. The same ingredients go in, but the exact same taste never comes out twice!

The combination of the margaritas and the Corinthian ambiance had definitely suited *The Alphabetties* that night – the perfect situation for that group of friends to be in. But to Zoe's horror the girls found that it had suited them so much that they'd felt compelled to begin singing songs from the shows! It has already been established that Zoe is not a fan of musical theatre although she will confess to having enjoyed *Miss Saigon* - mainly because she liked the staging and the helicopters. It has also been established that Kate loves watching and performing in them. This is just one of the reasons why Kate and Zoe often question how come they are such good friends. Their views on politics, religion, period dramas, adventure movies and of course musical theatre are poles apart. But they do share the same outlook on life and deep-rooted values. Although why Kate doesn't enjoy the *Star Wars* franchise is beyond Zoe, but she cannot imagine life without her, Kate is her rock.

Not surprisingly Kate led the sing song which attracted some, in Zoe's opinion, unwanted attention but mercifully the bar had emptied somewhat due to the now late hour. After renditions of "Memory", "Edelweiss", "I Dreamed a

Dream", "Some Enchanted Evening", "I Know Him so Well", "Any Dream will Do" and many more, Zoe had been at her wits end and she had never been so thankful to be told that it was closing time and that they had to leave – Praise the Lord!

⬜⬜Ⅱ✝⬜⬜⬜⬜∩⬜……⬝⬝:.·˙˙·.⬜∵·⬜⬜⬜∪⬜⬜⬜⬜

Mind you, Zoe would concede that Kate had the right to be singing her head off, as earlier that year she had passed her law degree with flying colours -what an achievement. Zoe had nothing but admiration for her friend who was clearly brilliant. For a woman who freely admits to being a numbers person, she had found her way through the intricacies of the British Law system and the incredibly complex language in which it is written and blown them out of the water.

Kate had asked Zoe if she could look after Francesca, Vincent and Kitty whilst she attended her graduation with Max and her parents. Zoe was more than happy to and managed to get them and Holly, Eric and Frank all to the impressive graduation venue in time to be waiting outside with champagne and plastic flutes. This really was a staggering achievement and even the kids knew they should be very proud of their mamma. Kate now had to think about where her future was going to go – the world was her oyster! The amazing skill set she had worked for, a law degree coupled with accountancy, meant her career options were wide open. But could she commit to more years of training and exams and go down the legal route? It would be challenging but rewarding, but the level of dedication that needed wouldn't affect just her – there was Max and the children to consider. She was going to have to do a lot of soul searching.

⬜⬜Ⅱ⚡⬜⬜⬜⬜∩⬜...·⸱⸱:.·˙˙·.⬜∵⬜⬜⬜∪⬜⬜⬜⬜

The musical margaritas had also taken their toll the next morning as Faye hadn't made it to breakfast - mind you this had turned out to be a very wise move. As hinted at earlier the hotel was not *The Ritz*. The waitress had resembled someone from *Acorn Antiques* and the breakfast buffet had looked more like a bush tucker trial. However, the friends aren't easily defeated, especially when they have already paid, so they'd bravely gone ahead and ordered four cooked breakfasts. Big mistake! Who knew that baked beans could be rock hard and fried eggs are meant to come swimming in vinegar!

After the horrific dalliance into the hotel catering capabilities the day could only get better and indeed it had with a visit to the *Art Lovers House*, designed by the fantastic Charles Rennie MacIntosh – another person Zoe greatly admired. Born in Glasgow he was an innovative Art Deco artist, designer and architect famous the world over. His wife, Margaret MacDonald, was also equally talented but of course you don't usually hear about her – ain't that always the way! The *House for an Art Lover* was on the outskirts of the city, so Sally had suggested they take a trip on the Glasgow subway or as it is affectionately known *The Clockwork Orange* due to its bright orange trains. It was one famous landmark after another that day as their subway stop is the *Ibrox Stadium* and the nearby famous Glasgow tenements of Dunolly Gardens.

⬜⬜Ⅱ⚡⬜⬜⬜⬜∩⬜...·⸱⸱:.·˙˙·.⬜∵⬜⬜⬜∪⬜⬜⬜⬜

As they'd travelled on the tram, Maggie announced that her commute to work had recently got shorter as she had got a new job. It had been a difficult decision as Maggie had struck lucky and had fitted in perfectly at her first hospital out of university. If it hadn't been for the logistics of her life, she would probably have stayed there a lot longer. But the lengthy drive to work was just too much along with the demands of her job and running the family home solo a lot of the time. So, when a job came up in the Maternity Services at her local hospital, she couldn't let the opportunity go by. She had applied and with the help of a great reference she had been successful. She was excited about the new challenges working in a large hospital brought and was glad to see an end to the long drive to work especially on a night shift. She was confident she'd made the right decision but did have feelings of trepidation as she would be a small fish in a much bigger sea.

☐☐⊔⅄☐☐☐☐⌒☐...⋯∶.⋅¨⋅.☐∴·☐☐☐⊔☐☐☐☐

Sitting in Bellahouston Park the *House for an Art Lover* is not surprisingly the venue of choice for fans of Charles Rennie MacIntosh. It was stunning especially the Music Room, which on the occasion of their visit had been laid out for a wedding reception later that day. The light had flooded in through the many pairs of glass doors and it had looked beautiful. Although they hadn't lingered there too long as Sally had got a strong urge to rearrange all the place names!

Sally had a deep-rooted need for some light hearted fun that weekend. Only days before she had attempted to get Gabe to face the fact that their marriage was pretty crap – certainly for her. Gabe too had begun to realise all was not well in paradise but was nowhere near as troubled as Sally. She hated failure and the thought of her marriage not working was eating away at her. It was hard for her to accept but she had reached the conclusion that they needed outside help. Sally had no intentions of throwing in the towel yet, but felt their relationship needed to be repaired – for their sake and their beautiful girls.

Being thorough and pre-emptive was in Sally's nature so before broaching the subject with Gabe she called on her professional strengths and had done some due diligence. She had come to realise that there are many things that are as important in a marriage as love – communication, honesty, loyalty and respect to name a few, she felt their marriage was lacking in some of these. So, one evening when Gabe seemed in a more relaxed and receptive mood, she suggested to him that they could go for couples' counselling to try and get back the relationship they once had – to reignite some passion and drive.

From his obvious astonishment this suggestion came completely out of the blue for Gabe. And he didn't see why they should ask an outsider for help with the relationship, they could work anything out between them. Sally felt his almost instant dismissal of her proposal just reiterated the lack of mutual understanding between them – she felt they couldn't give each other what they wanted. Gabe just felt they were going through a tough patch like all couples with a young family do, it would pass and all would be well. Sally didn't adhere to this and wanted more, higher goals for their partnership and family. But for now Sally left her feelings to fester, becoming increasingly emotionally disconnected from Gabe – she felt she was drifting away from him.

□□ⅠⅠ⅄□□□□∩…⋯∶.·˙˙.□∵□□□∪□□□□□

Before this year's trip, Zoe had heard Glasgow described as a city with a notorious nightlife, a famous live music scene, theatres and authentic traditional pubs, quirky themed nights to slick cocktails haunts and sleazy hideaways. This is probably all very true but that Saturday night in 2004 they had struggled, to say the least, to find a venue to meet their needs.

After a meal at an Italian restaurant during which the host had flirted outrageously with Faye (an occurrence that happened a lot on tour), they'd asked the waitress where she would recommend for further drinks and entertainment. She'd suggested a place called Madness as she had said it was great fun and just round the corner. After much kissing on the cheeks by the landlord, especially of Faye, they'd left and headed off excitedly. Madness turned out to be an appropriately named venue. The large bar had been full of hen/stag dos all singing loudly and being conducted by a drag queen dancing on the bar. As they'd stood in a line, motionless staring with their mouths open, the girls had realised that they had stuck to the carpet and they'd become acutely aware that they were officially old. They would have needed many, many more drinks before they would have joined in the frivolities going on at Madness and they'd turned tail and left the asylum!

After exiting from Madness the girls' night had not improved. In brief it went like this:

Back to The Corinthian Club, much enjoyed the night before. However, Saturday night you could only get in if you were on a guest list. *The Alphabetties*, weren't on the list and they hadn't got in despite mentioning Dave whose name seemed to get everyone in who was younger than them!

Followed by a gay bar recommended by a taxi driver; not one of them is homophobic but they'd decided against it due to the amount of tongue action going on in the queue by those wearing leather or very little clothing that all looked hideously uncomfortable and inappropriate for the climate. It all brought back memories of Mr Salami!

185

Then The Venue; a converted chapel that had been suggested by Rich. This too had a queue outside but with less bondage gear wearing clientele and the line had been moving quickly. This time the girls had got to the door only to be told the place was now full.

Getting frustrated they tried The Hilton Hotel Residents Bar; a drink was had but the atmosphere was diabolical and the hotel residents didn't look like they would loosen up – the antithesis of the clientele at Madness.

So, they consulted the Guidebook and headed to The Piano Bar; this was really creepy and everyone went quiet and turned to look at them when they'd opened the door which they had then immediately closed.

Despair sets in and they try a pole dancing club; the bouncers toyed with the idea of letting them in but then decided five housewives from Cheshire would do nothing for the image of their establishment. They were refused entry – again!

Finally, having lost all hope they try a sleazy all night diner; this place served drinks if you ordered food. Although still full of pizza served by the lecherous Italian the girls had ordered a portion of nachos and a round of drinks. The waiter tried to insist they each order food but backed down after he received their collective demonic glare.

As they'd sat in the far from sanitary surroundings of the sleazy diner, they had all started to lose the will to live. The horrible realisation that in the eyes of the drinking and clubbing world, they were old and no longer young, desirable females that they want in their hostelries. They were over the hill, not wanted on the cool guest list despite their considerable spending capabilities. From that night certainly Zoe felt that she just wanted to do what she enjoyed with the people she liked and no longer had any desire to be a part of the in-crowd. As long as she had these women to share adventures with, she would be happy. Zoe couldn't speak for the others, but she suspected she might not be alone in these thoughts. But also in her mind was the worrying thought that the nachos were extremely tasty and dubious diners should be added to the list of fallback places when on tour!

After their lack of success the previous evening, the next day retail therapy had been required. Sunday markets nowadays are often organic, environmentally friendly affairs all very rustic with homemade jewellery, jam and artisan bread. They can't vouch for it now, but The Barras when they had visited was shabby and a bit run down but it was where they had been assured they would experience 'a slice of pure Glasgow'. Everything purchased here was carried away in a flimsy plastic blue and white striped environmentally unfriendly bag and came from stalls with names like Betty's Pants.

⬚⬚Ц⅄⬚⬚⬚⬚∩⬚......⋮.⋅˙˙⋅.⬚⋅⋰⬚⬚⬚Ս⬚⬚⬚⬚

Choosing the best shopper amongst *The Alphabetties* would be quite a tricky call but on the whole Kate probably takes the crown. Don't get this wrong they all like to shop but Kate doesn't let money burn a hole in her pocket. She is a great believer in making hay while the sun shines and spends it when she's got it. On every flight Zoe has taken with her, as an *Alphabettie* or otherwise, she has made a duty-free purchase – having already cruised the shops at the airport. Very generously it is often an alcohol-based purchase which

Zoe is fortunate enough to enjoy but she also does like a nice set of small L'Occitane hand creams or a Touche Eclat. She's a sucker for *"luxury brands at unbeatable offers"*, but there is no denying she is a canny shopper and certainly won't take any crap from any retailer whose path she may cross.

Faye also a shopper of some repute, is a woman whose good taste is obviously reflected in her shopping habits. She is discerning and certainly doesn't buy rubbish for the sake of it. Uncannily she always seems to know where all the good shops are wherever they go to visit – she can home in on a good shoe shop like a bloodhound who's caught a scent. Also, if she sees something she likes she will buy it regardless of the circumstances. On one of their trips, she carried a king size duvet set around with her all day as she couldn't resist it. Mind you Kate also managed to successfully get a set of six wine glasses home unbroken in her suitcase after a weekend away.

Maggie knows what she and her girls like and purchases things for them with no fuss. When they're away she tends to buy things for herself more out of necessity, like a new pair of mules if her feet are killing her.

Sally always purchases and sends a postcard to her mum from wherever they go on tour and occasionally opts for a nice scarf or piece of jewellery for herself along with a gift for her girls.

Zoe tends to restrict her spending to a souvenir of the visit, some beer for Frank and if she saw something she thought they would like, a gift for the kids. Her family has never set a precedent for big gifts from holiday destinations. They all try to keep them cheap but tasteful and if all else fails a fridge (or in their case boiler) magnet will suffice.

All the girls are very generous so arguments over money are never a problem. As a rule, Zoe is probably the least affluent, but this is through her own career choice and Frank bless him has always supported her decisions and worked his heart out to care for their family. In this the seventh year of the *Alphabet Tour*, Frank and Zoe had been married ten years. Both these facts she found hard to believe and still considers herself blessed that she chose the sliding doors which led her to be where she was, with him and their children.

Frank was no longer working in Leeds but despite being based locally he still did long hours. Holly and Eric were now nine and six and like most kids in their pretty bourgeois area were doing loads of out of school activities. Holly was on the school netball team and played football for a local side every Saturday morning. Eric was also sporty and played football on a Sunday morning for a team which Frank was now managing and thrived on it. There were singing and drumming lessons, swimming sessions, golf, cricket, dancing and numerous birthday parties at Laser Quest, Jungle Gym or a local Chef and Brewer with a ball pit and climbing frame.

Although she hated the expression, Zoe was 'Mum's taxi' for a lot of the time. They had even taken the ultimate step into suburbia and bought a people carrier. Frank, as is his way, had researched these vehicles in depth and had found a great deal on a Toyota Previa. This vehicle was supposed to have revolutionised the world of people carriers and it certainly revolutionised their family life. With eight seats and a large boot going away with all the paraphernalia that comes with a young family was now a piece of cake. However, Zoe was rapidly discovering the downside of such a vehicle. As stated, it could seat eight so she increasingly became the go to mum for other parents to cadge a lift for their child. At first, she didn't mind as in her head she was going anyway and was notching up favours for the future. But sadly, few of these favours were ever reciprocated and she just got stuck with the role of minibus driver. The noise was the worst thing that got to her, seven kids all excited about their imminent activity. This, combined with the fact that she couldn't alleviate the mayhem by using the threats that she would use on her own kids on other peoples' offspring! Plus, she wasn't sure whether it was the treadmill aspect to this stage of family life, but Frank and she were spending less and less time together – with or without the children. They were both pretty knackered much of the time and had used up all their patience on the kids. This was creating pressure between them which she hoped was just a phase all married couples went through.

⬚⬚Ⅱℷ⬚⬚⬚⬚⌒⬚…⋯⋮.·˙˙·.⬚⋱·⬚⬚⬚∪⬚⬚⬚⬚⬚

Despite the fiasco of the previous evening, the group had managed to finish off their time in Glasgow with a culinary delight in the form of a trip to *The Chip*. The Ubiquitous Chip had been serving fine food since 1971 and was a really splendid restaurant with practically a botanical garden growing inside. *The Alphabetties* are good in this kind of environment and ordered food and wine a plenty. As a native Glaswegian Sally knew *The Chip's* reputation and as is her way had booked well in advance, long before the girls had set foot in her old stomping ground. When she was growing up, her father had owned a newsagents in the city centre. Every time they went passed she proudly showed *The Alphabetties* the shop which was still going strong. In fact, they had seen it so many times during the course of that weekend that they'd felt sure it must have been a decent sized chain not just one shop.

190

The Ubiquitous Chip hadn't disappointed, and the food, drink and ambience had lived up to expectations. Although Zoe recalled that they'd all been tickled by the group of people sitting at a table nearby. They had been, to put it kindly an odd-looking bunch who, from first appearances and observation of their behaviour, had seemed to be at a wake. However, when the cake had been brought out and the traditional song had been sung (albeit plaintively) it turned out they were celebrating a sixtieth birthday! Despite it being a million miles away from an experience with the girls, this scene had made Zoe think, by the time they'd reached the end of the alphabet Faye, Kate and Maggie would all be well on their way to sixty and for Sally and herself beyond that – but hell what a ride it was going to be!

Chapter 10

H for Health Spa

"The loneliest woman in the world is a woman without a close woman friend".
Toni Morrison

Some of life between tours.

Edna fell down the stairs when visiting Zoe and Frank and ended up in A&E on Christmas Eve. Thankfully she was OK. However, Kate was completely traumatized after having to take five kids to a Christingle service!

Vincent wanted to be Dobby at school on World Book Day. He insisted on complete authenticity and wore little more than a hessian sack. As it was early March the poor lad nearly froze his little testicles off!

Charlie and Abi were very excited to be bridesmaids for Sally's best school friend up in Scotland.

Kate celebrated turning forty with a pink themed party which she took and ran with to the extreme! She and everything else at the party looked amazing. Although there was quite a lively competition between the men in attendance over who managed to buy the cheapest, gaudy pink shirt!

Gabe was very happy as he got tickets for the British Open and watched Tiger Woods win at St Andrews.

Shane, to a greater extent, and Maggie spent time in Johannesburg setting up a South African office of the family firm.

When Zoe began to collect her thoughts to recount the latest edition of *Alphabettie* exploits, it struck her that before she was married, she had never indulged in the full health spa experience. She'd had a massage or two and maybe a facial but not a complete package of treatments to tone and work her body. The closest she had come was watching the episode of *Victoria Wood on TV* when they go to Pickneys Spa and end up sneakily drinking champagne in the sauna and escaping to the fish and chip shop!

As Zoe is what she likes to call an English Rose (pale and pasty to everyone else) she had in the past had a course of sunbed treatments to take the glare off her white skin, but she wasn't that comfortable with the experience. The now old-fashioned under and over sunbed made her feel like she was in a toasted sandwich maker – she got very tense and sweaty and came out in a bit of a rash. Although the sessions did give her a healthy glow for a while, she didn't repeat the experiment and nowadays such machines are pretty much frowned upon, they're likely to give you skin cancer or claustrophobia, that type of thing.

In preparation for a family holiday to Florida when the children were young, Zoe did have a spray tan which is the treatment that has replaced the human sandwich maker. Again, it wasn't a dignified affair. She had to stand in a large shower unit without a curtain in just a pair of paper knickers which had been given to her by a young girl who had a figure like Pamela Anderson. Despite Zoe's self-confidence already having taken a major hit, the young assistant then asked her to strike several ridiculous poses with her limbs stretched out unnaturally. All Zoe's nooks and crannies were then sprayed with what appeared to be cold coffee. Although there was a strange odour like yeast emanating from her for a while, the process seemed to work well, turning Zoe's usually insipid body into a sun-drenched version of its paler self. However, after enjoying the hotel pool and local beaches she reckoned she must be one of the few people to have come home from Florida paler than when they went!

So, Zoe was excited and a little nervous about this year's tour comprising a weekend at a fully-fledged, even featured in *Hello* magazine, spa hotel. As they weren't travelling too far Sally had offered to drive and had scooped them all up in Gabe's Mercedes. He is usually precious about his car, so this had been quite unexpected.

Relations between Sally & Gabe had been bearable recently but that may have been because Sally was pleasantly distracted. During her recent trips to London, she had found herself working with an old colleague, Mark. In the past they had successfully collaborated on various projects and enjoyed each other's company at the socialising which inevitably followed. Despite the initial attraction they were both married, and the relationship remained on a professional basis with flirtatious undertones. Sally certainly wasn't the kind of girl who had a quick shag in the stationary cupboard and never to mention it again – and thankfully nor was Mark. But the last time she met Mark, she had found herself wanting to spend time with him. Sally realised that she had missed him when he hadn't been at the previous work event and this time, uncharacteristically she asked if he would like to go for a drink after the meeting. She was glad when he seemed pleased that she had asked and that evening found herself inexplicably confiding to him her worries about her marriage and questioning whether she was happy.

Although Sally knew she had Faye to talk to, talking to someone removed from her life at home was comforting. Mark just listened to her, never interrupting, and genuinely seemed to be interested in what she had to say. She felt weight lift from her shoulders as she disclosed to a person who was present, not distracted and wanted to be there and hear what she wanted to get off her chest. They had talked, or rather Sally talked, and Mark listened for what seemed like hours.

□□Ⅱ✗□□□□∩□…··∴·˙˙·.□∵□□□∪□□□□□

The journey had gone smoothly and as they'd pulled off the motorway Sally had switched to the then revolutionary satellite navigation system and had put in the required postcode. Dutifully they'd followed the instructions voiced by the new-fangled gadget but when it had announced that they'd reached their destination they'd been very confused. Ironically, they were outside a nursing home, a very attractive, expensive looking one but nonetheless a nursing home! Had the Artificial Intelligence of the car got a sense of humour or had it made a judgement call and decided this was a more appropriate destination for its current passengers! After the hilarity of the situation had calmed down it was established that the health spa was a couple of hundred yards down the road.

□□Ⅱ✗□□□□∩□…··∴·˙˙·.□∵□□□∪□□□□□

Being a girl who likes to read a map, Zoe has never fully trusted satellite navigation. She likes to work out where she's going, where it is in relation to other places and what there might be to see nearby. The old people's home incident had only served to reinforce her distrust of A.I and led her to recall another far from smooth incident when a friend of hers brought her sat nav along to 'help' find the way to a new location.

Over the years Zoe has been coaxed and coerced into a number of ventures with Kate, one of which was Girl Guiding. Kate took over the Girl Guide pack Francesca attended to save it from disappearing. And yes, she needed someone to help her out running the unit. Zoe agreed as it meant spending time with Kate and Holly was in the Brownies that fed into this Guide unit, so she had an ulterior motive. Little did she know that twelve years and well over a hundred guides later they would still be at it. The need for a sat nav came in when they visited a possible destination to take the Guides to camp. Kate in her own inimitable way had managed to persuade the then Brownie leader, Pippa to progress up to help run the Guides when her two daughters finished at Brownies. Through this bond Pippa has been a firm friend ever since. And it was she who brought the navigation aid when Zoe picked her up one spring evening to suss out the adventure camp not too far away.

They managed OK to navigate across town and out into the countryside using Pippa's device. All was going well, and they'd turned off the main road onto a single width lane. No worries with this as they expected the camp to be off the beaten track. Then they reached a small lake and ran out of road. This is when Zoe's wariness of satellite navigation kicked in but she stayed calm and kept her mouth shut. Pippa fiddled about with the sat nav which informed them there was an alternative route if they turned round and took the right hand turn, they had gone passed not far back. They did this and climbed up a hill which after a while became cobbled and houses began to appear in the distance – phew! However, the road got narrower and as they came over the brow of the hill it also became apparent that it wasn't a road but a pedestrian only access to the quaint cottages on either side. What's more the 'road' had steps!

They panicked slightly but had really gone passed the point of no return. They considered their options and decided carrying on would be a lot less hazardous than trying to turn round or reversing back down the steep hill – and the steps were shallow and well-spaced out, they could do this. So, like a scene from *The Italian Job* they carried on bumping down between the terraced houses, eventually emerging into a part of the village where, from the look on people's faces, cars were not meant to emerge! Since then, Zoe has come to accept that, as there are now more satellites cluttering up Earth's atmosphere, navigational tools can give more accurate directions. Kate, by the way, found the place just by following road signs!

⬜⬜Ⅱ⸙⬜⬜⬜⬜∩⬜…⸱⸱⸱⸱⋮⸱⸱˙˙⸱⬜∵⬜⬜⬜∪⬜⬜⬜⬜⬜

To continue the travelling metaphor Kate's life and indeed Max's had gone in a new direction over the last year or so. Max's relatively new decision to become a contractor had already had some ups and downs. Max and Kate had obviously considered this change at length and had in fact spoken to Frank. Frank was contracting when Zoe met him and had been doing very nicely financially. The fact that contracting pays well, Max would confess, was the main reason he wanted to set himself up as a freelance business. Frank had given up contracting when the kids were tiny as, despite the money being good, he was working ridiculous hours and was missing too many of the once in a lifetime moments.

As their children were older, Kate and Max felt it was now a justifiable risk worth taking. But it was also why Kate had made the difficult decision to remain with her current employer and not branch out using her new qualification. It was true Max could make more money for the family taking contracts, but he could also be let go without warning and there was no sick or holiday pay or pension payments. They would need the safety net of a steady income in case a contract ended unexpectedly or there was an extended period between getting contracts.

As you would expect many of the jobs on offer were based in London and other cities, but Max is a home bird and hates to be away from his family for any extended time. This limited the number of contracts for which he could apply. Mind you, given the number of bombings in London that year, Kate wasn't keen for him to go there either. So, Max had been almost forced to take shorter contracts than he had hoped for in the early years of his new venture. But this was OK, it was all good experience to add to his CV. It would be the periods between contracts that would prove trickier. Kate had joked that the kids would always know when things were a bit tight as they would be eating Tesco 'stripey' baked beans and drinking non-brand soft drinks! Despite her bravado, Zoe could tell Kate was a little concerned about how they would cope with the uncertainty. So, as well as her new role at work of Company Secretary she also took on a great deal of the administrative work which came along with Max's contracting; she was happy to do this as the control freak in her wanted to keep a close eye on the running of Max's business.

Her role change at work had come about in recognition of Kate's hard work and achievement. Her company understood she could now easily look elsewhere for a new job with a better salary. To pre-empt such an eventuality, they had offered Kate the position as Company Secretarial Assistant and a decent pay rise. So, for now she had put her dreams of using her law degree on the back burner and took her in-house promotion and kept her watchful eye over Max's contracting.

☐☐Ⅱⱥ☐☐☐☐⋒☐……⋯∶.·¨˙·.☐∵·☐☐☐∪☐☐☐☐

The chosen venue for pampering had been a sprawling stately home set in rolling grounds - "a Jacobean House

Reimagined". Sally and Faye had been allocated a room with a lounge. Oddly as there were three of them, Maggie, Zoe and Kate had been in a smaller room a couple of miles away in the opposite wing. Following Victoria Wood's example, they had smuggled in a few bottles of fizz and once these had been safely stashed away in Sally and Faye's suite, they'd headed off to register, then get their activity itinerary and a nice lunch. Clearly lunch had been a priority. The place must have been refurbished since then, but at that time the décor of the spa restaurant had been Grecian inspired by the ancient architecture with many columns and the odd water feature. It had been inhabited by women of all shapes and sizes wearing fluffy white dressing gowns and wafer thin flip flops. The food had been a very tasty hot and cold buffet, but they'd felt like naughty schoolgirls when they'd asked for the wine list and were told in a very condescending manner that alcohol was not served with lunch. Their waitress had been very well turned out with immaculate hair and make-up but she'd had the personality of Miss Trunchbull and had clearly been a stickler for the rules. So, on that occasion Faye hadn't even tried to sweet talk her into a nice, chilled bottle of rosé.

When they'd organised the activities for the weekend it had become apparent that there were definitely sub groups within *The Alphabetties* – those who go to the gym and those who don't. Zoe had tried gym membership in the past, but she may as well have set fire to a pile of money. It would have been a lot easier than setting up a monthly standing order and would have at least kept her warm for a while! On the rare occasions she had ventured inside a gym she felt very uncomfortable and thought that she should have toned up at home before she even went there! Exposing her white, wobbly body next to muscly, motivated athletic types was excruciating. Many of these establishments have huge floor to ceiling windows exposing those inside to scrutiny by any

Tom, Dick and Harry who might be passing. Zoe thought that the last thing a poor unsuspecting soul wants to see as they go passed is the likes of her sweating profusely and gasping for air as they try to keep control of a cross trainer!

The group split was obvious, Faye and Sally had opted for sessions in the gym whilst Maggie, Kate and Zoe all preferred more sedate pursuits – yoga, relaxation, colour coordination and meditation. But they'd all decided to join up for swimming, golf and archery – for which three of them would obviously be able to wear the perfect colour coordinated outfit and push through any pain by focussing on their inner breath.

☐☐⊔⅄☐☐☐☐∩☐……⋮.˙ ˙˙.☐∵.☐⊔☐☐∪☐☐☐☐

One thing Zoe has always enjoyed is swimming and generally messing about in water. She lived by the coast when she was a child and her mother, in her own incomparable way, used to pick her up from primary school every day, drive to the beach and pretty much lob Zoe in the water – weather and tides permitting. This sounded quite idyllic as she wrote it down, but Zoe was pretty sure her mother would have been over the limit to drive and didn't keep a vigilant eye on her as she splashed about in the shallows. Zoe also recalled her father acquired a sea going canoe from a work colleague when she was about nine or ten. She was set adrift in this vessel again without any instruction or guidance. As the canoe had quite a wide hull and she was a lightweight child, thankfully she never had to go through the trauma of it capsizing. Although she did manage to lacerate several fingers on the side of the canoe as she grappled with the sizeable paddle and the width of the substantial vessel. Health and Safety were never a thing in the 1960's and 70s – well not in her family anyway. Still, she lived to tell the tale, spent many happy hours at the beach and has loved swimming ever since.

⬜⬜Ⅱλ⬜⬜⬜⬜⌒⬜…⋯⋮.˙¨˙.⬜∵⬜⬜⬜∪⬜⬜⬜⬜

So, Zoe had been keen to try out the health spa pool which they'd found with no trouble. The luxurious changing rooms had been equipped with large lockers, spacious showers, numerous lotions and potions for in and out of the shower and hair dryers – no hair straighteners in those days! However, the changing rooms had proved a little tricky to get out of. There had been numerous doors leading off them to various types of steam rooms and in their efforts to get poolside the girls had kept opening the sauna door much to the annoyance of its occupants. Thankfully after they'd reversed out of the sauna, apologising profusely for the third time, they'd finally made their escape. Entering the sauna had made Zoe feel a little self-conscious as there had been several men inhabiting it. She mused that maybe this male affinity with the sauna was because they were aware that a steam heated environment allows more blood flow to the penis which can mean better erections? But do they know that paradoxically, research has shown that saunas can reduce sperm health - so take your chances chaps!

The pool area had been luxurious, completely tiled with brass jets coming at you from all angles fired out of gushing lion heads – or possibly chimera heads if the pool designers had stuck to the décor theme. Again, Zoe had found herself feeling uncomfortable as they'd clambered into the jacuzzi. Once more she was sitting with complete strangers for a longish period but this time in a small pool which struck her as the perfect medium for growing germs – hot, bubbling water can sustain life out of volcanic jets at the bottom of the deepest ocean so a few million bacteria shouldn't have a problem multiplying in a jacuzzi! Although never thinking of herself as a germophobe, on the whole she reckoned she could live without the steamy, bubbly activities that go along with the swimming pool at a spa and would be happy just ploughing up and down notching up lengths. Mind you the hygiene at her local municipal pool was questionable. She once saw a lifeguard pouring household bleach straight into the water just before it opened to the general public including her good self. On that occasion she waited till a few other fellow swimmers had taken the plunge and had come out with their skin intact before she ventured into the water.

⬜⬜⛙⏝⬜⬜⬜⬜⏜⬜……⬝⬝⬝⬝⬝.⬝⬝⬝⬝⬝.⬜⬝⬝⬜⬜⬜⏌⬜⬜⬜⬜⬜

Thankfully, probably due to the number of minor celebrities who had visited the spa, their healthy hotel had still seen fit to have a Champagne Bar. So, you can imagine that was where they'd all met before dinner. The bar had been in the old library of the former stately home with high ceilings, wood panelling and not surprisingly many books. It looked like the setting for a game of Cluedo or a Murder Mystery.

Hotel etiquette had required that no jeans were permitted in the dining room. *The Alphabetties* had complied, and all had scrubbed up accordingly. Funnily they'd all worn black that evening, maybe subconsciously to make themselves look slimmer amongst the other spa residents. Zoe had always thought that it was probably a dieters' myth, but science says wearing black does actually work. Neurologists have confirmed that it is the way in which your eyes see colour. Apparently black does the best job of hiding visual interruptions – that's a polite way of saying muffin tops, love handles, middle age spread and so on. The eye can easily travel from head to toe with minimal to no visual interruptions. It is a super clean and cohesive look. But beware as black absorbs the light and pulls it away from people's faces which makes it a good colour to avoid as you get older.

As part of her background research Zoe had discovered there are hundreds of terms and synonyms for human lumps and bumps which include this very small sample:

Traditional: spare tyre (or a Dunlop), beer belly, boobs, paunch, girth, middle age spread.

Medical: adipose tissue, cellular fat, mammary glands, abdomen.

Sad: lonely handles or hate handles.

Street: side junk, lady lumps, big booty, ghetto booty, juicy.

Offensive: fat ass, lard arse, pork tits, fupa (fat upper pussy area), gock (over hanging fat between the stomach and genitals or gut and cock).

Funny: fun bags, melons, norks, baps (all seem to be breast related).

Zoe's personal favourites: tingle fat, love curves.

Zoe had hoped that after her weekend at the health spa some of her tingle fat would disappear and her love curves would be smoother – doubtful!

Once in the main dining room they'd all been presented with large leatherbound menus which thankfully had included a wine list. There had been a wide range of dishes to choose from, but each dish had been given a traffic light rating according to its calorific value. From what Zoe could remember the categorisation had been something along the lines of:

Red Star: danger high fat and/or calorie content.

Amber Star: not too bad, average fat and moderate calorie content.

Green Star: good low fat and low-calorie content.

Or put another way.

Red Star: you really don't care do you or you are one of those infuriating people who can eat what they want in copious amounts and never put on a pound.

Amber Star: you'd like to be eating red star courses but have guilt and you put on weight just looking at food.

Green Star: you're a skinny cow and want to stay that way and will deprive yourself of yummier food to do so.

You can imagine what colour most of the stars had been on their table!

On this tour Kate and Zoe thought they would have a go at meditation and try to get in touch with their inner soul. They'd both rather fancied the idea of being able to take themselves away from it all whenever they felt the need – certainly staying calmer would be a good thing for Zoe. After her mild episode of postnatal depression, she found she could still lose her temper at the drop of a hat. Weirdly this tended to be focussed on poor long-suffering Frank. Her outbursts could get mildly violent. We're not talking Quentin Tarentino type violence, but she did once empty a bowl of mashed potato down Frank's jogging bottoms and threatened him with a steak knife. Oh, and there was a dent in the kitchen wall caused by her hitting the wall rather than going for him. Guess the old saying is true *"you always hurt the one you love"*. Frank got a lot of stick from Zoe; she knew she was doing it but couldn't stop herself. Having said that, Frank wasn't the easiest person to live with. He was a pessimist and could always see the negative in anything Zoe, or anyone did. She had managed to beat it in to him that he mustn't be like this with the kids, but he still struggled to be enthusiastic about anything other than football. He was never openly hurtful, but he just couldn't pay a compliment if his life depended on it.

⬚⬚Ⅱ⅄⬚⬚⬚⬚∩⬚……⋮.⋅ ̈ ̇⋅.⬚∵⋅⬚⬚⬚∪⬚⬚⬚⬚

Finding the venue for the meditation class had been ironically quite stressful. Kate and Zoe had spent a furious ten minutes finding what had appeared to be a forgotten room at the top of the darkest tower at the furthest corner of the stately home. On entering they'd expected to find a cobweb covered spinning wheel highlighted by an eerie shaft of light. What they had found was a circle of women all looking as stressed as they were. The woman running the session had been predictably a child of the sixties with long hair in poor condition, a floaty tiered skirt and John Lennon glasses – she'd had a definite look of Professor Trelawney in the Harry Potter films. Considering the teacher had looked like she needed as many friends as she could get, she'd spoken in a very condescending manner which hadn't helped Zoe's attitude towards the exercise. Nor had the hideously uncomfortable chairs which hadn't been conducive to losing yourself and drifting away.

Professor Trelawney had begun her narrative by asking the assembled group to close their eyes and to start their journey into meditation by imagining they were in their favourite room at home. Zoe liked most of the rooms at home, so probably had spent too long umming and ahhing over which room to choose. Then she'd bet like most of the women there, when she'd chosen her favoured room, she couldn't get passed thinking how she really should dust more often. As her voice got softer and admittedly less condescending the tutor told them to feel themselves floating out of the room, up above the house and into the clouds all the time looking down on where they are floating from.

As she'd got older, Zoe had become increasingly unhappy with heights so to ask her to look down on things whilst drifting way above her house had not been a good idea. She had begun to feel slightly nauseous. Although, this path to enlightenment had seemed to be working a treat for others in the room and one woman had even begun to cry. But Zoe was pleased when the child of the sixties had brought them back down to earth and she had been heartily glad she hadn't thrown up. This wasn't the path to inner peace she was going to follow in future! Kate had agreed and had spent her foray towards enlightenment trying not to nod off and snore.

So, Zoe had hoped that the next activity they did together would ease her then troubled mind and get rid of all thoughts of floating away into the atmosphere never to be seen again. As it had turned out, a session at the driving range hitting balls really hard was much better therapy and far more rewarding. Swinging a golf club had turned out to be another of Sally's hidden talents and she credits her skill to Gabe who plays off a handicap of three. Maggie has dabbled with a few golf lessons, but Faye, Kate and Zoe had only ever managed miniature golf prior to this outing. However, after having been taught how to grip the clubs by a very patient man, they'd each found a pen and started whacking away. As expected, Sally's balls went straight down the middle of the range, Maggie's soared pretty much in the right direction and Faye did pretty well too but Kate's shots had been something else. As she'd unleashed her swing the balls had ricocheted around the pen bouncing off the sides before plopping on to the course just in front of her. She really had been lucky not to knock herself out and afterwards had conceded that golf wasn't her forte. Zoe's had been rather erratic but she had managed to hit the odd shot straight and far. When this had happened, she'd watched her ball disappear into the distance with great satisfaction and much whooping with glee. However apparently such behaviour was unbecoming on a golf course and the instructor had been none too impressed and the girls had got a bit pissed off too as Zoe's noisy ritual meant it had taken her a lot longer to get through her bucket of balls.

The atmosphere in the Health Spa restaurant and in general had seemed more relaxed on Saturday night – although dinner had again been colour coded. There had been a pianist playing mellow melodies in the long hall which was where most of the guests had gone after their meal. Listening to the ivories being tinkled whilst enjoying a bottle of wine was very pleasant but sadly had been short lived as the pianist wrapped up his set not long after *The Alphabetties* had arrived. So, for some reason and, as yet never repeated on tour, it had been decided that a game of charades was in order. Like golf, acting proved to be another activity that the girls could do with varying ability. A number of dodgy mimes had been performed much to the amusement of the other guests. But when Maggie had started to act out a very dubious sounds-like for *The Hunt for Red October* they'd felt it was time for them to retire.

⬚⬚Ⅱⱦ⬚⬚⬚⬚∩⬚……∵∴.·˙˙.⬚∵·⬚⬚⬚∪⬚⬚⬚⬚⬚

As well as acting out dubious rhymes, Maggie had also made another questionable decision since the group were last on tour. Unbelievably her twin girls were going to be eight this year and Scarlet was heading towards ten. There was no doubt that Maggie and Shane had produced three beautiful little girls. This had not gone unnoticed and out of the blue they were stopped one day by a complete stranger and asked if they would consider allowing the twins to do some modelling – with their voluminous curls and huge blue eyes it was easy to see why they were approached. At first Shane and Maggie were hesitant but after a further meeting with the modelling agency and many reassurances they decided this particular child exploitation would do Jennifer and Samantha no harm and make some money for them to invest for the twins' future.

So off they all went to a studio in the city centre to star in the latest magazine campaign for a new line of children's clothing. The twins were to be photographed both together and separately with other children and the final campaign would be chosen at a later date. Maggie and Shane were very excited, in fact far more excited than Jennifer and Samantha. As children the twins were quite shy and quiet when first meeting people, as are many children their age. But on this particular occasion they were as sullen and unsmiling as they had ever been. Despite Maggie, Shane and numerous photographers and photographers' assistants trying various means, they didn't crack a smile between them – in fact they both looked like they might burst into tears at any moment. As a result, greater attention was given to the more enthusiastic and willing kids also there and Maggie, Shane and the girls spent a long day watching other children making their way into the next upmarket catalogue you'd pick up in John Lewis Childrenswear. But this did give Maggie and Shane time to reflect, and as they observed the activities of the day, they decided that most of the other kids were precocious, spoilt brats with fawning saps as parents. By the time they were allowed to leave they had decided that this wasn't the world they wanted their beautiful girls to grow up in, one based on superficial good looks and blatantly competitive. They left and went home via McDonalds which made all of them smile, especially the girls!

For Maggie, Kate and Zoe their final day at the health spa had begun with a session on the toning tables, for which at that quite early hour they'd been the only customers. The young lady in charge had put each of them in a machine which to their horror had manipulated, stretched, jiggled and pulled them in all sorts of unnatural directions at an uncannily fast speed. Their legs hadn't been that far apart since childbirth and unwanted memories of stirrups and stitches came flooding back.

For Zoe, this meant recalling that cruelly after a twenty-three-hour labour with Holly, she then had to endure the indignity of a repair to her perineum. Although she didn't have an episiotomy (when a doctor or midwife needs to make a cut in the area between the vagina and the anus, the perineum, during childbirth) she did end up with a perineal tear. Zoe never forgave the midwife who realised too late that her baby's head was in fact considerably bigger than the orifice it was supposed to come out of. So, she ended up tearing, as do seven out of ten women apparently! You'd have thought they would have noticed this pattern and prepared better for this extra indignity.

Many years later, well after the birth of both her children, Zoe saw an advertisement in a magazine to "Peri Prep your Bits". The advert was for a softening and moisturising oil to massage your perineum from thirty four weeks pregnant. The manufacturer advocated either massaging yourself or asking a partner to do it. As this she laughed out loud. By thirty four weeks she hadn't seen her *Doris* for a long time and could just about manage to get on and off the loo without assistance. So finding her perineum let alone massaging it with an infusion of avocado, grapeseed and sweet almond oil, was completely out of the question. As to asking Frank to do it, although he showed an overly enthusiastic interest in watching their offspring emerge, there wasn't a hope in hell he was going to go anywhere near that area to massage it. He was definitely not one of the blokes that get turned on by a heavily pregnant woman and an orgasm was never going to be an aid in their birthing plan!

□□**ᒪᒪ**⅄□□□□**∩**□...⸱⸱⸱:.⸱⁚⁚⸱.□⸫⸱□□□**ᑌ**□□□□□

As it turned out the toning tables had also produced a moment which always makes *The Alphabetties* laugh a lot. Apparently toning tables are designed to increase the circulation of blood and oxygen throughout the body and increase lymph drainage, joint mobility and reduce poisons and toxins in the body – thank you *Google*! Whilst she'd been on the tables Zoe had managed to increase something else. As she'd taken up position on the machine which bent you over she had lost rather than gained muscle control, the amount of excess air in her body had increased and she'd broken wind loudly and clearly for all to hear! Zoe had been mortified but her fart had caused Maggie and Kate to completely corpse with laughter and the rest of the session had been a complete right off – Zoe certainly hadn't subjected herself to any more punishment for fear of further farting!!

Billy Connolly says that a fart is just your arse applauding and George Clooney thinks there is nothing funnier than a fart. Although mortifying Zoe liked to think on that occasion her arse had been applauding her for having a go at these ridiculous exercises and Kate and Maggie had definitely agreed with George!

The weekend at the health spa had certainly ended with a flurry of activity. Whilst *Thunderpants* and her two companions had been toning up, Faye and Sally had been on a bike ride taking in the local countryside. Apparently, Sally had questioned Faye's title as the fittest A*lphabettie* as she struggled along the lanes around the stately home. So much so that they'd swapped bikes only for Sally to point out that the gears on Faye's bike weren't working. Faye had been pissed off at this news but relieved she wasn't having heart failure.

☐☐⊔⅄☐☐☐☐⋂☐...⋯⋮.⋅ ̈ ̈.☐∵.☐∵☐☐☐⊔☐☐☐☐

Faye would certainly never have asked for the title of fittest *Alphabettie.* She is very modest and even self-deprecating but over the last year since returning to work she'd had cause to believe more in herself and realise she was in fact good at what she did. Obviously, she was still juggling work and being a mum. And she was clearly doing it successfully as she had been contacted by a local charity providing vision care for the homeless in the city. Recently one of the main players at the charity had to step away from their duties. The charity had consulted numerous optical practices in the greater area for their suggestions regarding a potential successor to the role - Faye's name had come up several times. When she was first approached, Faye was amazed, thrilled then panicked in that order. She had never seen herself in such a role. But when she told the girls they all agreed that they could absolutely see her doing it and she should jump at the chance.

Charities of this kind work on trust, people seeing a familiar face and a person with whom they feel safe and comfortable. Although Faye would admit she isn't the highest qualified optician, those in her profession and private life knew she could make people feel at ease and nothing was too much trouble for her. Despite this very flattering approach Faye contemplated at length as to how she could fit such a role into her life and hadn't accepted the position immediately.

⬜⬜Ⅱⅇ⬜⬜⬜⬜∩⬜...⸱⸱⸱⸳⸱⸱⸳⸱⸱⸳⬜⸱⸱⬜⬜⬜∪⬜⬜⬜⬜

Once the group had reassembled, the round of activities had continued at a pace and they'd headed off for a session of archery. They'd been kitted up with leather arm and breast protectors and of course bows and felt very Amazonian as they'd walked to the shooting range. Kate had turned out to be a lot better at this sport than golf and had been a pretty mean archer. They'd all serenaded her with "Everything I do, I do it for You" for quite some time afterwards. Zoe had thought it was the leather breast protection that brought out her inner warrior princess and hunting instinct and to be fair to the health spa it was impressive that they had protection that could accommodate Kate's ample bosom.

⬜⬜Ⅱⅇ⬜⬜⬜⬜∩⬜...⸱⸱⸱⸳⸱⸱⸳⸱⸱⸳⬜⸱⸱⬜⬜⬜∪⬜⬜⬜⬜

Unlike Kate, Zoe's bosom had not always been of current sizeable proportions. As a teenager she was a late developer and didn't even start her periods until she was sixteen. She had been desperate for it to happen and for her boobs to appear. She looked younger than all her contemporaries who happened to be the most developed girls in school. She looked like a little boy next to them and envied them when they managed to get out of showering after PE as they were "having their period Miss". Although she never resorted to socks down her bra, Zoe had lied once or twice to her sports teacher about having a period just to fit in. She couldn't have put socks down her bra because she didn't have a bra. She was fifteen and had tearfully begged her mother to buy her one. She was having a full medical at school and couldn't bear the thought of going in to see the nurse in a vest. So, her Mum agreed, and purchased two triangles of brushed cotton on a length of elastic which Marks and Spencer rather grandly called a starter bra.

However, after a very short space of time, once she had worn a bra for a while, Zoe had decided it wasn't for her. Not in a bra burning feminist type of way she just didn't enjoy wearing them. Obviously, Zoe carried on wearing a bra to school and sixth form college after that so as not to be mocked any further by her peers. But she could remember distinctly one Saturday night running to meet her friends outside the local pub and wondering why they were gesticulating at her from across the road. She was bra less that evening and it turned out that maybe now was the time to put the bra back on to save embarrassment and keep the bosoms she had developed since the school medical under control. Her friends very subtly told her it looked like there was a puppy fight going on under her top and her nipples were sticking out like pencil stubs – nice, thanks girls.

From that day to this Zoe has had to wear a bra especially after having two children and gravity taking over. She still finds them infuriating and there is nothing like the sense of freedom when she can 'release the beasts' at the end of a hard day's work. However, she could never be one of those completely liberated women who go bra-less and have their knockers swinging about their midriff. No, much as her bras are now more a feat of structural engineering than anything sexy and alluring, she cannot be that woman. Nor could she stop shaving her armpits, legs and *Doris* (only when absolutely necessary) or wearing makeup or having a fixation with shoes. Zoe believes in rights for women but won't look like a dog's dinner to prove it.

Chapter 11

I for Puerto Banus

"Friendship is the source of the greatest pleasures, and without friends even the most agreeable pursuits become tedious."
Sir Thomas Aquinas

Some of life between tours.

Holly, Vincent, Chloe, Scarlet and Abi all started different senior schools!

An idiot crashed into Shane's car which was written off. Thankfully nobody was hurt but Shane was very sad for probably longer than a grown man should have been.

Abi fell down a ditch during a moonlight walk on a Year 7 'bonding' trip to a YMCA Adventure Centre. The poor girl twisted all her ligaments and was on crutches for what seemed like months – to her and Sally anyway!

Kate fell asleep on the train home from a social event with work colleagues in Chester and ended up at Manchester Piccadilly. Being a full-time working Mum can take its toll on the best of us!

Eric hurt his wrist playing football for his weekend team managed by Frank. Both parents agreed he seemed OK at the time. A week later he said it still hurt and it turned out he had fractured it and was put in a cast. Zoe and Frank were mortified.

Kitty took her Grade 2 ballet exam and passed with flying colours. She looked adorable.

In order to begin that year's Tour notes, Zoe had consulted the dictionary. The *Oxford Learners Dictionary* defined the adjective tenuous as "so weak or uncertain that it hardly exists". That year *The Alphabetties* had reached 'I' the ninth letter of the alphabet and the link to their destination was firmly within the dictionary definition of tenuous! The letter I been for Iberian Peninsula, aka Spain, therefore the Costa del Sol, so Marbella and to be honest Puerto Banus. The vagueness of the destination was, in the main, down to Maggie for it was she who had timeshare weeks with a company offering properties in Puerto Banus.

The girls already knew that Maggie was very generous, and that year's trip proved it. She had done an excellent job of the booking and making travel arrangements. Despite the hilltop location, a bit of a distance from the main hotel complex, their adjoining apartments had made up for that along with a pool and a perfect balcony for sundowners. Maggie, Shane and their girls have travelled extensively both for business and pleasure. Although they enjoy the finer things in life, they are in no way ostentatious and in fact Maggie often ends up getting herself in excruciating situations.

◻◻Ⅱ⅄◻◻◻◻⋒◻……⋮.·⋯·.◻·⋰◻◻◻⋃◻◻◻◻◻

One such occasion, a few years ago, involved an invitation from a couple of male jeweller friends from whom Maggie and Shane had made several purchases over the years. They had been invited for dinner at the couple's city centre apartment and their hosts lived up to the premise that gay men are all natural domestic experts with inherent flair for tasteful interior styling. Their home looked like something out of *Vogue Living,* very minimalist with artsy walls, cream upholstery and not a speck of dust anywhere. They all had a wonderful evening and after a fashionably chic dinner they adjourned to the designer sofas. As the evening progressed and the drinks flowed, dancing was the next item on the agenda. However, Maggie had remained glued to her seat unable to join in with the *Pride* hits. As she had sat on one of the cream, upholstered chairs, she realised to her horror that she had unexpectedly started her period! And she could feel that it wasn't just a 'show' – this was a code red! She was horrified and as you can imagine terrified of moving from her perch. She gestured to Shane as discreetly as she could manage and once she had his attention explained:

"You'll have to come up with an excuse why we suddenly have to leave?"

"But why I'm having a great time, I haven't danced to Bronski Beat in years!"

"For God's sake just do it. I've had an unexpected flood!"

Shane now just looked at her with a blank expression.

"I've just started my period early and have no way to sort it out. Please just tell them the babysitter has called or something – JUST DO IT!"

As Shane unexpectedly made their excuses, Maggie composed herself and assessed the damage. She had risen tentatively and although there was a very slight sign of her predicament it wasn't the scene from *Carrie* that she feared. Shane played his part and told their friends that the babysitter thought Samantha had swallowed a small piece of Lego – strange what scenario comes into your head in this kind of emergency, but it did the trick. Maggie had put on her thankfully long coat and Shane ushered her out of the pristine apartment still apologising. Whether the jewellers ever sussed out what happened Maggie never found out as the evening was never mentioned by any of them again, thank God!

Having donned sun tops and flip flops *The Alphabetties* had headed out from their adjoining apartments and had managed to find themselves a quaint bar, oozing character right by the sea with endless views across the Mediterranean. They'd ordered sangria which had come in a clay pitcher, served to them under a terrace, sheltered under a palm leaf stoop which had filtered the sunshine perfectly. From where Zoe sat at that moment her life and the lives of the other *Alphabetties* had seemed quite idyllic. But an idyll is, by definition, unsustainable and it was Sally who shattered the illusion. When there was a rare lull in the conversation, Sally had quietly and sadly said:

"Gabe and I are getting a divorce".

⬜⬜Ⅱⅈ⬜⬜⬜⬜∩⬜…⋯⋮.·⁺⁺·.⬜∴⬜⬜⬜⋃⬜⬜⬜⬜

In order to get a divorce, you must prove that your marriage cannot be saved – Sally knew that under increasing strain their marriage could not be rescued. She was devastated for her two beautiful girls but recognised it was the best thing to do. Staying in a marriage that isn't working doesn't help anyone - it takes much more strength to let go. No other parties were involved although Mark was increasingly in Sally's thoughts. She knew her relationship with Gabe had shifted too far apart and no longer fitted together. It was time to go their separate ways – it would be less destructive in the long term.

Reminiscent of a Gordon Lightfoot song, she told them that she couldn't pinpoint what or when she thought their relationship had gone wrong, the love she had for him, maybe hadn't gone but had certainly changed. And despite her commitment to the family and her best efforts she wasn't going to get that back.

"I've done everything I can think of to make things better, I've given all I have but I've reached the point of no return. I don't want to keep repeating the same pattern in my marriage, but Gabe wants to maintain the status quo. That's not enough for me! "

The girls knew this was true as Sally loved her daughters so much, but the time had obviously come for her to think about herself and her future happiness – which in turn meant the future happiness of Abi and Charlie too. Over the last couple of years Sally had done all she could to save her marriage. She had managed her work schedule, so she didn't travel abroad as much, passing up career opportunities to be at home. She'd given up counting the number of times she'd tried to talk to Gabe. She had been there for all his successes and failures but whatever she did she just knew she wanted more from a lifelong relationship. He was still a great dad to his precious girls and still gregarious and the life and soul of any party - but that wasn't enough. Sally needed a life partner with her drive and lust for life and pushing herself to enjoy all that life had to offer.

Gabe couldn't possibly have thought there was nothing wrong with their relationship, he was a very intelligent man. But when Sally finally told him she couldn't do this anymore and wanted a divorce he seemed genuinely shocked and almost puzzled. After his initial reaction which was one of flight accompanied by a lot of alcohol, Gabe did manage at last and too late, to discuss things with Sally. He'd known his marriage was going over a cliff but just didn't know how to pull it back to safety. He confessed to Sally:

"As well as being in love with you, I've also been in awe of you. You're always so strong, I thought you didn't really need me."

How wrong could he have been. Gabe had left that night to spend time with his parents.

⬜⬜Ⅱ⅄⬜⬜⬜⬜∩⬜…⋯⋮.˙¨.⬜∴⬜⬜⬜∪⬜⬜⬜⬜

So, the weekend away with her girlfriends had come at just the right time, she had needed her spirits lifting and they were the ones to do it. After sympathy and reflection, the group had decided they needed a walk along the beach to a change of venue to liven things up. Their quaint little restaurant hadn't actually been on the beach but more on a rocky outcrop. To reach their chosen stretch of beach they'd had to paddle for a few hundred yards. But the tide had come in somewhat since they'd sat down and as they'd entered the water from the rocks, they'd all had to hoist up their shorts or skirt so as to not get completely soaked. Sally, being the tallest of the group, had made better headway and was soon out in front of the rest of them, but that hadn't been the only reason why she'd ploughed ahead. Maggie, Kate, Faye and Zoe had stopped in their tracks and were trying to maintain their balance whilst creasing themselves laughing as Sally had got further ahead.

When Sally had pulled up her skirt to avoid the rising tide, she had managed to tuck it into her knickers and in turn exposed a fair amount of buttock. She'd looked uncannily like the iconic Athena poster of the tennis girl made famous in the late 1970s! The situation, plus the need for emotional release, meant Sally too had stood in the Mediterranean up to her knees and laughed out loud – it had brought some urgently needed joy into her heart.

Looking like survivors of a shipwreck they'd finally managed to come ashore near the hotel complex affiliated to Maggie's timeshare. As they hadn't wanted to waste precious holiday time walking up hills, they'd thought they would enquire if there were any similar apartments nearer to the hotel i.e., at the bottom of the hill closer to the large pool, bars, restaurant etc. For some inexplicable reason

221

instead of just asking, Maggie and Sally had thought it would give the request more credence if one of them had an affliction which made walking up the hill difficult. So, on the spur of the moment as they'd approached the reception desk, they'd decided Zoe had a heart condition and explained to the receptionist that: "Her condition isn't life threatening but nonetheless debilitating, could you help?"

⬚⬚⊔⅄⬚⬚⬚⬚⌒⬚……∴.⠄ ̈ ̇⬚∵.⬚∵⬚⬚⬚⊔⬚⬚⬚⬚

Although at the time of visiting Puerto Banus, Zoe probably wasn't at her slimmest she was far from obese. She couldn't have run a marathon by any stretch of the imagination, but she could certainly manage your average fitness class. Irrationally, she became concerned as to why the girls had selected her as the invalid member of the group and questioned whether to them, she looked as if she had a heart condition. She knew that some people may not have any symptoms before they're diagnosed and heart failure can happen suddenly or gradually, over time.

Shit, so maybe she did have heart disease and just didn't have any symptoms and she could keel over at any moment. Maybe the girls are onto something here and have done her a favour. She couldn't recall whether she had mentioned to them that earlier in the year her brother Rich, whilst out mountain climbing in The Lake District had been rushed to hospital having suffered some sort of heart attack. When she had been told the news about Rich, Zoe had rushed to the hospital to be with her beloved brother expecting him to be unconscious and wired up to machines and monitors. Thankfully, when she arrived, he was sprawled across the bed in a very skimpy dressing gown and pyjama shorts looking ridiculously healthy and rather like a porn star. Admittedly he was hooked up to a monitor, but it was pulsating away with a strong, regular beat. It turned out that his heart muscle had actually been attacked by a virus.

☐☐Ⅱ⋏☐☐☐☐∩☐……⋯∶.⋅¨⋅.☐∵☐☐☐∪☐☐☐☐

So, with the incident of her brother's virus still fresh in her mind, Zoe had got completely illogical very quickly. Her state of mind hadn't eased when the hotel staff had shown them the only alternative accommodation they could then offer - on the 23rd floor! The height and the very unsafe looking French windows and balcony had given all of them palpitations, not just Zoe, and they'd decided to give it a miss. The room had looked like one you'd see in films where a minor actress is thrown out of the window into a pool handily located below or a balcony the villain is tossed over to plummet to his death on the poolside.

Probably not medically advised if you've just been told you have a heart condition, but after a trip up to the potentially unsafe and lofty hotel room they'd all felt the need for a drink. They'd made a quick trip to the local shop to stock up for prinks on their perfectly safe, spacious apartment balcony. On leaving the very local mini market, Faye had been pushing the trolley containing the supplies and strangely she'd forgotten to return it. She'd just kept on walking and boldly had pushed it up the hill back to the apartment. Her actions, although illegal had proved invaluable, and the trolley had accompanied them on all subsequent trips to the beach/hotel complex/bar/shop and had certainly saved a lot of moaning and groaning about carrying stuff up the bloody hill.

Puerto Banus is 6 kilometres west from the centre of Marbella and is known as the Costa del Sol's playground for the rich and famous. The Spanish Riviera abounds with boob jobs and bimbos. *The Alphabetties* had never seen so many big yachts and small overly tanned, elderly millionaires – all of whom had a young woman on their arm dressed top to toe in designer labels. Puerto Banus is the most expensive port in Europe. To moor your yacht here will cost you over 50 times the average wage in the UK. Such wealth is beyond Zoe's comprehension, she couldn't compute having so much money that you own a boat that has a crew of fifteen people.

So, you can imagine that Puerto Banus was a prime place for people watching and that evening they'd secured themselves an excellent vantage point. Faye had announced, maybe somewhat prematurely:

"Sally you're almost a free woman now you should start to think what kind of a man you'd like to partner up with in future. Look at all these specimens strutting by, it's like flicking through a catalogue!"

Not surprisingly Sally had been somewhat taken aback but could see the logic and entertainment value in Faye's suggestion and had responded:

"Although you're an insensitive cow I can see that your suggestion has some merit and may save me time in future".

So, between them, mainly under Faye's guidance, they'd devised the simple but effective Green/Red rating system for the members of the opposite sex that had been passing by. Hypocritically, they'd known that if men had been taking part in such a pursuit assessing the females walking by, they would have been outraged at such blatant sexist activity. The system, which is still used by *The Alphabetties* today is not in any way complicated. Green is for 'if you were single, you would contemplate sleeping with them if they weren't married or a complete tosser' and Red for 'not a chance'. This is a very shallow game but often brings forth surprising results.

After people watching for much longer than they'd anticipated the girls had gone in search of what else Puerto Banus had to offer, aside from wrinkly millionaires. Only a few yards further down the harbourside they'd found a great bar with excellent music which was heaving with people.

The place had been absolutely rammed, and they'd split up to secure seats upstairs whilst Kate and Faye had tried to get to the bar. Zoe had been pleased to be in the seat finding group, as squeezing past sweaty blokes in various states of inebriation or scantily clad women, so you have a skin-on-skin situation with a stranger was rather abhorrent to her. Kate had managed to make it to the bar first but whilst trying to attract the attention of the rather frazzled staff, she'd had to endure some creepy guy pushing against her and feigning an apology when she glared at him.

☐☐凵ᕦ☐☐☐☐⌒☐…⋯⋮.·˙˙·.☐∵☐☐☐∪☐☐☐☐

It all reminded Zoe of nights out years ago in her hometown, particularly on New Year's Eve. This is one of the annual holidays when you feel compelled to have a good time; you must stay up late and welcome in the next twelve months and what they might bring and be joyous about it or try to forget the last twelve months you've had. When she was young this meant going to the already packed local pub with all her friends drinking and shouting at each other until the midnight hour arrived and then kissing the person next to you – please God this was one of your friends but often it was some random stranger you just happened to end up squashed next to at that moment and would never contemplate touching lips with for any other reason!

More recently, New Year's Eve has been a lot more civilised, usually involving dinner with friends then drinks at their house so the kids could crash out when they were knackered and having champagne on the front lawn at midnight. This all made Zoe's life now sound very suburban and middle class, which she had to admit it probably was.

⬚⬚Ⅱ𝄡⬚⬚⬚⬚⋂⬚…⋯⋮.⋅˙˙.⬚∴⬚⬚⬚⋃⬚⬚⬚⬚⬚

Despite downstairs being a cattle market for the lecherous rich, upstairs had proved to be much more conducive to *The Alphabetties* needs. From the elevated vantage point, they were able to do more people watching from a different angle! This was great as the music had been pretty good in this place and the square footage they'd had managed to carve out for themselves had been used as an impromptu dance floor. So, this was where they danced, drank, chatted, drank and danced some more until the lights had gone up at 4.30am! This had been a first for *The Tour* and they'd been very proud of themselves, they could still party with the best of them.

⬚⬚Ⅱ𝄡⬚⬚⬚⬚⋂⬚…⋯⋮.⋅˙˙.⬚∴⬚⬚⬚⋃⬚⬚⬚⬚⬚

Zoe did like a good boogie and much to her delight so did Frank. He'd quite happily dance the night away if the music was right and although their kids would disagree, he has some good moves. Clearly the more he's had to drink the more flamboyant he becomes but Zoe would much rather that than a man who won't even shuffle from one foot to the other with her. Frank is great friends with Max and one of the main reasons is their mutual taste in music – which is often not to Zoe's taste or Kate's or indeed most of the population. So, on the occasions when one of their less mainstream favourites comes on, they have been known to clear the dance floor and dance quite happily with each other. It's a sweet bromance and one which extends beyond obscure punk bands of the 70s and 80s to a love of craft beer and sport, typical male stuff - shallow, but important to them.

◫◫ƛ◻◻◻◻∩◻……·:.·¨·.◻·.·◻◻◻⊔◻◻◻◻

That night in Puerto Banus, Zoe and her friends had really wanted to prove a point, that despite being mothers of thirteen children between them and in their forties, they could still pull an all-nighter. So much so that when they'd got back to the apartment they'd decided that to finish off a great night, a quick dip was needed – in fact a skinny dip. When the decision had been taken to go au naturel, Zoe had gone to the loo and was taken aback when she'd come out to find her chums running past stark naked towards the pool shouting:

"Get your kit off Zoe we're doing some night swimming!"

Not wanting to miss out she stripped off and jumped in. There is something wonderful about the freedom of swimming in the nude and under the Mediterranean moonlight, this really was a tour moment.

Predictably the next day to say the group had been jaded was an understatement – and to be accurate it was later that same day. They'd managed to limp from their apartments down to the pool, slid into the water to try to revive themselves then collapsed onto sun loungers. As they'd lay there trying to recover from the overindulgences of the night before, they'd all started to notice that Kate looked a little strange. Not green around the gills as you might have presumed but there was something different about her face. Maggie had been the first to notice it as she'd refrained from a second dunk in the pool and had been lazily watching the others somewhat pathetic efforts.

"Kate, do you feel ok, your mouth looks weird?"

Kate has a great sense of humour, a raucous laugh to go with it and usually manages to smile regardless of whatever life throws at her. And it was this propensity for laughter, combined with the Iberian sunshine which had caused her to look different that morning around the pool in Puerto Banus. Over the course of the weekend Kate had laughed and smiled so much that she had tan lines on her face. When she relaxed her face, there was a distinct line coming down each side of her mouth. When she examined herself in someone's hand mirror she had been appalled:

"Jesus Christ I look like a ventriloquist's dummy!"

Ironically, once they had all noticed, they couldn't stop laughing which made Kate laugh and so the situation had perpetuated. Luckily Kate's predicament had been easily solved with foundation and a touch up brush.

□□⨿⨪□□□□∩□...⋯⋮.⋅˙˙⋅.□⋰□□□⨆□□□□□

Zoe hates having sunburn and gets angry with herself if she's stupid enough to let it happen. Mind you, her legs could stay in the sun all day every day and would only turn slightly off white. The worst incidence of sunburn which she suffered happened on a trip to America with Frank before they got married. Frank had organised a road trip taking in Arizona, Colorado, New Mexico, Utah and Nevada. It was amazing and they had a wonderful time. They even did a horseback ride down Bryce Canyon in Utah. Their guides were genuine cowboys, one was called Dean and the other Martin which Frank and Zoe found hilarious although Dean and Martin didn't seem to see the reason for their mirth – but Zoe couldn't help humming "Memories are made of this" all the way down the canyon and, which looking back was very apt!

Despite being with authentic cowboys, Zoe and Frank didn't feel the need to wear the full outfit with Stetson and fringed chaps unlike a couple of Japanese tourists who joined them, but they did see the wisdom of wearing a hat as the sunshine was ferocious. So, with headgear and sun cream they thought they were pretty safe from the harmful UV rays and focussed on not falling off their horses as they made their way down the canyon along perilously narrow and crumbling paths.

However, Zoe had made a rookie error and forgotten to put sun cream on the top of her ears and the right one had stuck out the side of the baseball hat she had chosen for the day. By the time they got back to their RV Zoe had a huge blister which ran along the top and down the back of her ear. It was quite disgusting and very sore. Fortunately, she had longer hair at that time and could mask her stupidity under her then henna coloured locks – when the blister popped it was even more disgusting, but we won't go there.

And in fact, this incident paled into insignificance for one very special reason. This trip was one of several impressive gestures that Frank had pulled off over the course of their life. He had kept the nature of the trip and the exact destination a secret from Zoe until they were at the airport. It was an amazing trip seeing so many truly awesome natural and man-made wonders, the Grand Canyon being the most memorable but not just for its breathtaking, grandiose landscape – this was where Frank proposed!

As a man who can't bring himself to pay a compliment, he has over the years made up for his ability to appear to be indifferent by pulling off some really wonderful expressions of how he feels about Zoe and his family.

Anyone who has had the joy of visiting the Grand Canyon will know that you are encouraged to sit along the edge – at designated points – and watch the magnificence of the sun setting over this mammoth crack in the planet. And it was at such a spot, at such a moment that Frank had planned to pop the question. Zoe had noticed that Frank had seemed unusually flustered and on edge that evening but thought nothing of it and just nagged him:

"Hurry up Frank or we're going to miss it. What the hell do you do that takes so long?"

This was a phrase Frank would hear a lot over the years to come.

But they made it in time, found a designated bench to themselves and as the couple sat hand in hand watching the sun finally kiss the horizon over the Grand Canyon, Frank completely bottled it! Bless him he really struggles with displays of affection and despite having played all this out in his head hundreds of times and even though there was no one else there to watch him make his declaration, it was all too much for him. So, with Zoe still in blissful ignorance, they went for dinner in the nearby Canyon Rim restaurant as planned and with Frank still seeming perhaps even a little odder. They then went to finish off the evening with a few drinks in the local bar. And it was here Frank chose to finally make his move – and even then, he was prompted by a loud conversation at an adjoining table about a forthcoming family wedding. Zoe has tried to erase this detail from her mind but as they both eavesdropped on their neighbours, he actually said to her:

"How about it then?"

And gestured with his beer bottle to the next table so Zoe knew what he meant. After a couple of moments to absorb what Frank was trying to do, she said:

"Is that really how you're asking me to marry you?"

She then walked out, found a nearby wall, sat down and began to cry. This was not the romantic proposal every girl dreamt of – although Frank's original plan clearly would have been. Seconds later Frank ran out of the bar after her, realising he'd probably cocked up one of the most important moments of their lives. And as Zoe sat on the car park wall, now red faced and snotty, he went down on one knee and asked her to marry him. After telling him at length what a complete dickhead he was and questioning if he really thought that was a good place to ask someone to spend the rest of their lives together, she said:

"Yes of course I will!"

Looking back on it, retelling this story pretty much sums up their marriage. Frank doing nothing romantic for months, nay years, then pulling something wonderful out of the bag but somehow cocking it up whilst Zoe, after her initial surprise and amazement berates him for doing something to undermine the occasion. But Zoe knew how lucky she was to have a man who even thought about doing such things to please her. Her heart ached for her friend and what she was going through as her marriage came to an end.

Chapter 12

J for Jerez

"There is an unspoken bond you create with the friends you travel with."
Kristen Sarah (YouTube Star)

Some of life between tours.

Clive broke his ankle playing hockey. It was a trying time for Faye – like a lot of doctors Clive wasn't a good patient!

Faye turned forty. Clive was still in plaster - she wasn't happy.

Kate went to get two kittens as a present for Kitty's birthday. She returned home with two kittens and an Alsatian puppy!

Frank, getting steadily balder (but no less handsome in Zoe's eyes) managed to pull off an impressive impersonation of Harry Hill at a New Year's fancy dress party!

Charlotte turned into a teenager and developed many of the stereotypical traits overnight. Sally doesn't quite know what's hit her!

Maggie and Shane's neighbour purchased an ex-military armoured vehicle which he keeps on his drive. This isn't a great addition to their quiet cul-de-sac. But more worryingly Maggie has her suspicions he may be a peeping Tom!

J, Q, X and Z have been proved by, amongst others Samuel Morse, inventor of the famous code, to be the least common letters in the English language. The *Alphabet Tour* will certainly uphold this research. The main factor in choosing a destination each year is obviously the letter that has been reached along with things such as cost, accessibility and weather. This is easier some years than others. A for Amsterdam, B for Barcelona, both straightforward and easily to reach from local airport(s). Or there may be a financial reason such as a cheap apartment on offer. Or it could be that a member of the group stamps their foot and insists they go to the Champagne region of France as that is clearly the only place the group can go for C – or a similar strong locational desire.

This year is proving tricky. J and Z are equally the second most difficult letter for children to learn to write only surpassed by G. Likewise for the *Alphabetties* J proved troublesome. In the 2016 United Nations list of towns and cities estimated to have over 100,000 population, Zoe and the girls had only heard of a handful of those beginning with J. These included Jaipur, India, Jodhpur also in India, Jeddah in Saudi Arabia, Jakarta in Indonesia and Johannesburg in South Africa. There are only three countries in the world beginning with J – Japan, Jamaica and Jordan. None of which were feasible for just a weekend away! Staying in the UK there are a whole host of places beginning with J many of which sound delightful such as Jolly's Bottom (Cornwall) and Jingle Street (Monmouthshire). But none of these British destinations really ticked the boxes for a group of mums set free for the weekend. So, Zoe had to think what other priorities, apart from the alphabet the girls prioritise to decide their *Tour* destination - sunshine came next. Coming from a city with a reputation for high rainfall, *The Alphabetties* all like to feel the sun on their skin. Fortuitously, at this time Sally had contacted the group and attached a newspaper article about an annual sherry festival in Spain in a place called Jerez (phonetically pronounced Herez with an H).

"Look what I found in this week's Sunday Times – what do you think ladies?"

En masse they'd all though it looks great, very Spanish. I've never heard of the place - it'll be a voyage of discovery!

Zoe had felt very ignorant as she had no idea about the Andalusian city apparently famed for lashings of sherry, beautiful horses and Flamenco. But praise the Lord this is somewhere they had all liked the look of, it had plenty of sun and what's more could be reached by a reasonably priced flight from their very handy airport, and they could be there in a couple of hours – sorted!

As Zoe was recounting the trials and tribulations of securing a destination for the tenth *Alphabet Tour* it made her smile to think how other people love to spend time discussing where the *Tour* girls could go next. Friends and strangers alike all think the *Alphabet Tour* is a wonderful idea and have proffered destinations on many occasions. In fact, more than once friends have spent a considerable period working out venues for the entire twenty-six letters. When this happens, it reinforces Zoe's feeling of how lucky she is to know Kate, Faye, Maggie and Sally. People say how they wish they had thought of it or we should do that with so-and-so and what's-her-name, but to date Zoe hasn't heard of any friends or acquaintances who have. She could say hand on heart without hesitation that they are missing out. And clearly *The Alphabetties* are doers not procrastinators!

Once they have a destination, *The Alphabetties* find the other logistics of accommodation, and transportation, relatively straightforward. Five women with at least seven degrees and numerous professional qualifications between them can get these aspects dealt with pretty sharpish. At the time of writing up the tenth tour, Zoe had needed to compile an up-to-date CV and found herself surprised at how many qualifications she'd actually managed to acquire along the way. So as a digression from her scribblings and as an interesting aside she started to jot down the collective academic accomplishments of *The Alphabetties*.

Zoe herself had left university with a BA(Hons) Degree in Town and Country Planning. She had chosen this degree to maximise her time as a student whilst being fully aware her intelligence was limited. The course also offered a foreign field trip, a year out in practice earning money and on qualifying, a year exemption from the required two years' experience before gaining membership to the Professional Institute and thus more pay. However, this was far from the future Zoe had dreamed of, but one advised by her Careers Officer at Sixth Form College who, on looking back, was a terrible bore. She should have gone with her heart and studied Ancient History and Anthropology and gone on to discover a lost city in the depths of the Amazon Forest!

During the course of her working life, she had also managed to gain a BTEC in Management Studies, Foundation level PRINCE2 management training and much more useful, a Certificate in Childminding Practice and an Ofsted Certificate of Registration.

The motives which the others may have had for choosing to attain their various qualifications, Zoe did not know. However, between them they had notched up an impressive tally from academia;

Kate:

BA(Hons) Accounting Course which she managed to acquire with some ease and leaving behind her a trial of wild nights and broken hearts. Followed by a Bachelor of Laws (LLB) which astoundingly she did part-time whilst raising three small children and supporting a husband.

Faye:

Bsc Degree in Optometry followed by a Professional Certificate in Low Vision and several other certificates to hone her skill and interest providing holistic eyecare in the community.

Sally:

Bsc (Hons) in Information Technology Management followed by an Msc in Business Strategy and Innovation Management which easily qualified her to be a member of the Chartered Institute for Information Technology.

Maggie:

Bsc (Hons) Midwifery. Although she had never been particularly academic at school once she found her passion, she had soared, achieving this degree part-time with three rug rats running around and a husband who was increasingly travelling abroad for work.

No wonder these women had no problem booking a hotel and flight to the Mediterranean! Zoe felt honoured to know and love them all.

⬜⬜Ⅱ⅄⬜⬜⬜⬜∩⬜…⋯⋮.⋅¨⋅.⬜⋰⬜⬜⬜∪⬜⬜⬜⬜

However, there was one slight hiccup to that year's plans which had been the timing of the flight. Departures to Jerez had been limited and hadn't flown till mid-afternoon. Clearly

237

this ate into their weekend away, so over the passage of time when this eventuality is unavoidable, as a group they unanimously decided that being at the airport officially counts as being on *Tour.* They weren't at home, they were with other travellers, they could have a glass of fizz (albeit at ridiculous prices) and they could shop. So, the girls had just arrived early at the airport and the *Tour* had been underway.

⬚⬚ℍ⅄⬚⬚⬚⬚⬚∩…··⋮·˙˙·.⬚∵⬚⬚⬚∪⬚⬚⬚⬚⬚

Zoe rather enjoys waiting at airports, for reasonable lengths of time anyway and with the caveat that she's not travelling with small children. She likes to sit and wonder where everyone is going, with whom and to do what. Anyone could walk by you as you sit on your uncomfortable airport lounge seat. Young people off to explore the world full of excitement and wonder, families reuniting after months apart hugging and kissing each other and never wanting to let go, cold hearted paid assassins going to carry out a hit without thinking twice, celebrities in dark glasses with bodyguards – it's fascinating to think who is passing through. Also, on the rare occasions when she travels alone, she finds it thrilling, again for a short time, to be anonymous - nobody knows who you are, what you do or where you are from. She could be anyone, an international woman of mystery. Zoe thinks airports really are the gateway to the world – probably because she's not using them week in/week out.

Sally on the other hand didn't have such a romantic view. She regularly travelled abroad for work and had spent many hours in airport lounges, which was time she could have spent with her girls. The demands of her job had caused her increased anguish over the last year since she had told Gabe she wanted a divorce. To be fair to Gabe after an understandable period of anger and remorse, he had graciously agreed to a divorce with dignity and civility. This was to ensure his precious girls still felt safe and didn't have to witness their parents fighting and teaching them the wrong things about being married. Sally and he tried to deal with everything amicably to ensure they were both there for their children and reassuring the girls neither of them were walking away.

Gabe now saw his biggest job was to make sure the kids were OK and told Sally:

"I don't want the girls to feel any stress or anxiety or worry about what their relationships might be like in the future. And God they mustn't in any way feel guilty about what's happened – none of this is their fault Sally."

"OK Gabe but that means we must both make time to listen to them and let them have time to process their feelings."

Sally stopped herself there and didn't go on to berate Gabe about the past. She had to have faith that he would protect and love their girls.

They had sold their beautiful house with no problem and Sally had found a new home for her and the girls in the same area to minimise disruption to their world. The reality of events did seem to have brought out the best in Gabe and when Sally had to go abroad, he stepped up to the mark and looked after the girls without hesitation. Charlie and Abi amazed their parents with their maturity and understanding about what had happened. But they didn't want them to feel they had to protect their Mum and Dad from how they were truly feeling. Sally and Gabe were for once united in their approach and knew they must make sure the transition to the new family arrangement was as love filled and painless as it possibly could be – at least for Charlie and Abi if not them.

Despite it being her decision, Sally still felt bereft when the logistics and reality of what she had put in motion started to unfurl. It had taken all her considerable strength to function at work which was a double-edged sword - being busy allowed her to escape what was happening in her world for a while but took her away from her beautiful daughters more than she wanted. Irrationally she felt jealous of Gabe having the girls to himself and more than once she had questioned her actions. Faye had been a pillar of strength for her, and she had turned to her regularly.

Although Faye knew Gabe pretty well by now, she was emphatically Sally's friend. She was nonjudgmental, kind, practical, loving and had given Sally the strength she needed. Faye had listened a lot and said a little but one of the things she had said had hit home with Sally. Over one of many glasses of wine, Faye had very shrewdly told Sally a quote from Margaret Atwood she had recently come across:

"A divorce is like an amputation; you survive it but there is less of you".

Despite it being at her instigation, Sally was finding this very true. She hadn't appreciated how much it would still hurt and the heartbreak it would still bring. Normally Sally wasn't a big crier. But Faye had helped her realise the healing powers of a good cry. Sally found herself using Faye as a sounding board to rationalise the actions she had taken and the bewilderment that she was feeling.

"When I met Gabe, I loved his spontaneity and carefree attitude. I loved that he lived from day to day. When did that turn into annoyance and wanting more? How can something I found so attractive turn into something so destructive?"

Jerez had indeed proved very Spanish, as thankfully, when *The Alphabetties* visited it had not yet been discovered by hordes of tourists. What's more, their hotel was an architectural feast – Zoe got very excited. The building had been a former convent, tastefully converted keeping many of the original features including marble floors, cloisters and a bloody great statue of the Virgin Mary which had dominated the lobby. Jerez, or its full name Jerez de la Frontera is a pretty place with the action focussed on the main square. At first glance there had appeared to be plenty of restaurants but on closer inspection a communal shiver had gone down the spines of *The Alphabetties* as they realised, the eating places all seemed to be exclusively offering tapas. Their minds had collectively flashed back to Barcelona and the tapas incident on *The Ramblas*, and Maggie had spluttered:

"Shit that's a lot of Tapas!"

As they tried to resign themselves to sharing small plates of food, praying it would be more palatable than their previous experience, Kate suggested they should also try what Jerez is famous for:

"Girls, given where we are, we really ought to try its main export! I know Sherry at home isn't great, but it's got to be better here in its homeland."

This had brought on another collective shiver as Kate had clearly forgotten that they had tried this theory out before and had been sorely disappointed. However, the logic was still sound and had to pay off at some point, so sherry had been ordered. The sherry list in the restaurant had been extensive, but although their Spanish was non-existent, and the waiter's English was limited, they'd managed to ask him to recommend some sherry for them to taste. A tray full of glasses and liquids resembling bronchial cough medicine had duly arrived.

Sherry has never featured as a drink of choice on *Alphabet Tours*, so they'd all taken their first sip with some trepidation. The reaction had been mixed. When he died, Charles Dickens had over a hundred bottles of sherry in his cellar and he used to give his pet canary a thimbleful twice a day. Somerset Maughn described sherry as "the civilized drink". However, on the whole, Zoe thought *The Alphabetties* would have agreed with the anonymous person who said "I'll say this for sherry it really makes you fancy a vodka"! Zoe really hadn't liked it, Faye and Sally had finished what was in front of them, Maggie had just about managed her glass but only Kate had knocked it back and said it wasn't bad and had polished off all that was left over.

⬚⬚Ⅱ𝄞⬚⬚⬚⬚⬚⌒⬚…⸱⸱⸱⠅⸱⸱˙˙⸱⬚⸱⸱⬚⬚⬚∪⬚⬚⬚⬚⬚

Kate, God love her is one of those people who will have a go at anything and will always try to see the best in any situation, to the extent that her family have nicknamed her *Pollyanna* after the childhood heroine from the American novel who has a unique philosophy on life. Pollyanna's philosophy centres on what she calls *The Glad Game,* an optimistic and positive attitude she learned from her father. No disrespect, but Zoe felt sure Kate had come across Pollyanna in the Walt Disney film, which wasn't very faithful to the novel but nonetheless the heroine is still portrayed as a very cheerful, talkative and radically optimistic person who focuses on the goodness of life and always finds something to be glad about, no matter the situation. This is certainly Kate's outlook; life is too short to be miserable or to complain about your lot. This 'make the most of things' approach has, like it did for Pollyanna, made Kate many friends and a go to person for any event.

Zoe mused that Frank on the other hand was the antithesis of Kate/Pollyanna which Zoe increasingly found annoying and hard to cope with. Frank always sees the downside of any situation however joyous or uplifting, often to the point of being morbid. What's more, in any discussion he always sees the other person's point of view. When Zoe just wants to rant or needs the blind support of her husband, she finds it infuriating and sometimes hurtful that, rather than agreeing with her or defending her, he will defend or rationalise the actions of a complete stranger rather than just trying to calm her down or show her some unconditional love. And in any given conversation he always has to have the last word, however ridiculous those words might be, and he very rarely apologises when he is wrong – which is more often than he would ever admit. Zoe didn't want him to always agree with her blindly like some sycophantic yes-man, but she would have liked his recognition or agreement once in a while – or God forbid a compliment!

Unusually, maybe due to their ecclesiastical surroundings, they had all slept well that night. This occurrence was unexpected as hotel bedrooms are often ridiculously hot, you're in a strange bed and because Faye and Maggie are not good sleepers at the best of times. As has already been established Maggie often shares a room with Kate and Zoe. On several occasions they have woken to find her fully washed and dressed or not there at all, having taken herself off for an early morning walk. On that trip, Maggie's tiredness had in part been due to the rigours of her new role at work.

Although on paper her move to a hospital nearer home was a good idea it was proving to be a very traumatic change. The reality of working in a large NHS under-funded hospital had hit home to Maggie over the last two years. She had been on an unrealistically steep learning curve and frequently found herself in situations she felt ill equipped to handle and, on several occasions, had been scared for the safety of both herself and the patient, often rushing around the ward trying to find help which just wasn't there. She knew that the nature of the job would mean irregular hours, but she frequently stayed long after her shift had finished or found herself taking over situations from another midwife with minimal handover. Maggie was discovering that the work of a midwife was hard, underappreciated, and full of complicated patient scenarios and fraught relationships with other healthcare workers.

Her superiors would regularly ask her to deal with situations with which she had not previously been involved. One such occasion had occurred a few months ago. Maggie had her first experience dealing with the trauma of a stillbirth. The physical birth itself was uncomplicated but the emotional tidal wave that accompanied it was almost unbearable. This aspect of a midwife's work is of course covered in training but is hardly talked about amongst colleagues. Maggie had to call on all her inner strength to get through this deeply sad, yet deeply intimate time with the mother and family. She did her best to ensure the parents got everything they wanted and spent time with their baby. But she had felt inept and needed an ally with the skills to help her through this. An ally came but long after the event, the memory of which would never leave her.

In typical Maggie style, she had dealt with the family's ordeal with professionalism, compassion, and kindness. The parents and extended family, the latter often forgotten in this scenario, all felt a terrible loss and greatly appreciated that Maggie had made herself available to talk to them and allow the parents to take time to make memories with their child. All of which meant that Maggie had almost fallen into the role of a Bereavement Specialist on her ward. A role she had never expected, and which was making her once again reflect on her life path.

⬜⬜Ⅱƛ⬜⬜⬜⬜∩⬜……⸭⸰⸰⬜⸰⸭⬜⬜⬜∪⬜⬜⬜⬜⬜

Despite *The Alphabetties* not having taken to sherry in general, they'd felt a tour of a sherry cellar had to be done whilst they had been in a city known the world over for its production. And to be honest they had realised Jerez didn't have much to offer that wasn't sherry related – but they could have guessed that! The Tio Pepe cellar in the heart of the town, is the largest producer of sherry in the world and, more importantly their tour had included a little *choo choo* train – a feature which the wine-making industry seems to relish and which was rapidly becoming a *Tour* tradition. When they'd booked, they had been offered an option of tasting either two or four sherries during the visit – you can imagine which option they'd gone for! To be honest on this particular winery tour the train really hadn't been necessary as far too much of the time was spent getting on and off the train, as many stops were made with very short journeys in between. No sooner were they on than they had to get off the train to look at some more really old bottles or barrels in one of many dark, musty, cold rooms. As she was compiling her thoughts of Jerez, Zoe felt bad about been so disparaging of the Tio Pepe tour as she seemed to remember it had been pretty interesting and eventually after the many dark, musty cellars and a short lecture, they'd ended up at the supposed climax of the tour - the sherry tasting. But like many women find, climaxes can be disappointing and sadly they all felt the sherry on offer had been no better than the cough medicine they had sampled the night before! They'd all got a much bigger thrill in the gift shop purchasing unnecessary gifts – obviously not sherry!

⬚⬚⊔⋋⬚⬚⬚⬚⋒⬚…·⸱·⸱⸱·⸱·⬚⸪·⬚⬚⬚⊔⬚⬚⬚⬚⬚

As she gets older Zoe finds herself becoming less and less tolerant and her attitude is more selfish and if she doesn't want to do something she'll say so – like drinking sherry. Much to her offspring's horror she will complain if she feels she hasn't received the attention or goods that she has paid for or deserves. Holly and Eric will glare at her and plead with her not to say anything. Holly in particular thinks Zoe is very impatient. In the distant past Zoe had worked in the hospitality industry in various capacities and recollects that the philosophy back then was the customer is always right and efficiency and good service were very important. The summer after Zoe's first year at university she was, not heavily but somewhat in debt with an overdraft to pay off. Her father was in the Masons when he left the navy and cliched though it was he did have his connections. He managed to get Zoe a job that summer working at a local hotel owned by one of the brethren.

That summer she acted as holiday cover for nearly everyone who worked at the hotel. She would go in early to serve the residents their breakfast, then be a chambermaid, changing beds and cleaning rooms, then a kitchen help, peeling potatoes and fishing out banana from last night's fruit salad, then back to waitress for any funeral wakes or similar events in the afternoon. This would be followed by serving residents dinner and then being joined by many other waitresses to serve food at large functions such as a

Masonic Ladies evening or a charity dinner dance. After several weeks of this gruelling regime Zoe was completely knackered but debt free and even managed to finance a trip to France with a university chum.

Providing good service was drummed into her that summer but doing so, to some of the customers, was testing to say the least. Like the long-term resident who moved all the furniture around in their room every day and every day the manager insisted it was put back the way it originated. Or the woman at the dinner dance who refused to let the staff take her precious mock fur coat to the cloak room and then complained viciously when gravy was spilled down it. Or the lecherous men who leered at her because the waitress' uniform was uncannily like a French maid!

□□Ц□□□□□∩□…··∴.·¨·.□∴□□□∪□□□□□

This holiday job preamble brought Zoe to the recollection that after the sherry tour *The Alphabetties* had been very pleased with themselves as they had found a little restaurant full of character tucked away in a square by a huge church, off the beaten track. They loved it when this happened and had grabbed a table overlooking the square. The place had been buzzing with local people, and they'd felt this venue would inevitably result in a memorable lunch.

Well memorable it was, but not for the reasons they had hoped. They had appreciated that the place was busy and would have been happy to sit in the sun with a glass of wine (not sherry clearly) whilst their food was prepared. Alas they hadn't even got that far. The waiter clearly wasn't going to serve anyone who wasn't a regular or Spanish and resolutely had refused to serve the girls despite much gesticulating and even approaching him, he still wasn't going to take their money!

Each of them had tried to catch his eye with varying degrees of politeness:

Zoe: "Excuse me can we order please?" No reaction.

Sally:" Hello we'd like to order drinks" Nothing.

Maggie had got up, approached him and looked him in the eye:

"Sorry we know you're busy, but we'd like to order!" Vague head gesture from waiter giving the group some slight hope.

Several minutes later, after consulting google translate Faye had given her best smile and tried in Spanish:

"Hola, nos gustaria pedir bebidas y comida, por favor".

Still nothing at which point Kate had stood up announced:

"For Christ's sake this is ridiculous!"

And she'd then walked off with her companions in close pursuit. So, after their initial euphoria had been well and truly crushed, they'd taken their custom elsewhere. This wouldn't have happened in Zoe's day!

However, on a more positive note whilst they had been in Jerez that day, they had managed to find out details regarding the annual festival which Sally had first read about in the newspaper article a couple of months ago. They had seen several beautifully adorned horses pulling equally beautiful carriages driven by immaculately turned-out horsemen and women. It had transpired that these impressive carriages would take part in the culmination of the festival, a grand parade that took place that evening. This information had been gleaned from a very helpful lady at the Tourist Information Office, the antithesis of the grumpy waiter, who had also told them where a good vantage point would be to view the parade and where they could find a good Italian restaurant. Yes, *The Alphabetties* had decided to ditch tapas for a tried and tested favourite. They felt they had given tapas their best shot but after the earlier debacle they decided it just wasn't worth it!

So that evening they had taken up position at the recommended spot to watch the festivities go by. It seemed like everyone in Andalusia never mind Jerez had turned out to line the streets. The girls had high hopes for big things and had waited to be impressed. The atmosphere had been infectious, and the parade had been led by the beautiful horses with ornate carriages. Then whilst showered by confetti cannons they'd watch the inevitable marching bands go by along with numerous, huge inflatable animals. The parade had been extremely noisy and had made slow progress through the centre of the town. After half an hour or so, standing by the roadside repeatedly cheering, they'd come to realise that the parade pretty much consisted of the aforementioned inflatable animals and every marching band within a hundred-mile radius. So, when Faye pointed out that they had to leave to make their restaurant reservation they were happy to go as their enthusiasm, by then had well and truly waned.

⬜⬜Ⅱλ⬜⬜⬜⬜∩⬜...⋯⋮.˙˙·.⬜∴·⬜⬜⬜∪⬜⬜⬜⬜⬜

Despite the repetition of the participants in the parade, Zoe was really pleased they had been in Jerez that weekend. She loves taking part in or witnessing a local event that brings people together. She is the person who tries to push to the front and cheers, shouts and claps the loudest as people go by or who stops and listens as street performers entertain. She loves all that and although she is probably embarrassing to her kids now, she hopes that Holly and Eric will also grow up to appreciate other peoples' efforts to make everyone's lives brighter and happier.

All *The Alphabetties* have a similar outlook which is probably one of the reasons they get along so well – they all aim to enjoy the opportunities life presents to them. Faye in particular is very good at engaging with complete strangers and finding out their story. Often, one of the group will turn round in a queue at the airport or in a bar and she'll be chatting away to the people next to her. Sometimes it backfires on her, and they get stuck with the local loon or letch, but Zoe is glad Faye is prepared to take that risk and commune with her fellow man.

It is probably this quality that makes people confide in Faye and a definite contributing factor as to why she was doing so well in her new role at the charity eye clinic. Faye had accepted the appointment about eighteen months ago and was loving providing eyecare to those less fortunate in the community. What she wasn't loving was the amount of administrative work which seemed to have come her way with the role. She was in effect responsible for ensuring the considerable amount of paperwork involved in running a charity, was kept up to date. Clearly, she didn't do this single handed. There was a small but great team of volunteers to help her with this, but she had the final word. So, she was getting to grips with charity governance, legal documents for the Trustees, grant and lottery applications, lease and freehold property documents – the list went on. Much to Faye's delight, her former colleague and now friend Bridget had recently approached her to join the team of volunteers at the charity and had even expressed an interest in taking on some of the administration side – which although she found bizarre Faye was very grateful for. Bridget seemed to instinctively know when things had to be applied for, submitted or put before the Trustees. Marvellous. Bridget's skill and that of the other volunteers meant Faye could focus on the practical side of the charity which she relished and now managed to do alongside her paid work. After being initially overwhelmed by what she had taken on Faye felt she was now getting to grips with her appointment and was generally coping with life.

As well as being a gift when dealing with those that visited the clinic, Faye had found that her approachability had allowed Bridget to offload some of her problems. Bridget had recently trusted Faye enough to tell her how working with her at the charity had provided a respite from the difficulties she had in her personal life. It turned out that Bridget was an only child and had been brought up by her mother after her father left, as her mother said for 'a younger model' and never featured in Bridget's life. Bridget told her she'd had no complaints and she'd had a happy childhood with her mum but sadly her mother had been diagnosed with Early Onset Alzheimer's. Bridget recounted to Faye that her mum had her when she was forty two, the reason she always said her father left her for a younger woman. Now in her mid-sixties she needed regular care, but it had taken many years for Bridget to get a proper diagnosis as she'd discovered the symptoms are often incorrectly attributed to stress – not unfeasible if the patient has brought up and supported a child on their own. But all that time Bridget had known that stress wasn't what her mother was suffering, and she kept on insisting there was something else. Up to now Bridget said they were managing; her mother could still carry out her daily routine but Bridget confessed:

"I do worry what the future will bring and how we'll cope, mum relies on me so much. I need to find a way to sort her out."

An involuntary tingle had gone down Faye's spine when Bridget had said this, it had brought on a sense of foreboding in Faye. But Bridget told Faye all this one evening after a particularly busy stint at the clinic as they were having a quick drink to wind down before going home. Although Faye knew she should get back she felt Bridget needed her more than Clive and the kids at that moment. Despite her slight feeling of apprehension, Faye still felt privileged that Bridget had trusted her enough to share her very personal issue – one which she had kept from her professional colleagues at work. Although as Faye listened to Bridget talk about her homelife, she did come away with a sense that Bridget had almost partitioned off this part of her life and had to some level, objectified her mother – for example Faye realised she didn't know Bridget's mother's name and she hadn't seen a photo of her. The thought came to Faye's mind that perhaps Bridget was somehow ashamed of her mother and wanted her kept completely apart from her professional life and friends.

〰〰〰〰〰〰〰〰〰〰〰〰〰〰〰〰〰〰〰〰〰〰

Having left the parade behind, the girls were ready to eat and were looking forward to some tasty Italian food but they'd struggled to find the restaurant recommended by the nice lady in the tourist office. Although this was a part of town they hadn't ventured into, they'd all been pretty sure they had found the right spot. As she had spoken to the nice lady, Sally was unequivocal that:

"This is where the restaurant should be, I'm bloody starving for Christ's sake it can't be far away!"

Although the definition of madness is said to be doing the same thing over and over again and expecting different results, the girls did do exactly that. They all stood in the narrow street turning around and looking for the usual tell-tale signs of an Italian restaurant: red and white checked tablecloths, canopies and umbrellas, Italian flags, and geraniums in terracotta pots. But no, there hadn't been a snifter. Then, when things had begun to get fraught, as hanger crept in, Zoe had spotted a very small, very tastefully carved slate sign adjacent to a large, heavily carved wooden door a little further up the narrow street. She'd approached and beheld this was the place. It was clearly a local secret and certainly didn't rely on passing trade! The group, like the cast of a horror film, had slowly opened the imposing door and cautiously popped their heads round - only to be greeted by the warmest welcome from the concierge who had been expecting them and had showed them to their table.

After the initial difficulty finding the place, the girls hadn't been surprised that this wasn't a typical family run Italian restaurant. The restaurant was very swanky, very tastefully decorated with large replicas of sections of Roman art and sculptures around the place, the arm of Apollo, the bust of Caesar, that type of thing – not a candle in a Chianti bottle in sight. The girls had been seated at a corner table behind which on the bare plaster wall a replica of *Michelangelo's David* had been lovingly painted. The painting obviously hadn't been to scale but was still very impressive. However, as Maggie had sat down on the far side of the table Kate had blurted out:

"Maggie you can't sit there just look behind you! *David* is taking liberties!"

Much to the amusement of her companions, when Maggie had sat down it looked as if *David's* sizeable genitalia were resting gently on top of her head. Once the girls had seen this, they couldn't get it out of their minds, whichever way Maggie had turned and after several dirty jokes, *double entendres* and much hilarity, the group had asked if they could possibly move to another table. Luckily the staff were very accommodating, and they hadn't had to explain that they couldn't spend the evening looking at Maggie with a flaccid penis and large scrotum on her head!

Once relocated, the girls had studied the menu and ordered food, a meal each just for them on their own plate and no sharing! Of course, wine too had been ordered and as the evening mellowed the restaurant filled up – the venue clearly wasn't as much of a secret to the locals as the exterior implied. They had a fabulous time and hadn't wanted the evening to end. But Faye had this in hand and had become on first name terms with the lovely young Croatian waitress who had been looking after them. She had explained to Marta, their waitress, that they wanted to go on elsewhere after their meal and that as they were in Andalusia, they would love to see some Flamenco - did she know of anywhere they could go to tick this off their 'to do in Spain' list?

Marta had proved to be a little gem and had given Faye and the girls masses of advice and informed them:

"There is a traditional Flamenco bar nearby with live music this evening and then, after you can go just a few hundred yards further away to a night club which is also very popular."

The girls were so impressed with the young lady that they'd tipped her handsomely at which point she was so thrilled she said:

"Look it is only a couple of moments away. I will show you, as, like the restaurant it is quite hard to find".

Faye of course got very giddy by the potential for late night partying and invited the young waitress to join them:

"Why don't you come in with us, we'll have great fun?"

But the waitress had wished the girls good night and, after depositing the girls at the Flamenco scurried back to the restaurant – either something was lost in translation, or she could see the look in Faye's eyes and the possibility that a night with these women could get seriously out of hand!

At this point the girls had not fully appreciated that Jerez is not only famous for sherry but that the city is equally famous for its Flamenco dancing and is often called the birthplace of Flamenco. The bar to which they had been escorted had been a very popular place indeed, packed out with standing room only. Apparently, the singer that had been about to perform was famous in Andalusia as one of the best at his craft. They'd arrived just as the guitarist and the elderly male singer had come on stage to rapturous applause. The atmosphere had been charged as the performance began. The guitar playing (or correctly called *Toque*) was very impressive and the girls had begun to get swept up in the excitement waiting for the dancing (*Baile*) and singing (*Cante*) to begin. The dancer had appeared looking fabulous in a traditional dress with a ruffled skirt, scraped back black hair in a tight bun and block heels. Her dancing, stamping and finger clicking had also been amazing. They were so glad they'd managed to be present at this performance by artists who were clearly local celebrities.

That was until the singing had begun. From out of nowhere, making them all jump and with no relevance to the music been played by the guitarist or the rhythm being stamped out by the dancer, the elderly gentleman had begun what sounded to them, like very loud wailing! After his initial outburst he'd sat down on a stool and for a moment they thought he'd had a heart attack. But it appeared he had sat down to make it easier for him to begin frantic clapping in time with the foot stamping and to continue his incredibly untuneful 'singing'. None of them had been able to make out any words, although the girls had thought he might have been repeatedly singing arsehole but that hadn't seemed right. The performance had struck Zoe as very manic as well as dramatic. But if you'd gone by the look on their faces, the singer and dancer, weren't having a good time, both had deeply furrowed brows and appeared to have a bad smell under their noses. After suffering this for five minutes the girls couldn't control themselves any longer and like disrespectful adolescents had let loose several loud titters. Their behaviour had not gone down well in this the hallowed capital of Flamenco, so they'd made a swift exit. So, it had come to pass that Flamenco was another Andalusian activity the girls were unlikely to repeat!

The nightclub on the other hand had been a far greater success. Not only had the place been easy to find, mainly due to the two very large bouncers on the door, but it was an amazing place. It was huge and had multiple rooms all decorated on a Moorish theme – kind of Morocco meets Studio 54 but tasteful. What's more the clientele had been mixed in age and the girls hadn't felt like everyone's mother! Although, having said there was a mixed clientele, you could probably have guessed the age of the clubbers by the room you found them in. There had been a large room playing the then current hits Rihanna, Kaiser Chiefs, Kanye West and a lot of the Spice Girls – they had reformed that year. There had been another sizeable room predictably playing a lot of songs that the girls had felt sure were Eurovision entries and a belter called "The Show Must Go On" had been played more than its fair share. But praise the Lord, like any self-respecting nightclub should have, in Zoe's opinion, there had been an '80s room. So, that was where the girls based themselves and had drunk and danced until the early hours.

As the others had come to expect, Faye had attracted a fair amount of male attention during their time in the room and had been asked to dance by a couple of reasonably good-looking Spanish chaps. She is always polite and accepts a dance as she says it must take a certain amount of courage to come over to a woman and ask. She then of course makes it perfectly clear she's not interested in anything further. Zoe agreed in principle with Faye's take on this but also felt that many men were not that chivalrous and had only one aim in mind!

However, on this occasion Faye hadn't been the only one to gain the attention of a youngish man. Maggie had been the other lucky recipient of several attempts to coax her on to the dance floor by a persistent male. Although she really hadn't been keen and didn't feel the need to employ Faye's sensitivities, she had eventually relented. During her foray on to the dancefloor she'd established that her admirer had really been a bit odd and didn't warrant any more of her precious *Tour* time. He had been dismissed in no uncertain terms. Although she had to admit it's always flattering to be asked - by anyone really!

Chapter 13

K for Kinsale

"It is one of the blessings of old friends that you can afford to be stupid with them."
Ralph Waldo Emerson

Some of life between tours.

The twins started at the same senior school as their sister. Some more sibling rivalry but on a more advanced scale!

Nobody could believe it but Clive turned fifty – where are the years going!

Eric and Kitty played in their school's cup winning netball team.

Clive was very proud as Noah began showing an interest in and a talent for playing hockey.

Eric developed a talent for telling silly but surprisingly funny jokes. One of his favourites was: Why did the fish blush? Because the sea weed! There were many, many more!

Sally was in America on business when Obama was elected President. She was genuinely moved and felt she'd been a part of an extremely significant historic event.

Things in life do not always go according to plan. This had certainly been the case for the start of what had unbelievably been the eleventh *Alphabet Tour*. The girls had headed for the *Emerald Isle* to Kinsale, County Cork, the gourmet capital of Ireland. Zoe in particular had been really looking forward to it. She'd never been to Ireland, and had always had a soft spot for the Irish lilt and had to confess she found the accent very seductive although often bewildering. She had met various Irish people throughout her life and a couple were now dear friends, but albeit after a couple of drinks inside them, she sometimes struggled to know what the hell they were talking about – or as they'd say 'what the fuck' they were talking about.

⬜⬜Ⅱ𝔁⬜⬜⬜⬜⌒⬜…⋯⋮.⋅¨˙.⬜∵⬜⬜⬜⋃⬜⬜⬜⬜

His accent was among the many things that had drawn Zoe to Frank. Geordie was another regional accent that she loved, and which fondly reminded her of her days as a student. She had to confess she wasn't as keen on a Scouse or a Brummie accent but recognised that people may feel the same about her Cumbrian tones. But thinking about Frank's positive points felt good, as it was certainly something she had been doing less and less over the last couple of years. Although recently she and Frank had become closer with the sad death of his Mum the previous year.

Jack Common, a twentieth century essayist born in Newcastle said being a Geordie goes beyond mere geography and is "a quality of heart". This was certainly the case with Edna - her heart had been huge. A staunch Methodist with strong traditional views, although surprisingly divorced and married twice, she had doted on her family especially all her grandchildren and Holly and Eric certainly loved her to bits. Like most people from the North

East, she was very friendly and would talk to anyone. She had welcomed Zoe to the family with open arms and when they got married, told Zoe that her Frank was lucky to have her "as he's no oil painting!"

She had worked hard all her life, played team darts, and had risen through the ranks of the Women's Institute. She always spoke her mind which overall was a good thing but often her tact filter seemed to stop working. Zoe will always remember Edna's immortal line when she handed her the newly born Holly:

"I wanted a boy but she's beautiful."

Zoe could have flattened her then but missed her now. She and Edna had got on very well and Zoe had enjoyed talking to her and would tell Edna about her mum. Edna understood that Zoe missed her mother but didn't try to replace her. In reply, Zoe had listened to Edna and the stories she had to tell and didn't judge. Being their only grandparent, Edna was so special to Holly and Eric and telling them their beloved grandma had died was one of the hardest things Zoe had ever had to do. The thought of it could still make her breakdown and cry.

Frank and his sister, Jean, who was beautifully devoted to her mum, were with Edna when she had slipped away in hospital – her huge heart finally surrendering. Frank was strong for his sisters and Holly and Eric, but Zoe knew he was going to miss his mum terribly. He was the apple of her eye, and she was mightily proud of her son, the university graduate. Although he had never openly told his mum how much he loved her, Zoe felt sure she knew. Zoe also knew that she and Frank had drifted apart recently, and Edna's illness had made them reflect somewhat and brought them closer together again – Zoe hoped not just temporarily.

To maximise their time away and to fit in with cheap flights, that year the tour had started off on Thursday evening. The plan had been to arrive in Kinsale late evening between 10pm and 11.00pm which allowed plenty of time to settle in and chat over nightcaps. However, on arrival at Manchester airport their plans had gone awry. The navigation computer, or some such thing, at Heathrow had thrown a wobbly and many flights across the country had been seriously delayed or even cancelled. Fortunately, the girls' flight had only been subject to a delay, albeit one of considerable length and in fact had turned out to be the last flight scheduled to leave Manchester that night. So relieved that the tour would still take place the girls had decided to make the best of a bad job and had headed for the bar.

Steadily, as the night had drawn on, the airport lounge emptied until there had only been the Cork passengers left and only their solitary flight remained on the departures board. This is an experience few people must have at an international airport and as it got dark it had become quite eerie – Zoe was reminded of the film *Final Destination* with passenger premonitions and exploding planes, but she'd thought it wise not to mention this.

As they had finally boarded the plane most of their fellow passengers had been quiet and tired. But whilst waiting *The Alphabetties* had managed to polish off a couple of bottles and had been very vocal as they'd boarded. There'd been an audible groan as the girls pushed and barged their way to their seats. Of course, Faye had been smiling and wishing everyone good evening as she'd made her way down the carriage. But still the other passengers had prayed they wouldn't be the unfortunate one sitting next to these diabolical women! The girls had continued to disturb the in-flight peace for, oh at least ten minutes before pretty much in unison they'd all passed out totally zonked. Not another peep had been heard from them till touchdown in Cork.

□□⫫𝆏□□□□⋒□...·····⋮.·̈·̇·.□∴·□□□⋃□□□□□

In fact, Faye had quite a lot to be smiling about that year. Clive had been promoted and was now the Clinical Head of his unit. Credit to him he worked extremely hard and was certainly enjoying the perks which came with the job - which included him and Faye buying a new house. Tucked away in a leafy corner within walking distance of nearly everything they needed; they had found a gorgeous period home. When they had eventually moved in, they were both relieved as they had been looking for a property for many months and been gazumped a couple of times. But as they say everything happens for a reason and this house, they knew as soon as they saw it, was the one for them. Clive very sensibly had conceded, in the greater part, to Faye's skill when it came to decorating and fitting out their new abode. She could see the potential for the house and had plans for refitting the kitchen and other revamps around the place which would make it their forever family home and a great place to entertain – which thankfully they both loved to do and did regularly.

□□⫫𝆏□□□□⋒□...·····⋮.·̈·̇·.□∴·□□□⋃□□□□□

It turned out that Zoe wasn't the only one who swooned at the silky, sexy, sultry tones of the Irish accent. All the girls had been looking forward to being talked at by a silver-tongued Irish man and they'd anticipated the first of these would have been their taxi driver, but surprisingly no! As they'd all clambered into the pre-arranged minibus, which to be fair had waited for the delayed flight, Maggie had uttered, probably too loudly:

"For Christ's sake we've managed to find the only Jamaican taxi driver in Ireland! "

When they had ultimately arrived at their accommodation, it had been what might be described as bijou and somewhat smaller than they'd expected – women find things often are! The main cause for concern had been the single bathroom which was a lot more compact than imagined. It was inevitable over the course of the weekend that the modest bathroom had frequently become steamy and congested – and not mentioning any names, had also suffered a blocked loo and required attention from the caretaker!

The caretaker had turned out to be a very friendly lady who, the day before, had left them a small hamper of goodies – tea, coffee, milk etc. She had reminded Zoe of Mrs Brown of *Mrs Brown's Boys* fame, but taller. She had been very welcoming in a down to earth way and had set the girls minds at rest about the plumbing mishap:

"Oh fuck don't you worry girls, I've shifted more shit from the toilets in the houses I look after than this little pile!"

Although slightly taken aback, the girls had walked away from the house feeling matters had been left in very capable hands.

They'd wandered down into town finding their way through the mixture of old buildings and what appeared to be Council flats and houses. In the daylight, the centre of Kinsale was very pretty with traditional colourful Irish front doors, flower boxes, narrow streets and chunky slate buildings. Amongst it all the girls had found a lovely café offering many mouth-watering morsels. So, in the beautiful sunshine they'd sat themselves down at a table outside and had waited to be served by a nice young Irish man or beautiful colleen. But, once again the group were sadly disappointed. The young man who took their order, although not unattractive, was distinctly East European, as most of the staff appeared to be! Still, the breakfast and various coffees were very tasty, and they'd whiled away a very pleasant hour or so.

Finally, they'd mustered themselves and gone for a more extensive mooch around the place. They'd noted where the good-looking pubs were, where the food store was (you couldn't with any stretch of the imagination call it a supermarket) for the purchasing of alcohol, where the cash point was, and Zoe thought bizarrely where the cycle hire shop had been! Whilst they mooched, they'd done a little retail therapy and then it had been time to eat and drink again! A local seafood restaurant had been recommended to Sally and as they'd passed it on the way in, the girls decide to head there for a 'nice lunch'.

Despite the shaky start to the *Tour*, with the airport delay and the plumbing mishap, by this stage things seemed to have picked up. As they had approached the restaurant a table outside had become available and they'd plonked themselves down to soak up some more rays, drink wine and refill their tummies. The restaurant had lived up to its reputation and the girls had enjoyed a selection of *fruits de mer* including fish chowder and a very sophisticated prawn cocktail.

A little exercise had then been required to walk off lunch. The group had wandered off towards the water where they had spotted that they could take a cruise around the rather beautiful natural harbour next to which Kinsale had been built. The girls like a good boat trip so had checked out the times and realised that the next one would be along quite soon. They had waited so they got pole position aboard the boat.

The ship/tug/boat had duly arrived, and the girls rather forcefully had grabbed seats on the upper deck in front of the captain's bridge and had snuggled down under the thick Irish wool blankets that had been thoughtfully provided. As they'd headed out to sea taking in the scenery, the odd passing shag, and the choppy seas, the girls had realised that their trip was going to be even more idyllic than anticipated as wine was served on board. Marvellous! They had promptly purchased a bottle of surprisingly good wine and settled down to enjoy the cruise.

As the boat chugged out of the harbour a strange white shape had caught their collective eyes on the distant shore. They'd peered hard till eventually with one very loud clang the penny dropped and at the same instant it had dawned on the girls what they had been looking at. A naked man was standing proud on the rocks looking out to sea. Posing like Leonardo Di Vinci's *Vitruvian Man*, he really had let it all hang out (which was impressive as although sunny it was still quite chilly that day!). Then as the girls had continued to stare and giggle uncontrollably, an arm had appeared from the cabin behind them clutching a pair of binoculars! The captain had leant out of the bridge and offered the girls a better look. He had then assured them that the exhibitionist had not been a regular part of the tour saying:

"You lasses are lucky; we don't normally see that extra point on the fecking headland!"

The girls had begged to differ and had all agreed, after each had looked through the binoculars that he really had nothing to be standing there boasting about – maybe he had been apologising!

The rest of the harbour tour had seemed somewhat tame after that but had passed by very pleasantly and they'd returned to dry land feeling flushed but not just due to the sea air! Once back at the little house the girls had changed leisurely to go out for dinner. Faye had pre-booked a table at a restaurant she had been to on a previous visit to Kinsale for a wedding and which she'd known would be popular with the locals.

The restaurant was on the other side of the harbour but nonetheless the girls, or rather Faye, had decided they'd walk as it was a pleasant evening. As they'd passed the harbour the tide was out, and they were lucky enough to have seen an amazing sight – a whole host of herons all gathered in the evening sunshine to harvest what lay beneath the then very shallow muddy waters. As was her way, Zoe had wondered what the collective noun for a group of herons was and she later discovered there was some debate over it. It could be any of the following as far as she could tell, siege, sedge, hedge or scattering. As the herons she'd seen had been a good distance apart from each other, she decided she'd seen a 'scattering'.

⬚⬚Ɫɫⱥ⬚⬚⬚⬚∩⬚…⋯∴·˙˙·.⬚·∵⬚⬚⬚∪⬚⬚⬚⬚

Zoe knew that Frank would find this snippet of info interesting and the love of finding out useless facts and trivia was something they'd always shared. But over the years of visiting places, Zoe had honed her skill to pick out a juicy fact from exhibitions, museums, leaflets and brochures. She had developed this talent when the children were little and found that if she could get them interested in where they were visiting her life would be easier and the kids seemed to remember where they'd been. So, if there was a grisly beheading, hidden treasure or a toilet related story at any English Heritage or National Trust site they had visited, Zoe would sniff it out – so to speak. Then she, the kids and often Grandma would head to the gift shop and café whilst Frank meticulously read through every board and piece of text on display. Although, looking back at family holidays Zoe did think she may have taken things a little too far when she'd dragged the family to a chapel in Rome where the walls were decorated with the bones of the dead monks who had resided there – nightmare inducing holiday highlights for the kids!

⬜⬜⊔⋊⬜⬜⬜⬜⌒⬜…⋯⋮.⋅ ⋅ ⋅.⬜∵⬜⬜⬜⊔⬜⬜⬜⬜

Although not a great distance, walking up the hill on the other side of the harbour in heels had meant that the crew had built up quite an appetite. When they'd arrived at the restaurant it had been packed. There had been several large tables including one next to the girls that was celebrating an elderly gentleman's birthday. As the evening had progressed, and the family had become more intoxicated, the girls had been sucked into the adjoining celebrations. They'd been included in the traditional rendition of "Happy Birthday" and the elderly gentleman's relatives had tried to get the girls to sing along to other Irish favourites. The girls had recognised many of the songs that had been sung, very tunefully it had to be said. However, they certainly hadn't known any of the lyrics and although tuneful, after several drinks the diction of the elderly gentleman's family was never going to help with this! So, the girls made a cordial exit and headed back into town.

Kinsale certainly deserved its title of "Gourmet Capital of Ireland" and there were many, many pubs around the picturesque little town. But after their large meal and moonlit promenade the group had opted for a hotel bar with big sofas and comfy seats – they'd felt like real old farts but at that point didn't care. Mind you the selected bar had proved to be a rich seam for people watching, bitching and the Red and Green game – pastimes which all the girls enjoy. Although after a fairly short time these activities had clearly not been riveting enough for Kate as she had nodded off - which she does have a tendency to do.

⬜⬜Ⅱ⅄⬜⬜⬜∩⬜...⋯⋮.·¨·.⬜∴⬜⬜⬜∪⬜⬜⬜⬜

As has been mentioned before Kate has FOMO on a fairly impressive scale. Over the years that Zoe has known her, Kate has on many social occasions stubbornly refused to go to bed regardless of how tired she might be and of where she might be. Zoe has witnessed her fall asleep in numerous places on sofas, chairs, in a booth in the corner of a nightclub and even the floor on one particularly memorable night! Although whilst in Kinsale she did have a genuine reason to succumb to sleep.

Kate's eldest, Francesca, was now thirteen and having to deal with more than her fair share of teenage angst. Francesca is a very clever girl and had no trouble passing the entrance exam for the local grammar school for girls. She had fitted in well taking the expected levels of high educational attainment in her stride. Kate and Max were thrilled that she seemed to be in the right school for her to shine and reach her potential. Francesca too seemed happy. She is a perfectionist and driven to achieve the best she can – traits which had clearly been passed on from her mum.

But recently Francesca had seemed distracted and even angry, but Kate had put this down to usual teenage behaviour and raging hormones. Then one evening Kate had gone into Francesca's room to grab her washing to find her crying and obviously very upset. Kate put her arm round Francesca and asked her:

"What's wrong darling, can I help?"

And then the floodgates had opened. Apparently, Francesca was being 'mean girl' bullied at school. Throughout generations girls have been bullied by girls and an all-girls school would seem like an inevitable place for this to happen. One 'popular' girl in Francesca's friendship group had accused her of talking about her to another girl behind her back and spreading rumours. A 'she said/she said' situation had escalated, none of which was true. Francesca had openly denied ever saying anything unpleasant about the 'mean girl'. However, this girl had more control in the year and coupled with a deep nasty streak she had set about ostracising Francesca from her friends.

Poor Francesca was distraught and didn't know what to do. It made Kate's heart ache to hear her pouring all this out and from her own life experience could empathise to an extent with her feeling of betrayal. Only a few days ago this girl had been Francesca's friend. Despite her gut instinct to race down to the school and vent, Kate did her best to listen to her daughter and try to guide her towards finding a solution herself. She was also relieved that Francesca had felt able to talk to her and had not kept her pain inside and expressed it in a much more destructive way.

As they talked, Francesca told Kate that she did have one ally at school who was still talking to her – a girl that she saw when she walked to school who had noticed Francesca crying on her way home and asked if she was OK. Kate was incredibly thankful to this young lady and was trying to help Francesca build on this new friendship and to show the 'mean girl' she didn't need her. But it was an ongoing process as Francesca just couldn't understand why the girls she considered her best friends were being so cruel. Hence Kate was spending many hours lying awake at night worrying about what the next day at school would hold for her precious girl – she hated having to deal with things she couldn't do anything practical to fix. She was finding this situation of mental anguish unexpectedly harder than she ever thought she would.

⬚⬚Ⅰi🍸⬚⬚⬚⬚∩⬚…⋯⋮.⋅ˋˋ.⬚∴⬚⬚⬚∪⬚⬚⬚⬚⬚

The girls had awoken to another lovely sunny day. It had to be said they'd always been very lucky with the weather on tour. The good weather had been fortunate as this was the day the girls had decided to take to bicycles! Yes, Kinsale was where the gang got active, mounted up and headed off to Charles Fort out towards the mouth of the harbour. The wiry-looking guy in the bike shop had proved to be very knowledgeable and had them all kitted out with suitable bikes in no time. He had seemed very calm about letting them loose on the busy streets of Kinsale.

Not surprisingly Sally and Faye had taken the lead whilst Kate, Zoe and Maggie had brought up the rear. The hill up the headland that they had ascended the night before had once again featured on the way to the fort and had served to demonstrate the varying levels of fitness within the group. Faye and Sally had made it up the hill without even a single gear change, Kate had also managed well, and Maggie and Zoe did OK. At this point everyone had still been on their bike and hadn't yet started puffing and panting like an old boiler, but the day was still young. The next part of their route had taken them off road and along a very pleasant cycleway next to the coast for a little while. Zoe mulled that as they whisked along this stretch it had felt very much like being in a scene from an Enid Blyton book - *Five go Cycling in Ireland*. But as they had begun to climb through the trees Zoe's daydreams had turned to dismay. With her long legs Sally, accompanied by super fit Faye, had put some distance between themselves and the rest of the group who, when the gradient had become steepish had decided to dismount and had opted to push. They all caught up with each other, but things then took a turn for the worse. Bizarrely and without any warning it had appeared that they had to lift their cycles over a stile in order to get back on the road to the castle. This manoeuvre had proved tricky to say the least even for Sally with her extra height. However, they'd eventually managed to get all the bikes and themselves over unscathed, but this had only been achieved with the help of a poor chap who happened to be passing!

⬚⬚⛏ℷ⬚⬚⬚⬚∩⬚…⋯⋮.⋅˙˙⋅.⬚⋅∴⬚⬚⬚∪⬚⬚⬚⬚⬚

This hadn't been the only transport related predicament Sally had found herself in recently. Since moving house, she had obviously had a lot of clearing out to do. Gabe and she had spent a whole weekend dividing belongings up and allocating furniture and effects to each other. It had been hard, but they had managed to do this without the involvement of solicitors and legal agreements. Wrangling over who got what in a faceless office was not something either of them had wanted to do. Instead, they had allocated time to do this task together and overall it had gone harmoniously, and they had even managed a laugh or two at some of the horrendous things they had stashed away – wedding gifts from weird aunties, odd family heirlooms, that type of thing. There were things which clearly meant more to one of them than the other and, as they were both downsizing there was pretty much enough furniture for them both – well at least to get by for the near future.

On clearing out the loft they had inevitably come across all the girls baby clothes, toys and equipment which Sally certainly knew she was never going to use again. So after selecting the more treasured items she couldn't part with, she had asked around at school to see if anyone could make use of what remained. One of the more officious mum's had said she'd take it if Sally could deliver it to her house - her church was having a jumble sale. This particular Mum's persona frightened even Sally, which is saying something and on the rare occasions when they had spoken in the past Sally had found herself uncomfortable and behaving like a blithering idiot in her presence. So, Sally felt somewhat daunted when she dutifully loaded up the car with Abi and Charlie's baby things and headed off to the officious mum's house. And what a house, it was effing enormous and as Sally pulled up outside, she felt even more uncomfortable about passing on her possessions to this overbearing woman.

After Sally had scraped her mouth off the floor of her car, she began unloading the bags from the boot. The officious mum had obviously spotted her pull up and was purposefully marching down the drive to greet Sally who was by now ridiculously nervous. Thoughts were flashing through her mind about the quality of the items she was passing on to this rich, opinionated woman. Sally knew all the things she had bought for her babies had been cute and gorgeous, but she worried that far from all of them were designer labels. She had a mental picture of this woman going through the piles of baby grows, wearing rubber gloves, holding up items and tutting at the number of things from Tesco, Sainsburys, Primark and Asda!

Sally was hoping that maybe officious mum would be softer on her home turf but alas no. She was equally nerve racking and Sally spluttered:

"Good morning hope all of this is up to your standard?"

To which the reply came:

"Yes, let's hope so. I know it's the church jumble sale, but we don't want to be selling any old tat!"

Sally laughed nervously and backed towards her car and found herself actually thanking the other mum for taking these things off her hands – rather than as one would expect thanks coming in Sally's direction for the generous donation.

As she racked her brains in a panic to remember whether she'd washed the baby clothes since they emerged from the loft, she edged her way around the back of the car and opened the car door behind herself and slipped in. To her horror Sally found herself sitting in the back seat of the car behind the driver's seat – clearly not where she was meant to be. All Sally could do for several seconds was sit there thinking "shit, shit, shit!!!!"

In her panic to get away she had just opened the first door she came to and leapt in hoping to find some safety. But no and what's more there were child locks on the back seat doors, so Sally was trapped in this nightmare scenario. As she sat there swearing to herself, officious mum, looking perplexed came round to the car window, tapping on it and demanding to know if Sally was alright? She obviously thought Sally was having some sort of episode. Sally now sprang into action and with some difficulty, began to climb into the front seat laughing and mouthing:

"It's fine, I'm fine, silly me, durrr!"

None of which had helped the situation as officious mum was clearly humourless and just wasn't seeing the funny side one iota. Unlike *The Alphabetties* who quite literally pissed themselves when she recounted the tale at their next meeting.

◻◻⏄λ◻◻◻◻∩◻……⫶.·⃛⃛.◻⫶·◻◻◻∪◻◻◻◻◻

Once the girls were over the major wall and back on tarmac there was a super very steep hill going down to the coast which they all greatly enjoyed, before they headed up again to the castle. Eventually they all arrived at the castle, every one of them having spotted a very nice pub as they shot past it at the bottom of the hill.

The castle was actually quite impressive but not enough for the girls to fork out a rather hefty entrance fee and they'd made do with exploring the outer ramparts. They'd spent some time posing and taking various photos and had managed to nearly get stuck in a particularly narrow turret type thing. Then they'd just done stuff which *The Alphabetties* were extremely good at - they'd sat up there, enjoyed the view and had a really good laugh about something that they found highly amusing for quite a while. Laughter was always high on *The Tour* agenda!

They'd remounted and positively whizzed down to the pub at the bottom of the hill with its own little jetty and had refreshments whilst looking out to sea. From this vantage point they'd spotted a number of people on a beach across the harbour, some had even been frolicking in the water – it was a very nice day after all. They'd then decided that the beach across the harbour would be a lovely place for a picnic and that they would pick up provisions back in Kinsale for a nice lunch al fresco on the beach and had set off.

But they'd have to get back up the incredibly steep hill which they'd come down earlier and there was no alternative route, it couldn't be avoided. Even Sally decided this hill was just ridiculous and got off to push along with Kate, Maggie and Zoe. Faye however showed off how bloody fit she actually was and pumped those pedals all the way back to the stile. She must have had calves like Lynford Christie. The gang were very impressed and gave the girl credit where credit was due! The rest of the ride back was manageable, and the gang pulled up outside the food store in Kinsale having narrowly avoided being knocked off their bikes by the rather chaotic traffic in the centre of town.

They stocked up on bread and cheese, nibbles and of course a couple of bottles of wine to wash it all down with. Poor Sally had to carry it all as she was the only sensible member of the group with a rucksack type bag. The route to the beach was busier than their trip to the castle but the girls successfully managed to negotiate the bridge across the bay and back down the headland to the beach. Once there they'd got off their bikes to push them onto the sand, which wasn't that easy. What's more, it was whilst performing that manoeuvre that they'd seen a rather large notice explaining the local by-law forbidding the consumption of alcohol on the beach.

The girls made a unilateral almost instant decision to ignore the sign and proceeded on to the beach to find themselves a good vantage point for watching the seaside activities and yes maybe to be less conspicuous when drinking the wine! They'd also decided to keep it wrapped in the bag which did rather give them the appearance of a gang of winos.

They perched themselves halfway up the bank at the back of the beach on a kind of comfy ledge and settled down to lunch in the sun, swigging merrily from their poorly disguised wine bottle. This proved to be a very pleasant afternoon and the girls sat and watched people playing on the beach, arriving at the beach by canoe and even an old lady knitting on the beach. However, eventually the girls had to face the inevitable cycle ride back to Kinsale to return the bikes. So somewhat reluctantly they'd hauled the bikes out of the sand and headed back to town.

That evening they had decided to stay at the little house to watch both *Strictly Come Dancing* and the *X Factor* before heading out to the small but very pretty, Irish town. The group had decided to forgo eating out but to nibble and drink at home whilst watching TV. So, when they got back to the little house the TV was moved around until it was in the optimum position for them all to view whilst being able to reach the assortment of savouries and the hummus without having to get up! Faye was particularly enthusiastic about the *X Factor* and announced loudly as each contestant came on how fabulous they were, when to be honest some of them were, quite clearly crap. The champagne had obviously affected her judgement.

⬜⬜Ɫ𝔦⬜⬜⬜⬜⌒⬜…··∴·⸳˙˙·.⬜⸪·⬜⬜⬜∪⬜⬜⬜⬜⬜

Mind you it wasn't surprising that Faye was enthusiastic about the TV as she herself had recently been on it and could even make an appearance that very night! God knows how these things happen in the world of marketing research, but Faye, Clive and the kids had been contacted by an advertising agency to ask if they would appear in some new TV advertisements for a leading brand of breakfast cereal! Although the money offered wasn't as substantial as you might imagine, it was nonetheless exciting, and the kids could hardly contain themselves at the thought of being on the telly.

Although many would say that the importance of a traditional family life was declining, back in the early 2000's families were still popular in TV advertising – retro families sitting down at the table for breakfast together. Apparently, people hankered for 'the good old days' and family life was a rich source of imagery for the ad industry. Cereals were moving away from sugary, high fat products to more health-conscious cereals. So, Faye and Clive fit the bill perfectly; a medical couple with three healthy kids with the visual twist of ginger hair, living in a beautiful house in a respectable suburb – they practically made the ad themselves!

Faye had initially thought it was great fun and had told the girls when their advertisements were due to air. *The Alphabetties* all dutifully watched the relevant channel at the allotted time and laughed at how bizarre it was to see the

Rogers family on the gogglebox! But Faye did say how quickly the novelty had worn off as, even the miniscule amount of fame they unexpectedly found from being in the cereal commercial, had become annoying very quickly – people really do just come up to you, regardless of what you are doing, who you are with and where you are, point and say, "you're in that advert on the TV!". Faye had a taste of what it must have been like for Lynda Bellingham in the OXO ads and had thanked the Lord that she hadn't turned into "Britain's Favourite Mum"!

⬜⬜Ⅱ𝔵⬜⬜⬜⬜∩⬜…⸱⸱⸱∶⸱⸱˙˙⸱.⬜∵.⬜⬜⬜∪⬜⬜⬜⬜⬜

After tearing themselves away from Saturday night TV, the girls enjoyed their last night in Kinsale finally managing to find the lilting Irish brogue they'd longed to hear all weekend, courtesy of a large stag do. They'd struck up some friendly banter with the future groom and his friends in a pub where there had been live music and the Guinness had been flowing – Saturday night was clearly the night to be in Kinsale. However, once the live entertainment finished, their chosen venue had emptied somewhat and quietened down and not surprisingly the stag do and lilting accents had left too. But by then the gang had a sofa and a couple of comfy armchairs and were very reluctant to move. So, more wine was ordered and when there was a lull in the conversation Maggie had made an announcement.

⬜⬜Ⅱ𝔵⬜⬜⬜⬜∩⬜…⸱⸱⸱∶⸱⸱˙˙⸱.⬜∵.⬜⬜⬜∪⬜⬜⬜⬜⬜

She reminded them of how she had fallen into an unofficial counsellor role at work on the maternity ward. Although she had found this daunting at first, as time had gone on it was becoming more and more the reason she went to work – she was finding the physical side of midwifery less interesting, and she was increasingly drawn to trying to understand the emotional and psychological effects of birth and its related complexities.

She had become so fascinated by this aspect of her work that she had taken another life changing decision and enrolled to do a part time MA in Clinical Counselling back at university. She had pored over the logistics of making this move for months. The course had a modular structure delivered over three years on a part-time basis with just one full day a week on campus. Unbelievably her girls were now twelve and eleven and although still a handful she felt they could cope with her taking on this enterprise. The three of them were very close and could look after and out for each other.

Maggie's Dad had now pretty much retired from the family company and handed over the reins to Shane. Shane was a natural at the business, supplying mechanical parts around the world and making the best deal for his customers. Their website said, "communication is key to our success" and Shane certainly had the gift of the gab to secure contracts and deliver the goods. Zoe had in the past laughed to herself that he would probably make a good drug or arms dealer – she hadn't mentioned this thought to Maggie though! Shane also had more time to travel and build up personal customer/supplier relationships since he had employed a 'Woman Friday'. Sandra had been working at the company for a few months and had proved herself a great asset already, essentially working as Shane's PA taking up some of the home-based work to allow him to focus on customer service and client liaison.

So, Maggie thought overall this was a good time to change her life path. She'd handed in her notice at the hospital and was signed up to the National Health Service Professionals to do bank shifts. This would allow her to still earn a reasonable wage whilst giving her flexibility to work on her studies. Nonetheless she was still feeling somewhat anxious and full of trepidation at making this move. But to *The Alphabetties* it had come as no surprise that she had flown through her assessment interview and suitability checks and was embarking on more studies. Over the years of their friendship, they had all come to see that she would make an excellent counsellor.

Maggie had empathy and understanding in bucket loads and her manner was such that she always managed to set people at ease. In fact, sometimes the girls found themselves confiding things to Maggie that they thought were secrets they'd take to the grave! They would all have to stay friends with Maggie as she knew too much – although she didn't have a spiteful bone in her body so would never tell whatever happened. She also had a great sense of humour which they reckoned would help see her through what wasn't going to be an easy career move she'd need to stay strong. But she had thought long and hard about the pros and cons – emotional demands, long hours, difficulties of setting up your own practice versus job satisfaction, multiple career opportunities, flexibility and good pay. But the pros had won, and despite the potential hurdles she was ripe for the challenge!

☐☐⨅⅄☐☐☐☐∏☐…⋯∶.⋅˙˙.☐∵☐☐☐⨆☐☐☐☐☐

Like all the *Tour* weekends, K for Kinsale had come and gone in what seemed like the blink of an eye. The next morning the Jamaican Irish taxi driver had managed to find them and had deposited them at Cork airport where there were no delays or hitches, and they were all soon back in Manchester.

On returning home Zoe had received an email in response to something *Alphabet Tour* related she had done several months ago.

□□⊔ⱦ□□□□∩□……⋯⋮.⋅⋅⋅.□⋰□□□⊔□□□□□

Given the number of individuals who had now expressed their admiration at how far the girls had reached through the alphabet, Zoe had thought maybe even more people would like to hear about their exploits. So, she took it upon herself to write to her then favourite magazine – which is sadly no longer in existence. She had penned an email explaining who the girls were, how they'd met, what they were up to and how far they had been and sent it off to the features editor as listed in the magazine. And she'd heard nothing back – she had thought it was a long shot and left it at that. Until that was, she came back from Kinsale.

She'd opened her emails and there was a message from a journalist at the magazine. The message explained that they were running a feature on women's friendship groups and Zoe's email, which had been archived, fit the bill of what they were looking for. She asked Zoe to contact her to arrange a phone call to discuss the possibility of them appearing in the feature and what it would entail. Zoe screamed out loud at reading this – so loud Frank appeared in the study door to see what was going on. She immediately contacted *The Alphabetties* who all responded in a similar fashion to the news – maybe even more so as she hadn't mentioned to them that she'd contacted the magazine. She hadn't wanted to build up any false excitement.

Subsequently Zoe replied and a phone call was arranged for a few days hence. When she spoke to the journalist it turned out she was a local girl, which was one of the reasons she had been drawn to Zoe's message. She said how great she thought their friendship group was, where it had originated and how it had grown into *The Alphabet Tour.* She said several groups were being considered but for the reasons just mentioned this group looked promising. She explained that if they were selected, they would need to come to London for a photo shoot and asked if this would be a problem – Zoe categorically answered on behalf of her group that this would be absolutely fine! The journalist chatted some more asking about how things were in her old stomping ground and then asked if Zoe could send some recent photos of the group of friends for her editor to look at. Zoe could hardly contain herself and said that wouldn't be a problem. A gathering was immediately organised at Maggie's and Shane was roped in to take photos.

Given the connection with the journalist to South Manchester and the banter that Zoe had shared with her, the girls were very hopeful and giddily discussed what a photo shoot in London would involve. Things then went quiet for many days with nothing appearing from the magazine in Zoe's inbox. But she guessed no news was good news and things take time in the world of publishing. When she eventually received an email, she eagerly opened it expecting tickets to London to be an attachment. But she and the girls were to be disappointed.

The journalist explained that she thought they had been a very strong contender to feature in the magazine. However, they had lost out to a group of school friends who had supported a girl through a long illness and one of them had given her their kidney – FFS! She explained that on balance, not surprisingly, her editor had gone with this group and thanked *The Alphabet Tour* for their story and enthusiasm.

The Alphabetties were gracious in defeat – well after swearing a lot and repeating in many different ways how the hell were they meant to compete with sharing your organs. There was also much debate as to whether in fact the rival group's story was true. But Zoe didn't think people were that desperate to appear in a women's magazine with a then dwindling circulation! Still, they had enjoyed it while it lasted, planning their few moments of fame.

What's more they all knew that *The Alphabet Tour* would keep them friends for life which is very special – even if the magazine didn't think so! And of course, they would give each other a kidney, or any other organ they could if need be. Although Zoe did think that, knowing the girls for as long as she had, an *Alphabettie* liver might be a dodgy option!

Chapter 14

L for Long Boat

"Friends are the sailors who guide your rickety boat safely across the dangerous waters of life."
Sare and Cate

Some of life between tours.

Kitty and Eric starred as lead roles in the school production of *Robin Hood.* This casting had been a sign to all their relatives that they were destined to be future sweethearts! This was an ongoing belief for many years to come much to their annoyance..

Noah, Eric and Kitty all started different senior schools – although Eric had managed to go to the same school as his sister!

Frank turned fifty and celebrated with a great 'Black & White' party in recognition of his Geordie heritage.

Sally was asked to speak at an international conference on the changing role of women in the IT sector. She was very nervous but feedback following her lecture implied there were going to be a lot more empowered women in the computer based world from then on!

Eric, like most of the *Alphabet* children got a mobile phone for his eleventh birthday in readiness for senior school.

Holly had to have five baby teeth removed to allow her to have braces fitted. She was extremely brave unlike her mother who had to get Frank to take her to the dentist for the procedure!

As Zoe sat down to recollect the antics of this year's *Alphabet Tour*, she was strangely filled with excitement. She reckoned that this was because she would be writing about the most intrepid adventure the girls had embarked on so far - and indeed the most tenuous. C for Champagne had been a little left of centre, and although I for Iberian Peninsula was geographically correct it had been pushing it! But that year L for 'long boat' was really stretching a point.

However, in 2009 the state of the British Economy had not been great. The country was in the deepest recession since World War II, unemployment was at 10%, the stock market had plummeted, the housing bubble of 2007/2008 had collapsed and on average house prices had dropped by 15%. Everyone had felt the credit crunch including *The Alphabetties,* who having to cope with the cost of growing families, had made an executive decision to stay in the UK that year. And Maggie's timeshare company had once again come up trumps and had offered a fabulous deal on a canal or long boat. Actually a long boat is a ship the Vikings arrived in to slaughter our ancestors, but the girls weren't that pedantic – it was a boat, and it was long!

☐☐Ⱡ⅄☐☐☐☐⋒☐…⋯⋮.⋅˙˙⋅.☐∵☐☐☐∪☐☐☐☐☐

Bizarrely though, despite the economic downturn, at that time, Kate had found herself in a new situation at work. She had by now been at the insurance company for nearly four years and as had been predicted by her friends and family, she had well and truly made herself indispensable. She knew the workings of the company inside and out and her boss relied heavily on her skill set and dedication.

So, it came as a complete bolt from the blue when her boss had announced he was retiring and was in the process of selling the company. Initially Kate was surprised that she hadn't clocked on to the fact this announcement was coming. Then she was cross that he hadn't confided in her and sought her advice. Then she was perturbed about her future and her job which although she complained, was now somewhat predictable and not as challenging as she would like, she found herself eating her words now this proposal had come about. To be honest she really didn't like change, certainly not change she hadn't instigated and could not control.

It transpired that Wayne, Kate's boss, had entered initial talks some months ago with a wealth management firm, before the recession had got a firm grip on the country, with a possible view to them acquiring his company. Despite the recession, negotiations were well underway by the time the staff of the small insurance brokers, including Kate were informed. Wayne was very keen to retire and given the uncertainty of how long the recession would last, wanted to sell his business as quickly as possible and whilst it was still an attractive proposition. The firm he was dealing with wanted to take advantage of the benefits of buying a company during an economic downturn – fewer competitors, lower purchase price and cheaper assets. But Wayne was a good and indeed shrewd employer and wasn't going to let his staff down and wanted to maximise his assets and get the best price for his business – apart from anything he wanted to retire in a fairly high level of comfort. So, talks were still underway.

As a result, Kate now found herself dealing with a large firm from London who, in a process of "creating prosperity for the generations of tomorrow" bought up smaller companies, like the one she had so devotedly worked for and took over their clients and business. As the mediation went along, she was increasingly feeling like a small fish in a very big pond, her role within the potential new company deteriorating if not slipping away altogether. She didn't like the situation one little bit and had decided to set her mind and expertise to doing something about it!

□□⊔⋏□□□□∩…⋯∶.˙˙.□∵□□□⊔□□□□□

Maggie had not only provided the means for this year's tour to take place but had then, very nobly, offered to drive to the boat and the girls had travelled very comfortably in one of her family business's fleet of Mercedes! The destination had been somewhere in Nottinghamshire and with the aid of sat nav had proved relatively easy to find. Although upon first arriving the girls had been a little tentative, as first impressions were that the home of their boat appeared to be a couple of mobile huts and a large car park lurking in the shadow of several large cooling towers.

Once the formalities were over with and the girls had signed their lives away in one of the mobile huts to ensure the boat was returned, they had been directed towards the marina. And what a marina it had turned out to be. If you were a canal boat this was clearly the place to be. Somehow hidden behind the mobile huts were hundreds, nay thousands of canal boats all prettily painted and covered in flower boxes and watering cans all stretched out as far as their eyes could see. The girls had thought that obviously if you owned a canal boat this was where you had to be seen, this was barge central!

□□⊔⋏□□□□∩…⋯∶.˙˙.□∵□□□⊔□□□□□

Since the last *Alphabet Tour,* Maggie had had a mixed year. She'd started, and was loving, her MA course in Clinical Counselling. She relished the people centred approach to counselling and was already looking forward to her practice placement. Being on 'the bank' and the part- time nature of the course gave her the flexibility to handle work, study and look after her precious girls and Shane. She knew she had made the right decision and had been relishing what life was throwing at her.

Then sadly her father died. He had been the driving force of her family, hard but fair, a gentleman who took no nonsense. He had built up their business from scratch and just as he was able to sit back and enjoy the fruits of his labours, knowing the company was in Shane's strong hands, he had become very ill and died in a matter of weeks. Maggie had been key to ensuring he was cared for and looking after her mother who had to a great extent gone to pieces. As he always did Shane had stepped up, running the business and helping Maggie with her parents. Maggie's mum, who had never been overly affection towards her own children, really loved Shane and so he and Maggie worked as a team to ensure all the logistics of the death of a parent were dealt with, whilst explaining to and caring for Scarlet, Jennifer and Samantha. Luckily at work Shane could now rely on Sandra, who, over the last few months had proved herself invaluable, learning quickly and stepping up whenever needed. In fact Sandra was now more than a colleague but a friend to the whole family. Between them they had got through one of life's traumatic events, but it had been hard - Maggie loved her father deeply.

□□⨅⚡□□□□⌒□……⸱⸱⸳⸱⸱˙˙⸱.□⸱⸱□□□⨆□□□□□

Before leaving the hut, the girls had been told that their boat wouldn't be ready for a while and that they could walk to the other side of the marina to visit the restaurant for lunch. This the girls had done, taking in the ambience of canal life as they'd wound their way through the boats and over bridges to the marina refreshment complex. The restaurant had not looked great and unsurprisingly had been decorated with canal and barge paraphernalia. But unperturbed by the decor the girls had ordered hot beef sandwiches from the rather surly barman and of course their first drink of the weekend. The sandwiches, although Neanderthal in their size and presentation, had turned out to be mighty tasty and had been devoured with relish – well horseradish actually – and in a manner that had befitted their appearance.

After lunch the girls had been instructed that they could board the boat which in this vast marina had been some distance away. This meant they had to load their bags onto a large trolley and navigate said trolley down a long, quite narrow jetty to their craft. Their prowess at this task hadn't boded well for the trip ahead but eventually all the bags had been safely deposited on the boat. The company who owned the craft that would be their home for the next couple of days, had several boats in the marina with witty names like 'Knot so Fast', 'Soggy Bottom' and 'Moor Often than Knot'. Clearly someone at the boat yard had a dreadful sense of humour and loved a terrible pun. *The Alphabetties's* boat had been called 'Cor Blimey!' which on the whole they'd thought wasn't too bad given the selection of names on offer.

Once on the boat a very jolly chap who bore an uncanny resemblance to Captain Pugwash with greasy black hair, large joules and belly and an impressive black moustache, had welcomed the girls. Captain Pugwash had been tasked with explaining to them how the barge worked. Zoe had vaguely remembered what he was saying from her earlier trip on the canals that year with her South African relatives. However, on that occasion she had been more below decks preparing food and gin and tonic rather than anything topside.

Zoe's sister had come over to England a few months earlier with her husband Paddy, and their middle daughter Lucy, her husband Nolan and their two daughters Peyton and Eden. Rich and his youngest Tim had also come along with Zoe, Frank, Holly and Eric and they'd had all set sail on a huge narrow boat on the Cheshire Ring not far from South Manchester. Paddy had always wanted to have a holiday on a canal boat and he threw himself into his duties as captain and was very possessive of the rudder – mind you he had paid for the trip for them all so nobody was complaining.

The weather had been kind, so they'd had a really lovely time despite being on top of each other for the four day trip. The kids had played well together and were proper little canal urchins running along the top of the sizeable boat and jumping on and off at locks with no fear. The adults, including Tim who was now in his early twenties enjoyed sipping beer and wine as they leisurely made their way along the canal. They'd stopped for barbeques in the evening and then retired to the boat for board games before the kids went to bed and the adults caught up with each other's lives.

One night there had been a particularly memorable game of Scrabble. Given there were twelve of them they had split up into teams and Tim had partnered Holly. As the teams were of mixed ages and abilities a lot of the words put down during the game were not that impressive. However, on one round when it came to Tim and Holly's turn there was a long pause. Holly at this stage was eleven so had a reasonable vocabulary but nothing high scoring had come from her team. But Tim was sitting with a wry smile on his face which prompted the question:

"Tim why are you grinning inanely – what are you offering?"

He replied:

"We've got an unusual word which will give us a great score but I'm not sure it's appropriate for Holly's cousin to put this word down on their turn?"

Holly just looked blank, not having any idea of the word he had formed from their letters. The other grown-ups, having had a few beers by this point egged him on and agreed it couldn't be that bad.

So, Tim went ahead and put down his high scoring word:

V A G I N A appeared on the board

To which Rich announced:

"It's not every day you see a vagina on a canal boat dining table!"

A memorable word indeed made even more so as it straddled a triple word score bringing Tim and Holly 30 points! It clearly evoked much laughter especially from the kids who thought it was hysterical. After she stopped laughing Zoe had to say she was impressed with her children's, especially Eric's, anatomical knowledge – but she guessed that they probably referred to this body part as something else amongst their peers! At that moment she also looked around and thought how wonderful it was to be with her siblings. It was rare when they were all together and Zoe realised how much she missed being with them both.

⬜⬜Ⅱ𝔵⬜⬜⬜∩⬜…⋯⋮.·˙˙.⬜⋰⬜⬜⬜∪⬜⬜⬜⬜⬜

The girls had felt the training they had received for taking command of their canal vessel had been rather hit and miss. Captain Pugwash had left them merely saying:

"This video will explain everything you need to know about operating this boat girls. Pay careful attention and if you have any questions, I shall be back shortly to get you underway."

All very casual considering he was about to hand over a 50-foot-long vessel to a group of women who clearly didn't look like they had any experience of inland waterways! So, with good intentions the girls had sat down to watch, what had turned out to be a lengthy video on how to behave on the canals, how locks worked, the ways of water folk etc. After concentrating on this for nearly 2-3 minutes the girls had decided this was an ideal opportunity to sneak in a few drinkies before being let loose on the water. After this the video had seemed much more entertaining and the girls had sworn to the jolly boatman on his return that they had understood and processed every detail.

Having been told this, despite the number of empty glasses by then on display, remarkably he had seemed happy to let them take charge of a boat on the canal. Luckily, he had taken the boat out of the marina for them and on to the open canal. Otherwise, the girls were pretty sure there would have been a trail of carnage and destruction left behind them as they tried to exit the maze-like marina!

Once underway and on the right side of the canal the girls had all taken turns at the tiller and throttle with varying degrees of competence. It had been quite amazing how quickly the demarcation of roles on the boat had evolved, especially after they had navigated their first lock. The first lock had proved to be a bit tricky as the girls had forgotten to undo a rope at a critical point in the proceedings and had nearly ended up with a canal boat suspended in mid-air halfway up the side of the lock. But once the hysteria and laughing had stopped, and some quick thinking had been applied by Sally, the boat had been released! Luckily Sally had also experienced the canals before and seemed to have retained more useful knowledge than Zoe. Sally had taken control of the chaos without any argument from her companions. From that moment on she had become Captain of their vessel with the support of Deck Officers Faye and Zoe, and Maggie and Kate been chief machinery operators both on canal side and below decks.

⬜⬜⊔⅄⬜⬜⬜⬜∩⬜......⋮.·¨·.⬜∵⬜⬜⬜⊔⬜⬜⬜⬜

Sally's ability to step up as 'Commander in Chief' that weekend reflected how she was now feeling in general about her life. After her divorce having taken what seemed like forever to sort out, she was back in control of her destiny. It had been three years since she had broken the news to *The Alphabet Tour* that she and Gabriel were splitting up and since that point things had conspired to make the divorce process limp along.

There had been no problem in the beginning establishing grounds for their divorce. Of the options they could cite at that time – adultery, unreasonable behaviour, desertion or living apart – unreasonable behaviour was the one Sally had opted for. Unreasonable behaviour is the common choice as it applies to any behaviour as a result of which "you can no longer bear to live with your spouse". That pretty much nailed how Sally had felt. And so, they started down their path towards joining the 33.3% of marriages that end in divorce.

The process hadn't got off to a lightning start as Gabe took his time completing the matrimonial order – the decree for divorce. Initially this was fuelled by him just being disorganised but also coupled with some degree of reluctance and bitterness. However, eventually he came to realise the inevitability of things and they had filed a joint application for divorce and the court recognised their marriage had broken down irretrievably – although Gabe probably did still hold a thread of hope at this point. There were delays with the court processing their application but eventually their Decree Nisi was issued stating that the grounds of divorce had been established and the legal requirements had all been met. Sally and Gabe then had to get a financial and legal agreement in place before they could move towards a final divorce date – this opened up a whole can of worms.

As a couple they had to discuss what would be best for them and more importantly their girls. Sally had been the main breadwinner in their household so she was rightfully on her guard to ensure she wasn't fleeced through the course of this process. This was particularly as she knew she had no intention of remarrying but had always suspected Gabe might as she found it hard to picture him coping with life on his own. After what seemed like eons and forests of letters from lawyers spent haggling over pensions, tax consequences and restrictions to future financial claims, an agreement had been reached and they were able to apply for the Decree Absolute. Once again there had been some court delays but earlier that year they had been granted a divorce – Sally and Gabe were no longer married and after all these months and months Sally had moved on past any regret and had finally felt liberated.

□□⊔⅄□□□□⋒□……∴.˙˙·.□∵·□□□⊔□□□□□

By the end of the trip the girls had been working like a well-oiled machine and had been jumping on and off the boat like old hands and gliding in and out of locks without touching the sides. But before that there had been numerous occasions when they had incurred the wrath of the serious canal folk. Bizarrely this had been particularly from the women who had quite openly tutted in their general direction and thrown them venomous dirty looks.

Nonetheless the intrepid group had made it to the first canalside pub where they moored up and set to organising the sleeping arrangements for their weekend. That year Maggie, aka Dobby has been privileged enough to share a twin room with Sally as Faye had been more than happy to sleep in the living area. This had been due to the rather coffin like beds, their close proximity to each other and Faye's mild but definite claustrophobia. This meant that once again Zoe and Kate had been sleeping together, this time in the double room at the pointy front bit of the boat. As they'd wiggled their way down the length of the vessel, they'd been filled with trepidation expecting their quarters to be snug to say the least. How wrong could they have been! As they'd reached the tip, the boat opened out like a Tardis into what was for a canal boat, a luxurious room with a bed that went right across its full width with wall mounted lights and numerous pillows, set back into an alcove with matching bedside tables! It had looked just like a set from a soft porn film – even more so when music from the ships radio got piped in through the ceiling! Frank and Max would have been in heaven just imagining their girls together in this salacious canal boat bed. Zoe instantly went to thinking about names for the porn film in which this bedroom would feature and the best she could come up with was *Carnal Boat Capers*. But despite the X rated movie vibe of the room, Zoe and Kate had been pleased as this was, by far the biggest bed they had ever shared, and they considered that they'd struck lucky on this occasion.

Once refreshed and changed the gang headed towards a local Indian restaurant recommended by a fellow canal goer, only a short walk away – but which had involved a precarious traverse across a lock gate and wandering around the local village for a while which didn't seem to have a centre. Once they'd found the restaurant, the place had proved very popular, and the girls had been concerned that they wouldn't get a table for quite some time. Still, they were in no hurry, and they went in, were shown to a waiting area and were given menus to peruse.

After only a fleeting moment Faye had spotted that Bollinger was available on the wine list and she called over a waiter. She announced, "This will be my treat girls, no arguments!"

Then she told the waiter that she would like a bottle of Bollinger bringing over as quickly as he could. At this request the waiter looked a little flummoxed as if Faye had said something so shocking that he couldn't process it. However, the manager who had just happened to be passing the waiting area, had heard, and completely understood Faye's request. He appeared next to the blithering waiter like the fancy dress shop owner materialising in an episode of *Mr Benn*! The manager swiftly took control, clicking his fingers at other staff, who leapt to it and managed to find them a table, clear it and reset it and have Faye's bottle of Bollinger in an ice bucket next to it in a matter of minutes! The manager ensured that the girls received excellent service and his full attention for the rest of the evening. Once their glasses were charged Sally raised a toast:

"To the remarkable powers of champagne and Faye's staggering ability to use it to her and her friends' best advantage. God bless her!"

The following day, the girls had awoke to the sound of ducks quacking and canal boats passing by. Zoe had found it very disconcerting to see ducks swimming past the bedroom window and it had taken her brain several moments to get orientated that morning – the Bollinger may have also been a factor in her confusion. It seemed that life on the canal started early. Faye, who often woke at what her fellow shipmates considered an ungodly hour, had switched on the radio and piped Saturday morning radio down the length of the boat.

□□⫪𝔁□□□□⋔□…⋯∶.·⁘·.□∵□□□∪□□□□□

Faye was in fact a bit of an insomniac and often only slept a couple of hours a night. Recently whilst lying awake in the small hours her thoughts had turned to her career and how she was doing professionally - in particular her time at the charitable clinic. She had no regrets whatsoever about taking on the voluntary work. The relationships she had built up there with both clients and colleagues she had found immensely satisfying – providing eye care for vulnerable people she considered more rewarding than recommending the latest designer brand frames for the near perfectly sighted. However, she was spending more and more time thinking about one relationship that had grown from here – her friendship with Bridget. Over the last couple of years, she had come to know Bridget really well – or she thought she had. They regularly had drinks or lunch together and Bridget had, on a couple of occasions, come to Faye and Clive's home for dinner – although Bridget had never invited Faye to her home. Faye assumed this was because her Mum's condition made it difficult, and she didn't question Bridget on this.

But recently for some reason she couldn't pinpoint, her 'spider senses' were tingling again when she spent time with Bridget, a feeling of apprehension that she had experienced in the past when Bridget spoke of her homelife had reared its head again. Faye just felt uneasy about her and being Faye, she had noticed a few other things had changed. Bridget's appearance had been upgraded, she was definitely wearing more designer labels many of which Faye admired and she seemed to be socialising a great deal more with people outside of work and the charity. Also Faye realised

Bridget very rarely said anything about her mum nowadays and was vague when Faye inquired how her mum was doing. Bridget was becoming increasingly invaluable to the clinic and Faye probably had to admit she relied on her too heavily to run the financial and legal side of things. This reliance combined with the other changes to Bridget were making Faye increasingly uneasy. Or was she just being stupid, surely Bridget deserved a few of the nicer things in life and to forget about her troubles when she was with her friends. But Faye still told herself to be more vigilant both at and away from the clinic.

⬜⬜⎍⚶⬜⬜⬜⬜⋔⬜…⋯∶.⸳⋅⋅.⬜∵⬜⬜⬜⎍⬜⬜⬜⬜

Once they had stirred themselves, the girls got to grips with getting underway and had managed to successfully use the barge poles to push themselves off the bank without leaving anyone behind or anyone ending up face down in the water! They'd tootled along quite happily in the sunshine, sipped coffee and enjoyed idle chit chat until inevitably they'd come across the next lock of the day. It had been here that they'd run into (not literally but close!) an older couple who had turned out to be their nemesis! For some reason unbeknown to them this rather grumpy couple of hardened canal folk had taken an instant dislike to the girls and thought they had no right to be on the canal at all, never mind in charge of a boat! Clearly these canal folk made instant decisions, judging books by their covers. *The Alphabetties* hadn't looked like typical long boat owners – whatever that might be – with shorts, vest tops, Faye's espadrille high wedges and Raybans. Of course, the girls considered that the waterways of Great Britain should be welcome to all. But they had suspected the grumpy couple had been staunch Conservatives, who hated the youth of today, wanted out of the EU and certainly wouldn't welcome newcomers to this very British activity!

However, despite the negative vibe emanating from the grumpy boat, the girls had pressed on regardless and entered the lock alongside the odd couple. The woman clearly hadn't been happy about this and had spent her brief encounter with the girls telling them what they shouldn't do on the canal in a superior, unhelpful kind of way. The bloke, although looking unpleasant, was just about civil and had given the girls a couple of useful pointers – much to the fury of his spouse. Zoe may have made it up, but she seemed to recall, the grumpy couple had a big, ugly dog on board too - but she couldn't swear that this fact hadn't been her imagination elaborating the scheme for effect!

⬚⬚Ⅱ𝔁⬚⬚⬚⬚∩⬚…⋯⋮.·¨·.⬚∵⬚⬚⬚Ս⬚⬚⬚⬚

Another thing that Zoe had hoped was in her imagination but sadly wasn't, was the deterioration of her relationship with Frank. Increasingly she was finding him, the kids and life in general irritating – but mainly Frank. More and more she found herself getting irrationally angry with him and wanting to spend time away from him rather than together, the way a marriage should be. Her family was the most important thing to her in the world and the thought of it falling apart was almost inconceivable to her but still she couldn't control her growing feelings of resentment towards Frank – she just found him aggravating no matter what he did or said.

The last few months had been particularly stressful mainly because the local authority she worked for was merging to become a unitary authority with several other adjoining councils. Colleagues were losing their jobs or been reassigned to other roles, people were leaving before they were pushed, teams were moving offices, new officers were in charge, and everything was just very unsettling. An atmosphere of 'us and them' prevailed at work as people from the different councils were all thrown together and expected to smoothly transition into a perfectly functioning unit - clearly this wasn't happening and staff, councillors, customers, general members of the public and anyone working with the new authority weren't happy. All this plus Zoe still had a long commute and family life to sort out on her return home.

What's more in a few months Holly would be moving up to senior school and there was constant talk outside the school gates about which school the kids would be going to and the need to get your child tutored to pass the Eleven Plus and entrance exams. Thankfully, despite them clashing on just about everything at the moment, Zoe and Frank were on the same page about this and neither of them was elitist about which school Holly or Eric went to. Obviously, they wanted their children to reach their full potential, but they wanted them to be happy doing it. Frank and Zoe had let Holly decide if she wanted to take the entrance exam for the local grammar school. She said she would – all her friends were, and she was a clever girl. Frank and Zoe really didn't think a single sex school would suit her but gave her their full support – and they couldn't help themselves, they succumbed to getting her a little bit of tutoring to prepare her for the nature of the exam. This was unlike many parents and even schools in the area who had been tutoring children pretty much since nursery to pass these exams parrot fashion. Although Zoe and Frank believed children should be rewarded on their own merits, their school catchment area was not an even playing field and they too had to call on a couple of performance enhancing tricks.

Although desperate not to get sucked in to all this nonsense – none of the schools in their area were bad and the local school around the corner from where they lived had a great reputation – Zoe couldn't help getting neurotic. This was mainly down to the hysteria generated by other mothers who seemed to get off on instilling panic. Zoe had met one particularly obsessed mum whilst food shopping. Zoe couldn't escape as she only spotted her once she was well over halfway down the freezer aisle and had unfortunately made eye contact. They had exchanged a pleasant hello with the usual inane comments "Here we are again", "they never stop eating". But then the obsessive mum had said:

"What will you do if Holly doesn't manage it?"

Zoe was genuinely stumped and had no idea what she was referring to and wondered what massive responsibility Holly had been given but had failed to tell her about. All of this must have clearly shown in Zoe's face, as obsessive mum then pressed on, stepping right up close and speaking in an almost whisper:

"You know if Holly doesn't get into the grammar school? I can't sleep worrying about Naomi".

When the penny dropped, Zoe exclaimed:

"Oh that, well she'll go to Teddington Road School and really that would be for the best, make our lives a lot easier as it's so handy. Holly will do her best wherever she goes".

Then Zoe just smiled and breezed off casually. Honestly, from the look on the woman's face you'd have thought Zoe had told her to fuck off and mind her own business! The obsessed mum was clearly very uptight and had been expecting a long conversation about verbal and non-verbal reasoning and how unfair it is that so many foreign students get a place at 'our' local grammar school. As she walked away, Zoe had also remembered that she'd heard gossip from a supposed friend of this woman. Apparently on a night out with other school mums many months prior, the obsessive mum had got pretty tiddled and revealed she ironed her knickers and had never given her husband a blow job! The woman really did need to loosen up and Zoe's sympathy went out to poor Naomi – and Naomi's dad!

⬚⬚Ⅱ⅄⬚⬚⬚⬚∩⬚…⋅⋅⋅∶⋅⋅⁚⋅⬚∵⬚⬚⬚∪⬚⬚⬚⬚

After they had escaped from the lock and the ugly, grumpy couple, the gang plodded on down the canal – nobody goes fast on the canal, the maximum speed limit is 4 mph! That day the weather had turned out to be glorious and as lunchtime approached the girls had decided G&Ts were in order. Galley maid Kate was thus dispatched below decks where she'd rustled up some drinks and very soon the girls had been toasting the success of their trip so far.

However, this success had been short lived. Despite being long and on the whole straight, canals can still pull tricks on you and as the girls had tried to negotiate around a slight bend without spilling their gin, they'd somehow managed to get the boat struck on a sandbank which of course was surrounded by nettles and in close proximity to a herd of curious cows! Maggie had taken a brief turn at the steering wheel at this point and was profusely apologetic about their predicament – although she stressed that she'd pointed out earlier that such an event would be a distinct possibility with her in charge of navigation!

After an initial panic involving hysterical screaming and copious expletives, the girls took a big swig of gin and tried to compose themselves. However, regaining their calm had been hampered somewhat by the increasing speed the cows, of which there had been many, had approached the girls.

Cows, for the most part, are friendly, but can be dangerous. They are intelligent animals with an innate sense of curiosity, but they do not like to be surprised or startled by loud noises, they have a fear of the unknown and do not like change – bit like Kate really! The unexpected, noisy, arrival of *The Alphabetties* and their brightly coloured long boat into their field whilst quietly grazing had pretty much pushed all the buttons guaranteed to upset any nearby cows. Once up close to the, by then, stampeding cows, the girls realised that these animals are big – they can stand over six feet tall and weigh over 1200 lbs.

At this point, carrying on with the bovine theme, Sally had assertively taken the bull by the horns, shoved Maggie out of the way and slammed the long boat into reverse and ordered the rest of the crew to push down hard on the barge poles. Soon after the engine had been revved in reverse - perhaps a little more than it should have been judging by the cloud of diesel fumes that had appeared - and after much grunting and groaning and many nettle stings, the girls' team effort had freed them from the sandbank just as the charging cows had reached the water's edge!

Feeling relieved but duly proud of themselves and with Sally in charge, the gang had quickly moored up on the opposite cow free side of the canal to regain their composure. Here they had proceeded to celebrate with another drink and a nice lunch which comprised of a beautiful selection of cheeses Faye had brought along. This had all been very pleasant and once their heart rates had come down, the gang had chilled and felt confident that they could now handle whatever the waterways could throw at them. They'd had good food and drink, sunshine and great company - all that was missing had been music and a dance floor! When this thought had entered her head, Kate remembered she'd brought her MP3 player and had then proposed what seemed to her an obvious next move:

"Bloody hell girls the top of the boat makes a perfect dance floor!"

So, despite probably incurring the wrath of more canal folk the girls had all climbed on top of the boat and danced their hearts out to 1980s girl power hits – the canals of Nottinghamshire resonated to "What a feeling", "Girls just Wanna have Fun" and "She Works Hard for a Living". And as they were all "taking their passion and making it happen" guess who went sailing by – the grumpy couple had not been impressed!

□□⨇⨇λ□□□□∩□……∴.∙ˉ˙.□∴□□□∪□□□□

Kate had always been a person who lived life to the full and seized whatever opportunity had been available. She hated missing out on anything and would go to great lengths to try and make sure she didn't. But since the last *Alphabet Tour* her zest for life had been put on hold whilst she focussed on the life of her brother, Gareth. He had been diagnosed with cancer late the previous year and Kate's family had held their breath.

Like Kate, Gareth had always thrown himself into everything he did and had a good time along the way. Despite this meaning he nearly got thrown out of university he had managed by the skin of his teeth to qualify as a vet and now had his own local, highly reputable small animal practice. However, being a vet had never stopped him from enjoying a good steak and washing it down with a nice chianti. But this lifestyle may have been a contributory factor to his bowel cancer.

Kate cherished her brothers and was devastated by her eldest brother's illness and seeing the toll it took on him and his family. As is her way she needed to do something to help and had done all she could to support him. Although her frustration at not being able to do anything directly to ease his pain was tangible. But one thing she had done which eased her mind was research. She had spent many hours poring over medical websites investigating bowel cancer, its affects, and its usual prognosis. Comfortingly she had discovered that 53% of bowel cancer patients lived ten years or more after their diagnosis. Also, Gareth's cancer was Stage 2 which gave him a lot higher percentage chance of longer-term survival. Kate hated the term survival; she'd much rather have been reading cure but sadly that word didn't appear in her research.

Mercifully Kate's research had proved to be accurate. After a couple of operations and several rounds of treatment over the last few months, Gareth had proved what a fighter he was and not long before the latest *Alphabet* trip he had been told his cancer was in remission – it hadn't completely disappeared but "had significantly decreased" and his consultant was as confident as he could be that Gareth should continue on this path. So, Kate finally breathed out and had felt justified in letting her hair down and grabbing some fun when it was on offer.

□□⨇λ□□□□⋒…⸱⸱⸱⋮⸱⸱ ̈⸱ ̈⸱.□⸱⸫□□□⨆□□□□□

After the long boat roof disco had come to an end, the girls had needed to get serious for a minute as they had to work out how far they could keep going before they had to come back! They only had Sunday to get back from wherever they'd got to, and they had to find a place to turn to go back the way they had come - sadly there are very few circular routes on canals. After they'd considered the map supplied with the boat carefully and counted up locks, the girls had reckoned they could go on a bit further to a village where there appeared to be a pub and even a fish and chip shop if pushed.

They'd arrived at their appointed destination only to find it was a popular place to stop and it looked as though they were going to have to carry out some fancy turning and parking moves. In a rare moment of clarity, the girls had thought they would get the boat turned around so the next morning they could be underway as soon as they could. Once that task was completed, they would head for a mooring a little further back up the canal. Where they had decided to turn, the canal sort of widened out into a small bay like area which had allowed a three-point manoeuvre to be carried out. With Sally at the helm and everyone concentrating and doing exactly as instructed they'd turned hard into the wider area, praying they didn't get wedged across the canal or stuck on another sandbank and cause a major incident that would go down in canal folklore.

But with remarkable ease and skill on Sally's part, before you could say 'girls on tour' they'd nipped round and were coming up to the mooring. The girls now had to slide their craft gracefully into the space without crashing into the boats parked either side and knocking all their neighbours' possessions flying. Although this exercise had come with a certain amount of pressure the girls didn't even break a sweat and were by then dab hands at driving and mooring up. They didn't know the name of all the equipment, but they knew that they needed to bang the curly metal things and the straight metal things into the ground and tie the ropes around them nice and tight, so they didn't drift off in the night – and this they duly did.

⬜⬜Ⅱⅹ⬜⬜⬜∩⬜…⋯⋮.⋅¨⋅.⬜∵⬜⬜⬜∪⬜⬜⬜⬜⬜

That night wasn't a wild one given travelling along the canals is quintessentially a calm and tranquil activity, the length of which is, generally only peppered by the occasional country pub. But the girls made the most of it and listened with bated breath to Sally filling them in on her exploits over the last few months.

Unlike life on the canal Sally hadn't been hanging about now that she was divorced. Over the last three years her relationship with Mark had certainly moved on. Now unencumbered with guilt she had given in to her desire for this man and had actively made sure he knew it. It hadn't been too difficult as Mark felt the same way, his marriage having gone pretty much a similar route. He was now divorced and living close to the old family home which his wife had fought long and hard to retain for her and the kids.

Sally and Mark were by now regularly travelling up and down the country for romantic, sex filled weekends together and had planned a holiday sailing around the Greek Islands – another passion they shared. Passion certainly seemed to be at the forefront of their relationship at this stage and *The Alphabetties,* were vicariously reliving a new romance through Sally's escapades! They were all really happy for her but Zoe, and maybe the others, were jealous to a degree. Zoe couldn't help but think about the state of her marriage and ached for the thrill of a first kiss and the excitement of being the object to someone's unmitigated desire.

⬜⬜⊔⋋⬜⬜⬜⬜∩⬜…·⋯⋮.·˙˙·.⬜⋰⬜⬜⬜⊔⬜⬜⬜⬜

The next day the gang had once again been underway pretty damn early. The weather had been marvellous, and the girls had been raring to get under way and to ensure they got back to the marina for the allotted time. They soon found themselves whizzing along (well, as much as you can on a canal!) and were through a couple of locks before you knew it. They had also teamed up with another boat and become 'lock buddies'. This means that you try to keep together and go through locks as a pair in order to speed up the whole process and reduce waiting times.

Their 'lock buddies' had been a very nice couple who had seemed to pretty much spend all their free time on the canals and had masses of experience. Surprisingly this hadn't put them off teaming up with *The Alphabetties* and they had chatted happily as they'd waited for locks, gone through locks and left locks! However, during the course of the journey, the wife had quietly confessed to the girls that she didn't really enjoy canal life very much. Although the girls had certainly had fun on their current adventure, they had seen her point. The attractions of the canal life, they had all thought were limited to say the least and it was pretty much a given that none of them would be investing in their own long boat in the future! All the girls agreed that they liked life at a faster pace than 4mph – the average healthy 70-year-old human can walk 2.5 mph so would only be less than half an hour behind you, 4mph is the top speed of a hedgehog and a mouse can run at 8mph so it would get there twice as quickly running than if it had hitched a lift on your prettily painted long boat!

Chapter 15

M for Malaga

"Shared laughter creates a bond of
friendship."
W. Lee Grant

Some life that happened that year.

Holly, Francesca, Sophie, Charlie, Abi and Scarlett all got hysterical at a JLS concert.

Sadly the second of the Sloane Family's four cats died. Holly and Eric were very upset at the death of Vic, their black cat that loved to cuddle.

Shane had to cancel a business trip due to an ash cloud from a volcanic eruption in Iceland!

Scarlet became a prefect at her school and took her role very seriously - especially where her sisters were concerned!

Mark was introduced to Sally's mum, sister and brother. Although there were some reservations prior to the event, he was a hit and was welcomed on board.

Max & Frank shared their love of Punk music with a night out at Manchester Academy to see Stiff Little Fingers – recapturing their youth!

As Zoe started to write this year, she found it comforting that the girls were back on track alphabetically - Malaga does indeed begin with M. She just wished the rest of her life was heading in a similarly positive direction. But she knew recounting her latest adventure with her dear friends would help her mood. In fact, it had turned out that all the girls were particularly looking forward to the tour that year.

It was hard to believe that a random choice of destination had led five women on such an epic crusade as *The Alphabet Tour*. This year despite being on their thirteenth outing, and hence halfway through the alphabet, the group felt quite young as they'd joined the queue for their Costa del Sol flight. According to the Spanish Office of National Statistics there are nearly 300,000 Brits living in Spain of which 40% are over 65. From the people around them at the check-in desks it had seemed like an awful lot of these over 65 ex-pats had recently popped back home for a visit and were now heading back to hibernate in the Spanish sunshine. Obviously, Faye had immediately attracted the attention of one of the dapper old chaps and in typical fashion, through the medium of jolly banter, had found out his life history in explicit detail! This chap and his wife were actually very sweet and regular visitors to Malaga and had supplied the girls with some useful tips about where to go and the frequency of public transport. This couple still seemed blissfully happy together without a care in the world. Zoe found herself pondering if in fact that was the case and mused about what really went on behind the closed doors of a marriage that had lasted so long.

⬚⬚⊔⅄⬚⬚⬚⬚∩⬚…⋯∶.·⋯·.⬚∶·⬚⬚⬚⊔⬚⬚⬚⬚⬚

Zoe's marriage was undeniably heading towards a dark place. Communication between her and Frank basically consisted of the bare minimum required to ensure the kids were OK and any essential information relating to running the house and getting through the day. Anything else usually ended in an argument and often involved the exchange of hurtful abuse. Until now Zoe and Frank had told each other everything and made each other laugh on a very regular basis. Now for no reason at all, whatever Frank did, however minor, just irritated Zoe and she was pretty sure this feeling was mutual. Zoe longed for the days when she and Frank were courting, when she couldn't wait to see him and tell him every single detail about her day and fall into bed with him and be as close as they possibly could. Now they hardly looked at each other let alone touched and hadn't made love or had any kind of intimacy for months.

Thankfully the school holidays had brought some relief from the downward spiral they seemed to be in. Kate had asked Zoe if she and the kids would like to join her and her brood plus her parents, at a friend's holiday home in North Wales. Zoe had nearly bitten her hand off and was relieved to get away from home for a while. Frank and Max had dropped them off and stayed for the weekend whilst the girls stayed with the kids and the grandparents for the whole week. The plan was for the men to come back the following weekend and pick them all up.

Kate's friend had said many times that she was welcome to use her holiday place and, never one to look a gift horse in the mouth, Kate had finally taken her up on the offer. It wasn't a huge place, so the kids all slept in a tent in the garden which they loved. But the location of the bungalow was amazing, just a couple of minutes from the beach.

They had just about made it through the weekend being civil to one another, but once Frank had gone back to work and she didn't have to bite her lip and keep up appearances, Zoe could relax. Walking on the beach, playing with the kids and sipping wine with her best friend was just what she needed. Obviously, Kate knew there was a problem between Zoe and Frank. However, she didn't raise the subject unless Zoe wanted to talk, she was just there for her friend. The week had flown by with adventures in the Welsh hills, picnics on the sand and no worries. Then the men came back.

Frank and Max arrived on Friday night. After her week to emotionally detox Zoe thought maybe things would be good again with her man. But almost as soon as he set foot through the door, she could feel her body tense, her chest tighten and all the good the sea air had done just evaporated. Kate had prepared a fabulous dinner and had rearranged furniture so that everyone could sit together to enjoy the feast. Frank started to knock back beers at quite a rate which annoyed Zoe. Then Frank ate his dinner just using his fork which annoyed Zoe. Then Frank kept interrupting her when she was talking which annoyed Zoe. Then Frank laughed too loudly at Max's jokes which annoyed her. Then Frank told Holly and Eric off for shouting at the table which annoyed her. Then Frank kept on breathing which annoyed Zoe! She couldn't stop herself - every time Frank opened his mouth to say something she would contradict him or shoot him down. She hated herself for it but couldn't stop herself, she just wanted Frank not to be there. For the adults the tension around the table became palpable. Eventually after one more dismissive put down from Zoe, Frank slammed his cutlery down making everyone jump, stood up and announced:

"I'm not taking any more of this shit!"

And stormed out of the holiday home.

Zoe burst into tears and apologised to everyone as she fled the table and went into the bedroom. They had ruined the evening for everyone. She sat on the bed sobbing irrepressibly. Thankfully Kate had followed Zoe before either

Holly or Eric had come in to see what was wrong with their mum. She put her arms around her friend and just let her cry till she was exhausted and drained. Kate was a staunch believer in the sanctimony of marriage and that you had to work at keeping a relationship going. But Zoe was no longer sure her marriage could or should be saved. When Kate said to her:

"Don't worry Frank will come back."

Through her tears Zoe, without missing a heartbeat, had replied:

"I'm not sure I want him to."

⬜⬜Ⱶ⬜⬜⬜⬜⋔⬜……⋯⋮.⋅˙˙⋅.⬜⋱⋰⬜⬜⬜Ս⬜⬜⬜⬜⬜

After the usual procedures and rituals at the airport the girls boarded their plane with relative ease. And once in the air things continued to go smoothly, that was until a worrying incident had started to unfold close by. Zoe wasn't able to ascertain where exactly they were from but a couple of Asian ethnicity sitting a row in front of them across the aisle had clearly been in distress. The husband whose wife looked considerably older than him, had desperately been trying to attract the attention of a stewardess. His wife was breathless and quite pasty looking, and he had been genuinely concerned. Finally, after another passenger stood up, a member of the cabin crew had assessed the situation and things escalated. Although not on the scale of *Snakes on a Plane*, tension had mounted and there had been a lot of frantic comings and goings. Then the Captain had made an announcement asking if there was a doctor or any medical professionals on board. From their snatched glimpses of the distressed passenger, it looked unlikely that she was pregnant but despite this the girls as one all looked at Maggie. Maggie did roll her eyes a bit, but it was in her nature to try and help so she'd started to undo her seatbelt to see if she could assist. Just as she started to stand up a guy further down the plane made himself known to the crew. The girls turned around hoping he would be a true hero type with Hugh Grant hair and a modest understated but sexy demeanour. Despite him being more of a world-weary, middle-aged GP with receding hairline, Maggie made herself known to him:

"Hello, I'm a midwife and if I can I'm more than happy to help."

Maggie hadn't mentioned the several glasses of fizz she'd had but as is often the case in stressful situations she had instantly felt completely sober when she thought she might be helping with an emergency. As it was, after an initial examination of the poorly Asian lady, the doctor thanked Maggie but said he'd continue to monitor her and would call Maggie if the situation worsened.

Whatever the doctor had then reported to the cabin crew had led the captain to put in an emergency call to Malaga Airport and the passengers were informed that the plane had been given priority to land. At this point it wasn't the patient but her husband who had needed attention. He had clearly escalated the situation in his head and was harassing the doctor and cabin crew and generally getting in the way. It was then that the GP had come to Maggie with pleading eyes and asked if she could step in and try to calm the hysterical husband. The cabin crew had all been busy trying to keep nosey passengers in check and reacting to the pilot's request to prepare the plane for an emergency landing.

Maggie had taken herself off and had applied her recently acquired counselling skills to great effect. Despite the language barrier, she had managed to calm the husband down who when she'd first approached had grabbed her and was speaking frantically in a language Maggie was obviously not familiar with. But Maggie's general serenity, her soothing voice and overall ability to create calmness had broken down the cultural differences and was clearly understood in any language.

The rest of *The Alphabetties* had also sobered up by now and were all in awe of their friend's skill and proficiency in such a highly charged situation.

Once on the ground a team of paramedics had immediately boarded the plane. The Asian lady had been strapped to a trolley, given oxygen, and swiftly removed from the cabin with her husband in hot pursuit, now considerably calmer and escorted to the exit by Maggie. Although she had been happy to help, Maggie had let out an audible sigh of relief once the Asian couple were off the plane. The doctor had thanked her for her help and was genuinely grateful she had been there. However, Maggie was very relieved the incident was over and really could have done without this kind of start to this long-awaited trip with her dear friends.

██Ⅱ⅄████∩█…···∶.·¨·.█∵·███∪█████

Maggie's relief was, in part, due to the fact that she hadn't done anything medical recently and she was pleased no procedures had been necessary. She had completed her MA in Clinical Counselling and had taken herself off the NHS Bank a few months ago. So, she felt her nursing skills were a bit rusty. And what's more she really didn't need any more stress in her life.

At the time of her father's death the year before, she and Shane had been so glad that they had Sandra to help them ensure the company was running smoothly. Whilst they dealt with the family repercussions of her father passing - the emotional, legal and financial fallout – Maggie was relieved that they could trust Sandra to keep on top of things at work. However for some time after her father's death, Shane had been protecting Maggie from the truth.

For several months Sandra had been making increasingly suggestive advances towards him. It had started in a very mild flirtatious way in the office which Shane had no problem ignoring but she had started showing up at occasions he was attending outside the office and openly coming on to him when he had politely shown her to a taxi. Shane wasn't a great one for using social media but he had come to realise that Sandra had not only managed to get all his account details – which clearly he had never given her – but had also become 'friends' with Maggie and his beloved girls.

Sandra was a very attractive, slim young woman in her early thirties, unattached and to many men would have been extremely desirable. But Shane never had or would have eyes for anyone except Maggie and was quite frankly somewhat bewildered by Sandra's attention and clear desire. He was just an ordinary guy going about his ordinary life.

Over the last few months her fixation had escalated. Prior to his last business trip abroad, Sandra had taken it on herself to book two flights saying they worked so well together it made sense for her to be with him at the coal face. There was some logic to this and Shane was never one to quash initiative but combined with her previous actions this was going too far. He was definitely right to be concerned as when he checked the travel arrangements himself he discovered she had also booked them in to a double room! Shane immediately spoke to her about it and said it was highly inappropriate and she would not be accompanying him on this or any other trip - Sandra was very affronted. She almost screamed at him demanding to know why he didn't want her to go and saying:

"We're a great team, it would be wonderful to be away together free from the constraints of the office and home! You know it makes sense Shane."

Shane was perplexed and really didn't know what to do. So he spoke to Maggie, his true love and confidante, telling her everything and how things had spiralled and finally asking her what he should do. Maggie listened to Shane in disbelief, she really liked Sandra and had trusted her, she felt betrayed and sick to her stomach. But the one thing she was sure of was that Shane would never have led Sandra on in any way – he didn't have it in him to risk his beautiful family and the company. After a long talk they agreed that she would have to be given a written warning and if her behaviour didn't change she would have to be dismissed. If she was unwilling to carry out her job properly and she continued this inappropriate conduct, they had no other choice.

Shane was very apprehensive about telling Sandra all this but she seemed to take it well and apologised. She admitted she realised her behaviour was unacceptable and it would never happen again. But she lied! Things got worse, not at the office but everywhere else. From that moment on her work and behaviour towards him and all her colleagues was exemplary. So although it was painful to go into work with her everyday Shane had no reasonable grounds to dismiss her – although he had taken back charge of his diaries and online security.

Outside of work strange things that were happening which Maggie and Shane knew were down to her but had no evidence to prove it. The first odd thing to happen they didn't at first consider was anything to do with Sandra. Their cat, who was known to wander off, had disappeared for a few days. They thought nothing of it and even the girls weren't worried as that's what their cat did. It was when it returned wearing a different coloured collar that Shane and Maggie became suspicious. They threw this collar out straight away and actually destroyed it – Maggie thought Shane was being overly dramatic when he said it could be bugged but indulged him.

There then came a whole series of events which Maggie described later as basically being stalked. All the family would feel like they were being followed or would spot someone they knew was Sandra from a distance at places they regularly went, school, shops, parents homes. But this figure was always sufficiently far away as to have some plausible deniability. Although when Sandra 'bumped into' Maggie at her gym that was clearly not a coincidence but an act of intimidation. The way Sandra talked to her in an overly familiar way about her husband made Maggie's skin crawl.

It was what happened around Shane's birthday that finally pushed them to act. Before going away for the weekend, there had been the usual birthday celebration at work with cake in the office and then drinks at the end of the day. However, when everyone was gathered around to grab cake, Sandra had presented Shane with a beautifully wrapped gift. In front of all his staff, he could only smile and accept it graciously – he had been hijacked although he did manage to delay opening the gift there and then with the help of a timely phone call. He shoved the present in the drawer hoping never to have to open it. However Shane decided to take the gift home as he suspected Sandra was regularly searching his desk - if she found her gift discarded God knows what behaviour that would trigger.

So that evening before celebrating with his friends and family, Shane and Maggie opened the gift to find a very expensive watch. A personal gift admittedly but it was only when Shane turned it over that they were really freaked out. Sandra had engraved her gift with three chilling words:

"I can wait".

Shane was particularly unnerved and was ready to call the police there and then. But Maggie said not to spoil his birthday weekend. They were going away for a couple of days, just them and the girls, they could forget about this deranged woman for a little while. And they did manage to have a lovely weekend, free from paranoia with no glimpses of a figure following them, just focussing on their girls and each other. However on their return they understood why their weekend had been so relaxed – Sandra had clearly been busy at their home.

She had broken into their house and had daubed a big red heart on the wall of their kitchen. Clearly not the work of your average burglar and they knew it was time to get the police involved – they now felt they were in actual danger from this woman. Initially, once they contacted the police little action was taken as despite everything they had no physical evidence it was Sandra doing all these things. They were advised to keep a log of incidents they thought were connected to Sandra, to confide to family, friends, neighbours and colleagues that they were being harassed, to improve their home and phone security and alert their phone provider that they may receive malicious calls.

Shane and Maggie were somewhat reluctant to involve others close to them in this hideous scenario – they felt they were just putting more people in danger. So they only told those in their immediate circle and the staff at the girls' school. However Shane had decided he could no longer be in a room with this woman and was going to fire her. Although he did fear the repercussions, the thought of being anywhere near Sandra for another minute was unbearable. He called her in and told her straight she was being dismissed immediately, to clear her desk and leave. Bizarrely she just nodded, smiled and left the room without any retaliation she just said:

"Thanks Shane, I'll see you around."

The way she said it made Shane's blood run cold and he straight away updated the police on this latest development. However, a few days later events took a turn which Shane and Maggie could never have predicted. Not only did the police get in touch with them but two plain clothes officers turned up on their doorstep. In fact these officers were from the UK's INTERPOL National Central Bureau. Maggie made the guys a cup of tea but as she and Shane listened to what they had to say she felt a stiff whiskey would have been more in order. They had begun by showing Maggie and Shane a photograph of a woman who they recognised immediately and identified as being Sandra. The men looked very serious but strangely pleased and went on to tell them what sounded like the plot to the latest James Patterson novel.

When Shane had reported Sandra's activities to the police, one of the details he was asked for was the name of his company. Once the report was logged the company name was flagged up as a trigger against an INTERPOL Red Notice issued on a fugitive in connection with a series of international murders. Maggie nearly fell off her chair at this point.

The officer went on to say that three businessmen had already been murdered – one in Africa and two in America. The chief suspect in all these cases was a petite, single woman in her mid-thirties whom they had just identified in the photograph. Like any good crime novel, the policemen had told them that INTERPOL had even given her a codename *Pono* – after the dwarf chameleon native to the eastern cape of South Africa.

The nickname was significant not just because the suspect is small and manages to change her appearance to evade capture but also because of the point of origin. The first crime had happened several years ago in South Africa with the murder of a CEO of a company very similar to their own. Over the last couple of years there had been two further murders in America of men doing almost the identical job and each one had been the owner of the company as well as the CEO. As this unbelievable tale unfurled Maggie and Shane were becoming increasingly uneasy and not surprisingly concerned.

It turned out that the woman had been identified as the daughter of one of Shane's suppliers based in South Africa with whom he had ceased business many years ago – he couldn't even remember why. However he wasn't the only one to have dropped Sandra's father and eventually he had gone bankrupt, lost his home and after his wife left him, he had killed himself. Sandra blamed the companies who had ceased trading with her beloved father for his death and had set about a systematic campaign of revenge against those who had given the order to stop working with him – Shane being one of them on her list. The connection between the men had come about after the deaths in the US – the names of the victims could be traced back to the father's records found after his suicide. A Red Notice had been issued for *Pono* aka Sandra et al and all the other company names that her father had worked with had been flagged up with INTERPOL. Hence the two men currently sitting in their living room were essentially telling them Shane's life could be in danger! This was mind boggling.

Although through all this Maggie's strength of character had been incredible, she was like a swan – seemingly gliding through the water without a care in the world, whilst under the surface she was frantically kicking to just stay afloat - she definitely needed a distraction and a little joy in her life, if only for a brief time. Although she was very reluctant to leave

Shane and the girls she needed to put her troubles behind her for a while, so she didn't tell the *Alphabet* girls about the international plot of murder and intrigue that she was mixed up in. As far as she could she just delighted in being with them, carefree and laughing – things she hadn't felt or done for a while now. Although, despite the expensive roaming charges she had taken two mobile phones with her and made some excuse about a poorly relative to ring home a lot more regularly than usual.

⬜⬜⯬⯛⬜⬜⬜⬜⌒⬜……⋮.⋅ ⁚⋅.⬜⋰⬜⬜⬜⎨⬜⬜⬜⬜⬜

After the excitement on the plane, once on Spanish soil the suitcases were retrieved without incident and the girls had headed outside to suss out how to get into the centre of sunny Malaga. Taxis had seemed to be the way to go – frankly at this stage the girls couldn't be arsed to make sense of the Spanish bus timetable. And it was at this point that another slight hiccup in the journey had occurred. As the girls had jostled for a place in the taxi queue there had been a clink and then a sickening sound of breaking glass followed by the lightning realisation that one of their bottles of champagne had broken! They'd all stopped and gawped at the sad looking bag, and all fought back the urge to stay and somehow filter their favourite tipple from the carrier bag. But they had been forced to move on and leave the sad little scene as the growing crowd of pushy Mediterranean locals behind had forced them to move on. They were then ushered, quite forcibly into two taxis by an officious little Spanish chap – he reminded Zoe of Danny DeVito's character in the seventies TV series coincidentally called *Taxi*!

After being deposited by the taxis at two different hotels with very similar names but neither being their hotel, the girls regrouped and tried to find their accommodation. In a

Benny Hill fashion, they'd explored several quaint side streets, before they had come across rather than found their lodgings which turned out to be a stone's throw from the Cathedral, just off the main artery of Malaga centre – Calle Larios. The boutique hotel had been full of Andalucian charm with a traditional terracotta façade peppered with intricate wrought iron Juliet balconies. The interior, centred around an indoor enclosed patio, had marble floors, carved wooden doors and many pillars. Zoe had been ecstatic even when the room she was inevitably sharing with Kate and Maggie had a huge pillar right in the middle of it. The hotel blurb had described such rooms as "smartly fashioned urban style rooms with a fusion of original architecture and modern style" – aka rooms with a bloody great pillar in them, live with it!

Once they had shaken off the grubbiness of travel and felt revitalised the group had headed out to explore what Malaga had to offer. Clearly an alcoholic beverage had by then become a pressing priority. They thought the area around the Cathedral would be bound to have a wealth of characterful, but possibly a little pricier, bars. The beautiful cathedral which for a building of such mind-blowing enormity was mightily well hidden away, had in front of it a small, picturesque square with quaint shops and halleluiah, a charming bar serving marvellous G&Ts! The girls had settled themselves for early evening drinks.

Following their drinks, the girls had sought out a restaurant where they didn't have to share food – they wanted more on the menu than the dreaded tapas – none of them had still got over the Barcelona vegetable salad/roasted pigeon experience! They had been encouraged that the food in the restaurant they had randomly selected would be good as it had been frequented by many locals enjoying the balmy summer evening. The girls had felt extremely relaxed and pleased with themselves.

Their food duly arrived, and not before time as the girls were by then mighty hungry. But alas and alack the food had been far from great! Pretty much every dish had been swimming in grease and even their hardy constitutions had struggled to partake. The girls were gutted – in their opinion there was just too much olive oil. But this view certainly wasn't shared in Spain. Apparently, Spain is the world's top olive oil producer and Spaniards consume more olive oil than any other country in the world besides Greece. The girls could well believe it and had thought that a major part of that year's consumption had been used on their one meal!

Still despite the sebaceous offering and the inevitability of indigestion, the evening had been very pleasant and after they'd paid the waiter whom it had to be said had been charming, the group had wound their way back to the hotel and a lovely long sleep – although a sleep punctuated by the noise and odour of flatulence.

The next day the girls felt some sea air would help them feel healthier and less gaseous and they'd headed for the beach. Faye had gleaned from the informative pensioner at the airport that the best way to reach the beach was by bus. And after a quick trip to the tourist information office to ascertain which bus and the usual confusion over which side of the road to catch it from, the girls were on a bus and on their way. It was only once motoring along, that the girls had realised; they had no idea where to get off! They'd had to play it by ear and had to sense where to alight. Clearly this had been a very risky strategy for them but as the bus went along, where they should be thinking about getting off became more apparent as small bars, hotels and restaurants began to appear. After they'd played 'let's stay on for one more stop' a couple of times the girls had finally plumped, pressed the bell and jumped off. Miraculously they had alighted at the very place they wanted to be. They'd strolled down a backstreet and had come out on a lovely promenade right on the beach with bars and restaurants a plenty. Fairly swiftly they'd chosen a particularly quirky little bar to honour with their custom and sat outside and ordered drinks. This was marvellous and the gang were happy. They had a beautiful view of the sea and a gentle breeze had blown to keep them cool. However, after a while the breeze had also blown in a couple of African chaps selling cheap watches and jewellery. Not ones to miss a bargain and having had a couple of drinks by this stage the girls had succumbed to one of the African chaps and had let him show them his wares!

Kate in particular was interested as she could see Fran and Kitty in a couple of the watches the chap had amongst his plethora of goods. Unlike Zoe who hated the whole idea of bartering and much preferred to pay a recommended price, Kate loved to haggle and negotiate a bargain – and to be fair she was very good at it!

□□Ⅱλ□□□□∩□.....⸱⸱⸱⦂.⸱ ̈⸱.□⸪□□□∪□□□□□

A bit of bartering in a sunny beach bar was in fact light relief for Kate. Over the last few months her world had also been turned upside down. Earlier in the year Max's Dad, George had sadly died after a battle with bowel cancer. His condition had gone undiagnosed for some time and the cancer had spread to surrounding tissues and organs. He had been a tall, strapping guy with a great presence – much like Max. So, his deterioration had been painful to watch. Mercifully without too much protraction he had passed away peacefully. Nancy, Max's mum, had been very stoical and seemed to be coping remarkably well. Nancy and George lived in a small village in the Midlands and were very active in the community. So, Nancy was surrounded by friends and was busying herself with the church and Women's Institute. Although Kate, Max and his brothers were all keeping a watchful eye over her.

As well as family life experiencing change, her work life had also thrown things at Kate which she was struggling to get her head around. The company takeover had been successfully completed and over the last year Kate had worked hard to ensure her new bosses knew what an asset she was and that her talents weren't overlooked. Indeed, her new bosses had realised pretty early on during her company takeover that Kate had a "lot to bring to their table" but they just didn't know where to put her in their company hierarchy to maximise her potential. It was clear to anyone, not just those employing her, that Kate had the skills to soar with a company like this. Kate has the aptitude to grasp new skills and procedures remarkably quickly with minimal direction and her ability to multitask and organise is legendary. So, it came as no surprise to friends and family, that Kate's perseverance paid off and she was given a place in the company Mergers and Acquisitions team in their Cheshire office.

Despite the often prolonged working hours and commuting, Kate had taken to her new role like a duck to water. She grasped the new skills and procedures in no time and put her accounting and law qualifications to good use. Kate loves nothing more than a complicated spreadsheet and was adoring developing and executing acquisition strategy and procedures. What's more, although her new boss turned out to be a much younger version of herself, they got on like a house on fire – neither of them suffered fools gladly and they shared the same work ethic. The only thing Kate wasn't sure about was her unofficial role as office mum to her new young male colleagues. But she got over it as it meant that on the many social occasions organised at work, they bought her drinks and organised taxis to ensure she got home safely.

So, it would appear that all was going well work wise for Kate, but her success had brought with it a major conundrum. Although based in Cheshire, her new job required regular trips to HQ in London. Again, exciting for Kate and easily doable in a day by train so no major childcare issues. The work of the team meant they were often asked to keep in close contact with the company directors, advising them on the soundness of potential acquisitions and keeping them abreast of progress and impact of takeovers. On returning from one of these visits to HQ, Kate's Cheshire boss had called her into the office for a one-to-one chat. Filled with trepidation Kate feared the worst – she hadn't lived up to expectations and she was going to be let go.

So, it was much to her astonishment when her team leader had welcomed her into the office with:

"Well Kate I've got some great news for you. I've been asked to see if you would be interested in a promotion."

Kate was floored and incredibly flattered. This must have shown all over her face as her boss went on to say:

"Oh, come on Kate it can't come as a complete surprise – you've absolutely shone since you started here and the guys in London have seen it."

But it genuinely did come as a shock. Kate had hoped she was doing a good job but never felt that the work she was producing would warrant a promotion. She was thrilled, especially as the salary figure being thrown around was sizeable! But then as the new role was explained further to her something became apparent which made things a whole lot more complicated – the promotion would mean working full-time in London!

Obviously, Kate was given time to think about it – although not that long, she had to make a decision in the next few weeks. She'd gone home that day in a turmoil of emotions - so excited at the prospect of a promotion and so pleased with herself for making her mark with this international company. At the same time wondering how to tell Max and could they consider moving to London – Max was equally as bad at dealing with change as she was. He'd been through such a lot this year, losing his dad. Could she leave all her family and friends that meant the world to her and go to live in the big city? And the kids, could she uproot them and decant to London? They were all teenagers now – well Flo was twelve – such a sensitive time, emotionally and educationally. She had a lot to think about and was losing a lot of sleep doing so.

⬜⬜Ⅱ⅗⬜⬜⬜⬜⋂⬜…⋯⋅⋮⋅⸱⋯⋅⸱⬜⋱⬜⬜⬜⋃⬜⬜⬜⬜

Once Kate had beaten the African salesman into submission and a couple of knock off watches had been purchased the girls' thoughts had moved to food. A short distance away they had found a lovely restaurant with white tablecloths and silver cutlery where sardines were grilled on the beach and then brought to the table by waiters in penguin suits and impeccable service. They'd complemented this idyllic Mediterranean scene with a very quaffable bottle of the best cava on the menu – the lunchtime ensemble had reminded Zoe of a Jack Vettriano painting.

As the midday sun had got very hot, the girls had moved around the table according to their preference for sun or shade and the experience had been topped off with the waiter bringing them a tray of complimentary Ginja – a Portuguese cherry liqueur. Sadly, most of the gang weren't taken by the Ginja but it came as no surprise that Kate had felt it would be rude to leave them after such a wonderful meal and she diligently managed to polish most of them off.

As the afternoon had begun to draw to a close, the girls had felt perhaps they should make their way back to Malaga town. But as they'd got up to leave it had become apparent that they weren't completely sober anymore and after her Ginja intake Kate was in fact quite bladdered! They'd set off towards their bus stop but after a short walk decided that a tactical rest on the sea wall was in order. As they'd sat gazing out across the sea, Kate had thought it looked so inviting that she'd go for a paddle. In her head, she probably thought she was gliding down the slipway to gracefully dip her toes in the cool waves as they lapped on to the shore. In reality Kate had been swaying badly, looking like she could go arse over tit at any moment.

So, Zoe and Maggie had scooped her up and escorted her on to the bus where they had all prayed that Kate wouldn't follow through the grizzly retching noises she'd started to make once the bus had got underway! Back in Malaga the group had split up - Zoe shepherded Kate back to their hotel room whilst the others took themselves off to the rather chic shops on Calle Larios. And a very memorable shopping excursion it turned out to be.

Over the years *The Alphabetties* have done their fair share of shopping whilst on tour. Many, many presents have been purchased for the children, some presents for husbands – usually beer, sexy underwear on one occasion a lot earlier in the alphabet and various souvenirs and mementos to remind them of their fabulous weekends together. But the purchase made in Malaga was to go down in *Alphabet Tour* history.

It has been previously documented that Sally is the tallest member of the group and not surprisingly has the longest legs. On their slightly drunken shopping trip both Faye and Maggie had thought Sally would look absolutely amazing in a pair of thigh length boots they'd spotted in a beautiful shop only minutes from the hotel. Sally isn't normally one for statement clothing but on this occasion was swayed by the judgement of her friends and several glasses of wine. She had been wearing a fairly short summer dress which when paired with the extreme over- the- knee boots served well to show off the potential for this particular kind of footwear. If possible, Sally's legs looked even longer and slimmer, and she had definitely given off a sexy vibe – the girls had all thought Mark would probably see her more in the boots than they would! So, despite being considerably more expensive than her usual tour souvenir, the boots had been purchased. How often the boots have been worn since is questionable, but the girls had never since witnessed them on an outing!

◻◻Ⅱλ◻◻◻◻∩…⋯⋮.·¨·.◻∴◻◻◻∪◻◻◻◻

Sally's life since her divorce had been going well. Overall, her gorgeous daughters seemed to have come through the divorce unscathed and both were doing great at school. She loved her new house and work was going fine, although she was still travelling a great deal which had its pros and cons. And one thing was undeniable - she was falling in love with Mark.

Their romance by now had turned into a partnership. Despite the physical distance between them they were making it work and steps had finally been taken by Mark to show his commitment to his new love. Sally had been concerned, as the months had gone by that Mark had not yet told his children about her. But partly in fear of jinxing things, Sally had bitten her lip and hadn't pushed him to move things forward.

Another reason Sally wasn't pushing for Mark to tell his offspring about her was something quite bizarre – freakishly Mark's kids had the same names as her girls! Thankfully Mark's Charlie was in fact a boy, Charles and his daughter was just Abbey not a shortened version of Abigail. So, they did have options come the day they all met but Sally still found it very hard to get her head around. Since the day Mark told her many months ago she found it unbelievable and didn't bother telling other people unless directly asked what Mark's kids were called. It was too mind blowing – and *The Alphabetties* would certainly dine out on this fact!

Although being patient about not being revealed was very hard, especially as her Abi and Charlie were becoming increasingly fond of Mark, Sally's tactics had paid off. On a recent visit up North, Mark had passed on the news that he had told his children that he had met someone else and that they would like to meet her. Initially when Mark had plucked up the courage to tell his Charlie and Abbey, the news had met with mixed reviews. Not surprisingly they were predictably defensive and loyal to their mum, who as yet had not met anyone else. However, recently his kids had admitted very responsibly to Mark that they wanted to see both their parents happy and if he had met someone else he cared for they agreed to meet her.

This had all occurred several weeks before his latest visit to see Sally. When he arrived and told her about telling the kids Sally was delighted and thrilled that he wanted her to meet them as soon as possible. She was inwardly rewarding herself for being patient and not pushing to move their relationship on. Then she was somewhat cross that he hadn't told her this major piece of news earlier so she could mentally prepare. Nonetheless the two of them had celebrated that night with a romantic dinner.

Sally knew that a relationship with Mark was never going to be straightforward but talking about it that evening had made the reality hit home. Being with Mark meant she would be involved in his kids' lives and plans for some time – at least until they were both eighteen. They were currently thirteen and fifteen. She was going to have to take time for it all to sink in.

But Mark didn't give her any time to absorb anything as he then hit her with his other piece of news. Since his divorce, he had been looking for a new, better paid job, preferably outside of London but not too far from the kids. After several interviews and rejections on both sides, he had finally secured a new position in Berkshire which ticked all his boxes. He'd been to visit the area and had actually spotted a house he was interested in and which he could afford – even with all the financial repercussions of his divorce. As he had told Sally all this, she had been listening very attentively which was good as he had finished off his homily by asking her to come to Berkshire and move in with him!

So, for the last month or so Sally had been agonising over the logistics of such a move and the emotions it had invoked. She was thrilled that Mark wanted to be with her on a permanent basis but of course it wasn't just her that any decisions they made would affect. She had to think long and hard about her girls. Abi's life was about to change anyway. She had accepted a place at university in London and was imminently heading off to the *Big Smoke*. Charlie on the other hand was just turning sixteen and about to begin studying for her A levels and deciding what to do with her life. Could Sally ask her to uproot her world at this crucial time after everything else she had put her through?

□□ȴȴ入□□□□∩□……∵:.∙˙˙.□∵□□□Ụ□□□□□

The next day the girls had planned to visit the museum dedicated to Malaga's most famous citizen, Pablo Picasso. However, as they'd approached the museum located down a narrow side street, it had become apparent that Picasso was a very popular guy! The queue was ridiculous. Not known for their patience, the girls had decided that they didn't want to spend a large part of their remaining time on Tour queuing to look at modern art. Zoe was mighty happy about this as she really didn't like Picasso's work in any of his periods, Avant Garde or otherwise.

Instead, after contemplating their options over coffee in a nearby *cafeteria,* the group had decided they would partake in one of the guided walks around Malaga that they had come across in a leaflet. This was an activity they all enjoyed and had the advantage of being able to be carried out slowly and they could take in any shops and/or bars/restaurants they came across on the way. The walk had been interesting and had taken in lots of little backstreets and hidden gardens. Once back in the main part of the town their route had taken them right passed a fabulous restaurant with stylish tables set outside in a lovely square. The girls decided this was the perfect location to spend their last afternoon and sat down under the tasteful cream parasols ready to order and indulge!

And indeed, a very pleasant afternoon had been spent sitting there. The waiters were attentive, the wine was good and the food tasty - what more could they have asked for? Well as it turned out the afternoon had taken a very strange turn as they'd sat digesting their meal. From nowhere a drunken, grown man wearing only a giant nappy had appeared and stood shouting what the girls took to be abuse at the restaurant customers! He really had been going for it and had clearly been very perturbed about something. As they had no idea why he had been so affronted, all the girls could do was laugh at him – he was in a giant nappy after all!

However, their laughter hadn't helped the situation and several waiters had intervened and tried to move on the gentleman of the road. As soon as one of the waiters had put a hand on him, he had got very agitated indeed and he had begun flinging punches around – although being as drunk as he was, thankfully he hadn't made contact with anyone. As the incident had continued to unfold there had been a lot of shouting going on and some male diners had also joined in the affray. Just as the girls had started to get a little uncomfortable the *Policia* had arrived. Two armed policemen got to grips with the man in the nappy in no time and he had been unceremoniously hauled away – still shouting and protesting about whatever had upset him.

□□ᘢᕀ□□□□∩□……·:.·˙˙·.□·:·□□□∪□□□□□

The surreal David Lynch type scene in Malaga hadn't been the only uncomfortable situation Faye had found herself in recently. Since the last *Alphabettie* weekend things between Faye and her work friend Bridget had become increasingly weird. Despite her best-efforts Bridget was by now almost avoiding Faye.

Previously Faye had thought their relationship had been blossoming both personally and professionally. But now she was lucky if Bridget could give her the time of day. Although seeming a bit conceited, Faye thought this was very odd and didn't like it one bit. She always felt one of her strengths was her ability to get on with people and she had taken Bridget's recent behaviour to heart. Faye felt she had done nothing to warrant being snubbed and she certainly didn't like being disliked. Quite frankly Bridget's aloofness was really pissing her off and Faye was going to get to the bottom of why she was pushing her away.

Faye had asked around at the charity clinic and although people weren't as affronted as she was, a number of them – certainly the other female volunteers – had noticed she was a bit more off hand. Faye took a little comfort from this, at least it wasn't just her getting the cold shoulder. Although Faye's main concern was Bridget's wellbeing, she couldn't shake a feeling that there was something deeper going on – something more ominous at the root of the change in her demeanour. Although Bridget was reluctant to have a decent conversation with Faye, she was still more than happy to go along to any social events or fundraisers arranged by the clinic. In fact, Bridget had stood out at the last couple of events, as she arrived beautifully turned out and was happily buying drinks for her friends and fellow volunteers. So, Faye continued to be bemused as to why she was backing away when they had become so close.

For a long time, Faye had felt something was wrong with Bridget but had continuously put it down to the strain she must be under looking after her mother, who was suffering from Alzheimer's and wouldn't be getting any easier to look after. It occurred to Faye that maybe Bridget was doing something she shouldn't be to help her mother – maybe helping herself to the charity donations, which it was Bridget's job to process. Faye was now like a dog with a bone and wasn't going to let this go till she got to the bottom of it.

She had already asked Bridget informally if she was OK and if there was anything she or Clive could do to help. Hardly surprisingly Bridget fobbed Faye off saying it was still tough at home but with the Council help they were receiving; she and her Mum were doing OK. Faye did appreciate that Bridget wasn't going to break down and confess to swindling the charity, but she thought she might open up a little. But nothing.

Faye didn't sleep at night anyway, but if she had, her obsession with Bridget would by now have been keeping her awake. She had spent extra time after hours, which she really couldn't afford to do, going through all the work that Bridget oversaw at the clinic and checking the books. This was far from Faye's skill set but as far as she could tell everything was in order. Either Bridget wasn't cooking the books, or she was very good at it. No, there was nothing else for it, Faye decided she would have to pay a home visit to see for herself what was going on with Bridget when she wasn't at the clinic.

Ironically, Faye then abused her power and looked up Bridget's address in the HR files. Bridget lived not far from the opticians practice where Faye had first met her – years ago, when Faye first went back to work as a locum and Bridget was an optical assistant. So, one Saturday morning after giving Clive some excuse about meeting up with one of her old work colleagues for coffee, Faye took herself off to track down Bridget's home turf. She was a bit wary of going on her own, but she had her phone, and this was Bridget not Ted Bundy!

The street that Bridget and her mum lived on was a very suburban, middle class Victorian terrace. The majority of the properties looked well cared for and loved. But as she pulled closer to Bridget's home, Faye could see that it needed some TLC and clearly hadn't had any external work for many years. The small front garden was hidden behind a high, privet hedge and was very overgrown. The short, curved path to the tiled porch was cracked and Faye nearly tripped up as she approached the door. There was no sign of life, but she could hardly see through the grey, net curtains hanging limply in the front window. She took a deep breath and rang the doorbell. She really didn't know what she was going to say if Bridget answered the door – she was just going to wing it.

She pressed the bell again as it was one of those annoying ones you can't hear ring, so you press it several times in case nothing has happened. After what seemed like forever the door very slowly started to open. It wasn't Bridget who opened the door, but a very frail looking woman, was this

Bridget's mother? Surely not, Faye knew Bridget's mum could only be in her sixties.

Quietly but very clearly and lucidly she said:

"Hello, can I help you?"

After her initial shock Faye said:

"Hello yes I'm a friend of Bridget's – I was in the area, so I thought I'd pop round and say hi".

Opening the door wider, the woman said:

"Oh, how lovely but I'm afraid Bridget isn't in at the moment. I'm expecting her back shortly though. Would you like to come in and wait – I can pop the kettle on?"

Faye's curiosity got the better of her and she kindly accepted the offer:

"Well, if you don't mind, it would be a shame to miss her and I'm in no hurry."

The woman smiled and stood back so Faye could enter the house. As soon as she was through the front door, she was aware of a musty odour, and it was apparent the house was as neglected on the inside as the outside. This is not what Faye had expected and she was perplexed. The woman invited her into the lounge and gestured towards a very old sofa, the majority of which was covered in papers and laundry. As she cleared a few papers away for Faye to sit down, the sleeve of her baggy cardigan rolled up and Faye caught sight of a couple of nasty bruises on the lower part of her arm.

"My name is Barbara by the way, Bridget's mum. It's so nice to meet one of my daughter's friends at last. How do you take your tea?"

"White no sugar please – can you manage, would you like any help?"

Barbara said she could manage and told Faye to make herself comfortable. As she walked away towards the kitchen it was evident that she also struggled walking. Barbara was clearly suffering but the thing that surprised Faye the most was how alert she was – although clearly not in good health this woman did not appear to have any signs of early onset Alzheimer's. Faye didn't know what to think but as Barbara returned with two mugs of tea, she decided she would try and find out what was going on.

She told Barbara that she worked with Bridget at the clinic and how well she was getting on there and how helpful she was to the charity. Barbara smiled and said that was nice to hear:

"Bridget doesn't tell me anything about her work. She says I wouldn't understand and not to be nosey if I ask her about her friends."

Slightly taken aback by Barbara's response, Faye decided to get more brazen and asked how she and Bridget were coping with her condition and were they getting enough help:

"Bridget always turns me down when I offer to help out. She says the Council have been very helpful and that you manage."

Barbara looked completely flummoxed by Faye's question:

"I'm afraid I have no idea what you're talking about dear – what condition?"

"Oh, I'm sorry I can appreciate you don't like to talk about your Alzheimer's. My apologies."

"Don't apologise dear but I don't have Alzheimer's – not yet at least!"

Barbara followed up her last remark with a little laugh. Now Faye was completely confused; did she have Alzheimer's but was so far gone she didn't know or was she telling the truth – she certainly seemed on the ball. Faye then drew on her experience of watching TV detective series and asked if she could use the toilet so she could have a nosey around upstairs.

"Of course, dear, straight ahead at the top of the stairs."

Faye whizzed upstairs and quickly had a look in the first bedroom she came across. This was clearly Barbara's room – very old fashioned, cold with the bare minimum of furniture – austere even. Faye gasped and moved on to the larger bedroom at the front of the house. This room couldn't have been more different. A huge brass bed was at the centre of the room with a large double pine wardrobe and a dressing table draped with jewellery and makeup. The room had a deep soft carpet and luxurious cotton bedding – Faye recognised it as the same as she had at home! Clearly this was Bridget's haven. Faye quickly took a couple of photos of the rooms before flushing the toilet (like a good snoop would) and heading downstairs.

But just as she got to the top of the stairs she could hear voices – Bridget must have returned whilst Faye was looking around. Faye strained to hear what they were saying, she could tell the conversation was tense but could only catch a couple of words:

"What on earth possessed you to let her in? You know you're not allowed to talk to anyone when I'm out".

Then Faye let out an involuntary gasp. So, she started down the stairs in case they heard her. As she entered the room, she was friendliness itself:

"Hi Bridget, I was over here to check out that boutique I used to visit on the high street when we worked together, so I thought I'd pop in and say hello. Your mum has been lovely and made me a cuppa."

Barbara looked petrified when Faye had come back downstairs, and Bridget curtly replied:

"I didn't know you had my address."

Before Faye had to think of an answer to that, Barbara saved her skin and meekly piped up:

"It's been lovely to meet Faye, she has been telling me what a wonder you are at the clinic dear."

Bridget looked sheepish and said through a half laugh:

"Well, I don't know about that, but it's nearly lunchtime now Mum and I'm sure Faye has better things to do than talk to an old woman like you. Thanks for coming Faye it was a lovely surprise."

Bridget then thrust Faye's handbag at her and pretty much pushed her towards the door. Whilst this unceremonious exit was taking place Faye could see the look of terror developing in Barbara's eyes – they looked like she was pleading for Faye to stay. But that wasn't going to happen as Bridget clearly wanted Faye out of there. Just before she was shoved out the door Faye shook off Bridget and said:

"Hang on I think I've left my phone in the lounge."

She pushed back past Bridget into the lounge and pretended to look for her mobile which was in her coat pocket along with a number of business cards she always kept there. After acting out finding her phone, as she passed Barbara to leave, she turned and grabbed her hand pretending to shake it and thank her for her hospitality. She just felt Barbara needed help and as she looked Barbara straight in the face, she took her hand and pressed one of her business cards into it. As Bridget once again firmly ushered her towards the door Faye glanced back and saw Barbara put the card in her blouse pocket and look directly at her. Faye wanted to help; she hoped now Barbara knew that.

Once back at her car Faye was visibly shaking – there was definitely something menacing going on in that house. She was no expert, but Faye was sure Barbara didn't have any stage of Alzheimer's and although she found it abhorrent to even consider it possible, she was pretty sure Bridget was abusing her mother, financially, psychologically, and physically. She felt sick. She had never seen Bridget so intimidating and to say she was keen to get rid of Faye was putting it extremely mildly. What the hell was she going to do about this – what if she was wrong? She couldn't just accuse Bridget of domestic violence and abusing her mother. But Faye knew that was what was happening, and it explained so many things. Why Bridget had never invited Faye to her house and had curtailed their relationship keeping it on a relatively informal level. And if she was exploiting her mother financially it explained her clothes and beautiful bedroom – her mother certainly wasn't benefitting from any financial help they may be getting. Oh God what was she going to do, she needed evidence - she didn't think photos of a couple of bedrooms and her gut feeling would be enough to report this. She just hoped Faye's mum was brave enough to get in touch with her.

When she got home, she told Clive the truth about what she'd been up to – she expected him to go ballistic and accuse her of being irrational. But to her surprise, although he was angry she had done something like this on her own, he didn't lay into her for being a busy body. One thing he had certainly come to know about Faye over the course of their marriage is that she is a very good judge of character, and she can sense when someone is in pain or needs help. But although he may have believed Faye's suspicions, he too had no idea what they should do. Unless Barbara asked for help, they had very little evidence to approach anyone about their concerns and what Bridget might be up to.

After all that excitement created by the grown man in the giant nappy, the girls definitely felt that more wine was called for. As they had sat sipping wine in the sun Zoe had mused about what Pablo Picasso would have thought about the recent events in this picturesque Malaga square. In her brief research for the trip she had read that Picasso's artistic inspiration had taken many forms, working through emotions, a passionate love affair, difficult life events. She felt sure that if he had witnessed what had just played out, *Agitated Man with Nappy and Beard* would have featured in his body of work and gone down in history as a Cubist masterpiece of the Avant Garde movement!

Looking around the table Zoe could tell the rest of the girls hadn't been thinking along those lines. Although she did reflect at how relaxed this group of women were; completely at peace with each other – no airs, graces or pretences. In fact Faye had been so chilled she'd taken the opportunity to put her head down on the table and have a nap. It seemed sad to wake her, as nobody else in the restaurant seemed to mind, but sadly they would have to as it was time to once again head home.

Epilogue

(Sometime after returning from M)

Zoe was just applying the final touches to her makeup when she stopped and looked at herself in the mirror. She'd always had an inferiority complex about her appearance. At university she had felt she was the least attractive of her group of friends. This certainly wasn't down to them or anything they had ever said, but she never considered herself as attractive or appealing to the opposite sex. Although she probably came across as fairly confident, in that classic way she hid behind her sense of humour and considered herself more the joker of the group.

So, when one of the universally acknowledged good looking lads at sixth form had asked her out, she wasn't flattered but shocked and even questioned whether this was some sort of hurtful prank. It wasn't and they went out together for over five years. But during that time, she had changed to be what she thought he wanted her to be and forgave him anything. It turned out he was a complete shit and had been cheating on her – it was only with hindsight that she realised this had been many times. She had felt a complete fool and her confidence regarding men and generally had gone down the toilet.

After a lengthy period of time licking her wounds, she then thought, sod this just enjoy life – if someone was going to fall in love with her it was going to be on her terms, taking her and her life just the way it was – warts and all. Frank had done this. He hadn't put any pressure on her to change herself and she could take him to meet any of her friends and leave him to get on with it – and she loved him for it.

But now, as she stared at her reflection, she knew that the one person she so deeply wanted to really see her, wouldn't even notice her efforts to gild the lily or even care where she was going or with whom. Things with Frank had not improved, and she had to fight back the tears. She had by now accepted that she had played her part in creating the

346

current state of her marriage. She knew she could be a complete bitch to Frank but at this stage she couldn't help herself. Frank on the other hand seemed defiantly incapable of recognising that he too was instrumental in the collapse of their relationship. She put on her lipstick and put it in her clutch bag. She kissed and said goodnight to her beautiful children, then grabbed her coat and headed out to meet the girls. Her heart lifted as she jumped in the taxi.

One thing she did know is that her dear friends would care that she was there and would notice that she'd recently dyed her hair (yet again) and was wearing something new. Zoe couldn't begin to quantify how much these women had come to mean to her and each other over the last fifteen years. *The Alphabetties* were now a part of her life that she hoped would remain a constant feature and continue well beyond the limitations of the alphabet.

Each of them had experienced the marvels and hardships of bringing children into the world. And thank God for the antenatal classes so miraculously organised by the NHS or otherwise none of their adventures would have come about. The value of those classes then and now goes way beyond the practicalities of pain relief, breast feeding and nappy rash. They give women a forum to meet other pregnant women, see that they are not alone, a place where they can express their fears, receive, and give support, laugh, and cry at the wonders and horrors of being pregnant. For *The Alphabetties* these classes sparked a wonderful, strong relationship between five women that would endure through anything that life threw their way.

Zoe could talk to *The Alphabetties* about her fears that nothing was for certain. How everyone thought she and Frank were rock solid but how that had changed, and she now feared the worst. And she knew that the others had all looked to this group of friends to get them through - both in the past and even more so now.

Sally had certainly found strength from the group to cope with her divorce and would be calling on the girls again to advise her on the decisions she now faced – Berkshire was a long way and a very different world for her and her girls to inhabit. Strength had never been something which Sally had thought she was short of. She had always considered herself to be strong, reliable and dependable. But the whole prolonged process of going through a divorce, set in motion at her instigation, had drawn on her final reserves. She had found herself needing emotional support which had surprised her as she had always thought she could cope with anything alone.

Although, unlike Zoe she had never questioned her self-worth and didn't have trust issues. Despite his faults Gabe had never shown any interest in other women. Sally knew he had loved her – and probably still did. But she had never questioned that falling in love with Mark was the right thing to do and she was thrilled when he finally asked her to move in with him. Although she had to admit she had thought maybe that the living together bit would happen where she was based not where he was. Could she see a future with him so far from the world she had built – did she love him enough to give that up?

The support of *The Alphabetties* was always there whenever any of them needed it. Even though Faye was helping Sally with her dilemma as much as she could, she was also spending a lot of time over a bottle or two with the girls, trying to work out what she should or could do about Bridget. Was it any of her business, should she get involved, would she make matters worse? Dipping into someone else's life like this cannot be taken lightly and had certainly made her appreciate how lucky she was.

Faye had definitely come to realise that people aren't your property, and you have no right to control a person's life. But what do you do when you think a person is deliberately withholding care and support from another human being? Faye was one of the most compassionate and generous people all *The Alphabetties* knew. Despite her appearing somewhat frivolous, drinking champagne and being the life and soul of the party, she cared deeply for her family, friends and fellow man in general. Even Clive, who despite all his medical training knew that his wife beat him hands down when it came to understanding a person's plight and providing sympathy and care.

Although Faye too had self-doubt, which was a contributory factor to her desire to help Barbara and give her the love and affection she clearly lacked. But what if she'd got it wrong? What if Barbara did have Alzheimer's? If she did have the disease perhaps, she was prone to bouts of aggression that forced Bridget to manhandle her mother. Maybe Bridget's increasing aloofness towards Faye was the only way she could cope with people who were showing her kindness.

Faye felt like her brain might explode but she kept coming back to the same inevitability that she would have to take some sort of action and get involved. She also couldn't get away from the feeling that she might regret it if she did. And on top of that, along with the other *Alphabetties* she was so worried about Maggie.

Maggie had now told the girls her plight and that of Shane and their whole family. She had needed a vent through which to ease the pressure. Maggie and Shane were still in a hideous state of limbo waiting to hear news about Sandra's whereabouts – *Pono* seemed to have dropped off the face of the earth. Her friends didn't really know what they could do and felt useless, the whole episode seemed so surreal and the potential outcome was too hard to even contemplate.

With good reason Maggie was going to have faith issues for quite some time – if not forever. She still couldn't fathom how she had put her trust in such a person and not spotted anything sinister about Sandra before. But she was clearly a clever woman albeit scheming and deranged, she was brilliant enough to have them blindsided for a long while.

More than herself she was worried about Shane and the girls. Shane had gone into himself, full of guilt, punishing himself for his lack of vision and allowing this to happen. He had been brought up with traditional values and he was meant to provide for and protect his family not put them in life threatening danger. Whatever she said to reassure him that they all still loved him and there was absolutely no way of anticipating this, for now Shane was inconsolable.

Zoe couldn't help but think that *The Alphabet Tour* girls were now a million miles away from where they had been setting out on that first weekend to Amsterdam. They were all so grateful for some time away from their babies and duties as a wife and mother. The problems they faced then seemed so simple compared to where they all were now. When can I give the baby Sunshine Orange for breakfast, why has her poo gone that colour and why is he crying now – these all seemed like such simple problems to solve but at the time were monumental.

Throughout the years of *The Alphabet Tour* and indeed since she'd known her, Zoe had looked to Kate for guidance – a life coach almost. She knew that if Kate had given something the OK, she probably would too. But even Kate, who not just Zoe looked to, but also her parents and siblings, was now struggling to know what to do for the best. She was being pressed by her bosses to make a choice about whether she was going to take the promotion and move to London.

Kate liked a sounding board before she made up her mind on things. This was often Max, Zoe or her mum Louise but, on this topic, she also sought the wisdom of the whole *Alphabettie* group.

Kate is fiercely family orientated and couldn't imagine a life in which she didn't see them if not daily certainly weekly. Her rational mind was telling her that this strength of commitment would ensure that she kept the family ties strong and would see them all regularly and speak to her mum every day. She knew that Max would support whatever decision she made although she also knew that he too would desperately miss his friends and the life he had carved out in South Manchester. And there were the kids to think about. They were at a particularly impressionable stage now, in or on the brink of their teens, forging their way through the complexities of puberty, friendships, choosing subjects to study at school, whether to go to university – making decisions that would be the foundations for their lives, not that they appreciated that yet. Thank goodness Francesca had got through the horrible bullying she had suffered and was now maturing into a brilliant young woman with the possibility of Oxbridge being mentioned. Vincent wasn't putting in any effort but was still managing to pass all the tests required. His focus was more video game based than academic and Kitty was just about settling into her new school and working out where she fitted in with her contemporaries.

There was an awful lot to consider, a lot to change and potentially damage. But then Kate kept thinking to herself that her hard work deserved to be recognised and she shouldn't have to sacrifice her dreams. She had worked really hard since going back to work and studying for her law degree, she should be allowed to reap the rewards. And the rewards would be considerable monetarily at the very least.

They could have a very comfortable, exciting life in London she felt sure. Max would easily find work and they could probably afford to live in a decent area with all the comforts of a good life. So why hadn't she given them her answer, why was she so uncharacteristically hesitant? This was the question she was struggling to answer.

Zoe was also struggling to cope with the prospect of Kate moving to London. Selfishly she kept thinking how the hell was she going to survive if her marriage broke down completely and her best friend moved nearly two hundred miles away. But she had managed to quash this fear to some extent by reminding herself of what was central to this group of women.

Since that first day in the local health centre as they all sat nervously wondering what lay ahead, the bond that they had forged had become incredibly strong. Mere distance wasn't going to break their attachment and stop the humour, love, and laughter from flowing. These girls were now friends for life, cohorts who know too much, kindred spirits who could laugh at secret jokes without feeling they have to let anyone else share. But if Kate and Sally moved away, would it really be the same? What if the unhinged, murderous woman returned to reap her revenge on Shane and Maggie – Zoe couldn't bring herself to even think about that.

For tonight the girls would be focussed on the next letter on their wonderful quest. Zoe couldn't wait to get to Faye's house to start planning their next trip to who knows where - well obviously somewhere beginning with N! She'd had a couple of thoughts about next year's destination which she'd throw in with the others to be discussed at length - flights would be considered, dates would be finalised, and hotels would be scrutinised.

Zoe knew that, wherever it turned out to be there would be masses of fun without judgement and memories for her to write about. Although she knew she really didn't have to record how the girls felt about each other and the excitement that each year *The Alphabet Tour* brought them all – these were a given.

Printed in Great Britain
by Amazon